Life o

The Vikings are coming

Life on Mars

The Vikings are coming

Hugh Duncan

Elsewhen Press

Life on Mars
First published in Great Britain by Elsewhen Press, 2022
An imprint of Alnpete Limited

Elsewhen Press, PO Box 757, Dartford, Kent DA2 7TQ
elsewhen.press

British Library Cataloguing in Publication Data.
A catalogue record for this book is available from the British Library.

ISBN 978-1-915304-02-5 Print edition
ISBN 978-1-915304-12-4 eBook edition

Designed and formatted by Elsewhen Press

Contents

Masha's Map of Mars

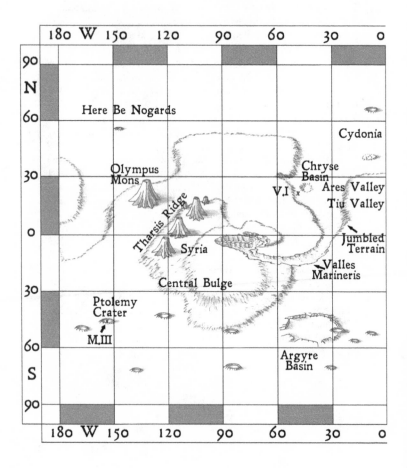

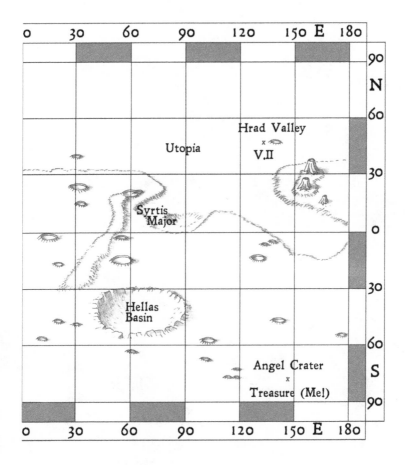

1

The Law of the Jumble

It all started with a sneeze. Great Uncle Syd had caught a *hot*, which is something like a cold, but with a lot more energy. The virus that caused the *hot* was rather primitive, but it did its job nonetheless. Great Uncle Syd sneezed and pebble-dashed the surrounding rocks with slime before he could get a flipper to his nose. The force actually moved him backward with the recoil, but he came to a halt with his butt buried slightly in the ground. No one had seen his unhygienic act, so he continued his clumsy crawl across the rock-strewn sand dunes, looking for somewhere a little colder to hide. Barely half an hour later, Nature sent the equivalent of a sneeze back at him by delivering a meteor headfirst into the Martian terrain, not far from Great Uncle Syd. Fortunately, he was protected from the sheet of ejected stones and debris having just ambled behind a suitably placed rocky outcrop. One stone that he'd sneezed on was launched into the sky, at far beyond the planet's escape velocity, and it orbited the sun for a further seventeen million Earth years, until it actually encountered the Earth.[†] There it fell and remained hidden in Antarctica, under layers of the last Ice Age, until it was dug out as part of a core sample in the Allan Hills, in 1997, and labelled ALH 84001. The rest is history, or geography, or possibly a similar word meaning 'rocks from Mars'. Maybe *aerology*.

And so, life was discovered on Mars, or *possibly* life, that *might* have existed once, in the form of very simple, small bacteria-like rods, if you squinted while looking at the rock sample and used your imagination. Of course, NASA had already sent spacecraft to visit the Martian surface a couple of Earth decades before Great Uncle

---

[†] A Martian year is about two Earth years; it might be worth remembering this.

Syd's sneeze had made a splash in the headlines. It was at that earlier time, in 1975, that Jade was about to keep a rendezvous she'd made with her dad about a million years before.

Jade kept stopping and looking behind herself, feeling she was being followed. She wasn't a very big *rock tortle*, but was still a tempting little crunchy aperitif for certain predators. She was only fifteen million Martian years old, nearly sixteen million, but this was relatively young for a rock tortle. Her dad, Elvis, was at least a hundred million, though Jade wasn't quite sure. Most adult rock tortles, she found, lied about their age. Either that or they became very forgetful and couldn't remember when they were born. Last year, she'd thought her dad had forgotten the rendezvous for her sixteen millionth birthday, until she realised she'd miscounted the years. Maths was a subject she was still mastering. She had tried scratching the years on her own shell to keep track, but ran out of space. Tortles of her age were known as *umpteenagers*. Jade was average sized for her age, somewhere between half and one metre long. She had the typical little beak of her species, big eyes and her carapace had the gentle sparkle of a subtle green stone that was dotted over the plates; the plates in turn were covered with an intricate dendritic fibrous growth, a bit like lichens growing on an old rock. Her limbs were somewhere between flippers for movement in water and claws for land lubbing, though more on the claw side than 'oar' side.

Jade knew this part of Mars quite well, the Chryse Basin, especially as she'd passed by only the year before. Though the air was thin, it cut like a sheet of paper through everything and she blinked against the mini-sandstorm that was trying to grow. It was actually a Martian summer at this time, though Martian summers were still pretty cold. The red sand dune patterns did shift with the prevailing winds, but the larger boulders always lay in pretty much the same places and Jade was using them to navigate. In fact, she had got to know some of the larger rocks so well, that she'd named many of them. When you've lived fifteen million years, you tend to pick up some odd habits to pass the time. The rock she was passing, a large craggy boulder with a thin layer of frost on the top, she called Thomas. Craggy Thomas. She remembered falling off it when she was only about two and half million. She still had the crack in her own carapace as a souvenir. Just next to it was a smaller rock, a triangular wedge-shaped one onto which she had fallen. She called this one Ben. Wedgy Ben.

'Hi Tom', she whispered nervously to the first rock, 'Hi Ben,' to the second.

She tried to sound casual and unafraid, in the way frightened, *uncasual* creatures do. She stopped and looked back again. She thought she saw a shadow slip behind the previous large boulder. But there was nothing there when she looked again.

* * * * *

Meanwhile, the boulder she had named Thomas turned to Ben. No one noticed it turning, as it did this in another dimension.

'I do wish she'd call me by my proper name,' said Amelius the Third, the rock Jade had called Thomas. Again, no one heard this, as Amelius the Third spoke in infra-sound, sounds far too low for normal hearing, unless you were a whale and there probably weren't many giant sea mammals within earshot. This was on account of the fact that there weren't any seas left on Mars. Certainly not any big enough to house a full sized whale. Probably not anyway.

'Yes,' said Turkan, the rock Jade had called Ben, 'but I don't think she realises that we are in fact four-dimensional beings and we intrude into her three dimensional universe looking like ordinary rocks sitting on the surface of Mars.'

'Oh yes? Yes,' Amelius the Third admitted, 'you told me that before, but I must admit I have trouble picturing a world with only three dimensions. You said something about party balloons, but I didn't think space was made of rubber.'

'It's quite simple really,' Turkan began, 'look, imagine you leant your elbow onto your glass coffee table top there. Any creatures living on *that* surface, say, would see what looked like a giant slug in *their* world ...'

Amelius the Third seemed to think about this for a while as the model sank in.

'You think there are creatures living on my *coffee table*? I cleaned it quite recently and I do use one of those cleaning fluids that says it kills 99% of 4D germs, dead.'

'That's not what I meant.'

'Ah, you think it's the remaining 1% that are still there. Maybe you're right.'

'No,' said Turkan in a fed up, we've-been-through-this-conversation-before sort-of voice. 'It was just a comparison.'

'Oh, like not real.'

'Yes.'

'Like the balloon?'

'Yes.'

There was a pause. Like most four-dimensional creatures, Amelius the Third was limited by his own number of dimensions. Those with such a wide field of view just wander in all directions and can't think in a straight line. Sometimes having too many dimensions to play with stops you seeing the finer detail, like three dimensions.

'So,' Amelius decided, 'you're saying my arm looks like a slug in two dimensions? And I thought me looking like a rock in three dimensions was bad enough...'

* * * * *

Jade thought for a moment that she heard some deep rumblings, coming first from the large craggy rock she had just passed, then it seemed to come from the wedge-shaped one. She put it down to mini Mars tremors, which occurred when meteorites hit the surface. She got her mind back to the problem in hand: that shadow behind the distant rock and the fact that it was becoming *not so* distant.

Jade was now worried. You didn't encounter many forms of life on Mars and when you did, you either ate it, or it ate you. She was a mineralist.[†] That just left the other alternative. Something was looking for lunch and *she* seemed to be the first course. Her dad had taught her that the only things smaller than her that could eat her were the *Eschers* and there wasn't much you could do to stop them anyway. Everything else that wanted to eat you was bigger, so the best thing to do was hide in the small crack of a cliff. The trouble for Jade was there were no cliffs on this part of Mars, certainly not within crawling distance for a small sized tortle. It was all rock-strewn, ochre sand dunes leading to dry-ice basins. So, 'hide behind something bigger than you', was the next step, but Jade realised that the largest thing she could hide behind was *herself.* She'd passed Craggy and Wedgy some moments ago and was now exposed and out in the open. This left the last resort: camouflage. When she thought the shadowy figure had darted behind Craggy Thomas, she quickly dug her head and four half-flipper, half-feet into the red sand, leaving only her over-scratched carapace exposed. She wasn't called a rock tortle for nothing. Rock tortles had survived on Mars for a long time because they looked very much like rocks, once the wiggly bits were hidden from view. Tortles were good at staying still. Jade had once remained in the same place for about twenty thousand years, sometime between her eleventh and twelve millionth birthday. She had never found out what caused the noise. Either it had been an

---

[†] *mineralist* – a creature that eats rocks. People of course eat salt as part of their diet and rats are known to eat dirt if they've been poisoned. This stops the poison being absorbed and so the rats run off to live to be poisoned another day. Heroes in many modern films always seem to advise their opponents to eat lead, so eating minerals is more common than you'd think.

innocent rock falling, or, whatever had been tracking her got bored and moved on.

Rock tortles' hearing was not outstanding in the thin whispering atmosphere of Mars, especially with their heads buried, but they picked up vibrations through the ground. Jade could feel the footsteps of her pursuer clip-clopping ever nearer. She held her breath, which was something she could do for months at a time. She knew she didn't have much of a smell: rock tortles didn't have a strong scent, for survival reasons, so if the creature couldn't recognise her shape, she knew she should be safe. And besides, she was ready to stay put as long as it took. And if she missed her sixteen-millionth birthday rendezvous with her dad, then there was always the next one, a million years later. Then she realised the creature had stopped next to her. 'KNOCK KNOCK' she felt on her shell and then she did something she hadn't done since she was six million. There was now a small pile of gravel behind her.

* * * * *

The environment on Mars had changed over the years. It used to be able to support millions of life forms and each lived for several tens of years. But all that had slowed down now. The air had thinned to suffocation point. The seas had all but dried up. Creatures had had to evolve to cope with the musical chairs of ecological change. Now, only a few tens of creatures could live on Mars, but the trade-off was that they could each live for millions of years. This meant that there were sufficient resources for such small numbers and it also meant that reproduction wasn't as imperative as it used to be. As long as a creature replaced itself with offspring every hundred million years or so, the species could avoid extinction. The downside for the majority of them though, was actually remembering how to reproduce.

* * * * *

Jade swallowed nervously. She could sense the other creature. It had stopped right next to her, which was too much of a coincidence. It must have detected her and now she was moments away from being the wrong end of dinnertime. KNOCK KNOCK! She suddenly felt on her shell again. The shock was enough for her to leave another sculpture of balancing pebbles behind her. Maybe this knocking was just the animal's signal of owning the surrounding territory, she hoped. Banging its presence out on a rock in its domain, to let other males (it was probably a male from what she knew about them), letting all the other males of its species know he was the Top Rock. KNOCK KNOCK! She heard again. She resisted the temptation to say 'who's there'. It might be a trick to make her think it was a friend; she'd pop her head out and then find she no longer had a head.

'You're not very good at hiding,' she heard, the voice sounding deliberately jeering.

Jade lifted her head out of the sand to look at what sounded like another rock tortle, then realised too late that it might have been another trick of the predator, mimicking a friendly voice and catch her in a moment of weakness. But it was too late, and anyway, the voice hadn't been that friendly in the first place. The sudden raising of her head out of the sand made the other young rock tortle step back in fright, then realising he was losing face, regained what he thought was an aggressive stance and puffed himself up.

'What?' Jade asked him.

'I said you're not very good at hiding,' he said again, slowly circling her and giving her a disapproving sneer. He looked at the ground in the direction she'd come from and said 'especially leaving all your footprints for a tortle-eater to follow…'

Jade looked behind herself as well and there it was, her trail. Groups of four plodding foot scrapes flanking a partially smoothed down middle track where her carapace had rubbed the ground. She too felt disappointed with herself.

'But you're *not* a tortle-eater!' she replied in weak defence, not able to think of a smarter riposte.

'How do you know?' said the youngster, in a cocky manner. 'How do you know I'm not a cannon ball or something?'

'It's called a *cannibal* actually.'

'Well I'm fast and, er, as tough as iron, so I could be one of those as well!'

'You're daft,' Jade decided, finally relaxing knowing her pursuer was just another tortle of about her own age.

'Not as daft as someone who leaves their trail behind!'

'But, but our predators are not intelligent enough to follow tracks are they?'

'Not if they're like you!' the other tortle jeered. 'And you're not even the right colour. Green. You stick out like a sore claw.'

Jade hated this little whippersnapper for pointing out her mistakes. Especially as he was right. But she hated herself more for being careless. Her dad had drummed it into her for millions of years to cover her tracks. What would he say of her now, that a young slip of a tortle, barely out of his eggshell had followed her marks in the sand? Probably that she was a turkey. She didn't know what a turkey was but was sure it was something best not to be. If she wanted to see her sixteen millionth birthday, she was going to have to tighten up on personal security. She snapped out of her daydream and tried to regain a bit of her posture to be ready to reply to her Martian stalker after his personal remark about her colour.

'I'm *supposed* to be green okay,' she said, not quite hiding her irritation. 'It's my name, Jade, which means green and anyway, it's the lice that do it, you knew that already, so don't get personal.'

'Do they?' asked the youngster with obvious uncertainty.

Jade picked up on this and her earlier defensive approach turned full circle. She looked at him more closely, he sensed it too, and he backed away.

'What's your name?' she asked accusingly.

'What, Oh, Grit.'

'So, *Grit*, you haven't got your lice yet, have you?' she asked with a touch of victory.

The young rock tortle's eyes searched wildly into the thin Martian atmosphere for help, but there was nothing.

'... I have!'

'Where?' and she approached him yet again.

'... er, they're not here, um they're on holiday.'

Jade turned away. She didn't have to hear any more. A tortle hadn't come of age until he or she had got their lice. Tortle lice were also called pyrites on account of their original love for fool's gold. Plus they were also a thieving bunch of rogues at the best of times. Jade had only had hers for a couple of million years and she'd picked them up in the usual way: a close encounter with another tortle. It was an old spinster of about a hundred and seventy-two million called Chalybete whom she'd literally bumped into on the edge of the Hellas Basin one rather windy autumn morning. Chalybete veered into Jade as if she hadn't seen her and Jade had assumed she was just turning a bit short-sighted. The harmless old dear claimed her own lice had covered her eyes deliberately to cause the crash. Insurance companies would have had a fun old time arguing about who was responsible. Anyway, the moment the collision had happened, half of the lice were seen to 'jump ship' and take up residence on Jade's carapace. Chalybete explained to her that this was how they spread. When they became too numerous on one tortle, the colony would split in two, one half staying, the other half finding a new home, a bit like bees or ants.

That was when Jade started to really turn green. She'd been born with tiny flecks of green crystal on her shell, which was why her parents had named her Jade. And, sure enough, she later became greener. She noticed from time to time the lice would hop off and pick up a green stone or green piece of gravel, hop back on and fix it into place on her shell. They also coated her shell with that strange cobweb of fibres, like candyfloss, though she never understood why. It seemed to cling tightly to her shell and never caught on anything so she assumed they were just decorating and making themselves at home. She didn't really mind having lice – she knew it was for a good reason – it's just that when they moved around a lot, it did itch. Her dad had said something about them being *symbiotic*, but she didn't know what that meant, so he explained that the extra stuck-on rocks added protection for tortles against predators as well as against the deadly cosmic rays from space, while at the same time the lice benefited by being on top of what was effectively an armoured personnel carrier. The captain of Jade's pyrites was called Raffi, Raffi Rehab. The pyrites were only a few centimetres high, but there could be thousands of them on a tortle, so what they lacked in size, they made up in numbers. Plus they made it up in aggression too. Being insectoid, somewhere between grasshoppers, ants, a preying mantis and human, the extra pair of limbs meant they could hold an extra pair of weapons – purely for protection of course – and they could carry many times their own weight, though most were too lazy to do that.

Grit followed her, trying to justify why he had no evidence of his lice.

'They got lost... um ... they, they hopped off to get a closer look when I visited Olympus Mons, they...'

'You never went to Olympus Mons!'

'I did!'

'Okay, who lives up there then?'

'Er, no one, cos it's too cold and the air's too thin.'

'Wrong! Fionix does, but look it doesn't matter if you haven't got your lice yet.'

'But I have!'

'You just have to be a bit more alert until you do.'

'I sacked them because they itched me! I didn't want –'

'Shh!' said Jade suddenly, stopping in her tracks.

Grit hadn't been paying attention and ran into the back of her.

'Oww!' cried Grit.

'Shh!'

'What?'

'Can you hear that?'

'No.'

Jade scrutinised the surroundings. Grit tried to stand behind her as she turned, like some comedy act with Jade as his living shield. Looking back in the direction from where they had come, she could have sworn that the two rocks next to Craggy and Wedgy had been not there before and seemed to be further from the original outcrop and closer in fact to herself and Grit...

'What is it?' said the worried youngster.

Jade scanned the horizon again and then heard a WHUMP! WHUMP! When she returned her gaze to the two suspicious looking rocks, she noticed that...

'They've gone!' she cried.

'What have?' asked Grit.

'The two rocks...'

Jade frantically looked round, straining first to see if the offending boulders were not still in the same place but somehow she'd missed them, or that they were lying elsewhere and it had just been a trick of the light, like a mirage.

'Where are they?' asked Grit with genuine worry.

'I don't know...'

Rocks couldn't just disappear, she thought. Her heart was now pounding fit to burst with the realisation that she was experiencing an experience she hadn't experienced before. Missing Matter. It didn't seem right or in fact it didn't feel safe. Think, she thought, what did her dad tell her? He said, 'act like a dead rock in these circumstances, but think like you don't want to end up like one'. Rocks that could disappear? She vaguely remembered her Great Uncle Syd mentioning *jumping* rocks, but... her thoughts were interrupted by something momentarily blocking out the sunlight. Blocking the sun!

Jade glanced up and in spite of the glare of the late afternoon sun and the red bloom of light surrounding it, she found her two rocks. They had jumped into the air and were now falling back down, heading straight for her and Grit.

* * * * *

Grit had not noticed them and Jade knew there was no time to explain, so she took a running dive at Grit and like another motoring accident, Grit got shunted out of the way by the collision, while Jade herself bounced back in an undignified recoil, landing upturned on her back. This also gave her a full view of the two carnivorous rocks heading back to land not quite on herself or Grit.

THUMP! Then a fraction of a second later THUMP!

Puffs of auburn coloured sand plumed into the air, obscuring the view for a few seconds before they settled back on the ground.

'Grit!' cried Jade. 'Help turn me over!'

There was no answer. Jade knew Grit hadn't been touched, her quick thinking had saved both of them, though she wasn't waiting for a thank you, she just wanted saving herself. Now! Being upside down, she was very vulnerable to another attack and now she had had to add *killer rocks* to her list of things to avoid.

'Grit! Where are you?!'

Jade strained to look at the upside down world and managed to make out a half-buried Grit in the sand a few tens of metres away. He was trying to act like a dead rock, but that seemed pointless, as these killers now knew quite clearly that they were far from dead and close to being dinner.

WHUM! Then a fraction of a second later WHUM!

Even looking at the world upside down, Jade could see that the two rocks had become airborne once again. That meant she only had a few seconds to solve this problem before she wouldn't have to solve any problems ever again.

'Grit! Help! Quick!'

But Grit remained motionless in the ground.

Great, she thought, having just risked her neck to save this lily-livered youngster he wasn't going to return the gesture. She waggled her limbs in all directions, like an upturned, well, an upturned tortle, but she couldn't quite get her claws to make contact with the ground. The two jumping rock silhouettes came into her view, rising above her and blotting out the sun again for a moment, before they started their downward descent to have yet another close encounter with her upturned body.

'Grit, if you don't move your butt over here, you are going to be hit by something bigger than a big falling rock!'

Just as Jade was resigning herself to never reaching sixteen million, she felt a sudden rush across her body and then noticed that all her lice had just jumped off her shell to the ground.

Oh, so this is what it's like to die, she thought, *the lice sense danger, dad said, and here they are, abandoning ship and saving their own necks. Well, I guess Grit will get his lice after all. This is so unfair!* Then she heard one of the lice shout out, but wasn't sure what it said. It sounded like 'capsized!', but in the delirium of her life flashing before her eyes, she assumed it was a bit of hysteria and she was *hear-lucinating*.

The outline of one of the jumping rocks gradually filled her view as it approached to make final contact with her. Before she knew it, she felt herself being uprighted and caught glimpses of what appeared to be her lice, using the wispy cobweb of fibres on her shell, like ropes and, working as a team, they had done what Grit had been powerless to do. And it wasn't a moment too soon. The gravity on Mars was weaker than on Earth and this had given Jade enough time to sidestep her attacker and –

THUMP! Then a moment later in the distance THUMP! Then a faint 'ow!'

Jade looked over to see that Grit had got one of his claws stuck slightly under his attacker's base. She went waddling over to Grit as fast as her short stubby legs would allow, then she heard the now familiar WHUM as her rock took off again.

* * * * *

In the past on Mars, there used to be a species of bird of prey that would drop rocks from a great height onto its dinner-to-be, in order to crack it open, much like some birds still did on Earth. However, the Martian rocks evolved when they realised they were getting a raw deal and cut out the middle man, so to speak, and got rid of the birds, (first by jumping on them), then they decided to catch their own food. How rocks were able to do this was not at all obvious, but it seemed to start when the Martian climate took a turn for the worse. The upshot of it all was that the rocks were evolving to be more like the living creatures while the living creatures such as the tortles were evolving to be more like rocks.

* * * * *

On another part of Mars, in the back lighting of a cool but red sun, the outline of a rather grand and majestic looking rock was silhouetted against the skyline. As a rock it was roughly hemispherical and it differed further from the average kind of rock in that it was moving gently (not jumping as the killer rocks). Actually, it was more angled than curvy, with a large groove running along its crest, as if someone or something had tried to cleave the creature in two and nearly succeeded. It moved slowly, climbing up the shallow incline to a small, local peak. This mobile rock also had legs, four in fact, one in each corner. It was another rock tortle. It was probably the size of a comfy settee, but perhaps not so comfy to sit on. It was much larger than Jade or Grit, so quite likely an adult, two metres long or more. Occasional movement by the creature caused the sun's rays to glance off its rough and quite eroded surface and, though mainly blue-grey, it glinted with tiny flashes of gold. On the rock tortle's back, nestled in the groove, was what looked like a plant, somewhat skinny and suffering from a possible lack of protein. In fact, it could well have been dead, though on a planet such as Mars, the states of being alive or dead tended to overlap. It wasn't unknown for rock tortles to have organic growth on their shells, much like crabs and limpets might have barnacles and sea weed, as natural camouflage, but a plant this size seemed out of place as it swayed wildly – it was as if this veggy life-form was looking for attention, saying 'hello here I am, come and eat me!'

The golden rock tortle stopped its shuffling up the hill and looked round. His name was Elvis. Well, his *nick*-name was Elvis. His real name was Joseph Presley, and he had been called 'Big Joe' at one time because of his size, but then it became Elvis after he'd formed a band. He surveyed the magnificent view of the Chryse Basin from this vantage point. Though he hadn't been born here, he did grow up in the Basin and he found his mind slipping gently back to the days of his youth, nearly a hundred million years ago. The rock-strewn basin of the present moment filled up with water in his mind until there was a sparkling blue sea under an equally sapphire blue sky. He felt his flippers knee deep in the cool, refreshing liquid. In the present, his claws try to sink into the cold, dry, ferruginous sand and barely sank at all, meeting the permafrost and the jagged rocks just below the surface, brought by the flash floods of the last round of volcanic activity. Elvis could see himself swimming, diving under the surface, holding his breath and being chased by Uncle Syd. Yes, Uncle Syd was fun in those days, before his health deteriorated. And there were so many other rock tortles on the water's edge and in the sea itself. His own mum and dad were basking on the beach, watching their children enjoying the family holiday. But even then the drying up had already been going on for some time. Each year, they had had to travel that much further from the hills to reach the edge of the Chryse Lagoon. Elvis himself had been born in one of the little lakes of the Jumbled Terrain in the Western Highlands. He huffed a small laugh as he remembered his dad's old joke. 'It's a tough life on Mars son,' he'd say in his big, advisory way, but it had the tone of a joke about to arrive. 'It's rock eat rock you know. Yep, it's the Law of the Jumble out there.' Elvis didn't understand the joke at the time, but that wasn't important; his dad always laughed at it and he laughed as well. His mum didn't laugh – in fact she always had a dig at his dad for telling the same jokes. However, her jibes actually seemed to be full of affection and not really a criticism, but at that young age Elvis hadn't understood grown up talk – nor long term relationships, for that matter. Then, he himself hit puberty and also had the added task of evolving to keep up with the drying of the planet. And boy, if his own tortle problems of acne weren't bad enough, Olympus Mons became the biggest spot on the adolescent face of Mars itself. The Mother of all Volcanoes. Suddenly the imaginary water round his feet disappeared and he popped back into the present. He sighed and took a deep breath.

'Is this high enough?' Elvis asked, seemingly to no one in particular. There was no answer.

'I say, Starkwood?' he asked again. 'Wake up!'

This time, the half dead plant on Elvis' back came to life, raised its flower-like head, stretched out its arm-like leaves and yawned in a very un-plant-like way.

'What time is it?' said Starkwood in a sleepy voice.

'Summer.'

'Is there any water, or was it all a dream?'

'It's like my humour out there I'm afraid,' said Elvis.

'What?'

'Dry.'

2

The Gospel According to St Arkwood

'So, my dear friend, is this peak high enough?' Elvis asked his flower-like passenger.

'Hang on...'

Starkwood regained some semblance of being sentient and stood as tall as he could (between half and one metre), and did something that looked like listening. He stayed like this for several minutes.

'I've got a bad feeling about this,' he said.

'You've *always* got a bad feeling about something,' said Elvis from somewhere below.

'Well, there is a change in the field, you know, but there's not even a whiff of a solar storm brewing.'

Starkwood didn't know if he wanted to admit everything to Elvis; he was worried Elvis would rip him up by his roots and give up on their fairly successful symbiotic relationship. Being an electrostatic plant, Starkwood was sensitive to the weak but battered-by-the-solar-wind magnetic field of Mars. In fact, Starkwood lived off the incoming solar wind's energy and that's why he was able to detect what was happening in the Martian magnetic field. Starkwood had a punk hairstyle of fronds sitting untidily atop what could only be described as a flower of a head. These delicate fronds seemed to wave and waft in unison in the almost empty Martian atmosphere, like a sea anemone's tentacles, but they didn't lean the way of the prevailing winds. No, they followed the lines of Mars' magnetic field. And this let Starkwood know where his next meal was coming from. He had a sort of frilly-ended snout, as might be seen on a mole or a shrew and it was all twitchy like a bat, forever reassessing the surroundings.

'Hearing any of those angel voices again?' Elvis mocked him.

'Well thanks a lot, you old rock *has-been*. You're just like that bunch of witch burning weeds that used to be my friends.'

'Just teasing. So nothing to report?'

'…No. Nothing.'

'You never really told me why you were shunned by your own, um crop.'

'You promised you wouldn't ask.'

'I was waiting for you to open up.'

'I didn't.'

'I know. That's why I'm asking you now.'

'I never asked *you* about your past.'

'Nothing to hide. Started as an egg on the edge of the Jumbled Terrain, when there was still water, had flippers but they grew into legs when there was more land than sea and, voila, here I am. So, come on, your history can't be any worse than your claim that 'Vikings' are coming to attack Mars, can it?'

'No, but okay, only if you promise not to throw me off the next cliff if I tell you.'

'I told you we have a deal. You keep me informed of any solar storms and I keep you out of trouble.'

Starkwood paused, seemed to think about it, then took the plunge.

'Well, it was shortly before we teamed up, what about a million years ago?'

'When I found you close to death on the edge of the Great Rift Valley?'

'Yes, they tried to sacrifice me to appease their gods.'

'So what had you said to them?'

'Well,' began Starkwood, 'I used to live on the Equatorial Bulge, you know, where the magnetic field gets pushed so hard by the force of big solar storms that the outer edge of the Martian field actually reaches the ground.'

'And there's good eating in one of them storms, isn't there,' Elvis remarked.

'Manna from heaven. There were crops of us covering the plateau; well you must have strolled into them on your travels.'

Elvis nodded but explained, 'Tended to avoid them as I found a lot more dust would stick to me, what with all that static flying around.'

Starkwood agreed.

'It was pretty crowded at one time, all of us competing for the best spot to catch the best cosmic rays. Although we all had our roots firmly entrenched, an agile static plant could lean over, stretch to full length and snatch the rays from a neighbour's patch.'

'Naughty.'

'Survival of the naughtiest.'

'But you're not that tall for an electric plant?' Elvis pointed out.

'Exactly! I was missing most of the best particles and jostled by all the other plants that were so much bigger than me. Anyway, one time I was straining so much to get an incoming cosmic ray, I uprooted myself! I thought I'd done myself a permanent injury and didn't expect to ever have any offspring of my own.'

'Sounds like it was painful.'

'It was. But after lying on the ground feeling sorry for myself, I tried to get up and found to my surprise that I had *prehensile* roots! I could walk! I was no longer a static plant, I was *dynamic*!'

* * * * *

Jade didn't have the time to analyse what had just happened, what with two carnivorous rocks trying to stamp on her head. She looked at her immediate surroundings and saw that she had drifted to the edge of a slight decline, a gentle slope down to lower terrain. In the far distance, there were cliffs, with the possible tortle-sized nooks and crannies that her dad had always advised her to head for when in danger. But it was a long way off. She looked at the ground stretching out in front of her and thought the rusty red sandy regolith seemed to have a little white coating on it and decided to...

THUMP!

A sliver of her carapace had just been chipped off by the almost direct hit of one of the pouncing rocks. The gash was only a centimetre or so wide, but the crack cut deep into her shell, exposing her delicate fleshy insides. While the dust was settling and Grit was dazed by the second rock that landed close to him, Jade shuffled over to the bewildered young tortle and spoke to him.

'I have an idea!' she shouted to the confused Grit, who was barely following what was going on. 'Quick, grab onto the back of my shell – we're going for a scrape down this slope.'

'What do I grab on with?' he asked.

'Your mouth, now come on!'

WHUM! WHUM!

The two rocks were airborne again.

'What, you want me to bite your *butt*?!'

'No! Well, yes, but,'

'That's gross!' said Grit. 'My parents told me not to talk to strange creatures, and I never believed it would be a girl tortle!'

'Don't be such a stupid rock head!' cried Jade in frustration. 'We need to get to safety!'

Grit didn't have time to resume his monologue before the young female rock tortle had actually bitten onto *his* butt with her beak-like jaw and was now scooping him off down the mild slope.

THUMP! THUMP!

It was only going to be a matter of time, thought Jade, before the chance jumps of the killer rocks would actually land on one of them. How the killer rocks ate was not clear to Jade – perhaps when sitting on their catch after the final splat, they would be *osmosising* them up by capillary action. Dish of the day, soupe à la tortle.

'Stop biting my butt!' cried the now irritated Grit, but Jade held on fast to her reluctant companion and she started off down the slope. She wasn't going that fast but she soon hit a patch where the permafrost met the surface and the sandy groove she'd been carving out with her shell suddenly lessened and she slipped down on the almost frictionless thin layer of ice, picking up the all-too-needed speed she had been after. The rocks *thumped* and *whumped* in her wake and they had to increase their strides in order to keep up with her, but Jade kept just out of their reach. Still they were dangerously close.

'Let me go!' cried Grit. 'I'm too young to die! I'm only fourteen million! Why won't you let me go!?'

Mumble mumble.

'Answer me!' insisted the young tortle.

'I gnustn't talk gnith gny gnouth hull!' said Jade, unable to speak comprehensibly.

'Kidnapping me!' cried Grit. 'Ha! You're gonna be in big trouble about this!'

'Good greesh!' cried Jade, rolling her eyes to the heavens, then she continued trying to navigate herself and the reluctant cargo to safety. There was another *whump* then another *thump* just in front of them. The sudden ejecta that shot up from the jumping rock showered the twosome with unwanted sand grains and shards of ice, and Jade had to negotiate round the killer obstacles as if she was on a slalom ride. There was enough of a wind for Jade to squint against the cold black breeze, and she could just make out what appeared to be a more icy patch ahead. In fact the incline was part of a descent into a

21

natural geographical basin, or more technically (as it was Mars) an *aerographical* basin. Maybe it was an old crater.

A thump shook Jade from her surveying of the scenery as one of the carnivorous rocks landed just in front of her and she barely swerved enough to avoid it and hit its side and broke contact with Grit, both of them spinning and rotating in their chaotic slide towards the bottom of the depression. Grit screamed as he landed on his back and he instinctively retracted his head and limbs. Jade, still slipping and scraping along on her stomach, brought her head down to ground level and tried to make herself more streamlined, to catch up with her new found and even more newly lost companion. She managed to hook her beak onto the rim of his shell, then drag herself in a clumsy way to end up perched on top of him. He was sliding on his back, while Jade was now standing on his stomach – the underside of his carapace. Her stance was one of some kind of Shelled Skateboarder.

It didn't last long as the second Killer Rock thumped in front of her again and she and Grit separated, both now sliding gracefully along on their stomachs, but Jade managed to catch Grit again in her mouth. Jade then thought she heard a tiny voice on her back that said something like 'hoist the main sail, yer bilge rats!' and to her surprise, the web like strands that draped over her carapace, seemed to spring up like a catapult, catching the wind and she accelerated away from the Predatory Rocks. She stole a glance behind and, though she was losing the hunters, they were not giving up. She peered over Grit's rather dormant body to see where they were heading and it was the bottom of the bowl. The lowest section actually seemed to be a flat, circular patch of ice with no rocks or even any soil showing through. Strange. A circular patch of ice about thirty metres across. She peered over the top of Grit again. The frozen pond didn't look white and all *crystally*, like the ice on the bowl's higher slopes. No, this layer of ice was actually *transparent* and looked *very dark* below. Dark, as in probably a deep, deep hole underneath, which was possibly full of water. Deep and dark like an ice covered well. Jade had never been around when there were real seas full of water on Mars, so she wasn't sure if she could swim. She looked at her flippers, which had evolved halfway to becoming clawed feet to move on dry land – the emphasis on *dry*, and they didn't look flippy enough to push against water. Plus her body felt more on the *sinking* side of swim than on the *floating* side – even if she held her breath. This was not looking good.

They hit the frozen pond like a pair of reptilian ice skaters and the ridges on Grit's back scraped along the ice, sending up a spray in an attractive arc. The two of them skewed to the left and ended up spinning, probably doing a triple half-swivel-turn in ice skating terminology, which would have scored a 5.9 from the Ukrainian jury had there been Winter Olympics on Mars. But actually, it was a Martian *Summer*. Anyway. They came to an ice screeching halt, dizzy and dazed.

The two stalking rocks had just landed on the frozen lake's edge and were taking off for a final pounce. Jade tried scrabbling to move on the ice, but there wasn't enough friction and she merely scratched claw-marks into the surface. For that moment, she hated her dad for not teaching her more about the laws of physics, so she could have used them to her advantage just when she needed them. She ignored the fact that she had often ignored her dad when he went into his *physics is fun* mode. So there they were, stranded on the ice. Which started to crack. Things were not looking good. The two boulders were at the top of their flight paths and about to land on the two tortles like sitting ducks. Yes, the ice was cracking, and as Jade looked at the spider web fractures in the frozen surface below her, she thought she could see a pair of eyes. And a huge, twenty metre wide mouth. Smiling with big white teeth showing.

* * * * *

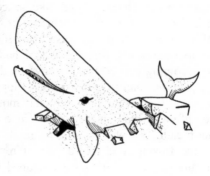

Chryssie was a lung whale. She had been asleep for, well she wasn't sure, but it was a long time and at least twenty thousand years but could have been several hundred million years for all she knew. She had just been woken by vibrations through the ground that resonated in her deep ice-lined water-well of a cocoon. The approach of a long overdue meal, she thought. A two course meal actually. She couldn't remember the last time she'd eaten, but she was damn hungry. It must have been at least the last time she woke up. Life was a bit on the boring side for a Martian lung whale. These days anyway. In the past, when there was enough water to make one big ocean, she remembered meeting up with other lung whales and swimming together in herds – or was it shoals, or swarms? Well it was something that hinted at a big crowd of things. A flock? No. But when the seas began to dry up and evaporate, her lung whale friends became separated and imprisoned in their remaining patches of water. Chryssie dug her own well to ensure she could sit upright and still be under water. Then it got colder, as Mars lost much of its atmosphere, so the only thing to do was to let the top of her well freeze shut with her inside and at least ensure her own survival through hibernation. She held her breath then went to sleep to conserve energy. The idea behind evolving into a lung whale was that when the climate improved, the atmosphere would return bringing warmer temperatures and water; this would melt her ice cap and she'd pop out and get some sort of long overdue take away. But that hadn't happened yet and Chryssie was pretty fed up. Well not fed, food-wise, but now the sound of a two-course meal had just given her the wake-up call. Plus she was dying for a pee and her parents had warned her before the climate change that it was a bad idea to drink Martian seawater in view of what all the animals did in it. And she couldn't be sure she hadn't already had an accident during her long sleep.

* * * * *

'And I said unto my followers,' Starkwood continued, 'hark now,'

'*Followers*?!' asked Elvis, bemused.

'Okay, well they couldn't actually *follow* me on account of the fact they were still fixed to one place, but they were my sort of *metaphorical* followers if you get me.'

'So what *didst* thou say then, oh holy bush?'

'I said; my fellow static plants, pull up thyselves and cometh with me, for this is how it is to be.'

'And did they *picketh* up their roots?'

'Er, no, they pickethed up some rocks and didst throw them at me...'

'Oh,' reflected Elvis, 'is *pickethed* actually a word?'

'Probably not, but it fitteth into my tale.'

'So, what happened next?'

'Well I tried to physically uproot some of my static friends and get them to move but mainly I kept my distance, on account of the rocks that the others were throwing at me. Besides, none of the ones I freed from the ground seemed to have the same dexterity in their roots like me, so I planted them again and went away.'

'So,' said Elvis thoughtfully, 'do you think you are the next evolutionary step for your species of plant?'

'What? Are you calling me a missing link or something?'

25

'No, you're not missing anything, as far as I can see.'

'A mutation?!'

'No. well yes, but a *positive* mutation. I mean in every generation, individuals are born with slight differences, most are actually worse off, but the occasional one is an improvement and it would mean *their* offspring would have a better chance of surviving.'

'Oh,' said Starkwood. 'but I thought that since the big climate change, us living creatures just started evolving, like *live on stage*, so to speak and not waiting for the next generation to change as, well, we don't, um *pollinate* that often do we?'

'Quite right,' confirmed Elvis, 'though us tortles don't pollinate at all. We, er, well that's another story. It involves lots of grains of sand and a round pebble, but what goes on between tortles stays between them. So maybe you started off with normal roots when you were, er, um, how *did* you actually come about?'

'Oh, er, a dad plant puffs his pollen out on a windy day, a mum plant picks it up, a seed pod pops out into the topsoil and here I was, well there I was.'

'And when was here? I mean there?'

'Well I remember seeing the ocean's edge from my plateau top and Olympus Mons wasn't there yet.'

'So your roots could have mutated anytime in the last hundred million years or so. Did you feel a change in them at all?'

'Well I did feel something tickling them about twenty five million years ago, but I thought that was just one of those rare Martian QT worms wriggling about beneath the surface.'

'Okay,' Elvis carried on, 'so how did you end up here, I mean, where I met you?'

'Right, yes, you see, I decided to try and convert some of my brethren plants into my new way of life – a life of motion. So I started the *Movement* Movement.'

'Is that what you called it?!'

'Not many plants wanted to join.'

'I can understand that.'

'I tried to get them to do these exercises with their roots, which I called anaerobics.'

'Another catchy name!'

'A few of the other static plants were actually interested and I had some fanatical disciples.'

'Really?'

'They called me Saint Arkwood, which is how I got my present name.'

'I didn't know that.'

'Yes, I was originally known as Arkwood, but the Saint bit got shortened to St and the title fused into one and voila here I am: Starkwood.'

3

The Rock Less Travelled

Sometime earlier, we zoom into the vibrant blue globe of Earth and head towards Europe. Aiming for France. Heading for the south coast in fact, down through a sprinkling of wispy high, thin clouds that are rapidly evaporating in the bright morning sun. North west of Cannes on the coast and towards Fayence, to the little village next door: Tourrettes. The houses clumped together on the side of the hill, leaning against each other like old people trying to remain upright. The village square: well not much of a square, and it wasn't the real centre of the village, it was where the road emerged out of the north of the village, ready to head for Mons towards the foothills of the pre-Alps. There was the square, the butcher's on one corner, next to it the bar and on the opposite side of the road, a recently opened flower shop, run by the postman's wife. The road leading into and out of the square was barely wide enough for one car, the square itself just about wide enough for two and there was the intermittent flow of morning traffic coming both ways, the occasional shaking of fists between confronting drivers, until one would give in and let the other car pass by. Or both would stop and shake hands with the clump of neighbours buying their meat or early morning coffee and twenty Gitanes. On the south side of the square was sitting Madame Helene, the fat lady of the village. She had already brought out her own chair from her house next to the ancient water fountain and was watching the world go by. Or not go by, depending on the cooperative nature of the drivers. Double parking was an almost permanent feature of the village and it would have been triple parking if there had been space for a third vehicle in the square, so usually it just built up in both directions with a chorus of honking horns.

Above the square, criss-crossing the air space were several telephone cables. Sitting on one wire were two birds. They were house martins. They both watched the traffic go by. The smaller of the two was actually called Martin – not the most imaginative of names for a house martin admittedly, but certainly an easy one to remember. Almost as bad as calling your pet dog 'Dog,' I suppose. Martin's slightly larger and older friend was called House. Was that cruel, or just a joke on the part of his parents?

'Morning,' said House, not taking his eyes off the laid-back people sitting at the table outside the bar, with their tiny espressos and ribbons of smoke unwinding from their filterless cigarettes.

'Morning,' said Martin back to him, their voices barely audible above the chattering cicadas that continuously reminded them they were in Provence and summer was coming. There were long pauses between the birds' comments, but that was normal. Nothing was hurried down here. It was the South of France after all.

'Madame Helene's put on weight...'

A glance down to the character in question and one could see the retired lady's blue and white checked dress just peeking out from her ever present pinny. Below that, her amply wide legs could be seen planted steadfastly on the ground, somewhat weatherworn and showing signs of varicose veins growing up from her ankles.

'Nah, it's just the dress…'

Martin then looked at the wall to their side, at the upside down mud 'igloos' that were the homes of his friend and his next-door. He continued after another long lazy break; 'I see you've got some wind damage from the Mistral last night…'

House took his eyes off Madame Helene's legs and looked at the offending hole on the top right hand corner of his home.

'Yes, I'm going to have to go and find some mud… not an easy task in this dry spell…'

They both returned their gaze to the village square below. A long pause followed.

'Below the bridge next to the old railway station…' suggested Martin, 'there's usually still some puddles of water. And the dirt's quite tacky there due to the horses…'

A woman went into the flower shop, so they watched her eyeing up the bouquets in the window display.

'So, Martin…' House started, 'you got anything interesting lined up for today?'

'Yes,' replied Martin, 'indeed I do. I'm expecting a communication from a distant cousin…'

The woman in the flower shop was pointing to a bunch of yellow roses. The postman's wife was carefully gathering them together, ready for wrapping.

'Really?' said House, even including some genuine surprise. 'Where does your distant cousin live?'

'…Mars.'

This reply generated a slight twitch from House but his cool was not lost,

'… that *is* quite distant…'

* * * * *

The face below Jade moved further down into the darkness, as if preparing to pounce, while in the mirror-like layer of ice the reflection of the two predatory rocks could be seen hurtling back down to the ground. Jade just closed her eyes and said one last prayer to her god: the Prairie Tortoise. Jade had completely forgotten about her recently found companion, Grit and he could have been anywhere for all she knew.

There was not a lot to the tortle religion. There was one basic question: which came first, the rock or the tortle? The main school of thought was that the rock came first, hence the name 'rock tortle'. I mean, they weren't called '*tortle* rocks' were they? But then others would ask 'does that mean a rock, which is sort of dead, came alive to become a tortle in the past? That would be a miracle if it happened, no? Then the counter argument was: living things die so it makes more sense that the tortle came first, *then* it died and became a rock. I mean, isn't that what fossils are? Rock versions of dead living things? I mean, living things grow, but dead things don't. Rocks don't grow?! Okay then, what about stalagmites and stalactites, they're rocks, they grow? That's different! Okay crystals grow! Tortles aren't crystals! But they do each have a special crystal sprinkling, like jade, or sapphire, from which they get their individual names. Well, okay, carnivorous rocks grow. But they aren't tortles! Yes but if they *eat* a tortle, the tortle becomes the rock. So you're saying every rock was once living then? Huh? The whole planet? Huh? Huh?! Look, is this the right time to have a debate about the meaning of existence? A tortle's life is hanging in the balance. Or maybe it's about to be born as a dead rock? This is not helping! Let's talk about this later.

Hopefully it should now be obvious that tortle arguments are rather circular, which is why they don't really discuss it much. Well, they do, but they don't get very far.

The ice below Jade suddenly cracked into huge slabs, which moved upwards in the middle and Jade found herself sliding down the smooth slope away from the epicentre of this mini-marsquake. A twenty-metre wide mouth rose out of the newly formed crater lake, displaying the biggest grin on the planet. At the same moment, two falling rocks fell into the splash of the lung whale, who then fell back inside her vertical bath and sent a tsunami of a wave outwards. This wall of water overflowed the crater's rim, pushing away the ice sheets, that had once been the plug on the top of the frozen lake, and sending them scraping and spinning slowly over the outer edges of the ice field. Jade had been on top of one of these pirouetting plaques of ice while Grit was nowhere to be seen.

Jade found herself on an ever-inclining sheet of ice, with the downward side now tilting back towards the very mouth that had broken through in the first place. Instinctively, Jade dug her claws into the almost frictionless surface and hung on for all she was worth. The ice slab became more and more vertical and Jade looked at her feet to see with horror that they weren't holding. Little chips of ice pinged into the air as she inched, almost imperceptibly in the bad direction. She whacked her head against the ice and her beak plunged satisfyingly deep into the frosty surface like an ice pick. Until the ice round her beak cracked and off she began sliding towards Mars.

'*Man* the ropes ya weevils!' came a little cry from somewhere behind Jade's head.

'What about us *women*?' came a little cry back.

'*Women* the ropes then!' snapped Cap'n Raffi Rehab and the next moment, dozens of little ropes with tiny anchors on the ends were thrown overboard. Jade was amazed by this unexpected rescue operation as she saw the anchors pierce the slab all around her and the ropes starting to go taught. Then they went slack and the next moment she was slipping down the ice leaving her rescuing ropes behind.

'Ya bunch of useless flotsam!' cried Raffi. 'You're supposed to keep hold of the damn anchors!'

'But you didn't say that Cap'n!' came a dissenting voice.

'Grab the loose ends!' Cap'n Rehab screamed and the

next moment there was action. Hundreds of lice jumped overboard and linked limbs like ants do on Earth to form chains long enough to grab a number of the anchor ropes that were whipping about in the chaos. Thud! Jade came to a sudden halt and the slack was taken up by the now well-educated, well-taught pyrites. A few lice chains snapped and individuals pinged randomly around Jade but soon regrouped until equilibrium was established.

'Worry not Ma'am!' said Raffi Rehab in Jade's ear.

Jade had just enough time to sigh with relief before the section of ice that she was hooked to snapped loose from the whole slab and, like a sledge, she and her crew of pyrites made a rapid shift in the wrong direction.

'HEY?' called out Chryssie, in her voluminous, whale-sized voice. The ground and air shook with the sonic boom. 'DID I JUST SEE JADE?'

As the water flowed back into the slightly emptied sinkhole, Chryssie leaned her chest on the unbroken ice surrounding her hibernation home and lay there, half in, half out and she looked around for the person she thought she'd seen. She saw a movement nearby so peered closer at it and it was a cowering little tortle, hiding behind a pile of gravel created from … well, let's just say the tortle was scared.

'IS THAT YOU JADE?' came the decibellion wail from the megaton mammal in a shock wave that swept the gravel wall away from the quivering Grit and exposed him to the elements. He opened an eye and peered at this mountain of a leviathan, showing just enough face for Chryssie to come to the right conclusion.

'OH YOU'RE NOT HER, SON. I THOUGHT I SAW HER JUST NOW. I KNEW HER FATHER, YOU KNOW. ELVIS. I THOUGHT I RECOGNISED HER GREENY COLOUR. NOT SEEN HER IN, WELL, ICE AGES… WHO ARE YOU CHILD? NOT SEEN YOU BEFORE.'

As if not wanting a land mine to go off, Grit tried to make himself as light on his feet as possible and whispered so quiet as if miming.

'I'm Grit...'

'SPEAK UP SON, I'VE GOT WATER IN MY EARS – PLUS I AM GETTING ON A BIT YOU KNOW!'

This reply actually caused such a rush of air that it made Grit slide backwards a few metres on the ice.

'I'm Grit!'

'STILL CAN'T HEAR!'

'I'M GRIT!' he cried with all his might, taking an aggressive stance, then, realising the enormity of the being that he was shouting at, he scrambled to run away but stayed comically on the same spot like a cartoon character trying to run with fear.

'WELL HELLO GRIT! I COULD'VE SWORN I SAW JADE.'

'She... was... here...' said Grit sheepishly.

'OH...' said Chryssie, then they both started glancing round to see if she was lying spread-eagled on or under a slab of ice, all bedraggled and perhaps knocked out from the shock of Chryssie's own geyser-like appearance.

'Jade?!' cried Grit with concern. There was no answer.

'JADE?!' thundered the whale. The sound echoed and lingered for a few seconds.

'Jade?!' said Grit again but Chryssie interrupted.

'SHHHHH! I THINK I HEAR SOMETHING... A MUFFLED SOUND...'

They both listened harder. Sure enough, there was a muffled voice coming from somewhere. They looked around the shattered lumps of broken ice but the focal point of the noise seemed to be coming from elsewhere. They even peered down through the unbroken ice to see if Jade had somehow slipped under the surface and was trapped in the water. No. The sound seemed to be coming from close to Chryssie herself. She raised her chest from the ice, in case *she* was lying *on* Jade. No. Grit looked at Chryssie's chest. Chryssie saw him looking. She stared down. Grit sidled up to Chryssie's blubbery thick skin and knocked on it with his claw.

Tap tap!

There was a muffled response!

'Come in,' came the sarcastic reply from inside the whale.

'GRIT,' said Chryssie, 'WE HAVE A PROBLEM...'

'You... You, you *ate* my friend!' said Grit.

'I DIDN'T DO IT ON PURPOSE DEAR! I WAS AFTER THOSE TASTY ROCKS!'

Grit backed away in utter fear, which is pretty much what he'd been doing ever since Jade encountered him (and probably for several millennia before that – though as a safety mechanism it had clearly worked up until now).

'DON'T BE FRIGHTENED!' pleaded the lung whale 'I WON'T EAT YOU.'

'Not now. You're already full up! But when you're hungry again...'

'THAT COULD BE HUNDREDS OF YEARS FROM NOW.'

The shouting conversation was interrupted by more muffled noises coming from the inner space of this gravitationally attractive creature.

'Hello?' came Jade's voice through the thick fog of flesh.

Grit looked at the belly of this baleen beauty and then into her eyes and seemed to hesitate in his cowardly stance. He slowly made a pace forward, his clawed half-feet, half-flippers scratching in the ice like chalk down a board, though since no creatures in the vicinity had hairs there were none to stand up with irritation. Then he scrabbled a bit until he was sliding forwards and he put a fierce look on his face. Chryssie watched him with curiosity. With the fact that she was thousands of times larger than him, she wasn't too bothered at what he might be about to do.

'Don't worry Jade!' he cried, 'I'm coming to save you!'

'?' came the silence from the whale's stomach.

'Let her go, let her go!' wailed Grit with all his might as he aimed for a head on collision with this monstrous marine mammal.

Grit closed his eyes and waited for contact.

BOING!

He rebounded, much as one would have expected from a semi-elastic collision, he scraped and slewed a bit to the left before coming to a halt.

He tried again. And again. Chryssie sighed. It looked like this might go on for some time. Let him get it out of his system, she thought. But it was touching that this little pip squeak of a tortle was willing to risk his life to save his friend.

'Let!'

BOING

'Her!'

BOING

'Out!'

BOING

Ten minutes later, Grit was lying on his back, legs in the air like a dead upturned beetle. He was panting and gasping out the same mantra: 'Let ... Her ... Out!'

'HONEY?' asked the whale, 'YOU DONE NOW?'

'She... Was ... My ... Only ... Friend.'

'DON'T WORRY WE'LL GET HER OUT...'

'How!?'

Chryssie wasn't actually sure about that. Things that tended to go in one end, her mouth, then either got digested, or they would come out somewhere where the Martian sun didn't shine. There was Chryssie's spouting hole of course, that used to be on the top of her head when she swam in the Chryse Ocean but it evolved to become a nose when she ended up vertical in a water well of a prison. Not only that, it wasn't a very large hole anyway so she couldn't imagine sneezing Jade out that way. Her mouth was the obvious choice but with all her internal valve systems, nothing normally ever came back out her mouth. This she explained to Grit.

'Okay,' he decided, 'then I'm going to pull her out.'

'BUT YOUR CLAWS AREN'T LONG ENOUGH TO REACH MY STOMACH.'

'I have a way...'

And with that, Grit turned his head as far to the left as

possible and with his beak he pulled out the end of a long stringy thing from inside his shell.

'WHAT'S THAT?' asked the whale.

'A rope.'

'WHERE DID YOU GET A ROPE?'

'I found it near a dead white tortle.'

'WHITE?'

'Yes. I think she died on her wedding day.'

'WHAT MAKES YOU SAY THAT?'

'The rope was attached to her huge wedding skirt.'

'OH…'

Chryssie didn't really understand this, so put it down to delirium. As they spoke, Grit tied the rope around his waist then looked for a hand-sized rock among the ice debris on the semi frozen Crater Lake.

'WHAT ARE YOU GOING TO DO YOUNG MAN?'

'I'm going fishing for a friend…'

The rock found and tied on, Grit swung it round his head like a hammer throwing heptathlete until he was sure he'd got the technique right.

'Okay, er, Miss Chryssie… or is it Misses?

'LADY…'

'Oh, sorry your ladyship. But now I must ask you to open wide… if it pleases you…'

Chryssie realised what the heroic little ninja tortle was about to do, so obliged. Grit picked up the end of the rope with the little rock tied to it and began to swing it round his head, faster and faster with a larger and larger radius.

'Here we go!' he exclaimed then launched the rotating rock on a rope and, sure enough, it flew through the thin atmosphere, arcing gently into the gaping chasm that was The Lady's smile. Plop! The rock hit the tongue and bounced along it a few times coming to a halt, the rope mimicking the same pattern, like a gymnast's ribbon on a stick. Grit then braced himself and crouched low on the ice for a better purchase.

'Now my lady, could you swallow it?'

There was a pause.

'I'LL NEED A DRINK WITH IT. HANG ON.' and

with that Chryssie reversed and sank momentarily into her well, the water overflowing a little with displacement, then she was up again and gargled a little before swallowing her 'shot on the rocks'. Grit felt a sudden surge pull him forwards and though his heels dug into the ice, he headed towards the entrance to the tunnel of no return. He came to a halt with his back feet pushing hard against one of Chryssie's bottom teeth, him leaning backwards to try and counteract the swallowing force of the whale. Then Grit started to shout into the monumental mouth of the aristocratic whale, his simple words echoing back as if he was singing in a cavernous cathedral.

'Jade Jade Jade… Grab the rope! The rope, the rope!'

Jade had stopped banging her head against the inside wall of Chryssie's stomach. There had been no answers from outside for several minutes. She was so frustrated, she felt like banging her head against… how had it all gone wrong? She'd spent the last however many million years barely encountering anyone and it had been heaven. Nothing exciting had really happened in that time and then, suddenly, her world had turned banana shaped. All she'd planned to do was meet up with her dad for a birthday, that's all. She felt she was getting a bit too old for such parties, but it made her dad happy. And then in no time at all she meets another tortle, a slightly annoying one at that, is chased by blind, biting boulders, only to end up inside what was probably the last lung whale on the planet. Jade remembered her dad telling her about them and from what this one said, they'd actually met before – though Jade couldn't remember her. What were the chances of all these things happening to her on the same day? Clearly in hindsight, the chance was one.

It was dark in the stomach of a 300m long lung whale. There were odd dripping and gurgling sounds and a bit of sloshing which was unpleasant to hear. Jade felt herself knee deep in a gooey liquid, that seemed to be making a quiet fizzing sound and she could feel gas bubbles tingling up the sides of her legs. She realised this was not a good sign. Her lice, who had gone overboard after the ropes, had all made it back on to her shell and were hanging their heads in shame.

'Beggin' yer pard'n ma'am,' said Raffi, 'we did our best. We be doin' this manoeuvre for the first time, like for real, an…'

'Don't worry,' said Jade, feeling sorry for the poor guy, 'we'll get out of this,' she said positively, though inside she wasn't sure how.

The next moment someone threw a rock on her head. A rock tied to the end of a string.

Jade was pretty sharp, which was useful, as she worked out what her newly found companion was trying to do. It was actually sweet of him, she decided, and she felt bad for thinking he was irritating.

While Jade thought this, she searched for the rock on a rope in the dark, acidic swamp of Chryssie's belly. She found it, and duly tied it round her middle. The cries of 'pull, pull!' were faintly making their way down the oesophagus and into the very large stomach of this sizable sea creature. Jade braced herself, which was difficult, as the mucus lining the stomach walls didn't give much friction back in return. Then she pulled…

Jade felt the string go taut for a second or two, then loosen like a kite string when the wind dropped. She found she was pulling on it and bringing more and more turns of the rope to herself like some silly magician pulling out an endless string of silk handkerchiefs…

Meanwhile topside, Grit had braced himself and shouted for the final time 'Pull! Pull! Pull!'

The next moment, that's exactly what happened. But he was no longer at rest in the safety and comfort of the outside world. No, he now watched himself in slow motion as he followed the majestic path of a ballistic projectile (himself!) through the air, a slight rotation, then the loose rope suddenly pulled tight again, whipping him further into the gaping black hole of this local universe. Grit gave a confused glance at some imaginary camera filming this spectacle, thinking that this was not how it was supposed to go. The hero comes to the rescue of the damsel in distress and they all live happily ever after. Well, he thought, at least he'd be with his friend again in a moment or two.

WHACK!

It wasn't often that Jade got hit on the head by another tortle. In fact this was the first time and probably something worth writing in her diary had she kept one.

'Hi Jade,' said Grit awkwardly, 'I was trying to rescue you.'

'And how's that going?

'I HAVE AN IDEA,' said Chryssie, trying to swallow her own words so they could hear her properly. 'HANG ON A MINUTE...'

Chryssie squinted around her at the jumbled mass of broken ice and a few odd rocks that were scattered across the floor of her ice-capped crater. Her gaze then rested on two out-of-place boulders. They stood just under a little overhang at the crater's edge as if they were lurking. It's hard to imagine that a rock could lurk, but these two did it like it was second nature to them. Chryssie also got the feeling they were trembling a little. She took a deep breath then slumped most of her body weight out of her water well, so she was lying on the ice floor. Now her face was only a few metres from the shaking rocks. One lost its cool and decided to make a jump for it. It took off but, barely a fraction of a second later, hit its head on the overhanging cliff of the crater rim. A few small bits of itself fell off and curiously, these little shards were also sentient and hopped around like jumping beans and gradually dispersed into the background. The rock panicked and flew upwards a second time, only to repeat the daft head-hitting routine, with more chips and splinters of itself pinging around randomly. Maybe that's how carnivorous rocks propagated their species: in times of danger, bits break off like a lizard loses its tail, but in this case, the little bits can escape to grow and carry on the family line while the bulk left behind doesn't. Or maybe that was how the Eschers formed? The second suspicious rock also began to jump vertically and it too banged against the ledge a few metres above its head and the next moment both were bobbing up and down like popcorn in a boiling pot.

The two ridiculous rocks were put out of their misery a second or two later when the twenty metre wide lips of a lung whale closed around them and the tongue dragged them to the back of her throat to swallow them whole. Chryssie let out a very un-lady-like burp but did excuse herself.

'LOOK OUT BELOW!' she cried to her unfortunate inmates.

BANG!

'Oww!' cried Jade. Grit sniggered cruelly at her misfortune until –

BANG!

'Oww!' said Grit as he too suffered the slings and rocks of outrageous fortune, by being hit on the head in a whale's stomach, by a tortle-eating rock.

The fizzing and bubbling that Jade had mildly experienced was many times greater for these two rocks as they started to dissolve readily in the acidic juices of Chryssie's digestive system. The two rocks wriggled helplessly as their parts below the surface of the acid lake melted away like a sugar cube standing up in a shallow cup of coffee.

'NOW RUB THE RESIDUE ONTO YOURSELVES!' explained Chrysie. 'IT'LL STOP YOU BEING EATEN AWAY. LET IT HARDEN AND WHEN IT'S READY, YOU'LL BE ABLE TO ESCAPE. WELL, EVENTUALLY YOU WILL. OUT THE EMERGENCY EXIT, THOUGH IT MIGHT TAKE A WHILE...'

* * * * *

Elvis and Starkwood stopped talking and looked up to the sky. For a moment, the sun's light was eclipsed from their view, even though neither of the Martian moons were around at that moment.

'Ah, I think she's back,' said Elvis.

'What, already?' quizzed Starkwood.

'Can't you sense her?'

'Well there's quite a cosmic wind blowing at the moment, plus those Viking messages I keep getting.'

Suddenly there was a rush of air and a sheet of darkness descended just over their heads, like the curtain closing after a West End show. It was like a pair of curtains – huge, flat – but almost horizontal, and about the size of two football stadiums side by side. There was a slight whooshing sound and the two ground dwellers watched as the flying object glided off into the distance and down the gentle slope. The two graceful football pitches were in fact a pair of wings that belonged to the largest ever flying creature (or machine) that had ever been created. The wing tips, over a hundred metres apart dipped close to the ground and picked up some red dust that entered and highlighted the two vortices that emerged one behind each tip. Somewhere between the leathery bat-like dark wings was what could just be seen as the bird's body, but very small in comparison to the cloak-like appendages that flapped in the wind of the touchdown. The head was pointed in both directions, a long sharp beak but also a backwards pointing spike. Fionix wasn't any ordinary flying creature. She was a kind of living dinosaur known as an aerodactyl, though she preferred to call herself a bird of paradise as it sounded much more appealing and friendly. Technically she was an *agros duabus ex paradiso*. Like other Martian life forms, she had evolved to keep up with the ever-worsening environmental conditions. Back in the old days of a thick atmosphere, she'd only needed regular sized wings, but as Mars lost its grip on its gas molecules, Fionix's wings expanded to fill the space required. Her 'arms' had been much like bats' arms, with the skin stretched between her fingers to create the lift she needed but, with time, the claws had grown so far from her mouth that she could no longer eat with the etiquette she used to enjoy. Even folded up, her wings were somewhat like two baggy umbrellas and she waddled most ungracefully on the rubble-strewn plains of Mars. So clumsy was she and so cumbersome were her wings that she couldn't easily take off from a flat surface. Well, horizontal surface. She'd tried before and her actions made the Earth's albatross look quite elegant. That's why she lived on the top of Olympus Mons, the tallest volcano on the planet. Not only did she have a head start on the launch height, but there were still gently active calderas up there and, using her voluminous wings, she was able to ride on the up-currents of the gases venting out of the planet's insides through the top of this super-sized shield volcano. When the fancy took her, Fionix would lodge herself tightly in one of the vent holes and let the pressure build up to the point that she'd pop out like a champagne cork – sometimes she could reach orbital speed if she put up with the discomfort of an overheated bottom.

Two feet could be seen now poking forwards as they made contact with the Martian regolith and churned up two grooves of top soil like the spray from a water skier. The apparent gracefulness of the manoeuvre was then lost as Fionix went tail over beak and rolled helplessly along the ground, the oversized wings crumpling like a newspaper caught in a sudden gust. Not much could be seen of the creature within the cloud of red dust that rose to the occasion for the audience, but as the cloud settled, her silhouette emerged.

Elvis and Starkwood noticed a trail of items that seemed to have been dropped along the path behind the gracefully *ballerining* bird. The two land dwellers followed after the crash landing but at a leisurely pace, with Starkwood on Elvis's back waving from side to side with each step like a drunken cowboy. Yes, the ground was strewn with several objects and the travelling companions eyed them with curiosity. One thing looked like a golden rectangle, another was a book; it was as if she'd been to a boot sale.

'Welcome back Fionix,' said Elvis with genuine delight.

'There's no place like Mars,' said the aerodactyl as she

picked herself up and shivered, sending many waves through her marquee-sized wings, shaking off all the grains of rubiginous dust. Standing there, Fionix was quite formidable in height, some four metres tall and not a creature you'd like to meet in a dark alley at night.

'It's been a while,' noted the tortle as he approached his friend, getting momentarily covered by one of her wings as she endeavoured to fold them down to a more manageable size.

'Was it fun?' asked Starkwood.

'Oh hi there,' realised the bird, 'well, it's been quite an adventure. I left, what, a couple of years ago no? Time goes by so quick when you're speeding around the solar system.'

'I see you've brought back some souvenirs...' said Starkwood, holding up a yellow metallic rectangular plate.

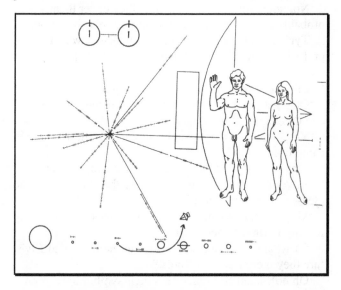

'Oh yes!' cried Fionix with delight as she tucked the final folds of her wings out of sight and waddled over to look at the very item Starkwood was holding.

'A postcard from Earth?' asked Elvis curiously.

'Well, actually I spotted one of those metal ships they keep throwing off the Earth and dumping into space, so I hopped on board and ripped off this picture.'

'You stole it?!' said Starkwood accusingly.

'How can I steal something that's been thrown away?! Those Earth people throw their stuff everywhere. Not only do they do it on their own planet but they've already littered their moon. It's like a breaker's yard there and now they're sending their wrecks to us and beyond!'

'So what's on this picture?' Elvis asked as the three of them perused the unusual engravings.

'Oh, this thing here is a drawing of the shipwreck I pulled it from.'

'And these odd looking shapes?' said Starkwood.

'Oh, they're examples of the Earth creatures,' said Fionix. 'They're called a man and a woman.'

'And they go around naked?!'

'No, not really. Most of the time they cover themselves, probably as protection from the intense solar radiation.'

'Typical isn't it, the whole universe over. Give a graffiti artist a chance and they'll draw all their rude parts on a public surface.'

'Like our very own Hanksie,' said Fionix

'Oh I get this part,' said Elvis, 'this is our solar system and there's our home, Mars.'

'Yes,' agreed Fionix, 'and you can see the metal ship came from Earth.'

'Maybe they *didn't* throw it away,' pondered Starkwood, 'Maybe it got lost and this says "if found please return to us Earthlings"?'

'Maybe,' said Fionix, 'but the way these objects keep leaving Earth, I rather doubt it.'

'So what are these round things up here?' asked Elvis, 'are they more Earth creatures?'

'Oh no!' laughed Fionix, 'it's their symbol for carbon!'

'But it's not made of carbon,' the rock star pointed out.

'Maybe they need some and it's some kind of postal request.'

'Ooh,' pointed Starkwood, 'this looks like an Earth

creature! Some multi-legged creepy crawly…'

The three of them peered closely at the unusual image in the centre of the plaque. If it had a body it was very small and there seemed to be a dozen or so legs of different lengths coming out in all directions and they were covered in tiny short bristles sticking out at right angles.

'Did you see any creatures like that when you were on Earth?' asked Elvis.

'No, but I'll look out for them next time.'[†]

'Did you remember what I asked for?' said Starkwood.

'What, a book about life on Mars?'

'Did you find one?'

'I don't think they know much, but I found this one…'

Fionix with her beak passed the book on to Starkwood, who accepted it with curiosity. He looked at the cover then showed it to Elvis.

'Life on Mars,' said Elvis out loud. 'Interesting. I wonder if we get a mention?'

'Not really,' said Fionix matter-of-factly, 'they only talk of little green men and –'

'What, not even little green *women*?' said Elvis

'Well they give all the reasons why we can't exist.'

'So much for them being an advanced race,' said Starkwood.

'Agreed,' said Fionix. 'I mean what intelligent species would keep blasting their metal junk out to contaminate other planets?'

'Why, are there other bits coming this way?'

'Oh yes,' said Fionix, again ambivalently, 'I passed two more of their shipwrecks on my way back home…'

Both Elvis and Starkwood looked at each other with realisation.

'The Vikings…' said Starkwood dreamily.

'…are coming…' Elvis completed his chant.

[†] The image was actually a diagram that was pointing to all the nearby pulsars, so aliens could use it like a map to find the solar system, but it still looked like a spider.

'How did you know they're called Vikings?' asked Fionix confused.

'So they *are* coming?!' stated Starkwood, not believing his equivalent of ears. 'Wait, how do you know about the Vikings?'

'It's written on the side of each ship…'

'Were there any passengers with horned helmets?' asked Elvis.

'Didn't see any. Ghost ships again.'

'Oh,'

'Like the others that came a few years ago…'

Elvis and Starkwood looked at each other again, then at Fionix.

'What others?!'

4
Muddism, Monopoles and Scarlet Siblings

Two months later…

'BYE!' boomed Chryssie.

'Bye,' waved Jade awkwardly. Grit waved but said nothing. Neither of them quite made eye contact with the whale, which was quite difficult to do, what with her having eyes the size of small moons. When you've passed through the digestive system of someone you know, it's still actually hard to face the truth.

'GIVE MY REGARDS TO YOUR DAD! AND HAVE A HAPPY BIRTHDAY!'

The rock tortle duo made it over the crater's rim and heard Chryssie slip back into her watery cocoon, pulling the larger bits of ice back over the top to speed up the freezing process and sealing herself back in for the next who-knew-how-long.

* * * * *

Chryssie thought about her old school friends, as she settled back into her hibernation hole. Memories of a time before the oceans dried up. There was so much sea, so much space in which to roam around. Hundreds, maybe thousands of lung whales in those days. Then, as the water disappeared, they each took to looking after themselves. Her friends had been a bit jealous and envious of her own regal lineage, but they did help her to dig her vertical suspended animation chamber and seal it with ice as the temperature dropped.

Chryssie wondered how many of her crowd were still around. She had tried calling out using her infra-sound cries, that could be heard over thousands of kilometres, but it had been radio silence since that day. Maybe they had replied while she was asleep. Her 'friends' on the other hand, knew exactly where Chryssie was and kept very quiet if they ever came within hearing range of her address. Most of the remaining lung whales were to be found under the ice in a twenty kilometre wide sea in a crater far, far away from Lady Chryssie, far enough to feel safe from her slightly superior attitude. A few hundred of them enjoyed a calm existence in this communal body of water, but they had also dug many kilometres of subsurface tunnels that interconnected across the planet, avoiding coming too close to their aristocratic ally. It was actually a little sad the way they excluded her, but that's unsocial media for you.

* * * * *

'How do we cope with... um ...' Grit started.

'We *don't* talk about it,' interrupted Jade, clearly perturbed.

'But,'

'No!'

'Aren't we supposed to live in the present?' asked Grit. 'Aren't we supposed to *mudditate* on our experience?'

Jade stopped and Grit bumped into her butt. Again. She turned to face him and pointed at the same time in the direction from where they came.

'I *am* living in the present. *That* over there is now the past. If *you* want to mudditate on it, then that is the direction where your future lies young man...'

'Well,' Grit risked, 'do you fancy talking about *past* experiences instead...'

'We will *never* talk about this again. You will *not* mention it to me. You will *not* mention it to anyone we meet, you will *not* talk about it for the next hundred million years, do you hear?'

'Okay...'

'Now,' Jade sighed, 'before I see my dad, there's one more thing to do,'

'Yes?'

'I want to see for myself this white dead tortle you said you saw.'

'Right.'

Jade turned south again and headed off with purpose, the purpose being to distance herself as far as possible from the out-of-this-world trauma she had gone through. Although she knew that she was still on Mars, for some reason she couldn't stop thinking about the planet Uranus...

The two of them did not exchange comments for the next two months.

* * * * *

Meanwhile, Back In Tourrettes...

'So let me get this straight' said House, as he placed the last piece of mud from under the old railway bridge into the damaged area of his house under the roof, 'you have a distant relative... on *Mars*?'

Martin watched his friend finishing his masonry work as they chatted, and interjected.

'I think you've missed a spot. Up there in the corner.'

House looked at it and shrugged.

'It'll do for now.'

'But you'll get a pain in the neck from the draught, if you ask me,' Martin suggested.

House was loathe to go back down to the bridge again, and was a little irritated by his friend noticing the omission – even though he was right. House sighed.

'Okay, I'll do it in a moment. Perhaps when the sun's gone down a bit – it's scorching out there. So Mars you say?'

'Oh, yes, Elvis...'

'Birds live on Mars?!' asked House incredulously.

'Oh yes, well birds of a sort, but Elvis isn't a bird.'

'What?! But he's a relative of yours and he's not a bird? How can that be?'

'Long story. I guess we were the same species before, but we've sort of evolved apart.'

51

'You never told me about this before!'

'Well it never came up in conversation.'

'Well what species is this Elvis now? And how come you're here and this auntie Elvis of yours is over there?!"

'Actually, he's more an uncle, a male if you follow. He's half turtle, half tortoise and it seems our related ancestors emigrated to Earth some time ago…'

'You're pulling my tail feather!' claimed House in disbelief.

'No.'

'So let me get this straight,' said House, scratching his head with a claw, 'you have a distant cousin on Mars –'

'Yes, a very distant one.'

'– and he's a turtle?'

'Well he used to be.'

'A tortoise then.'

'Not quite.'

'And you're a bird.'

'Same type as you buddy.'

'And you evolved from a turtle into a bird?'

'Well we all did,' said Martin, matter-of-factly.

'And Elvis told you all this then?'

'Oh no, not me. He's been communicating with my ancestors down the generations for millions of years.'

'And you know this because…'

'The tale has been passed down from father to son and mother to daughter, though sometimes father to daughter and mother to son. I must admit I had wondered if it had all been just a story.'

'So how is the message supposed to arrive?' asked House with curiosity, but also with much doubt.

Before Martin could say anything, a huge lump of something akin to guano droppings, descended from the sky and landed, with a kind of SPLAT on top of Martin, who ended up being completely enveloped in the offending material. Martin's wings sprouted out through the goo and they wiped his face clean.

'Um, a kind of pigeon post…'

House looked at his friend for a few seconds and,

without batting an eyelid, said: 'Looks like your Uncle Elvis has got a lot to say...'

* * * * *

It had been a long climb across the Equatorial Bulge and a lot of the motion had been upwards. So much so that the air had started to get even colder than the overhead summer sun would have suggested. In the bright glare, Jade and Grit could see the sparkling evidence of frosty, jewelled, dry ice on the ground. They could even see their breath as it immediately sublimed into a misty cloud that gently descended, like fairy dust, to the ground. The wind-worn layered rocks that marked the summit of this particular plateau were almost silhouetted against the glare of the midday hazy light, like a crazy psychologist's inkblot, with the symmetrical 'other half' missing. It was curious how the layered rocks jutted in and out – and to think that possibly each layer was once a sedimentary deposit of an ancient ocean. All the way up here! And it was also peculiar to see the outline of a sort of hemispherical lump of rock loitering in the shadow of the overhanging layer of rock above it. A rock that was *loitering*?! And it was doing it with such coolness that it instantly annoyed Jade. There weren't many rocks that annoyed Jade – she was usually quite tolerant of most of them. She stopped and as usual, her shadow of a friend bumped into her again while his brain was on its own autopilot. Grit had light-heartedly called this his auto-Martian mode to himself, but he'd never shared it with anyone as he didn't really know anyone. Until recently that is. And he dared not speak to Jade for the time being, not until she chose to break her own silence. He saw what she was looking at: the sentient-like boulder, the living shadow that nonchalantly and ambivalently exuded such indifference that was saying 'I don't care if you notice me, but you will anyway because I am going to make sure you do, without appearing to make it happen.'

Smokey breath was seen falling from one end of the

rock, the end that had a sleek, head-like protrusion. The head then looked over to them, as it came out of the shadow and was suddenly sparked to full life by the high altitude sun.

'Wow...' said Grit.

'Stop it!' said Jade, clearly irritated by the rock and Grit's reaction to it.

The head was that of a tortle. A tortle of a similar size and age as Jade, but tiny orangey-red flecks of ruby crystal in the grain of the face and shell, along with darker shadowy streaks, giving a kind of warning danger sign of colours, like on some road markings and poisonous insects seen on Earth. She (the tortle here was clearly a *she*), yes, *she* had almond shaped eyes and managed such a sultry look, you either wanted to rip her to shreds, or fall hopelessly in love with her. Sticking out of her mouth was a solid white, almost translucent object and as she breathed in and out, thin, heavy mist poured from it, flowing over her fore-claws and down the slope towards the visitors. The most noticeable feature though was the patch she had over her right eye. It actually made the visible one seem more powerful.

'Who... is... she?' Grit managed to say without taking his eyes off her.

'It's Ruby,' Jade said with both disappointment and disapproval.

'Hi sis,' said Ruby and somehow managed to say it with a subtext that sounded like a victory. 'Who's your new boyfriend?' she continued.

Before Jade could reply, Grit spoke: 'We've just come out of a lung whale's bottom!'

* * * * *

'Are you sure we've got time?' asked Starkwood, fussing as he usually did.

'Months, don't worry,' said Elvis.

'It's a little out of your way, the Equatorial Bulge,' Starkwood pointed out.

'It's worth it. Have you never seen the Monopole Meteor Shower?'

'Just the odd one in flight,' admitted Starkwood. 'They're not really my friends. We're competing for the same food aren't we?'

'It's a nice natural phenomenon. Worth a front row seat.'

As they chatted, Elvis was already plodding due east, not really bothering to avoid the larger football-sized rocks so he was seriously leaning from side to side like a boat on a stormy sea. Starkwood in turn was also swinging, a little out of step with the tipping movement, his head tilting left while his roots and the carapace leaned to the right; bowing forward as the tortle taxi encountered a little rock, then leaning back as he passed over it – like a contestant on a bucking bronco, filmed in slow motion. The red rays of the rising sun caught the wispy fronds of Starkwood's head and made them look ginger.

'Fionix said she'd be there?' asked Starkwood.

'She wants to get her house in order first,' explained Elvis, 'and then she'll invite us over to see her collection of trinkets.'

'It's a long way to Olympus Mons you know, it'd take even longer than going to the Magnetic Fields of Gold.'

'Well,' said Elvis, 'all sorted out apparently. We're going to get first class treatment. Fionix has offered to carry us there, it seems…'

'Flying?!'

'That's the plan.'

'But I've barely got used to walking!'

'You'll be on my back.'

'But is it safe?!'

'Safest form of transport, flying, so she's assured me.'

'For something with wings, yes.'

'Well, try not to think about it for now. Why not check out the book that Fionix brought you from Earth.'

'Okay,' and with that Starkwood sat down and perched the book on what seemed to be his knees, which were fused into his bulbous pear shaped butt and he flicked through a few pages. Actually, his lower body was more onion shaped, though a bit knobblier like a garlic and his legs were very much like a rabbits or kangaroo's hind legs. He read the book out loud.

'*Life on Mars*, it says, *is very unlikely…*'

'But still good odds,' put in Elvis.

'*The atmosphere is too thin. What there is of it is mainly carbon dioxide with small amounts of nitrogen and even less oxygen. It retains very little heat and the magnetic field is so weak, there is barely any protection from the dangerous cosmic radiation and solar wind.*'

'They've got that right,' said Elvis. 'Let's hope that puts those Earthlings off from moving here.'

'So we shouldn't really exist according to them.'

'Maybe we don't…'

Starkwood stopped reading and looked sideways at his transcendental transport.

'What do you mean?'

'Maybe we're just characters in a book that someone's writing.'

'What? That's ludicrous! What mind would come up with nearly impossible lifeforms living on the edge of *being*, with a plant travelling around on the back of an evolving rock tortle, who has a flying friend with wings large enough to wrap up a minor planet?'

'What mind indeed? There are some pretty weird creatures out there I'm sure.'

'Are you saying we're fragments of the imagination of something actually *in* our imaginary world?! That would be even more bizarre!'

'That's not what I meant, and it's *figments*, but I suppose that's a possibility too…'

'I can't accept that,' said Starkwood dismissively.

'I didn't say I believed in these ideas,' admitted Elvis, 'you know my faith is Muddism.'

'Yes, you've mentioned that before. What exactly does *that* entail?'

The two of them had just reached the highest point on

the southern edge of the Valles Marineris. This was the Great Rift Valley running west-east near the Martian equator – evidence that Mars had tried its hand at some plate tectonics, but didn't quite make the grade.

Elvis and Starkwood both stared down into the seemingly bottomless pit of the chasm and remained silent for a few moments. The rays of the rising sun were taking the opportunity to dip a toe in the cold depths of this natural foggy wonder. Early morning mist filled the deepest depths and the wispy, cotton-wool-duvet-covering, reflecting the light back and scattering it, making it look salmon pink.

'This,' said Elvis gently, 'is one of the most amazing sights we're ever going to see…'

Starkwood nodded in agreement, his own face lit up with an orange glow, his eyes reflecting back tiny little images of the scene below. Though the valley was almost 200km wide at this point, it was so deep that they could see the other edge of the rift valley on the horizon, in spite of the curvature of the planet's surface. The dawn sun sparked the copper coloured ridge to life, lit from below as well by the misleadingly steamy mist that looked like a hot bath. The valley disappeared into the distance both west and east and they could feel the sun's rays on their own backs and looked round to squint at another glorious morning.

'Never gets boring,' said Elvis and sighed with satisfaction.

'Is this the essence of Muddism?'

Elvis snapped out of his dreamy breakfast scenery and returned his attention to his friend.

'Oh, well, we were taught to appreciate the beauty of even the simplest things. It's a very ancient tortle faith, actually created to cope with the change of life from sea to land.'

'So it's been around a long time then!'

'Indeed. With the seas fading away, we ended up living in the marshy, muddy terrain that surrounded what used to be our home sea.'

'Oh, so the *mud* in Muddism is about *real* mud?!'

'It was. If we could cope with the mud in our lives we could cope with anything.'

'So, what, you're supposed to have daily mud baths?'

'The mud is actually metaphorical, though the real mud was a physical representation of the internal mess.'

'Are you tortles really that messed up? You've always seemed so calm to me, almost irritatingly so.'

'Thank you. That's what we aim for – a sort of *Whole-ier-than-thou* aura. We aim to reach '*delightenment*'.'

'Was it that hard being an evolving wet-to-dry land creature back then?'

'Actually the worst part was when we realised that as our numbers dwindled, the rest of us were living longer and longer. Our bodies were changing and we weren't expecting that. Well you know how that feels yourself. You stopped being stationary,' said Elvis.

'True. You don't expect a static plant to be mobile. Anyway, your transmogrification brought on the counselling?'

'Big word! You've been at that thesaurus again haven't you!'

'Well,' said Starkwood, 'it was a while since Fionix's last trip to Earth and I needed something to read. So was it the species change that was hard to deal with?'

'No it was living longer, more than a million times longer: that was the biggest trauma to overcome.'

'But isn't being alive what we all strive for? Even the inanimate rocks seem to be trying it out?'

'If we'd started out knowing we were going to be around for a while,' Elvis mused, 'our minds would have been more accepting, but they've been slow in catching up.'

'Oh…'

'Imagine you're used to having a bite to eat three times a day, then find out it's going to be once every million years, what do you do in the meantime?'

'Your metabolic rate slows down?' Starkwood suggested.

'Oh yes, that happens, certainly. But your mind's been buzzing up in fourth gear in survival mode and has to suddenly put on the cerebral brakes so to speak.'

'Oh...'

'Hence Muddism. We had to learn to think in a different way. Empty our minds.

'Oh, I've read about this... mindfulness?'

'Not quite. We call it *mindlessness*,' said Elvis

'Mindlessness?! So you think of just one thing?'

'No. Even less than that.'

'What, nothing?'

'Not even nothing. Even the absence of nothing.'

'Is that even possible?!' asked Starkwood.

'Well it's a bit like thinking like a rock. Rocks don't think. Well, the sentient ones do, but the inanimate ones don't...'

The sun was now well and truly awake, spotlighting our two travellers in a glorious blaze of golden sunrise as they slowly descended a little south of east in the general direction of the magnetic fields of the Central Bulge. Just then Starkwood saw a light blue flash in the sky and pointed.

'Oh! A monopole-cat!'

Elvis looked up to see the streak of bluish/lilac light and hear the faint distant cry of the love drunk Romeo: 'Nati!'

'A sporadic,' Elvis commented knowledgeably and Starkwood gave him a sideways glance so he explained: 'the poor guy got over excited and lost his grip. He's struck out for this season... Unless a female does the same thing...'

They both watched the unfortunate premature polecat arc and disappear over the northern horizon. They heard it cry again, 'Nati!!!' before it was lost from view.

'So,' resumed Starkwood, 'where did you learn this extreme form of meditation?'

'Actually we call it *mudditation*. We learnt it in the mud fields on the edge of the Chryse basin, when I was just a lad.'

'But there aren't any more mud fields left! How can you do it now?'

'Oh the mud was just a ritual. We just slowed down our minds so much that we could become like 'dead' rocks. This helps conserve energy of course. It also helps us hide from predators, as we can appear to be actual rocks for thousands of years at a time.'

'I see,' said Starkwood.

'Also helps to avoid the boredom of near immortality.'

'And it works for you?'

'I'm still here aren't I? And I haven't gone crazy yet.'

'Well apart from the weird theories of us being someone's fictional characters...'

'Ah, maybe that's just part of the *same* story...'

* * * * *

'*Just*' was a reasonable word for Grit to use, even though their 'rite of passage' had happened four months ago. They *had* just passed through a whale's digestive system four months ago. For such long-lived creatures, four months is a mere blink of an eye on the geological scale of things. But it wasn't something Jade had ever wanted to hear about again.

'Why in Hellas did you say that?!' she tried to ask out of the corner of her mouth but her sister still heard.

'Going boldly where you've never gone before, sis?' said Ruby, smiling as she moved smoothly out from her natural sunshade and approached the two of them. Ruby then looked at Grit then back at her twin: 'he's a bit young for you isn't he?'

Technically Jade and Ruby were twins, though clearly not identical. They had come from the same batch of eggs, but Jade hatched out a couple of years before her sister, making Jade the older one and Ruby the younger, more fashionably late one.

'It's not like that!' snapped Jade, but that was clearly not going to stop her sister's tease. 'And anyway, you know you shouldn't be smoking dry ice. Too much is bad for you!'

'Yea yea,' dismissed Ruby, 'it'll freeze my heart. You sound just like dad!'

BUMP!

The two sisters both stared at Grit, even Ruby lost a little bit of poise after this moment of contact. Grit looked up at them after having just head butted the recent girl of his dreams.

'What are you doing?!' demanded Jade.

'Yea, weird kid, what are you doing?'

Grit seemed momentarily lost for words.

'Um…'

'Yes?!'

'Um… I couldn't stop myself…'

'Don't you know how to act round other tortles?!' Ruby demanded.

Grit looked at them both, clearly embarrassed.

'I guess not…' Ruby finished. Without warning, Grit bumped his head against her carapace again. The focus of his unexpected behaviour scraped some of the dry ice frosting from the top of her shell then flicked it at the young Casanova. There was a curious hissing sound as his body heat caused the solid carbon dioxide to turn into gas and cool down his amorous advances.

'Sorry about that,' Jade said, as if she had been responsible for her friend's odd behaviour. Grit looked suitably self-conscious as he tried to understand his reaction. He didn't realise that it was a natural instinct – bumping a female's shell is exactly what male rock tortles did when they felt certain biological urges. How well it worked on the potential 'mummy' tortle would only become clear with two interested parties; in this case, one of the parties was not interested. Ruby's flicked dry ice gesture was a literal giving of the cold shoulder, and equally literally cooled his ardour.

Ruby brought her face within a hair's breadth of Grit's.

'Don't ever do that again!' said Ruby.

Ruby was now so close their beaks were almost touching and her eyes were staring harshly into his – well, one eye was piercing through Grit's skull; the patch

over the other concealed half of her intentions. Grit
swallowed nervously. Having spent most of his life not
seeing another tortle, apart from his parents and little
sister, and the slightly older Jade, to suddenly be a hair's
breadth away from one his own age was most unsettling.
A dangerously attractive one, at that. A claw suddenly
grabbed some of the loose wrinkled skin hanging around
his neck and scrunched it up, dragging Grit until their
beaks were definitely touching.

'Watch yourself or I will make sure you're the end of
your family line. Get my drift?!'

At that moment Grit noticed another eye staring
hatefully at him. A tiny figure standing on the front
edge of Ruby's head. It was a pyrite, and a female one
at that. She wore a captain's hat. Yes, this was the
captain of Ruby's pyrite crew. Captain Masha. Her real
name was Marina Bay des Anges, which means Bay of
Angels, as she had come from an angel-shaped crater
near the Martian South Pole. Masha had the same sultry
look on her face as her vessel. If it wasn't for the scowl,
Masha wasn't bad looking for a pyrite. The eye that was
visible was quite piercing but, like Ruby, the other one
was concealed by a patch. Masha didn't have a parrot on
her shoulder, nor a wooden leg, but she had one pair of
arms on her hips in a power stance, while her other pair
were wielding some fairly excessive cutlery. The male

pyrite captains like Sam Biosis and Raffi Rehab were not as healthy looking as Masha, being much older and more stereotypically bearded, beer swigging, pot-bellied slobs in lifestyle, with Sam being the more senior of the two.

Then Masha spoke.

'Yea, what she said,' and Masha gestured with her two cutlasses – a crossing of the blades like a pair of scissors, then a slicing motion as if cutting something in half.

Grit swallowed very nervously and strained not to move a muscle, while saying quietly '...Noted...'

Ruby released the scruff of Grit's neck and just so slightly pushed him away. Captain Masha looked Grit in his eye, lifted up her eye patch, first pointed two of her fingers at her own eyes (the one below her patch seemed as perfect as the other one), then pointed a warning finger at Grit, letting him know that he was being watched. This was all over in the blink of an eye patch. Ruby then did exactly the same thing with her own eye patch, which left Grit feeling confused as well as petrified.

Ruby turned back to Jade (eye patch back in place) and finally answered her.

'No harm sis,' Ruby dismissed it, 'I have that effect on the boys. So, what's this about your recent speleological journey?' and a beaming smile came across Ruby's face.

'Nothing!' defended Jade, 'He's talking out of his... his tiny little mind that's all. So how have you been?'

'Chilling,' and as she said this, she moved gracefully down the slope, Grit backing away sensibly as she passed by. 'I heard about you going to celebrate your birthday too soon...'

The dry ice frost that had settled on Jade's shell seemed to evaporate very quickly at this. She hadn't wanted to give her overly fashionable sister another reason to class her as the nerdy one, though it seemed that that geek ship wreck had sunk a long time ago.

* * * * *

'Ooooh stop!' cried Starkwood, so Elvis put on his brakes, though at the speed he was moving it didn't mean much of a deceleration.

'Another Viking message?'

'No, I feel a nice little storm brewing...' and Starkwood watched his own hair waving in the thin air, 'ah, no, keep going. It's a little further south-east...'

'Aren't you frightened of being zapped by a particularly energetic cosmic ray?' said Elvis.

'Well this one's actually a *solar* storm, so not quite as violent as those ones that come from exploding stars.'

'You're quite an expert in sub-atomic particles now aren't you?'

'Well,' Starkwood pondered, 'partly instinct, but also these books from Earth. Why aren't you moving? I said it's a few metres further along?'

'I'm stopping here if you don't mind,' said Elvis calmly. 'I can't afford to risk being hit by a Big One. Again.'

'Come on, they only happen, what, once every one hundred million years or so? When was the last time you got hit?'

'Ninety nine millions years ago – see this scorch mark here...'

'So you've still got another million years before there's one with your name on it.'

'It doesn't work quite like that,' explained Elvis, 'so how about you hop off and shuffle the rest of the way yourself. You need to exercise those root muscles of yours anyway or you'll never become part of the flower power movement in your own right. I'll stay outside the blast zone, thank you very much.'

'But you told me life was about taking risks. You told me to live on the edge!'

Starkwood hopped off his now stationary transport.

'I was talking literally my friend,' explained Elvis, 'not metaphorically.'

'What?'

'The top *edge* of a sharp-*edged* cliff. You told me the

field is much stronger at pointed corners and edges, so they're the places to attract your favourite charged meals.'

'Suit yourself,' said Starkwood, slightly dismissively, as he started to shuffle, triffid-like then hop, kangaroo-like towards the jagged rocky outcrop that seemed to be a focus of this present storm. Another sporadic monopole-cat flew overhead with the distinctive meowing scream, Doppler shifting in the background. It sounded like it was shouting 'Frankie!' as the red, glowing feline followed the field lines. There was even a crackling sound, and a couple of bluish sparks could be seen running through the spider web-like hairs covering Starkwood's body. As the sparks ran up to his head and into his waving hairstyle, the like charges on each fibril caused them to repel and Starkwood had a most unique hairdo that lasted until the electricity discharged through the ground (the effect here is called, not surprisingly, being '*marsed*'. Not 'earthed'). This gave Starkwood an obvious mini-shock but he seemed to glow like a plasma ball for just a moment, both literally and with joy. There was also a deep humming sound that accompanied the effect. For a few seconds, Starkwood himself rose a short distance above the ground by some kind of momentary repulsion before being attracted back to the ground again. It was almost like he was running in slow motion.

'Don't get carried away,' said Elvis, both for real and metaphorically, but Starkwood seemed to be completely absorbed by his present 'cordon bleu' cuisine.

'Out of this world...' said Starkwood, wide-eyed, as the fireworks of blue sparks and the soft orange glow plasma lit up his face.

ZAP!

Something like a bolt of lightning hit the ground a few metres away from the walking weed. All his hairs first pointed towards the place of contact that the cosmic ray made with the ground, then all pointed radially and again Starkwood gently bobbed into the air and slowly came down again.

Elvis squinted against the overly bright laser light
display that was going on, hoping it was still out of reach
of his slightly jagged and attractively '*marsed*' body.
Elvis had been struck a few times in the past, in fact he
had been hit by a Big One when he was only a million
and he had the body sized scar to prove it. Being
'cosmically rayed' had always made him feel nauseous.
Having angled and partly stellated ridges to his pock-
marked and weathered shell, he was a walking lightning
conductor and being a biggish rock tortle meant he was
often the highest local point whenever he was out in the
open.

Elvis started burying himself in the loose topsoil and
flicked as much of it up onto his back as his ageing old
limbs would allow. He heard another ZAP in the distance
and a yelp of half-pleasure, half-pain echoed in the now
darkening skies. Elvis could even see faint evidence of
the weak Equatorial Borealis that accompanied these
waves of energetic solar wind. On Mars, they were not
called the Northern Lights, or Southern Lights for that
matter, as they didn't happen near either pole. Mars just
didn't have the same classy field of the bigger planetary
bodies in the solar system. Something to do with an iron
deficiency in its diet. But what there was of the field
tended to happen around the Equatorial Bulge. Which is
why the monopole-cats were found not too far from this
high flux density plateau. Elvis would have avoided it if
he'd had a majority vote in this symbiotic partnership, but
he accepted his friend's special dietary needs and as
Starkwood also doubled as an early warning device, then
it seemed a fair deal.

ZAP!

Owww!

That did not sound like the cry of a Plant in Paradise, a
Gladiolus in the Garden of Eden a Hyacinth in Heaven, a,
wait, there isn't time for this free forming prose. Okay
one more: this Narcissus in Nirvana. Right, Elvis opened
his eyes… Oh dear…

There was his flowery friend floating, as if in an ocean,

but the rising smoke and burning embers coming from what used to be Starkwood's arm broke the illusion.

'Starkwood!' shouted the tortle, which did bring the whacky weed back to consciousness.

Meanwhile, Elvis was unburying himself from his shallow grave and went almost galloping towards the overcooked salad that used to be Starkwood. Starkwood himself dreamily opened his eyes to then focus on the spontaneously combusted arm and horror filled his mind as he quickly started patting at the smouldering injury with his remaining sepal-like arm, the little glowing orange edges of hot light, eating their way back through the veil-like wisps that surrounded Starkwood's spindly stem of his upper body. Elvis took a sudden slow leap into the air, but kicked up a huge tidal wave spray of Martian soil as if he was some strange Ninja surfer. In the slow motion action a couple of cosmic rays like blue-white Christmas lights hit the ground around them, creating a dome of interlocking forked lightning strikes that could have won a geodesic architectural prize had there been such a thing on Mars. The blanket of ejecta reached Starkwood before the slower, heavier, rock star tortle and it did its job of snuffing out the last flames of the once in a hundred million year mega-ray. A million years too soon. When Elvis' outline followed behind the dirt spray, it landed on top of Starkwood, just as another cosmic ray was about to break the laws of physics and strike in the same place twice. Instead, it hit Elvis' already over-scratched and pock-marked shell, vaporizing away a small hemispherical lump of the carapace. Admittedly, there wasn't very much combustion *per se* on Mars, what with there being very little free oxygen. Most of what was going on was, in fact, due to the high temperatures reached in the energy exchanges. However, a little yelp of pain came from between the plates on Elvis' back, as an unfortunate pyrite caught the full blast of the cosmic ray and fell frazzled and lifeless to the ground. The tortle louse, a female as it happened, was called Swift. Sailor Swift, clearly was not swift in nature.

Unless one considered the rapidity of her demise.

'Are you okay Starkwood?' Elvis asked with concern to his friend, who was mainly squashed under the tortle's weight.

'Mars moved...' said Starkwood in a daze, but with a drunken smile on his face, oblivious to any pain he might have been feeling.

'There must be an easier way of eating,' suggested Elvis, looking at his partly maimed friend. 'Smaller snacks maybe?' he offered.

'Strike while the cosmic ion's hot,' replied Starkwood, panting a little, 'well at least that won't happen again for a hundred million years. My arm'll grow back long before that...'

'Probability doesn't work like that my friend, I keep telling you. It'll happen when you least expect it!'

'Well I least expect it now!' cried Starkwood. Elvis quickly looked up, and at the same time lay himself spread-eagled over Starkwood, as if just saying the words would anger the gods of chance that were waiting to catch someone out.

'Come on universe, give me all you've got!' cried Starkwood as he pushed Elvis off with his one remaining good sepal arm.

5

Squatters and Perpendicular Universes

In another dimension, a pair of four-dimensional friends were sitting down to watch their 3D television screens.

'This is my favourite program,' said Amelius the Third, 'Professor When.'

'Oh,' said Turkan, sitting next to him on their 4D sofa, though, due to the extra dimension, they seemed to be upside down compared to each other and slightly passing through each other at the same time, occupying the same space so to speak but not the same hyper-volume. 'Oh,' said Turkan, 'have I seen it before?'

'It's about a dentist who travels to a perpendicular dimension and has many adventures, backwards in time,' explained Amelius.

'Ah,' commented Turkan, starting to drink from a Klein bottle, 'I feel I've lived it, read the book and acted out the play before. I think I'll play some 1D chess instead...'

'Fair enough, but there's one thing I don't understand,' said Amelius, somehow scratching the inside of his stomach with his finger.

'Only *one* thing?' asked Turkan, as he set up the chess pieces in a very long, thin, one square wide board that stretched off into the distance.

'I know you've told me about parallel universes and I think I get them now.'

'Oh you do? Explain it back to me then...'

'Well,' Amelius began, 'you said we're living in some kind of soap bubble, though I've looked outside and can't see the soap film. Anyway, you pointed out we're just one bubble in a foam and apparently there's another *me* and *you* in each bubble and in each one I'm asking the same question, but in a slightly different way. But, I'm not sure about the parallel bit. I think you said all the bubbles are moving in the same direction, parallel to each other, but where are we going?'

Turkan hesitated. His friend had *sort of* grasped a *sort of* understanding, albeit oversimplified and distorted, but he didn't want to take that away from him.

'Forwards in *time*,' Turkan said safely. 'We're all travelling forwards in time.'

'Ah!' said Amelius with delight, 'well, in Professor When, he actually *is* a bubble, a tesseract-shaped sphere that goes backwards in time, so I guess everyone will see him passing by the other way!'

'That's a possibility…'

'But what I don't get is how can you have *perpendicular* universes? Won't that mean they'll cross over each other at right angles and then everyone will be bumping in to everyone else?'

'Um,' reflected Turkan, looking for an easy solution to what might become quite a convoluted discussion, 'well perhaps they only share *three* dimensions but are perpendicular in the *fourth* so they never meet.'

'Ah okay, though I guess they have to meet at some point, like when Professor When jumps from one space bubble to another…'

'Amelius?' said Turkan, having now placed all his chess pieces in what appeared to be a random way along the 'single file' board, with some small gaps, large gaps, three pieces in a row and some on the underside (though to Amelius they would have looked to be on the top side in view of the 4 dimensional positioning, a bit like a Mobius strip). 'Amelius?'

'Yes?' he said, now offering him some nuts, by extending his hand down below him and then seeing his hand appear from the opposite direction *above* and in front of Turkan.

'Thanks. Why are you called Amelius the *Third*? Is it because your father was Amelius the Second?'

'No.'

'Oh, well, was your grandfather Amelius the Second and your father had a different name?'

'No.'

'So why are you called Amelius the Third?'

'Oh, because two thirds of me is *not* here…'

Turkan did a little double-take, then thought about it.

'I'll go first,' he said to Amelius and he picked up his first pawn by reaching to the left and his hand came up from below to grab the white piece on the lower side of the strip. He moved it to the top surface and placed it between two black pawns. 'Your turn…'

'Ok,' said Amelius, then he looked thoughtful as he surveyed the placement of the pieces, making out he knew how to play much better than he actually could.

'So,' continued Turkan, 'where are the other two thirds?'

This third of Amelius had picked up one of his black pawns and was fingering it absentmindedly.

'What?'

'Well, if only a third of you is here, where are the other two thirds of your body?'

'Um, well like you, I'm also on Mars.'

'I know,' said Turkan, 'but that's only a tiny bit. Where's the rest?'

'Oh, well, my parents told me I have several holdings rolled up in those off shore hidden dimensions.

'You must be *huge*!' said Turkan, looking at his friend and trying to consider the big picture.

'Big boned my mum said,' replied Amelius, still toying with his first pawn.

'Where are they?' Turkan asked.

'What, my bones?'

'The rest of you?'

'Oh,' he thought then pointed using the pawn in his hand, 'over there somewhere…'

Amelius' arm stretched off out of the right of the bubble, then came down from the ceiling through the floor and came in and out several times, crisscrossing itself around him and Turkan.

Turkan tutted and shook his head four dimensionally, which looked odd as it grew and shrunk and split into many parts like he was caught in a kaleidoscope.

'No,' he corrected his friend, 'that's the way to Mars, where your rocky butt sticks out!'

'Ah,' realised Amelius, retracting his arm, 'then it's in the opposite direction…'

As he was about to indicate the hiding place of his missing mass, Turkan grabbed his wrist and looked with concern.

'Where's the pawn?!'

'What?'

'You were holding your black pawn when you pointed. Your hand's empty now!'

'Oh,' said Amelius, examining it then looking in all his other hands in case he'd passed it on.

'You didn't let go of it did you?!'

'Um I don't know, maybe it slipped out…'

'This could be serious,' said Turkan.

'But I saw you had some spare pieces in the hypercuboid box where you got them from…'

'No Amelius,' said Turkan in a worried and annoyed voice, 'you rub anything from our world against the three dimensional universe and there could be consequences. I told you this before!'

'Sorry,' said Amelius awkwardly, 'but you did say the chance was very small.'

'Yea, a hundred million to one I know!' said Turkan. 'Let's hope nothing comes from this…'

* * * * *

The story so far: Elvis had just been pushed into the air by his cosmically crazy friend Starkwood. Elvis steadied himself after the push, which was hard to do both in the low gravity and also as he'd already left contact with the ground so he had nothing to grip onto. He made circular motions with each of his feet, all seemingly in different directions, but it was clear he had not yet evolved enough for flight.

'Don't provoke the laws of physics!' said Elvis, as he finally remade contact with the solid surface and slid to a halt, fortunately face up and only a few metres away from Starkwood.

'That's the silliest thing I've heard in a long time! Physics wouldn't dare to hit me again with a hundred million year wave.'

'Yes but if there's an infinite number of universes, then in one in a hundred million of them you get hit by a second cosmic canon ball!'

'What?'

'And a hundred millionth of infinity is still infinity!'

'What?!'

ZAP!!!! BANG!!!!!

There was a blinding flash of more blue-white light. The smell of burning Martian cellulose. Something serious and probably irreversible had just happened.

'I'll never walk again!' cried the detached head of Starkwood. The *head*?! Yes, the head. Sitting there by itself. No *body* to be seen. Only Starkwood's head seemed to remain in existence...

Elvis thought about looking on the positive side, like saying: 'well you won't have to worry about things like sore feet for the time being,' but decided against this line of Muddist thinking.

'I'm sure you will walk again,' he said instead, though not having any idea how that might happen. 'I mean has anything like this happened to you or any of your kind before? Like an accident when one plant loses a leaf, or petal, or... a body?'

'I'm going to die!' Starkwood cried in a most un-hero-like way.

Again Elvis considered pointing out that everyone was going to die anyway and being hysterical about it was not going to change anything, but also decided it might be a touch insensitive. Especially as he didn't know how long electrostatic plants lived – he didn't think they lived as long as rock tortles in view of his own species seemingly being an optimum one for longevity.

'I'm sure you won't die just yet,' he lied again, 'look, you were saying before the second blast that you could grow your arm back, no?'

'But there's no body to grow it back on to! I'm going to

be armless for the rest of my life! And body-less. Crippled and deformed for ever!'

Elvis realised his friend was contradicting himself about dying there and then and also living the difficult life of being handicapped for an eternity, but he didn't point this out either.

'Well, perhaps your body will grow back…'

'How?! What do you know about our biology?! How?!'

'Well you started from a seed didn't you, or a spore or something no? Well seeds get planted so maybe if we plant you, we…'

'Bury me alive?! You want to bury me *alive*?! You're ashamed to be seen with me, now I'm deformed! I thought you were my friend…'

Elvis let him rant and rave. There was no way he was going to convince his perturbed partner into thinking straight, so gave up for now.

* * * * *

Suddenly, in the 4D dimensional world, there was a flashing light and a 'wooga wooga' alarm sound and Turkan and Amelius III looked at each other in shock. But there was nothing they could do about it. Their world started to get all wavy and distorted like they were on drugs, as they felt themselves being ripped out of their cosy little bubble universe. Their 4D forms started to collapse in on themselves and they found themselves (well part of themselves (well another part of themselves)) heading for a small red planet (where another part of each of them sat there, disguised as rocks). Yes, a small red planet orbiting a yellow dwarf star in an average common or garden spiral galaxy in a mini cluster of galaxies on the edge of the Virgo Supercluster. Something was wrong.

* * * * *

Starkwood's head slowly rolled to one side again, as if

there was no stable position – or the most stable one was face down, his face being the heaviest part of his head. He no longer looked in the direction of the monopole-cat shower but was looking at the dirt below.

'Now I won't even be able to see that shower before I die!' he cried. As he spoke and cried, he dribbled from both his mouth and his nose and this got orange Martian sand sticking to his face like Earth sand would do to a fallen ice cream at the beach. The soggy end of where his head used to be attached to his body was also caked in dust like a breadcrumb battered fish finger. Elvis wondered how on Mars his friend was still alive, but realised over his long life just how many creatures cut in half still seemed to be able to regrow their missing bits.

Fionix, who'd just arrived, looked at Elvis and said: 'is he always like this?'

'Well,' said Elvis, 'ever since I've known him he's been a bit of a weeping willow, but I must admit losing one's body is a fairly good reason to be upset. I remember when my brothers hid my shell for a laugh when I was asleep and I was crying that I'd been burgled! I was only about five million then…'

They looked back at Starkwood, who was looking so sorry for himself. The poor *bebodied* plant was forced to stare at the rather uninteresting amber sand beneath it (bebodied is like beheaded but from the head's point of view). As it was now night, the sand didn't really have much colour, much like Starkwood himself, who was at the opposite end of the greyscale, and seemed a pale, almost zombie-like shadow of his former self. He was like an Earth plant that had been hidden from the sun and lacked its healthy green chlorophyll.

At that moment, Starkwood's hair started to rise, as if he was being pulled out of the ground and uprooted by some invisible hand, like he was a prize turnip. His hairs then spread out as if gaining a static charge again, which made him open his eyes wide, looking around a little worried.

'Oh dear,' he said, 'something's happening to me! Something bad! Again!'

His two friends looked at him and they could also see some blue static light crackling between the hairs on his head again.

'This doesn't feel good...' said Starkwood.

'Why, what's wrong?' asked Elvis, also looking round to see what demons were pulling his strings this time.

'I feel funny, like my stomach's up in the air.'

'Maybe it's like a phantom limb you feel when it gets cut off,' Elvis suggested.

'No, this is the feeling I get when I feel weightless, like when we go over a bump...'

'Well you have lost a *bit* of weight,' said Elvis, walking round his friend's head and eyeing him closely, 'most of your body in fact.'

'No, this is different. I'm feeling so light-headed... that... that...'

They watched with curiosity to see that his hairs were now pointing vertically.

'Have you seen this happen before?' said Fionix, looking back at Elvis.

'Well not exactly, but his hairs often stand on end. They follow the field lines.'

'Yes I understand that,' Fionix agreed, 'but if you look, he's not actually touching the ground anymore...'

They both looked and Starkwood looked too. Fionix was right. He was hanging in mid-air.

'I'm floating!'

'Yes you are! *This* is different, *this* is new.'

'I shouldn't be able to float!' screeched Starkwood, 'I'm not a lighter-than-air creature! My spores float but why aren't I touching the ground?!'

He tried turning his head to face upwards and to blow that way, which made his head drift down slightly, but like a balloon filled with helium, he started floating up again. Elvis came up to him and tried putting his claw on top of Starkwood to bring him back to Mars but he got a sudden shock and withdrew his hand in surprise.

'Ow! That kind of hurt,' he admitted, shaking his forearm to get the feeling back.

'I'm floating away!'

Fionix watched out of curiosity.

'Why do you think this is happening?' she asked Elvis.

'I guess if he's charging up again, and what with this storm raging, he might actually be behaving like one of those monopole-cats himself…'

'I don't want to be a monopole-cat! I don't want to change species!'

'I said *like* a polecat – I don't think you'll be evolving sideways for the moment, though, maybe he *is* evolving…'

'But I'm floating away. I'm losing my head! Soon there'll be nothing left of me at all…'

'Well let's not get too worked up about it,' said Elvis, then he turned to Fionix: 'I think you better bring him back down.'

'Okay,' she sighed, 'but now he's out of reach. I'm going to have to get airborne and that's going to take a little while.'

'Help! Don't leave me up here! Don't let me disappear, I'll get vertigo!! Then I'll be *vertigone*…'

'No you won't,' sighed Elvis.

The two friends watched as Starkwood's head floated, with some kind of purpose, in the general direction of whatever field lines there might have been. At the same time, the monopole-cats whizzed back and forth, occasionally colliding with each other. It became quite a firework display that night.

* * * * *

In another part of the Central Bulge, where the field lines were pointing into the ground, a lone male monopole-cat could be seen with his prehensile tail clasped to a rock. He, Frankie, was using his front paws to pick up the rock and hump it onto his shoulder. He was mumbling to himself and his bluish glow was actually quite faint: the look on his face a little downhearted.

The next moment Frankie threw his rock, shot-put-like,

in a southerly direction. Monopole-cats being relatively weak and delicate creatures his throw was not record breaking, in spite of the low gravity. As the rock followed its low trajectory, it pulled Frankie's tail behind it and barely lifted his body to follow in the arc, like a gymnast swishing one of those ribbons around on the end of a stick.

'Why are the elements against me…' muttered Frankie to himself as he landed. He picked up his rock again and 'putted' once more in the general direction of south. He thought of his fair maiden, Nati and sighed. He'd first noticed her several seasons ago, when he saw a beautiful creature arcing across the sky – well, *beautiful* to him. Unlike most monopole-cats, Nati had a long mane of hair, longer than her body, so when he first saw her, she looked like a comet streaking across the heavens. How could Frankie not get tangled up in that hair?

In yet another part of the Central Bulge, stood another lone monopole-cat, softly glowing red. Her name was Nati and she too was looking a little glum. She picked up the rock to which her prehensile tail was attached and instead of placing it on her shoulder and under her chin as Frankie did, she started to swing it round in a circle. Using her own tail as the connection to the rock, she started turning her own body around, like a hammer thrower, one of her back paws scraping out a small, circular depression in the top soil as she spun. The next moment, rock, tail, then Nati went flying in a northerly direction, her hair streaming behind like an advert for shampoo. She thought about how many times she'd missed her soul mate Frankie. The first time she'd seen him, he did a sort of Snoopy dance as he performed his mating flight through the Martian atmosphere. She thought he was cute. Most monopole-cats had the philosophy: 'if you can't be with the one you love, then love the one you crash into,' and they didn't seem to mind which partner they ended up with, but Nati and her chosen Frankie were a little different. Their conversations over the last few years had been sporadic and very brief, like an extremely slow, long distance game of chess, with about one move a year. Each time they took to the air, they tried to reposition their respective launch sites so they would encounter each other in mid-flight, a bit like trying to fire matter and anti-matter particles at each other by sending them in opposite directions round a particle accelerator and hoping they'd hit. Frankie and Nati still had to hone their navigational skills.

So, as they passed each other in the sky each time, they managed to exchange names and a few other essential facts, like their favourite colours and where they'd like to go on their honeymoon (both said Syrtis Majoris – it's a popular destination for newly weds). Frankie had tried to recite a poem, but with an average of one word each passing, he'd barely got to the end of the first line.

After landing in a heap, Nati picked up her tail rock again and repeated the spinning motion to re-launch herself, hammer style, to gradually get back to a more suitable starting point to encounter Frankie. Her hammer spinning method did actually get her moving about five times further than Frankie's shot put style. It was a generalisation that the male monopole-cats mostly used the shot put method while the female ones the hammer spinning style. Was this because the females were cleverer, or were the males just too lazy?

* * * * *

Starkwood's face was pointing downwards again as he floated in the thin Martian atmosphere, so he couldn't see the very monopole-cat display for which he'd been waiting so long. Instead, he saw Fionix running along, waddling a bit, in little leaps and bounds, gradually unfolding her wings. As they caught whatever breeze was there, they flapped open like huge sails, or more like one of those para-gliders running off the edge of a cliff. She had many false attempts to leave the ground as if gravity was trying to tell her something and she wasn't listening. She thought to herself that she should learn how to become statically charged herself while on the ground, as it might help take off procedure having that extra repulsive, anti-gravity force.

Of course, electric and magnetic fields were something she'd used once she was *already* in flight. That helped her move through the Martian skies (and beyond – even as far as other planets, but more about that later). She knew she could use monopole-cats (and had on occasion), but was loathe to take advantage of them without their permission. She did entice them with a 'you lift my body in the air and I'll get you to meet up with one of your potential pole mates' offer.

In the end, Fionix used the first segment of each wing like a pole-vaulting pole and levered herself into the air like she was using crutches and this gave her just enough height to flap her wings and complete her take off. With a sigh, Fionix began her pursuit of the bebodied plant.

* * * * *

Later, as Fionix sat and meticulously folded her wings again and before Elvis and Starkwood knew it, there was a little green man standing in front of them.

'Oh no!' cried Starkwood, 'there's a little green man! I'm starting to hallucinate!'

'No,' said Elvis calmly, 'I can see a little green man too.'

'You're hallucinating too!' cried Starkwood.

A second one appeared.

'There's a second one now!' shouted Starkwood '*Multiple* mass hysteria! More multiple mass hysteria! We're going to be surrounded by little green men! Hundreds of them, thousands of them, umpteen millions of them!'

'There don't seem to be any more,' Elvis observed, 'though two is already quite a lot, when normally there aren't any.'

The first little green man looked over himself, inspected his little green arms and his little green body and said: 'I'm a little green man...'

Starkwood cried out: 'You're hallucinating too! Even the hallucinations are hallucinating!' Then the little green man looked over at the second little green man and said: 'You're a little green man as well!'

'Yes that's normal. We're supposed to fit in wherever we appear.'

The two aliens turned their attentions back to the confused inhabitants.

'Good evening, I'm Officer Turkan and this is Officer Amelius and we...'

The other green man interrupted: 'No, Third...'

'What?'

'I'm Officer Amelius the *Third*, remember?'

The first little green man looked stumped for a moment.

'Um, I thought it'd just be Officer *Amelius*,' said Turkan.

'No no,' said the first little green man, '*the Third* is my public name.'

'Okay,' said Officer Turkan, getting back to business, 'yes, so we are the Physics Law Enforcement and...'

'What?' said Elvis. 'I've never heard of that before!'

'That's no excuse for not knowing the Law.' said Officer Turkan.

'But I didn't even know that physics laws had to be enforced – I thought they just happen.'

'Well yes, of course you did. Everyone thinks like that,' said Officer Turkan, 'we're here because one or more of you have broken a Law of Physics in the most recent past.'

'We've not broken anything,' Elvis replied casually.

'That's what they *all* say,' said Officer Turkan.

'Yea!' said Officer The Third. They both looked suspiciously at the suspects, as The Third continued: 'Shall we start with a body search?'

Turkan looked at his colleague and then looked at Starkwood, who took it very personally and started wailing.

'I don't have a body!'

'Well,' said Officer Turkan, 'we can skip the body search then. I think it must be something else…'

He looked at them and said: 'it's not likely to be speeding, unless…' and he looked at Elvis with a smile, 'you were going faster than the speed of light…' and gave a little chuckle. 'I'll check my positronic notes. The crime should be coming through shortly…'

While the Physics Police officer opened his digital flip top, there still seemed to be some of the blue static sparks flying around as an after effect of the cosmic storm. A few crackled under his feet.

'This must be some kind of mistake,' said Elvis, again in his calm, Muddist way.

'Not at all,' said Officer Turkan. 'We wouldn't be called out of our 4D bubble and whipped into your 3D world if something serious hadn't just happened. Ah, here it is,' said Officer Turkan, as he watched his little mobile pocket-sized digital note-book, 'yes… breaking the laws of probability without a licence.'

'*Licence*?' said Elvis.

'You viciously and maliciously broke the laws of probability, allowing yourself to get hit by *two* one hundred million year cosmic rays within a few moments of each other. That in theory is extremely unlikely don't you think?'

'Yes,' said Elvis, 'but that doesn't mean to say it won't happen. It just means…'

'Are you arguing with an officer of the law of physics?!'

'I don't think I'm arguing, officer. I'm just pointing out that the laws of physics allow some rare events to happen at some point sometime somewhere, as the universe is so big and of course there may be many universes, so…'

'Let's not get technical here son,' said Officer Turkan, 'there is evidence that your friend, a *Mister Starkwood* has broken the laws of physics and there is a fine to pay.'

'Fine?!' Starkwood said, 'I didn't want to be hit by cosmic rays!'

'You *taunted* them sir, according to the information here.'

'What information? What witness do you have then?'

'The Universe itself, it lets us know when the laws are going wrong.'

'A *fine*? Isn't there a trial?' said Starkwood.

'Er yes sir. You are allowed a trial.'

'Then I demand a trial!' cried Starkwood. 'I'm innocent! I'm innocent!'

'Anything you say, sir, will be taken down and used as evidence against you.'

'But I'm innocent! I didn't make it happen!'

'That's to be decided in a court of law.'

'Um, when,' asked Elvis, 'when would this trial take place?'

'Um,' said Officer Turkan, flicking through the virtual pages on his digital notepad, 'ooooh, well there's quite a back log I see. A number of cases.'

'A number?' asked Elvis,

'Yes.'

'How many would that be?

'Er, two,' said Officer Turkan.

'Okay, so when is the estimated time for his trial?'

'…In about seventeen Martian years…'

'Ah ok. Thank you officer. And what's the punishment likely to be if he's found guilty?'

'Um,' said Officer Turkan, flicking through more pages then he said 'Officer The Third, do you know what the going rate is for breaking the laws of probability?'

The other little green man looked so shocked that he'd been asked for some information, that he was stumped.

'I don't think we've ever had a breaking of the laws of probability before. I don't know off the top of my head. We'll look into it and let you know.'

'Thank you officer,' replied Elvis

'Be careful,' warned Officer Turkan, 'a third offence and you get imprisoned straight away!'

'Yes Officer…'

Starkwood had been almost completely out of this conversation – still seriously disturbed by what had happened to him. Elvis, on the other hand had taken it all in and decided, well, seventeen Martian years should be enough time to get over this traumatic event, plus it might give them time to find a decent lawyer who could defend Starkwood's innocence in this matter, though he wasn't sure where to find the best attorneys on Mars. Maybe at the Bar. Meanwhile, there seemed to be a little dispute building up between the two officers.

'Why do you keep calling it a positronic notepad?' asked The Third.

'Because that's what it is!' Turkan replied, still with the continued background of little blue flashes of light from under his feet and the occasional one on his body.

'But I thought it was called an *electronic* notepad,' suggested The Third.

'It *would* be,' Turkan pointed out, 'if this was a *matter* universe,' he said sarcastically. 'As it's an anti-matter universe, it's not electrons that carry the charge it's *positrons*!'

Officer the Third wasn't convinced. Elvis was overhearing this conversation and looked again at the crackling sparks that were building up beneath Officer Turkan's feet.

'But,' said Officer the Third, 'I think this *is* a matter universe…'

Turkan looked down at his own feet then at the little blue sparks that were igniting all around himself as realisation began to dawn. Elvis too was coming to the same conclusion.

'Oh dear,' said Elvis.

'I need to get out of here fast!' shouted Turkan, but the next moment, there was a large explosion. The anti-matter version of Turkan annihilated with an equal amount of local Martian matter, causing the equivalent of an 80 megaton nuclear explosion, that made a crater of several kilometres diameter, thus destroying all life within the hundred kilometre ejecta radius.

Well, that brings our story to an unexpected and rather abrupt end…

6
Space Invaders

In a closely parallel universe, where Turkan had appeared as a *matter* version of himself (with the clearly labelled *electronic* notepad so there was no confusion) and not the deadly anti-matter version, there had been no explosion, so no one was killed. Of course, in half of the parallel universes, this unfortunate event would have happened, but let's stay in one which might have a happier ending.

Elvis looked round, a bit confused.

'Did you just feel that?' he asked his seriously injured friend.

'I feel nothing...' Starkwood admitted negatively.

'Funny,' said Elvis, 'I had an odd feeling like a déjà vu, but it's gone now...'

'And I'm almost gone...' said Starkwood, snapping Elvis out of his daydream and back to giving his neurotic neighbour the attention he was looking for.

* * * * *

'That was embarrassing,' said Amelius, appearing as one of his 1D chess pieces back in his 4D bubble.

'Sorry, my fault,' said Turkan, also different and appearing to be an image inside the screen of his 3D television. 'I got confused with what type of universe we were being called to. Matter, anti-matter, an easy mistake to make...'

'Yes, but like the Moth Effect,' explained Amelius, 'we don't know the repercussions.'

'Don't you mean *Butterfly* Effect?'

'No, *Moth* Effect. We're going to be in the dark about what happens, until it happens...'

* * * * *

Grit and the two sisters finally reached the brow of the ridge they'd been climbing and they were now looking south-west to the plains of the Ptolemaeus Crater. Ruddy ridges as far as the eye could see, with the odd boulder of blue grey, scattered like chocolate chips in a chocolate chip cookie. The three travelling tortles scanned the horizon, taking in the beauty of the pebble-strewn panorama in front of them. Sunlight caught on a distant object in the plains below. It was something shiny, more shiny than any crystal you could find on Mars and Grit pointed it out.

'There! There it is, there, the dead white tortle!'

The two sisters squinted but it was too far away to see any detail. However, there did seem to be several bits of something scattered around the main object in the middle of the mess, as if some Martian Humpty Dumpty had had his final fall just here, without the king's men nearby to put him right.

'Look there,' said Grit, 'further north, that's where there was that huge round sheet I told you about …' then he tailed off and said: 'oh, it's not there…'

'Maybe you imagined it,' said Ruby.

'No no it *was* there,' said Grit, 'that's where I got this rope from. It was attached to the big round wedding dress-sheet-thing.'

The rope was still around Grit's neck and shoulder: the evidence was there for all to see.

'Maybe it blew away in the wind,' said Jade helpfully, then stopped. Did the shiny thing just move slightly, she thought to herself, or was it just the sunlight flickering off its bright surface? Well, she thought, the wind *was* blowing so it could have shaken it, causing a wobble in its reflection. They slowly walked down into the plains and headed towards the mysterious shiny object.

'Wait,' said Jade suddenly, 'there *is* something there…

'Where?' said Grit.

'Where you said there was the sheet, but it's not a sheet it's some markings on the ground!'

Ruby looked and saw it too and smiled. She could see

what it was, but didn't let on. She had quite good vision, helped by the heightening effects of the dry ice inhalation and in spite of the single eye.

'What is it?' said Grit trying to hop a little bit into the air to get a better view of the markings.

He even hopped onto a large rock nearby to get a better view: the markings were an approximately round outline, though looking oval from this shallow angle: a circular trace, looking about the same size as the original round sheet Grit had seen on the ground a few years back. In the middle of the circular patch there seemed to be a couple of other darker markings as if the ground had been dug up, plus some scribbly dug up soil near the circle's edge.

'I can't see enough of it,' said Grit, disappointed.

'Wait until you get there then,' remarked Ruby, bemused.

The three of them encountered the engraving in the dirt and eyed it with curiosity.

'It was exactly here,' protested Grit, as they slowly circled the outer perimeter. 'Look,' he pointed just to the south, 'the other ropes are still there...'

True they were, though half buried in the red sand and covered by the soil that had been moved by the Martian winds over the past year or two. Their minds returned to the missing sheet and continued to walk round it. Inside this circular groove, about ten metres across, were three separate larger rocks, about the size of a fully grown tortle (a metre or so). One was right in the centre and the other two were placed roughly symmetrically in the top half about north-east and north-west. Below the central stone, there was a curved line of smaller rocks, creating an upwards curving circular arc.

'Is it an ancient temple?' asked Grit.

Ruby 'pfffd' and smiled her superior smile.

'If it wasn't there when you got your rope, then it can't be very ancient can it, pebble brain?' said Ruby.

'Hidden by the cover?' he defended his theory.

'Could it be one of those gastronomical calendars?' suggested Jade.

'*Astronomical*!' corrected Ruby, gaining such delight in knowing more than her companions.

'Okay *astronomical*!' Jade admitted, 'but dad told me they used to eat the rocks on their calendar when they were done with it. So there wouldn't be any evidence...'

'Gastronomical... pfff,' Ruby muttered with a sneer.

Jade wanted to hit Ruby over her smug head with one of the rocks, even if it did mess up this ancient cosmic calculating device. Jade continued.

'Dad said they usually used rocks with a high silicon content as they were better at calculating the seasons and the major events...'

'It's a face!' said Ruby in frustration. 'It's a smiling face, that's all!'

This silenced the other two. The three continued to follow the rest of the perimeter without a word until Grit said: 'but maybe the face's symmetry is matched in the seasons?'

'Someone drew a big face,' Ruby stated and silence fell again.

As they arrived back at their starting point, Ruby pointed at some scribblings near the chin of the face.

'There, I thought so,' said Ruby and she left the others reading it and she headed further south, following the remaining ropes. Grit and Jade read the scribblings.

'Hanksie' said Grit aloud. Jade had a realising moment.

'What's a Hanksie?' Grit asked.

'You don't know?' said Jade but tried not to sound intolerant like her sister.

'Is that the name of an ancient stone circle?'

Ruby laughed but carried on in front and didn't turn around.

'You haven't seen one before?' Jade asked.

'No. Well I've seen some rock patterns before but...'

'No. Hanksie is an anonymous artist who...'

'Everyone knows who he is,' Ruby butted in.

'He's created some art works all over the planet. Writing or painting on some rocks or making shapes in the sand or in the ice, you know balancing rocks and stuff.'

'I've never seen one before.'

'Well they usually get destroyed soon after they appear.'

'Oh, is it the God of Mars who doesn't approve or something?'

Ruby smiled to herself again but said nothing.

'Probably the artist doing it himself,' said Jade. 'Dad told me artists can be quite emotional.'

'So who is Hanksie then?'

'He's Herman.'

'Who's Herman?'

When it was clear that Ruby was not going to waste her breath on this one, Jade did the honours. She caught herself sighing like her sister then vowed she'd be more patient.

'Herman is a kind of tortle, but he isn't. He hasn't got his own shell so he lives in the shells of dead tortles…'

Grit looked horrified and shivered, looking round in case the squatter was still in the area.

'That's horrible!'

'Well they say he was born without one, so the only way he can protect himself is to use an empty one.'

'And he goes round killing tortles to take over their shells?!'

'I don't think so,' said Jade, weighing up what she knew about this homeless nomad. 'I think he goes round looking for discarded ones, as he grows out of his old one.'

'That's creepy,' decided Grit, 'wearing someone else's clothes like that…'

The travelling trio stopped in front of the 'out-of-place' item on the Martian regolith. It was a row of small metal rings, one linked inside the other and leading towards a half-buried metallic cylinder with a pointed, cone-shaped end.

'This is not from Mars…' Ruby remarked, now actually starting to take the spectacle more seriously.

'So where's it come from?' Jade asked, looking round like Grit did and she even looked vertically up.

'Maybe it was made by the creatures that made the rock circle…' said Grit.

'It's a sculpture Grit!' Ruby snapped at him. 'Made by Hanksie!'

'Maybe Hanksie made this metal tube...'

'It's not a Martian thing,' said Ruby, 'we don't have this kind of technology on this planet.'

'What's tacticology?' Grit asked.

'Wow, you have been living under a stone kid!'

'Ruby's right,' Jade had to admit, as they continued to eye this unique construction, 'everything I've ever seen on the ground has been made of rocks. Not metal. Maybe flecks of metal in the rocks like our shells. And all the white stuff that we have is either frozen water or dry ice.'

'It's not natural,' Ruby continued. 'I can't see this being cut into shape by wind erosion. Certainly not water, as it looks like it appeared recently and we've hardly had any running water for a long time...' she stopped herself then looked at her two companions, 'not counting your recent swim in a lung whale's lake!'

Jade caught herself about to react, but held it in and reminded herself that Ruby would never let her forget her passage through the hidden tunnels of the largest creature in the solar system (not counting those in the sub-surface ocean on Europa).

The three continued to circle this foreign object.

'So where did it come from then?' Grit asked openly, 'I mean how did it get there? Everything, wherever it is, has to have got wherever it is by moving there itself or someone or something put it there...'

This was true, Jade thought. It was the sort of argument her dad had used when she was younger and asked where things came from. It was part of the Muddist teaching and if it wasn't one of the Martian creatures putting a boulder in a certain place, then it was the wind or the ancient rain or whatever, or the rock was actually alive. Ruby turned her gaze vertically.

'Up there,' she suggested.

'But normally only rocks fall from the sky,' said Grit confused.

'Or monopole-cats following the field lines,' Jade put in.

'Or one of those birds of paradise that always lands badly,' said Grit, having met a couple in his relatively short life.

'It looks like *this* one landed badly,' said Jade, looking at the object then also staring upwards.

Grit looked at what was a clearly damaged object and he too gazed to the heavens. His face lit up with an idea.

'The Gods!' he cried. 'A gift from the Gods!'

'Gift?!' said Ruby, 'it looks broken.'

'A *broken* gift from the Gods!'

'Looks like they threw it at us,' Ruby smiled.

'The Gods are angry!' Grit continued in his single-minded deduction. 'We must do something!'

'How about a sacrifice to appease them?' suggested Ruby, looking menacingly at him.

'Yes!' then Grit realised. 'What?! I mean no! I'm too young to die.'

'Death is as old as you get,' mused Ruby as she carried on walking round and looking at the object.

'Look,' said Jade, pointing at the apparition from above, 'there are scratch marks on its body.'

'Yes,' said Ruby dismissively, 'we can see it hit the ground and slid along a bit.'

'Maybe it got hit by flying rocks that it kicked up, or it rolled and scraped along on its top for a while,' suggested Grit.

'No,' said Jade, 'no, the scratches seem to be in groups, like claw marks...'

Ruby saw them and realised her nerdy sister was right and this ruffled her non-existent feathers. Ruby always felt she was much smarter than her goody goody twin, as she had never had to try hard to understand the world around her. She tried to hide her discomfort at missing the clue and picked up the morsel as it if had been hers all along.

'Yea, thanks for pointing out the obvious sis. We can ask Fionix if she knows anything about it.'

'Maybe one of the birds of paradise had a fight with it in mid-air!' said Grit with nervous excitement.

'Well if it was alive,' observed Jade, 'it's dead now.'

Jade stopped dead in her tracks and as always Grit bumped into her butt and Ruby did likewise to his. Jade even backed away which meant reversing into Grit who had no choice but to do the same to Ruby.

'Get your butt out of my face, punk!' said Ruby.

Grit couldn't side step fast enough and was caught between the fear of upsetting this formidable female umpteenager again and wanting to know why the sweeter of the sisters had retreated from the alien space carcass.

'Look!' said Jade, 'Tracks. Something slithered out of the empty space shell!

'Maybe it's a space egg!' said Grit and the three of them unconsciously formed a sort of circle for protection, looking outwards in three directions for whatever it was. Ruby didn't want to show she was worried, but this was not something her book of cool had prepared her for. She even looked upwards in case a flying creature had come out of the egg.

'No,' said Jade, seeing where her sister's attention was going, '*that* way, along the ground. Something came out of that thing and scraped along the ground, look two tracks, as if it slid along…'

They surveyed the surroundings, but apart from these traces of movement, nothing was there as far as the eye could see, which was as far as the northern rim of the Ptolemy crater.

'Or maybe it just slithered *in*!' said Ruby, finding an alternative and slightly more worrying scenario. Grit moved so Jade was between him and the alien object. Ruby moved behind Grit as she felt important enough to need two layers of possible sacrificing material: just two square meals to keep the slip-sliding creature's belly full, long enough for her to escape.

'Hello?' said Jade via the open entrance, to the astonishment of the other two.

'Who in their right mind would seek the attention of an unknown, and who knows, potentially dangerous creature, sister?' asked Ruby rhetorically.

The metallic white carapace moved. Not a lot, but more than could have happened if it was the wind. Which incidentally wasn't even blowing at this moment. The object had moved! There was a scramble as each of the three terrified tortles tried to climb backwards over each of the other two. It was not a pretty sight. Nor was it very dignified.

'Someone has to go and inspect it,' decided Ruby, with a tone that was clearly excluding herself.

'Not me!' snapped Grit. 'I don't want an alien clamping itself to my face then planting eggs in my stomach that burst out later and letting all my insides pour out on the ground.'

The other two looked at him with surprise at the graphic nature of his imagination.

'And aliens do that do they?'

'I don't know,' said Grit, 'but I don't want to take the chance!'

'Don't you want to protect us poor helpless *girls* from the big bad monster?' said Ruby, fluttering her eyelashes into the bargain.

Even Jade gave a disbelieving sideways look at her sister's sheer audacity.

'Ladies first!' shouted Grit.

'Who says it's a face sucking alien?' asked Jade. 'I mean, to this creature, it's *us* who are the aliens! Do we clamp ourselves on other creatures' faces and lay eggs in their intestines? I know I don't't!'

The carcass of the white metallic thing rattled again and the three reluctant heroes jumped a little and stepped away again.

'So let's draw lots for who looks inside,' said Ruby, again with the confidence that there was no way she was going to lose.

'What?' asked Grit, confused 'and then we choose the best one?'

'What?'

'And anyway do we have enough time to do some sketching?'

'No you block of pumice!' cried Ruby, 'Not *draw* as in drawing, we play 'Rock, Gravel, Sand'.'

'Oh. I know that,' Grit realised, and Jade reluctantly said 'Okay'.

'On the count of three then,' said Ruby, 'one… two … three…'

The three tortles quickly held out a front claw, showing either one of three shapes.

Both Jade and Grit held out bunched claws, while Ruby held up three separate clawed fingers.

'I win!' said Ruby.

'No!' said Jade. '*Rock* covers Sand.'

'Oh I thought I was I doing Gravel,' said Grit looking at his own limb.

'No, Sand covers *Rock*,' insisted Ruby 'and I did Sand so it won't be me.'

'Look!' Jade protested, 'all the rocks are sitting *on* the sand! Rock covers *sand*!'

'But what about all the rocks you *can't* see?' defended Ruby, 'the ones *below* the sand? The sand storms blow and *cover up* the rocks.'

'But…'

'Mars is one big rock,' explained Ruby 'and it's *covered* with sand! Accept defeat. Go on, you two go again.'

Reluctantly Jade and Grit gave in and as Ruby counted to three, they held out a front claw again. Jade held up one claw while Grit held up two.

'Rock crushes Gravel!' said Ruby, delighted the boy lost. 'Off you go, Sir Grit, protect us poor damsels in distress…'

Grit was still inspecting his losing claw shape as he slowly approached the biohazard. Suddenly 'Hello!' came as a cry from an opening, a gap caused by one of the object's huge white petals having been peeled back at some unknown moment in the past. A small head peered out, with a simple smile on its face. The head was almost skeletal, sunken cheeks but with a high bone structure and the face curving out then curving in to a finely pointed chin. Above the eyes of the face seemed to be a hat, but might have in fact been just the structure of the creature's head. This possible 'hat' looked like a ribbed woolly, bobbly hat but without the bobble, somewhat akin to the armoured plating on a triceratops' head but a lot more fashionable: shorter and with pleats and no backward pointing spikes. The unknown creature's eyes were big and sparkling and the creature, whatever it was, did not ooze any kind of dangerous vibes whatsoever.

'Oh you're Hanksie!' Jade realised and just as suddenly as her fear had come, it evaporated with the realisation it was someone she had heard about.

'No, not Hanksie' said the stranger, 'Herman. Hanksie a famous but very unknown *Gravity Artist*. Herman just a nomad.'

'Herman,' Jade corrected herself, 'sorry my mistake. You gave us such a fright you know.'

'And not only *nomad*, also *not mad*. Stories not true about Herman.'

'I shall remember that Herman,' Jade said politely. 'So do you know what this thing is?'

'This my new home,' said Herman proudly.

'Um, nice place,' said Jade. 'Do you know what it was before?'

'Abandoned home. Herman always lives in abandoned homes.'

'A squatter,' said Ruby, a little accusingly.

'Not squatting. Herman's legs don't bend like that.'

Ruby huffed. Jade ignored her sister and continued her fact-finding mission.

'Well how long have you been living here?'

'Since I arrived. Nobody in here. Herman always lives in abandoned homes.'

'Yes I heard that,' said Jade, 'but don't you usually live in an old rock tortle shell and move around – that's what my dad told me…'

'The Golden One.'

'How did you know?'

'You have his claws, Green One. And you, Red One, you have his beak.'

'I dark red,' said Ruby, already fed up with this strange stranger and impolitely impersonating him at the same time.

'Herman prayed to Ocean God in Heaven for new home and home fell from sky…'

Meanwhile Grit had disappeared and it was only then that Jade realised this, and looked round. They all heard some rummaging around coming from inside the white maisonette.

* * * * *

Let's just go back a little bit in time to the site where Starkwood had recently been hit by the cosmic ray. The plant, the tortle and the huge bird were already leaving the area. Elvis' outline was still visible in the distance, as several of his lice stood in a circle round the shallow hole they had just dug in the still slightly charged ground. The remaining piece of Starkwood's smouldering sepal had finally gone out and the last smoke signals had unfurled from the charred remains, the smoke signal probably saying something like 'smoking is bad for your health'. There were also several other pieces of Starkwood's body that had been through the cosmic blender, many tiny bits in various states of being cooked, from the sushi end of the scale to the BBQ burnt to cinders setting.

The lice hung their heads in respect as Captain Sam Biosis raised his head for the reading of the Last Rites.

'We be 'ere to mourn the loss of Sailor Swift,' began the captain in all reverence.

'Ahaar,' came the subdued reply from the congregation.

'She's gone to that Great Dry Sea In The Sky…'

'Ahaar.'

'Gave up 'er life in the line of duty…'

'Well,' whispered one voice to another, 'I 'erd he pushed 'er in front of the cosmic ray to defend his-self…'

'Shhh!' said the captain, 'she did be sacrificing 'erself for the crew!'

'Ahaar,' they agreed as the captain stared at the dissenting voice.

'It be the only 'onourable way for a pyrite to go…'

'I saw 'im grab 'er by the mandibles and 'ee 'idd behind her…'

'Who be saying that?!' demanded Sam Biosis. 'Twas Swift who grabbed me by the…'

'Ooerr…' sniggered a couple of the crew

'…mast and she be throwing 'erself in the path of that canon ball from space! And she gave up 'er life for 'er cap'n…'

'Ahaar…men.'

With that, the lice carefully put the charred remains of Sailor Swift into the hole and covered it with the red soil. They took the remaining piece of Starkwood's sepal and stuck it in the ground to act as a kind of headstone for their lost shipmate. Someone had scratched a message on the leaf: ''ere lies the soul of Sailor Swift, she didn't see it coming so is probably miffed.'

A final glance at the grave then they all hopped, much like grasshoppers, back towards the disappearing image of their rock tortle clipper. When there used be liquid oceans on Mars, the pyrites would have been thrown into the sea, weighed down with rocks (sometimes even if they weren't dead). Nowadays, throwing them onto the ground didn't seem to be the right thing to do, especially if they were still alive, so a proper burial was the official procedure (deep enough to make sure they couldn't claw their way out again).

* * * * *

House perched at a safe distance from his odd 'alien' friend Martin. Actually he felt like calling him *Martian*. House was still on the same telephone cable above the village square, but he clearly didn't want to be anywhere near the 'fibrous fax' of a second class letter delivery system. Martin seemed to be sifting through the manure from heaven and examining it with care.

'And you say it's a message?' doubted House.

'Yes,' confirmed Martin, 'from my distance cousin El-'

'...vis, yes you told me,' said House a little impatient, 'and you're reading it by looking through it?'

'Yes?'

'But it's just a load of sh...'

'Don't say it!'

'Shimmering slime!'

'To the untrained eye, yes, but you've seen those humans haven't you, that go looking for tracks and signs of animals?'

'Oh yes,' agreed House, 'naturists I think they call themselves.'

'Yes, well haven't you seen them looking at footprints and teeth marks in nutshells and stuff?'

'I have noticed that.'

'Well some of those naturists actually examine animal droppings and –'

'Really?! That's disgusting. Weird even.'

'Well they can identify a species from the type of droppings. And spot what they've been eating, like those owl pellets which contain the shrew bones.'

'Ah,' realised House, 'I think I see what you're getting at. So when you look at this postie bird's poo, you can read your letter in it.'

'Exactly.'

'But how does the message get into this Martian bird's droppings?' asked House.

'Fionix,' said Martin. 'Her name's Fionix...'

'Did *Fionix* listen to your cousin saying the message and, like, the thoughts that she had, got encoded into her own waste material?'

'No,' explained Martin, 'my cousin would have engraved his message on some small stones,'

'What, like Scrabble pieces?'

'Yes, and Fionix swallows them and well her digestive system turns those scrabble squares into this message I'm reading now...'

'Hang on, are you winding me up?!'

'No, seriously.'

'It still sounds like a load of cr –'

'Don't say it!'

'…cracked rocks to me.'

'Look at this bit here,' and Martin pointed to the material that was just in front of him 'Elvis is telling me about his travelling partner Starkwood.'

'Really? To me it just looks like a dark patch, then a lighter patch. What kind of creature is it?'

'Starkwood's a plant that's hitching a ride on his back. They sort of live in symbiosis.'

'Ooh! And the neighbours don't gossip about them?!'

'Not living in sin, *symbiosis*! Oh and Elvis says he's looking forward to meeting up with his daughter soon for her 16 millionth birthday…'

'Sixteen *million*?!' said House in surprise.

'Oh,' Martin corrected himself, 'that is Martian years.'

'Oh right,' said House, recovering 'their years are different to ours.'

'Yes, so that would be about 32 million Earth years…'

'What?! When did you last hear from Elvis?'

'Oh I haven't,' admitted Martin. 'My great grandmother Cottage did.'

'Cottage?'

'Yes Cottage.

'Your great grandmother was called Cottage?!'

'She'd made her nest under the eaves of a cottage. Anyway she told my grandfather, who told my mum and the messages have been sent down through the generations…'

'Crazy…' said House, shaking his head.

'No, there's even crazier stuff. Elvis heard about this sea full of lung wales under the ice in a crater…'

7

Visiting Volcanoes and
Zombie Vegetables

It was a slow, but thundering start. Fionix waddled along
the southern edge of the Valles Marineris. Elvis rode on
Fionix's back, much like a dragon rider, but he used his
beak to bite onto a tuft of thick skin on the back of
Fionix's neck. Starkwood's head was buried almost
completely in the soil-filled niche on Elvis's shell where
the blast had gouged out a small crater in the already
existing groove from his first cosmic bull's eye, ninety-
nine million years ago.

'We're gonna die!' cried Starkwood. 'We're gonna die!
Ahhhhh!'

With the immense size of Fionix's wings, the two
passengers could not see very much of the world below
them, only the odd glimpse, otherwise it was just a huge
expanse of leathery wings as far as the eye could see.
Being so large, the wing surfaces were a bit like the
surface of a liquid, with waves and ripples caused by the
air currents and the prevailing winds. It looked like the
passengers were sitting in a flying ocean.

'Getting there...' Fionix panted as she plodded along
the cliff top, the occasional rock or boulder loosened by
her pounding feet, wafting up dust and sending a little
shower of pebbles down into the depths of the seemingly
bottomless Canyon below. Elvis half-opened his right eye
and he could see, between wing flaps, the deep chasm
below them and he tried to remain calm with thoughts of
mud. And more mud. His head buried in mud.

'Now...' Fionix began, 'safety procedures... Please
remain seated during take-off. No smoking, and that
means you Starkwood. In the event of a crash,
everywhere is an exit –'

'Have there been many crashes?' Elvis asked casually.

101

'A number,' said Fionix.

'That number wouldn't be zero would it?' Elvis asked hopefully.

'No.'

'How many then?'

'Not that many,' reflected Fionix.

'Like once every…?' Elvis offered her.

'Um…' reflected Fionix, '…once every trip?'

'Once every *trip*?!' cried Starkwood?!

'About that…'

'Ahhhhhhhhhhhhhhhh!'

'Shh!' said Fionix, 'you're putting me off… here we go!'

The next moment, Elvis felt his stomach jump up and sensed he was going over the highest bump on a rollercoaster. Even Starkwood could feel his stomach too, but it felt to him like it was buried in the ground back where he'd been struck by cosmic lightning. He put the feeling down to the phantom limb effect that he'd been told about.

With a final hop, flap and a jump, Fionix rose into the air and reached the apex of her arc, before then turning groundwards like a poorly made paper plane. Down she went into the murky depths of the Marineris Canyon. Starkwood's scream could be heard Doppler shifting to a lower pitch as they fell further into the valley. Fionix was flying, that was for sure, but unfortunately, the direction of her flight was downwards. This was the opposite way she wanted to go. She would have liked to have used the excuse that it was due to the extra weight in the form of a rock tortle and a flower-head, but no; she had always had trouble taking off.

'Can we do anything to help?' Elvis asked with genuine concern.

'Pray to your Mud God,' said Fionix.

'Already doing that,' said Elvis.

Meanwhile on Elvis' back, the lice were not sitting round doing nothing.

'Ahaar!' cried Sam Biosis the captain.

'AHAAR!' his crew cried back in unison.

'Baton down that figurehead of a plant ya bilge rabbits!'

'Aye Aye Cap'n!' came the reply.

In no time, the pyrites had woven a criss-cross net of fibres across the crater in which Starkwood's head had been planted, thus making sure he would not fall out in the event of the flight ending upside down. Other lice had already been throwing their vine-like threads overboard and were tethering Elvis more securely to whatever purchase they could find on Fionix's back.

Fionix had hoped that she might avoid her 'back up' launch plan. She'd managed not to use it while any of her friends had been watching in the past, but this time, she might have to lose face in order to save lives.

'This is your pilot speaking...' began Fionix, 'um... Elvis, Starkwood, we have a problem...'

'Can I hazard a guess at what it is?" asked Elvis.

'No not now. I want you to take up crash positions...'

'If that involves screaming hysterically,' said Elvis, 'then Starkwood's one step ahead of you.'

'Ahhhhhhhhhhhhhhhhhhhhhh!' confirmed his chlorofilic friend.

'No. I want you both to hold your breaths, shut your eyes and block your ears...'

'Is this so we hear no death, see no death and smell no death?'

'No. Well, if things go wrong, yes, but it's never gone wrong before...'

'Never?!'

'Well okay, it's gone wrong, but I've always made it go right in time.'

'That should be comforting,' said Elvis, 'but somehow it isn't quite working.'

'Hey how old am I?' said Fionix, clearly insulted by Elvis's lack of belief in her.

'I never ask a lady her age.'

'Centimillions, that's how old!'

'Shouldn't that be hecta-millions?' Elvis asked.

'Anyway, we're in your safe hands: hands, or wings, flaps of skin, webbing – whatever it's called, officially, we're safely in them.'

'Please close all senses down now. And no peeking!'

By now Fionix had reached a sort of terminal velocity, which was quite fast in the thin Martian atmosphere and she prayed it didn't end in a terminal injury. She peered over her shoulder to make sure her friends were following orders and not looking. Elvis was using his elbows to grip the clump of neck skin, while putting his claws over his ears, and his eyes were squeezed so tight that his mineral-based scales round his eyes were starting to crack. Starkwood's head did not have its eyes closed but the faintest zombie expression on his face suggested that he wasn't picking anything up from the conscious world.

'Here goes...' said Fionix, as she opened her wings wide, angled them upwards and tensed up to cope with the soon-to-arrive centripetal forces. Sure enough, Fionix stopped descending vertically and instead took a circular trajectory – like a pendulum swinging – that would have caused some screeching if it was wheels on the ground going round a tight bend. Martian creatures weren't used to strong gravitational fields, so Fionix knew that her friends were feeling uncomfortably heavy. With her trips to Earth, she had experienced 'weight', but this still hurt.

By now Fionix was flying horizontally along the canyon and quite near to the southern cliff face. She looked down and noticed that she was so close to the valley floor that her wing tips were lifting up sand into the vortices, creating horizontal dust devils. Now she angled her wings further up and she started to climb, but also noticeably losing speed. This was the moment she was dreading. Switching on her jet propulsion while other creatures were within earshot. She strained herself in a very unlady-like way and a moment later there was a deep rasping sound. Before it went on for too long, Fionix brought her leg claws together and let them rub against each other. Sparks flew from her toenails and trailed behind her like very cheap fairy dust. There was a popping, crackling sound, a few putt putts and a momentary blue flame could be seen which snuffed out just as quickly, then suddenly a whoosh and a roar. Fionix's whole body was shaking like a Mars quake, but by then she was accelerating in the right direction. Out of the canyon's darkness and now rising higher and higher above the surrounding plateau. A large blue flame shooting out of her, well, what one might call her *rectorocket*.

The roaring sound became more noticeable when it stopped and silence filled the air. By now Fionix was many kilometres above the Central Bulge and was gently flapping her voluminous wings. With the sun setting over the horizon it was quite a view from this altitude.

'Um...' said Elvis, 'can we open our eyes yet?'

'If I say yes,' decided Fionix, 'you shouldn't be able to hear me, if you've still got your ears covered.'

'...ah... um ... pardon then?'

'You peeked!' said Fionix with horror.

'Aw come on,' said Elvis, 'we've seen you use your jet propulsion before. Heard it even. And well, the smell –'

'We're *not* talking about it!' snapped Fionix.

'Thanks for saving us,' said Elvis.

'... you're welcome. So get used to the ride, it's going to take a few days to get to Olympus Mons.'

'No problem,' said Elvis, 'I'm not going anywhere and I don't have any plans until my daughter's 16 millionth. Plus I still haven't read my distant cousin's letter yet.'

'Martin, no? Oh, let me give you some light,' and with that, Fionix unfolded a crinkle in each of her wings and suddenly a string of red lights could be seen along one wing and blue lights along the other.

'Oh!' said Elvis with surprise. 'I forgot you had a monopole-cat colony.'

There they were, clinging on with their prehensile tails and swinging from side to side in the breeze caused by Fionix's flying.

'No need for light,' said Elvis, 'remember I don't need to *see* the message.'

'Sorry, forgot,' said Fionix. 'Your cousin Martin's a

sight reader, that's what threw me. How's our cabbage patch doing?'

Elvis peered back over his shoulder to see what looked like a petrified petunia, a fossilised foxglove, a thunder-struck thistle, a – no wait, it isn't really the right time for this. Actually, it fits in perfectly as nothing else is going on: um a horrified hollyhock, a confounded conifer, a shocked shamrock, a –

'He's okay,' said Elvis.

Fionix refolded her flaps and the monopole-cats' lights cut out. In the darkness, Fionix could hear Elvis sniffing.

* * * * *

Tortles were not built to gallop. They had survived for millions of years by not having to move fast. In fact quite the opposite. Standing motionless for eons and impersonating rocks was standard practice for rock tortles on Mars. It was one of the unwritten rules and already built in as part of their evolutionary instinct. So, to see not one, but *three* tortles scampering most inelegantly across the dusty plains and highlands of the southern hemisphere was quite a spectacle. Actually, one of the tortles was far too cool to gallop and so she sauntered in a kind of sultry cat-walk way, with the air of not really being interested in getting wherever they were going, on time. The dark red one that is. Her sister, though, was doing her best to move at a high speed, but it wasn't a pretty sight. That's the greeny one. She was doing the right movements for it to be defined as galloping, but with the Martian gravitational field barely two fifths that of the Earth, it was all in slow motion and her legs would continue pedalling in mid-air like a long jumper, before she made contact with the ground again. Plus, she looked less like a racing horse and more like one of those Earth monkeys that bounds along sideways.

Grit, for some unexplained reason, was making the most progress forward. Was it because he was a boy and, whether it was umpteenaged tortles or teenage humans, there was still a reluctance for adolescent girls to be sporty? Or was it because Grit was slightly smaller and able to push more often against the ground? Or was he driven by some as yet unknown reason for wanting to catch up with the crazy *Gravity* artist Hanksie ('He Herman, he not Hanksie!').

It had been several weeks since Herman had hopped onto the little motorised skateboard thing that had come out of the crashed Russian Mars 3 craft and whipped the parachute into the air, which caught the prevailing winds and dragged the lone stranger westwards. Over the old cratered plains, uphill and down dale; well, up ejecta blankets and down inside crater rims went the rock tortles. Herman the skateboarding, paragliding house-sitter was getting further and further away from them but they could see the dust trail that he kicked up, just like the cowboys and Native American Indians chasing each other on horseback in the Wild West. The little Russian Rover didn't have wheels but two strips like skiis, which turned on wheels like the linkages of a steam train, and they slapped the ground. This made the mini rover hop and half slide along, a bit like one of those bounding gazelles in the African Plains.

Jade was actually questioning why she was chasing after this relatively harmless eccentric, but she was just following Grit, who seemed to have flipped into panic mode. He'd shouted something about a hedgehog egg when Herman shot off. That made no sense to Jade.

By now, Ruby had slowed down to walking pace then crawling pace and finally a nonchalant plod, which she liked to call 'vagueing'. Captain Masha was standing on Ruby's beak, back feet slightly apart in a power stance and some kind of harpoon weapon in one of her four forearms.

'Why are you slowing down?' Masha asked her hostess.

'What's the rush?' replied Ruby, eyelids closed through lack of interest, 'a silly little tortle boy chasing after a not very good Gravity Artist and for what?'

'Something's troubling him,' suggested Masha.

'Herman?'

'No, the young tortle.'

'Are you getting soft?' asked Ruby, almost with distaste.

'Instinct I guess,' said Masha, matter-of-factly, now sitting on one of Ruby's eyebrow scales and leaning her four elbows on her own knees, 'we pyrites are naturally tuned in to the feelings of tortles. We can sense these things.'

'I thought that was only for your host tortle?' said Ruby, slightly interested in this new piece of information.

'Obviously not,' replied Masha. 'Looks like it extends further…'

Just then, Masha was interrupted by the arrival of one of her crew.

'Cap'n Masha!' cried the enthusiastic pyrite, stumbling as he arrived.

Masha recognised his voice without even turning round.

'Piccolo,' she said with a slight, *what is it now* tone.

Piccolo was chuckling to himself but said nothing, though he bumped into her, so Masha was forced to turn and look at him. There were several of his crew mates a short way behind him. Her face remained deadpan. Several seconds passed.

'Nice patch over your left eye,' said Cap'n Masha, with almost no emotion.

'I thought you'd like it Cap'n,' he replied.

'I'm not so sure about the patch over your right eye though…'

'Who said that?' asked Piccolo looking round.

Masha sighed.

'Me, your captain,'

'Where are you?!'

Captain Masha sighed again, hating herself for what she was going to say next: 'Piccolo, why two eye patches?'

'Well Cap'n,' he started with excitement 'as you be a

108

badass cap'n with one eye patch, I am thinking I'd be *twice* as bad with havin' *two* eye patches!'

'Grief,'

'Yes Cap'n, grief is what I'll be givin' our enemies if they dare come near us with eye patches!'

'You'll probably scare them away. Okay Piccolo, I need to be alone to talk to our figure head.'

'Thankin' yers kindly ma'am,' said Piccolo who then turned only about 90 degrees and started walking off the side of Ruby's head. Fortunately, a couple of his crewmates grabbed him and momentarily saved him the full embarrassment of being a pyrite-overboard, only to live to embarrass himself another day. Masha could hear them talk as they returned to the carapace.

'I want to be as badass as you,' said Terry the Terrible.

'Well you can't be copyin' mee two eye patches!' said Piccolo.

'I know what I'll do!' decided the Terrible, 'I'll get two *ear* patches!'

'That's not a thing!' claimed Piccolo.

'You're jealous because you be not thinking of the idea yerself!' said Terry the Terrible.

'Who said that?' said mid-shellman Piccolo.

'It be mee, the Terrible One!'

'Where are you?'

'Take off an eye patch so you can see me!'

'No! I'll be losing mee street credibility!'

Masha looked to the heavens and wondered how she'd managed to navigate all this time with a crew like this.

* * * * *

Meanwhile, back at the graveyard...

No one had really noticed the grave of Sailor Swift, RIP (rest in pieces): it was small and insignificant, but also no one had really passed by this way since her remains had been interred several months before. However, all was not as it seemed. Beneath the surface, things were happening. The burnt and *apparently* lifeless shard of Starkwood's sepal that was Swift's tombstone had not been idle. Tiny little roots had started to wriggle their way down into the sand, which would normally have been rather depleted of anything worth growing in. But here, the normally bland soil was rich in nutrients in the form of the recently deceased Swift, plus side salad Starkwood. Not only was the sepal growing below ground level, some tiny shoots were also starting to appear in the part that was sticking *out* of the ground. Little hair-like fronds were already waving slightly in the ever-changing Martian electrostatic field and gaining that all-so-needed electrical energy to create the neural networks that turn a lifeless wooden plank of deadness into a real boy. Or girl. Or into whatever this hybrid was going to be…

Not far from the grave of the not-so-well-known Sailor Swift, were the remaining pieces of Starkwood's partly cooked body. While his still living head had headed off, the charred embers of Starkwood's body had been left scattered where they fell, like an overcooked lettuce. Whether it was the energy from the cosmic ray blast that was the catalyst for making the sepal come back to life, or at least *resurrected* life, wasn't clear, but the other seemingly overdone pieces of vegetable were doing the same trick. Wherever any part of Starkwood's carbonised torso had touched the soil was now a hot bed of activity. A very *slow* activity mind, but fast for Martian standards. Little thread-like roots were burying their little toes into the cold sand below each morsel, while equally small pale green shoots were sprouting and heading skywards. Sadly, this event, along with the Swift gravestone growth, went by unobserved.

8

To Hellas and Back

'These are definitely the same scrape marks,' said Grit, examining the roughly one directional ruts in the Martian top soil.

Ruby gave them a cursory glance but her body language was clearly saying she didn't give a Tharsis Ridge about the present pilgrimage to track down a runaway Herman the head case. Pyrite Captain Masha did try to peer over her nose to look for herself, but Ruby turned away too fast for her to get a good glimpse.

'Tut,' said Masha, 'you could at least try to take an interest in the world around you.'

Eyes closed as she turned away from the tracks, Ruby raised her nose slightly in a gesture of indifference.

'What?' Ruby snapped back sarcastically, 'a crazy crustacean does a runner on a skateboard thing and we're supposed to waste our time trying to track him down?'

'I think it goes deeper than that...'

'Oh and you know this *because*...'

'I don't know,' Masha said, a little frustrated, 'we've not seen anything like this before. Big white shells falling from the sky, with big sheets and a moving platform with round legs, unlike a caterpillar. All made of materials that don't seem to come from here.'

'Oh and we're in danger are we?'

'I don't know!'

'Exactly – you *don't* know. So why don't you just stick to what you do know – keep your crew under control and keep my carapace ship-shape. That's something you *do* know.'

'And we just leave your sister and Grit to get to the bottom of this themselves?'

'Sounds like a plan.'

'And we have something *more* important to be getting on with do we?'

'Hmm, a little bit of aimless wandering in the ice fields sounds *just* right.'

'Aren't you the least bit intrigued?'

'Let the winds blow and cover up these distractions.'

Masha sighed and was clearly torn.

'How about setting a new course, *Captain*?' asked Ruby, more as a command than a request. There were a few moments of silence, then –

'Yes ma'am…' replied Masha reluctantly.

Meanwhile Jade was examining the streaks in the sand more closely, like a true Martian Shellrock Holmes.

'Yes,' Jade confirmed, 'there isn't much wind erosion, so we're definitely catching up with him.'

Both she and Grit looked off into the distance to where the tracks seemed to be leading.

'You know where this leads?' Jade asked him.

Grit nodded while staring at the horizon

'Hellas Basin…'

'Yes …' Jade confirmed, 'I've not been this way in a long time. A few thousand years actually.'

'Really,' said Grit, a little distracted in his own thoughts.

'Yes,' Jade replied, now heading off in the general direction of the tracks. 'Last time I came this way, Fionix had started training her Hellas Angles…'

'That's nice… hang on, don't you mean *Angels*?'

'Er no,' Jade pointed out, 'Fionix made a joke about it, which I didn't understand. Something about them being the Hellas Angles, as they all just got their degrees…'

'Oh…'

'What about you? Have you been here before?'

'Oh just a few years ago…'

'Wow!' said Jade, stopping for a moment to look back at him, 'you're lucky you missed that huge storm here around that time. You wouldn't be here now to tell the tale!'

Grit didn't answer. Jade just carried on.

'Yes,' she explained, 'I heard the Eschers wiped out every living thing – Oh! Look!'

Her monologue was self-interrupted, as she pointed

ahead. Grit looked but his mind was obviously elsewhere.

'Dust!' Jade confirmed. 'Over there. It's not a dust devil – it's *him*!'

As they got closer to the object that they had been chasing these last few months, Jade realised their mistakes.

'That's not Herman,' she said with disappointment. Grit looked at the silhouette of a boulder-like object in the dust cloud that enshrouded it and realised himself that it didn't have the right shape to be the crazy Dune artist.

The boulder stopped in its tracks and turned to face them. It was quite a large boulder, certainly somewhat larger than these umpteenaged tortles. It looked a lot older too.

'Great Uncle Syd!' said Jade, both frustrated at it not being their quarry, but also pleasantly surprised to see a long lost family member.

Great Uncle Syd looked at his Great niece Jade and he almost smiled.

'Hey there,' he started 'um... no don't tell me, you're green, so you must be... Emerald, hey long time no see my dear!' and he coughed and wheezed a bit as he tried to laugh a happy laugh.

'I'm Jade!' she cried, not hurt, as she was used to his forgetfulness. 'It's a different green!'

'Yes *Jade*, I remember now. It must be over ten million years. How are you?'

'Something like that. Fine, great Uncle. How are you? The last time I saw you, you had caught that nasty virus. Has it cleared?'

'Oh yes thanks my dear. I think that meteorite that nearly hit me back then scared the bugs out of me!'

'Good, oh this is Grit by the way, uncle. I met him not that long ago...'

'Oh yes Grit' said great Uncle Syd. 'I remember you from a while back...'

Grit seemed all the more subdued and gave the merest acknowledgement that he knew the old codger.

'We're looking for a crazy tortoid called Herman,' Grit

said, changing the subject, 'he was heading this way – we thought you were him…'

Great Uncle Syd seemed to stop and think about this for a few moments, before saying; 'I've not seen anyone lately, sorry…'

'Oh,' said Jade, 'well just to warn you he was in this area.'

Meanwhile, The Tortoid Trio spotted a huddle in the distance. There was the accompanying dust in the air.

'Ah,' said Jade with a little smile, 'that must be the Hellas Angels…'

Grit looked towards the little dusty air force gathering…

* * * * *

'Right,' said one of the gang. The members looked like four smaller versions of Fionix. Almost vulture-like, a little bit pteradon with a couple of tennis pitch sized wings thrown in for good measure. The wings were between bat and dragon and so expansive, billowing in the wind. The fifth aeranodon looked, well looked a little different. Same sort of head with the beak and the backward pointing 'spike' that was typical of aerodons, but the body, well not enough wing and far too much leg… well, too many actually.

'Right, I hereby open the Hellas Angels' meeting,' said the one holding a sheet of ice and using one of her claws to scratch something onto it. This aeradon had green eyes and was a little taller than the others, with a sort of mane of light brown hair.

'*Hellas* Angels?!' said one bird of paradise, the one with dark brown almond eyes and long black hair, clearly not happy. 'I thought we agreed *Syrtis* Angels?' she continued pointedly.

'No,' said the Hellas candidate, '*you* decided the Syrtis Angels. Anyway, Hellas was more popular.'

'Really? And it's nothing to do with your name being Hell is it?'

'No!' said Hell, 'we're based in the *Hellas* Basin, look we're even having our meeting here!'

'Syrtis seems much more suitable,' said the brown-eyed bird, 'what with *Syrtis* Basin being much more, um darker, like we're *Dark* Angels! Sounds more *menacing...*'

'Really *Syrena*,' said Hell, wing claws on hips, 'and it's nothing to do with your name...'

'Guys guys,' said the smallest one of the flock, a more compact looking one than the other two, 'it's like we're always arguing and –'

'Liar,' said Syrena.

'*Layer!*' cried the smaller aerodactyl, 'you know my name is Layer, Syrena. You're doing that on purpose!'

'Sorry,' began Syrena with a cheeky smile 'I mean *Princess* Layer...'

'You don't need to use my title,' said Layer with a sigh, 'I'm just Layer. I'm trying to be like all the other birds of paradise,'

'Yes... Your Majesty.'

'Stop it!'

'Ignore her,' said Hell, 'and let's get back to the meeting.'

'Yes, let's get back to the meeting of the Hellas *Angles...*' said Syrena with calculated tease.

'It was a mistake!' shouted Hell, 'a spelling mistake! That was what, about 75 years ago and you're still bringing it up!'

'I quite liked it,' said Layer. 'Hellas Angles... well if we are angles, then me being the smallest in the squad I'd be *acute* angle...'

'And I'd be the *right* angle!' said Syrena with glee.

'No,' retorted Hell, 'you're *obtuse*!'

'Very funny Hell. Would that make Dasha a *reflex* Angle?'

The three of them looked at the fourth, most athletic member of the team. She was like Layer in that she had a long mane of blonde hair and she certainly did look sleek and sporty.

'Well,' said Dasha 'I do have the frame for speed.'

The others sniggered.

'Pity you don't use it!' said Hell.

'I do!' said Dasha, a little hurt.

'Yes you do,' agreed Syrena, 'but you take so long to make up your mind what to do, it does kind of bring your average velocity down a bit.'

'That's not true!'

'If I recall,' reflected Hell, 'when Fionix asked us to erase those canals that Hanksie created, it took you seventeen Martian years to decide what to do!'

'I was mudditating!' defended Dasha, 'Elvis taught me to think about things before making any rushed decisions…'

'Fine,' said Syrena, 'but would you take that long if I was to suddenly slap you round the face like I'm about to do right now?'

'What?'

SLAP!

'OW!'

'Clearly you would!'

The next moment there was a scuffle with wings flapping and dust raised, creating a rusty cloud, as Syrena and Dasha went through an alpha female confrontation, which also included a bit of claw swiping claw. They probably would have swung handbags at each other if they'd had them. Hell pulled them apart like a referee in a boxing match and held their loaded sharp nails apart.

'Enough of this!' cried Hell, 'It was only a spelling mistake after all…'

The sparring birds shook their wings to remove the fine copper-coloured silt that had settled on them, then they regained their posture. In that truce, a quiet voice piped up.

'What angle would I be?'

The four fully formed birds of paradise all looked at their fifth team member, with fairly blank faces. Looking up at them, all-forlorn, was the member who had a head very much an aerodon, but her body just didn't scream flying material. Her body was longish and sort of sausage shaped, segmented in a way and several of the segments each had a pair of short, stubby legs.

'Sorry,' said Hell, 'I don't think you're ready for that kind of nick name...'

'But it's not my fault I had arrested development!'

'We know,' said Syrena.

'I am trying to catch up,' said Catapilla, the Unfinished One, 'I'm trying to have a growth spurt...'

'Trying? Then you can be a *try*-Angle!' said Hell with pride at her own creative imagination.

Catapilla attempted to smile, but fell short. Yes, birds of paradise were not so much birds but a sort of cross between birds, dragons and butterflies. When they first hatched out of their eggs it was only a stage on the way to greater things. They were land born, so to speak before they became airborne.

Catapilla was a very quiet member of the team. She seemed to be less of a talker and more of a contemplator. She was similar in size and shape to Hell and also had a mane of mousy brown hair. Catapilla just looked at her friends and said 'If you say so...'

'Look,' said Hell, 'can we get back to matters in hand. Fionix asked us to take on another mission...'

Before Hell could go any further, Catapilla piped up.

'Unidentified bodies at nine o'clock...'

The other three team members all looked in completely different and possibly random directions.

'Where?' asked Syrena, irritated that she couldn't locate anything of interest while looking vertically up.

'Are we on summer time or winter time?' asked Princess Layer, holding a claw to her forehead to block the sun as she peered roughly east.

Hell was looking under her own wings and this lack of knowledge of direction did make one wonder what kind of crack team they were supposed to be. Maybe it was a *cracked* team after all.

'Over there,' pointed Catapilla with one of her many legs.

They all looked and could now see the rag-tag terrestrial troop of rock tortles slowly making their way towards the Hellas Angels.

* * * * *

Elvis had been a 'flying' tortle for a few days now, so having done travelling on land (solid), swimming when there were seas (liquid) and now moving through the air (gas), he wondered whether he'd ever try the fourth state of matter as a form of motion: *plasma*… He concluded that his body would probably vaporise if he tried it, so he put the thought out of his mind until such a time as it was needed again. He also wondered: if he stayed up in the air long enough, would he start evolving wings? He looked at one of his half-flipper, half-feet and gave it a waggle in the wind but realised it wasn't likely to happen anytime soon.

During the day, Fionix uncrumpled the folds in her wings that had served as a kind of tent for Elvis and his half-friend the fried vegetable. This way they could now see the amazing view from tens of kilometres above the ground – well Starkwood couldn't see, as he had been buried (*alive* as he put it) in the soil in Elvis' shell niche to make him grow faster. Fionix flew north-west across the Valles Marineris then the equator and was just passing over Ascraeus Mons. This was one of the huge shield volcanoes, the three in a row known collectively as Tharsis Montes, with Ascraeus being the most northerly of the three. Elvis had never seen it from above before and in fact on several occasions when he'd been passing by the base of the 25km high monolith, he'd looked up (never being able to see the top) and decided 'I think I'll walk round it again…'

There were no clouds blocking the view of this natural wonder and neither was there any out-gassing or smoke coming from the caldera at the peak – Ascraeus had stopped having major 'wind' problems several tens of millions of years ago. Elvis peered over the leading edge of Fionix's left shoulder at the splendour of the land formations below and the wind would have been in his hair had he had any, but he was just delighted to experience something a little different to the previous hundred million years. He wouldn't want such a change to happen too often though – he did like his routine. He could wait another hundred million years for the next change – but the way things were going, there were likely to be several unusual experiences queuing up in the coming months.

Elvis looked back over his shoulder at his quiet companion, whose head was sitting snugly in the niche created in the top of his carapace. Starkwood was staring upwards and mumbling to himself. Meanwhile several of Elvis' lice were fussing round the half-planted half-plant, trying to make him as comfortable as possible.

'All okay?' Elvis asked lightly.

'It hurts!' whined Starkwood.

'Where?'

'Everywhere?'

'Be specific…'

'On the ground. In the air. Everywhere!'

'Growing pains?'

'Ahhh!' grumbled Starkwood

'Oooh!' came an unknown voice from someone else.

The sudden appearance of a different voice that said 'oooh', surprised both Elvis and Starkwood. A creature was standing next to them on the top of Fionix's back.

'AHHHH!' cried Starkwood at seeing the apparition, the plant still seemingly in panic mode. 'A green cat! I'm hallucinating again!'

'I'm actually a *lustella viridis*,' said the feline phantom, 'the name's Katya,' she continued enthusiastically and held out a paw.

'The cat wants to eat me!' cried Starkwood. 'That's why she's green! She eats plants!'

'My friend,' interjected Elvis, 'I think she's a monopole-cat.'

'Indeed!' agreed Katya, 'that's the common name. Well my old common name. I was just an ordinary *lustella magneticus* but I seem to be going through a species change…'

'There's a lot of that about,' Elvis commented.

'She wants to eat me because of my electrostatic energy!' Starkwood shouted accusingly, 'We're sworn enemies! We're after the same food source!'

'A common misconception,' said Katya, moving closer to Starkwood to get a better look. 'You're an *electrovore*, while I'm a *magnetovore*. We're at right angles to each other when it comes to the food chain, so you've nothing to worry about. You are an electrovore no? A very unusual specimen in fact!'

'She called me a *specimen*!' Starkwood protested. 'She's going to do unspeakable experiments on me! Elvis stop her!'

Katya had now used one of her own paws to open wide one of Starkwood's already wide open eyes. Starkwood would have fended her off with his sepal hands, but he hadn't grown any new ones yet. The next moment, Katya somehow switched on her own green light, coming from all over her body, which she beamed into Starkwood's eye. His pupil shrank with the sudden increase in light level and the additional green spotlight lighting actually gave him an even more sickly look than he already had.

'Interesting!' said Katya and quickly pulled out a pencil from behind one of her triangular ears and produced a notebook that neither of them had noticed before and started scribbling notes.

'You're a *flos vestibulum* aren't you?"

'What?! Get off me!'

'An electrostatic plant no?'

'He was,' Elvis confirmed.

'Was?! Ooh he's changing too?! Let me write this down... and where is his body... is he going through the budding phase of his life cycle? I've not yet witnessed that stage, oh you must let me watch you changing!'

'Get this weirdo away from me!'

'Stay calm my friend,' said Elvis, 'I don't think Katya means any harm...'

'Not at all!' she confirmed. 'I'm trying to catalogue all the biodiversity on our planet. I'm the patron of the Friends of Mars Society.'

Elvis observed Katya more carefully, not having had such a close encounter before, certainly never with a green monopole-cat. They'd always been bluish or reddish. Another one of those once in a hundred million year events that was starting to happen all too often.

Katya was green. Not an 'in your face' green, except when she was beaming herself as she did while examining the half-dead dandelion. Her head looked like a cute kitten, her ears, cheek tufts and chin making the all too familiar star shape that was typical of these flying magnets. There were darker lines across her face, tiger like, but with a cuddly kitten's face she was the opposite of menacing. Her body, which was also greenish with tiger like stripes, seemed small in comparison to her head and she had paws that... well the front pair were scribbling away in her notebook while the back pair were suitably clamped to Fionix, her baby claws gripping onto her free ride just enough not to be whipped away by the wind. Her most curious feature, the most curious for all monopole-cats, was her prehensile tail. Much longer than her body, also greenish with faintly darker rings along its length and ending in what were neither fingers nor toes, but more like roots, which Elvis guessed she used to grab onto rocks, as did other monopole-cats, in order not to be suddenly dragged off into the Martian magnetic field before she was ready to, well, 'make babies'. But, for the moment, her tail wasn't latching on to anything, it seemed to just ripple a bit in the wind caused by Fionix moving through the thin Martian atmosphere – even thinner up at this height.

'So your friend *is* an electrostatic plant?' Katya asked Elvis.

'Yes, but not so static anymore.'

'What do you mean?'

'Not static as in not stationary anymore. He started moving around a million years ago...'

'I knew it!' cried Katya with joy and she waved pencil and notebook in the air. Elvis looked at her sideways, pausing, as he hoped for further details. Katya saw him so obliged.

'I'd heard about this evolutionary step and there have been rumours of some *flo vestibulae* uprooting themselves and becoming mobile and... but hang on,' she said, looking below Starkwood's head then lifting his head up to look underneath, 'no body, no appendages that allow motion – oh do they retract into your neck?'

'Get off!' Starkwood cried again. 'Anyway, where did you come from?' Elvis finally asked, a little surprised at the greenish monopole-cat's sudden entrance, but a little slow to follow up.

'Oh that's a fascinating process,' started the magnetic field feline, 'it involved a *southern belle* and a *king in the north* and a chance collision in mid...'

'I know how you polecats breed,' said Elvis, 'I meant where did you just come from *now*? I mean one moment you weren't here and the next moment you're on the back of ...'

'Fionix, yes I know...'

'You know her?!'

'Yes she knows me,' Fionix piped in, having just been enjoying a flying sleepwalk and now woken due to all the commotion, 'Hey Kat!' she greeted her.

'Hi Nix.'

'Nix?'

'Pet name,' Fionix explained, 'from where I was born, Nix Olympica.' 'Oh,' realised Elvis, 'But anyway, Kat, how did you get here and how come you're green and not, well, red?

'She is well-read,' said Fionix, not missing the chance for a joke.

'So many questions,' said Kat, delighted, 'and so many answers to give! I was flying to meet Fionix and I jumped on board.'

'Flying? But don't you have to follow the field lines? I mean I thought you guys had very little say in where you're going to go?'

'Yes I know!' said Katya with her endless enthusiasm. 'But it seems I've evolved, like your symbiotic friend here. I look green but I can change my polarity at will when it comes to travelling, so I can go backwards and forwards, mostly where I want.'

'That's useful,' commented Elvis then suddenly there was a putt putt sound and Katya seemed to flash a couple of different colours like a disco light, from green to blue to red, back to green. For a moment, she looked worried, then there was another splutter like an engine starting and her colour changed to red, then before she knew it, she shot off Fionix's back with a whoosh and a few fairy dust sparkles and disappeared into the distance. Elvis could just about hear her cry of 'Damn!' before the field had catapulted her out of earshot. Elvis squinted off into the distance but couldn't see anything.

'She hasn't quite got the hang of this free-moving, polarity-changing super power yet,' remarked Fionix, seemingly unperturbed by the rapid exit of her friend.

'I guess so,' agreed Elvis, 'so how long have you known Katya?'

'Oh a few years…'

'You've kept quiet about her.'

'It's a need to know basis.'

'This sounds intriguing – are you keeping secrets?'

'Actually…' Fionix started, then paused, 'quite a few. In fact a number of secrets.'

'Is that number bigger than one?'

'… it is…'

'I assume you have your reasons.'

'I do, *did*,' said Elvis' flying friend, obviously a little uncomfortable with her admissions, 'Trying to keep the peace, but now the proverbial Katya's out of the bag…'

'Is there a problem with that green polecat?! Is she contagious or something?'

'No, she's no trouble, quite the opposite in fact.'

'Okay, but I get the feeling that you are about to let us in on whatever trouble is brewing…'

'I think I have to,' admitted Fionix, as she started to bank to the right, 'I'm going to need help to avert a disaster for our planet…'

'Oh,' reflected Elvis, 'so nothing too serious then.'

Fionix looked at him sideways.

'Nothing that a flying carpet, a rock tortoid and half an electrostatic plant can't sort out…'

* * * * *

As Fionix banked, Elvis could finally see the top of the most amazing volcano in the solar system (possibly the greatest in the universe). There it was, Olympus Mons. It used to be called Nix Olympica, one of a handful of monumental shield volcanoes that pockmarked the face of Mars, like some huge planetary adolescent acne. Olympus Mons dominated most of Elvis' view of the north-western horizon, which was no longer a horizontal line that nicely split the land from the sky. Instead, it was composed of two inclined horizons, each leading up to the flat volcanic peak in the middle. The huge caldera was also visible now, showing that the very top of Olympus Mons was adorned with a roughly circular depression, a bit like the inverse of a plateau. This extinct volcanic crater was some 50km across or more and was now the main feature in view. It pretty much filled the whole scenery and the horizon was now the almost vertical cliff faces of the caldera's inner edge. Nothing else of Mars could be seen.

Elvis gasped quietly as Fionix just cleared the caldera's rim and slipped over the top like some Fosbury flopping high-jumping Martian bird.

* * * * *

Starkwood's head was falling; it seemed like a lifetime. Well it probably was the end of his life, the way he was going. They must have been some 25km above the surface of Mars. Starkwood had never bothered to learn much physics as a stationary plant and though he had been reading some Earth books over the last decade or so, the laws of gravitation were still a mystery to him. He did know it was going to be downhill all the way for the time being. The physics was something about freefall and terminal velocity and drag forces but he knew he didn't need to calculate it all. Nature was going to make it happen anyway. He'd already lost his body, there wasn't much left to lose.

Starkwood could feel the wind rushing past his ears, his electrostatic fronds pulled upwards with the air resistance like the tail of a little comet. The same air was streaming by his severed neck hole, which started an embarrassing whistling sound, adding an eerie foreboding nature to his situation. Starkwood wished that the ground would just open up and swallow him and it soon would, so actually he didn't have long to wait. It was going to be a couple of minutes, if anyone was counting.

Just then Starkwood hit a bit of turbulence, which caused his head to flip so he was now face down and looking at his own death coming up at him at high speed. Eyes even wider and mouth open wide enough to swallow a lung whale.

'AHHHHHHHHHHHH!' he cried but, at this speed, he was almost overtaking his own voice. Up until that moment, he was happy to just let nature take its course.

Being disfigured beyond recognition, he didn't want to live anymore, but he certainly didn't want to see his own demise. And now, with the atmosphere rubbing so rudely against his face, the effects were heating him up. There was a chance he could burn up before he reached the ground. Well, the original fire from the cosmic ray had started his fall from grace, so why not let it finish him off now? Then he recognised where his doom was aiming him.

'NO! NO! ANYWHERE BUT HERE!'

'Hello!' came a jolly voice alongside Starkwood. It seemed to be moving with him.

Starkwood gave a quick glance sideways and saw what might have been another one of his hallucinations – a green monopole-cat. Oh, no, actually, it was the *same* one. He then looked death back in the face and –

'AHHHHHHHHHH!'

He said this for want of something better to add.

'You're in a hurry to get to the Tharsis Ridge, Holy Flower Friend of Elvis…'

'NO!!!!!!!!!! I don't want to go there! AHHHH!'

'Well why not? It is quite lovely this time of year, with all those meadows of static plants, waving gently in the Martian electric field?'

'They'll kill me! They hate me!'

'Surely not,' said Katya, 'you seem a nice enough plant to me, pretty harmless, though you might hurt some of the plants if you land on them at this speed.'

'I don't want to die here! Anywhere else bu…'

'So why are you rushing to get there? Oh is this part of your growth cycle. Oh! Are you like those seeds on Earth that pop open during a forest fire?!'

'NO!'

'Oh, well, like those flowers that use the wind to spread their pollen?'

'NO!'

'Yes I can understand that. It would be unusual for the whole plant to become wind borne in order to disperse its seeds…'

'AHHHHHH!'

'So why are you in a hurry to get there?'

'I'm falling!'

'Oh I do that sometimes,' reflected Katya, 'though usually I fall *sideways*, well, whatever way the magnetic field lines are tilted when my green polarity flips to red or blue…'

'I'M FALLING TO MY DEATH!'

'Oh well, why don't you stop?'

'I CAN'T!'

'Ah,' Katya realised, 'that is a problem. And from my calculations, you have about fifty seconds before you reach the top of the ridge – sixty if you miss it and hit the bottom…'

'AHHHH!'

'I think I can help you,' Katya decided and she approached Comet Starkwood and started rubbing his hair fronds with her little paws.

'What are you doing?!' cried Starkwood, 'I don't need a hairdo!'

'Well,' reflected Katya, 'actually you do. You'll never attract a mate the way you look, but we can sort that out later. No my dear friend, it's friction-charging. Just watch…'

'Should you be rubbing me? It doesn't seem right!'

'Don't worry,' Katya dismissed him, 'you won't get pregnant or anything!' and she laughed.

Katya glided a short distance away to admire her work and within seconds, Starkwood was sporting an enviable bouffant quiff (well, some creatures would have been envious of his hairstyle) and he looked even more like a mad scientist. Katya had to slow herself down as her shampoo and set was putting on the brakes for her reluctant client. Starkwood was slowing down but he wasn't stopping. There wasn't much left for Katya to rub.

'At this speed,' she told him, 'you're still going to make a bit of a mess.'

'Not here!'

'You will enrich the topsoil though, which will supply

nutrients to the other plants…'

'Don't let them eat me please!'

'Okay,' said Katya enthusiastically, 'I'll try. I've never done this before so let's see what happens!'

Starkwood could not believe that his life was in the hands of a crazy green cat.

'Right,' said Katya, 'here we go…'

With that Katya approached him again and this time with her prehensile tail, grabbed a tail-full of his hairy fronds and then squinted hard. Her greenish glow fluttered a little like a light with a dodgy connection then flipped back and forth between red and blue. This made her swing to one side then the other, like a pendulum with Starkwood's head as the bob, until she got the right balance of magnetic polarity and suddenly, like the opening of a parachute, Starkwood was screeching to a halt and would have left serious skid marks in the air if that was possible. He and Katya were shuddering. Katya was straining herself, her paws grasping at what seemed like empty space but looking authentically like a mime artist pulling on a rope. Whatever invisible cord was there, it actually seemed to be working. Maybe she was grabbing hold of a bunch of magnetic fields lines, both proverbially and literally.

'AHHHHHHHHH!' said Starkwood helpfully.

'I don't think my engines can take it!' said Katya more calmly, but the words still carried as much terror. Then without warning, Katya's *Green for Go* colour started to blink on and off and the red and blue glows interchanged and the next moment she had shot off horizontally with the word 'Sorry' leaving her lips. Starkwood was on his own with this problem, seconds before contact with the top of the Tharsis Ridge. He could see the fields of his old neighbours swaying gently in the electrostatic breeze but as he approached, they all started leaning a bit towards him. They looked up to see what wonderful meal was heading their way, only to find with horror it was their ex-Saviour.

Starkwood hit a large angled rock which, tilted at about 45 degrees, caused him to bounce almost horizontally and there his head flew, spinning in the air like a hairy football. He hit the actual ground and bounced back into the air but as he'd hit at a shallow angle, he didn't bounce very high. He was too dizzy to follow what was going on, but the random outcrops of static plants were in a frenzied panic. Most ducked out of the way or hid their faces in their leaves but one managed to get a sepal to the side of Starkwood's face and slapped him out of the way. Another had crouched low and then sprung up and head butted the lone 'Godhead' and deflected him in a different direction. Two plants pulled a third one up by the roots and lifted it in the air, as if in a rugby throw-in, but fumbled the catch and Starkhead carried on. With each collision, the bouncing bomb of a fallen saint was running out of energy and gradually he bounced, skidded, scraped and ploughed up a spray of tawny soil along his crash landing path, uprooting a few of his kind on the way, until he finally came to the end of his crash landing.

There were cries of disapproval and sepals clasped and shaking like fists and one could hear the occasional 'witch' and 'burn him'. Starkwood's head finally came to rest with him face up, but he had his eyes shut, as a gentle rusty red rain of falling dust coated his already beat up head. As he opened his eyes, Starkwood's view of the sky above was eclipsed by another face looking back down at him. An angry face. The face of a powerful flower, a volatile vegetable, a boiling bush, no! We haven't got time for this. Well just a few more: a terrifying tree, a horrifying hedge, a –

'Welcome back *Saint* Arkwood...' said the face, with quiet menace.

'Um, hello your greatness,' he replied to the leader of his old allotment.

'We have some unfinished business to attend to...' said the Head plant, who was called Hedgewood.

129

9

The Dirtiest Race in Space

Fionix had made worse landings than this one. She shook the dust off her Mylar-thin, mega-wide wings, with waves rippling to the tips and back for several minutes after she'd reached the ground. Those waves ended in a whip cracking sound when they reached the narrower tips. Once done, Fionix started to retract her wings as if folding up a very large umbrella or putting away a tent and, as if by magic, she managed to fit her wings into a not too bulky packing space, much like beetles doing the same thing hiding their wings under their elytra. Next, she picked up the dislodged monopole-cats with her beak and flipped them back into her wing folds before they were whooshed away and forced to follow the local field lines. Well, a few got ejected, but she didn't seem too bothered – they were temporary lodgers anyway. Her final task was to help her Chelonian Chum and she waddled over to his side, then turned her head upside down so she could speak to him the right way up.

'Thank you for flying Fionix Airlines,' said the aircraft herself, 'come again soon...'

'...' came the silent reply.

'Okay there sir?' she asked Elvis, 'monopole-cat got your tongue?'

'Sometimes it helps to see the world from a different point of view,' Elvis reflected, 'though I'd rather be back on my own four feet...

Fionix used her beak as a lever and gently flipped Elvis the right way up.

'Welcome to my home...'

'Hmm,' said Elvis, looking around at the fairly featureless, flat-bottomed caldera, 'I like what you've done with the place...'

The plateau-like plain was all one could see until the

horizon, which was actually the almost vertical edge of the volcano crater itself. Across the unimaginative plain, there was the odd vent where gases of various shades, from colourless to smoky white, were adding to the anorexic atmosphere, replenishing what was being continually lost to space due to the all too gentle gravity and sissy soft escape speed.

'Hot and cold running gas I see,' said Elvis impressed, 'and no noisy neighbours…'

'Indeed,' said Fionix, 'and very few creatures can actually get to this altitude, whether by land or air and those that do, like the polecats, have other things on their minds.'

'A secluded sanctuary…'

'So how is our partly present parsnip-head doing?' Fionix asked.

Elvis peered back over his shoulder then said, 'well the pyrites said they buried him deeper in the niche, so he's sort of hibernating for now. I guess we won't see him again until he's grown a bit. They did add a rather powerful manure which is supposed to speed up his growth rate but it smells pretty bad so I imagine Starkwood's going to be holding his breath for a while. I'll miss those staring, crazy eyes of his… hey! Of *course*! *Stark* Staring Mad! I just thought of it! It'll suit him. I'll tell him when he wakes up. So we should get a bit of peace and quiet now…'

'Good,' said Fionix, cutting him short, 'because I have some important business to discuss with you and it's about planetary security…'

'Oooh,' said Elvis, 'sounds ominous…'

'It is,' said Fionix with foreboding, 'the continued existence of life on Mars…'

'Not again,' said Elvis half-heartedly, clocking up another one of those once in a hundred million year events that were rapidly becoming so mis-named.

* * * * *

'Who's going to be a tellin' him?' came the whispering voice from between the little cracks and crevices in the plates on Elvis' carapace.

'Whoever let it happen,' came another accusing voice.

'Well don't you be lookin' at me!' said another voice.

'The Cap'n is going to notice sometime and our glorious King will eventually find out...'

'Unless you be gettin' 'im back.'

'Like that's going to happen soon!'

'You were on watch!'

'The plant said he be wantin' some fresh air!'

'And you believed him?!'

'Well he did! I just didn't know he was going to throw his-self head first into the fresh air!'

'Being only a head, he couldn't exactly be a throwin' anything else in first could he!'

'The Cap'n'll be mad! He still hasn't got over losing Sailor Swift and that was months ago...'

'Then you better get him back!'

* * * * *

Meanwhile back in the celery cemetery...

In a lone grave on the edge of the Magnetic Fields of the Central Bulge, something was brewing. The remains of the sepal from Starkwood's arm that had been a headstone had continued to grow roots deep into the Martian soil. They had entangled themselves around the brave but demised pyrite. This curious growth was having an unusual effect on the surrounding area, the roots cocooning Swift's remains as if she was a silkworm. On the part of the sepal gravestone that was sticking out of the ground, two lumps, like buds, had started to appear about three quarters of the way up and each seemed to be covered with two close lines of hairs, a bit like... *eyelashes*! Such an event on Mars was unheard of before, not that creatures on Mars talked about such events in normal conversation. Though, having said that, it could have been a suitable topic of a conversation about evolution going for Elvis and Starkwood on one of their many philosophical random walks.

A few metres away from this budding sepal, Starkwood's other remains were growing in their own unique way. Roots had been rooted, though a closer inspection would have made it clear that they were more foot- and toe-like than any leguminous equivalent. Not roots, but feet and toes… Above Ground Zero, the new stems that were appearing also seemed to be sprouting limbs rather than leaves. What was clearly going to be the top part of each creature was still curled up and clinging close to each main stem.

* * * * *

Elvis followed behind Fionix as she led him across the Olympus Mons caldera plateau that was basically Fionix' living room floor. They passed a crack in the ground that was hissing gently and a misty cloud was jetting out. Fionix saw Elvis looking.

'Mainly carbon dioxide…'

'…hmmm…' said Elvis, 'explains why there's so much of it in the atmosphere…'

'Replenishing it,' said Fionix, 'Mars has a problem with gas. Gravity can't keep it down – not even a heavy one like CO_2.'

The outgassing vent suddenly whooshed then settled down again.

'Also good for having a shower,' Fionix continued, 'blowing off the dust of the day…'

'Nice,'

'And those pesky parasites…'

'I don't really get them,' said Elvis, 'but sand in my joints is a constant problem.'

'Feel free to use it while you're here. I also use these vents to launch myself off the planet.'

'I see,' realised Elvis, 'I did wonder how you got up there. Your take offs have never been, er, well…'

'What?!'

'Um as, er "uplifting" as your chats…'

'Hmm, nice recovery…'

As Fionix half-bounded (she was not a creature built for grace on the ground – nor in the air for that matter. In fact she was quite lacking in both. One wondered how she might move on, or in, water), yes she half-bounded as she used the elbows of her clumsy wings to move and looked a bit like a clothes horse being blown along in the wind that had lost half of its washing in the process. Other items came into view as they continued their walk down Fionix's hall of flame.

'What's that?' said Elvis, looking at the shiny, glinty rectangle that was propped up against a rock, then he recognised it 'Oh, that's the plaque you ripped off that Earth craft Voyager…'

'It's not stealing!' said Fionix defending herself, 'they'd sort of thrown it away.'

'I'm not judging,' said Elvis, 'I get the impression they were hoping it would fall into the hands of an intelligent lifeform-'

'Well it did!' defended Fionix.

'One that might *return* the gesture and pop in for a chat and a cup of something tasty.'

'I think that would be a bad idea…' reflected Fionix 'and this is one of the reasons why I've brought you here.'

'I've had a feeling about this my friend,' said Elvis. 'You seem to have been building up to something explosive, much like the gas in that vent of yours.'

'I'm afraid so…'

'You don't want these humans to find what they are looking for…'

'That's true…' Fionix started.

The next objects in the Olympus Mons Museum looked like large black plastic bags.

'What's in these?' asked Elvis.

'You don't want to know.'

'Well I do, if it'll help me understand what this is all leading up to.'

'I went to the Moon, the *Earth's* moon Luna on my last trip and, well, I was pretty annoyed.'

'Why?' asked Elvis, 'there's not much going on there you told me from your previous trips. Not much night life, or day life even.'

'Certainly not topside,' Fionix agreed, 'but that was up until four years ago. Humans have been to their moon now. Several times.'

'Well that was on the cards,' said Elvis, circling the pile of bags and sniffing but not picking up anything special.

'Good job most of the Lunar creatures live below the surface,' Fionix pointed out. 'But those humans! Their first visit off their own planet and what do they do?'

Fionix said this, shaking her head while eyeing the pile of bags.

'I'm guessing these are not bags of presents left for future lunar visitors?'

'They left all their space crafts scattered across the planet, even a *car*! Dumping their rubbish everywhere, just like they do on their *own* planet!'

Elvis could see that Fionix was getting worked up, so he came up to her and sort of stroked her wing with one of his front paws.

'Well, the spaceships, you told me they won't corrode over the years, so they shouldn't really damage the environment no?'

'No, but it just looks ugly. Spoils the scenery. No, worse is these bags…' Fionix pointed with a wing claw, 'these are filled with … all the human being waste they left behind…'

'What?!' said Elvis, stepping back from the pile. Fionix qualified her point.

'Their *poo*! The beings who visited the Earth's Moon! They left all their manure in bags, just lying around on the lunar landscape!'

'That is more gross than I was expecting.'

'They didn't even have the decency to take it back with them,' Fionix sighed, then carried on hobbling to the next item. 'They obviously don't promise the same promise that we Martians make to the universe: Take Nothing But Memories. Don't Even Leave Any Footprints…'

'I'm sorry they're like that,' said Elvis, with genuine compassion.

'They don't deserve to meet up with any other intelligent lifeform out here.'

'I can understand that reasoning, but what can you do about it? I mean for a start what are you going to do with these bags of sh–'

'I'm going to put them in the vent over there…' and she pointed a claw to another steam hole, 'that one has lava at the bottom and it will make this all disappear.'

'A happy ending!' said Elvis, trying to sound positive.

'For now. But the problem won't stop.'

'You told me they've stopped visiting their moon.'

'That's temporary. They'll keep looking for life, visiting other planets and then leave them all in a mess like they're messing up their own place and their own moon. They're sending their craft out in space without even thinking how they might be interfering with the eco-systems of other planets. No one out here is safe!'

'Sounds worrying,' said Elvis.

'It is. And I have to stop them!'

'Well we all have a choice in our lives and –'

'No Elvis, I don't. This is my job…'

'You're sounding all ominous again. Surely our job is to live our lives, have babies if we need them and leave enough resources on our home planet for future generations to use, though the way evolution's been going, we ourselves will be the ongoing, maybe *eternal* generation.'

'I haven't told you everything my friend…'

'I'm realising that.'

'I'm a Guardian of Mars…'

'… Oh. That sounded like it was capitalised…'

'It was.'

'And Mars needs guarding?'

'The *whole* solar system needs it from these *inhuman* beings.'

'Is this an official title or like did you just declare yourself a –'

'Official. It's a long story. But I had to swear to protect the planet from a threat like this. Well you've met my Hellas Angels…'

Elvis nodded, 'A pleasant bunch of environmentalists…'

'More than that. That's just their peace time occupation. You remember the task that went on for decades?'

'Yes of course, the Hanksie Grafitti. The unsightly artwork he spread planet wide. I like his little projects but that was–'

'Those huge lines he drew across the planet caused hysteria on Earth!'

'They weren't that badly drawn, I thought –'

'No! But an astronomer saw them in his telescope about 50 years ago, some guy called Schiaparelli and he mistook them for *canals* built by *Martians*! Humans believed there *was* life on Mars!'

'Well there *is*, though not building water channels yet! Well, not above ground…'

'But we can't risk humans finding out there *is* life here – they will come and destroy it like they're doing on their own planet!'

'I see,' Elvis realised, 'so is that why you had your little Angels erase Hanksie's Lines?'

'Yes, it took them years to do that. Fortunately on Earth the resolution of their telescopes was too poor due to the atmosphere, so it gave us time to make the lines disappear before the first spacecraft arrived here a few years ago. The humans saw nothing with their new cameras so assumed it had all been an optical illusion.'

'That was fortuitous.'

'But now, over these last few years, human activity in space has been getting worse. I've done my best to knock some of them off course, or damage their cameras, and at the same time I was trying to keep this human activity quiet from the rest of you guys. I didn't want to worry you.'

'Ah,' Elvis realised, 'I see. So has Mars been visited already?'

'Yes, a number of times…'

'Is that number more than one?'

'I'm afraid so. One group of humans, the Russians, have sent a handful of craft here.'

'Really? You've certainly kept them quiet from me! So what have they seen?'

'Fortunately nothing crucial,' admitted Fionix. 'My team and I have managed to sabotage all the ones that were trying to land on Mars. One called Mars 3 I think, had actually managed to land in one piece and just started to take a picture when it … *accidentally* got knocked over. There've been a couple of things orbiting up there taking pictures, but they're too far away to notice details like living things down here. Certainly things smaller than a lung whale.'

'I see. So now you've told me this I'm assuming the situation has reached a critical point?'

'… yes. I can't fulfil all my duties as I thought. There's too much to do. Another bunch of humans, the Americans, have sent two spacecraft and they are coming here. Soon.'

'Ah,' Elvis realised, 'is this anything to do with Starkwood's voices in his head?'

'I think so. He seems to have been picking up the radio signals from the spacecraft.'

'The Vikings? He called them the Vikings.'

'Yes. The crafts are called Viking I and Viking II. They both have a section that'll orbit Mars and each has another bit that is going to land on the surface! I can't deal with so many at the same time!'

'And they're coming soon?'

'Very soon!'

'Okay,' said Elvis, remaining in his usual Muddist calm, 'well, would you say the orbiting halves will be far enough away not to worry about?'

'Not sure,' said Fionix 'they have better cameras than before. They'll be able to see more detail…'

'Enough to see us creatures?'

'Probably not, but we must make sure our friend Hanksie doesn't advertise in big letters that there's someone here.'

'Okay, so it's the landers we have to worry about.'

'Yes. I mean if I can track one I can probably knock it out of action but there's two and I don't really know where they're hoping to land.'

'You found all this out on your recent visit to Earth?'

'Well yes, with the help of those birds and my chief science officer Katya...I wonder where she's got to now...'

'That green monopole-cat? You've taken her to Earth?'

'Sure. She does all my calculations for me. I know she's having polarity problems but she should be trying to get here so we can make an action plan.'

'I'm impressed that my long time faithful flying friend is actually some kind of superhero.'

'Oh I don't feel like a superhero,' Fionix admitted. 'I haven't succeeded yet. And I think in this line of business it's never over.'

'So what other super powers do you have, apart from interplanetary travel?'

'Oh,' Fionix blushed modestly, 'well, I...'

'Okay, if you can't reveal any I respect your privacy. But do you like, wear a face mask when you're super powering so your friends don't recognise you?'

'No.'

'Do you hide in a crevice when you're changing into your superhero outfit?'

'It's not like that. I do have the ability to camouflage myself so I can't be seen...'

'Oh that's nice. What, like us Tortles can pretend to be rocks?'

'Actually more sophisticated than that. Us birds of paradise share an ability with some Earth creatures, like some lizards, geckos and chameleons.'

'Ah, I remember Starkwood reading about them in the previous book you brought him. Yes, they can change colour to blend in can't they? That's useful trick.'

'There's others on the Earth, like sea creatures, the squid and cuttlefish. They can make much more elaborate colour changes. Well, myself and my fellow Angels can do that too.'

'Oh, is that how you manage to visit the Earth without being spotted?'

'Yes. When I'm flying in the Earth's atmosphere, I can make the underside of my wings light blue like their sky, though I usually try and travel at night to avoid the risks.'

'Okay,' said Elvis, 'well I can see how that is quite a useful skill to have, but getting back to the arrival of these unwanted guests, we have to stop them somehow, with or without your cloaking magic...'

'That's why I'm calling you up to join the squad...'

Elvis looked at his friend sideways and considered this. He'd never thought himself suitable material for 'Mars Wars'. He was more the peace protesting kind, but he realised his planet needed some kind of protection, so was not going to shy away from his duty.

'Okay, ma'am, so, er..., well what do we have to do? Warn every living creature on the planet to hide away for a while?'

'I'm not sure that would be the best move. It might cause planet wide apprehension and then those humans would see panicky plants, rioting rocks and batty birds flying around in a mass hysteria display and the next moment they'd be dropping some of their peace keeping bombs on us...'

'So, the opposite would be to tell no one anything? '

'Somewhere in between...' said Fionix thoughtfully. She was looking off into the distance so Elvis tried to look in the same direction but couldn't see anything but the slight henna-coloured haze of the Martian sky, with some of the brighter stars poking through the light pollution.

'A need to know basis?' proffered Elvis.

'Something like that... We know that two of these Earth ships are heading our way and they each have a landing craft, so we only really have to concentrate on the two landing sites. Make sure they see nothing in those areas.'

'Okay, that sounds more doable,' Elvis perked up, 'keep all the creatures hidden in those two places. Do you know where they're going to land?'

'Not exactly, but I'm hoping to get that information soon.'

'Okay and do you know *when* they're landing?'

'Not yet, but I'm hoping to get that information… soon … too…'

'I guess you weren't able to find it out on your trip to Earth?'

'The ground work's been done. Katya came with me to give me a hand and that distant cousin of yours has also got involved…'

'Really?' said Elvis, 'Martin didn't mention anything in his last poo-mail…'

'I didn't tell him until after he'd finished it.''

'So you mentioned there are some orbiting craft as well. Won't they be able to see us creepy crawlies, as we, um, creep and er crawl all over Mars?'

'As I said, probably not. Katya told me they'd be too high up to see such things your size or smaller. They might see someone like me if I had my wings fully opened, or a lung whale if one happened to pop out of its ice well.'

'Oh, well that's one good piece of news then. Lung whales don't tend to come out very often, certainly not since the seas dried up. And you said you can camouflage yourself so you can do that, or fly at night, no?'

'Indeed, my friend. Otherwise, those orbiting bits could only see larger objects, which is why my Hellas Angels spent so long covering up those fake canals that Hanksie made last century. That's a point, I need to make sure he's not done any more large scale adverts again.'

'Right, boss,' said Elvis, 'or is it captain or what?' and at this he did a salute with his claw.

'Flight Officer Fionix to you…'

'Really?!'

'No, I'm messing with you! We're a rather informal bunch, this protection force. A kind of Rubble Alliance.'

'So what's the first step? Who do we tell?'

'First I will need my science polecat. Then we will need your electrostatic friend. We need to set up a listening, hmm what did Katya call it, magnetic telectroscope or something similar.'

'Sounds complicated.'

'It means bringing together the plants and the polecats.'

Elvis looked doubtful.

'Sworn enemies I know,' reflected Fionix, 'but there's a bigger enemy coming…'

'Well let's not waste any time,' said Elvis enthusiastically, 'I'll wake Starkwood up…'

Elvis strained his neck and turned his head to try and look at the soil-filled niche in his shell and called to his friend.

'Wakey wakey! Starkwood. Mars calling Mister Plant!'

Nothing stirred. Elvis changed tack.

'Captain! Calling captain to the bridge!'

There was a quiet scuffling sound and then the pyrite leader emerged from between the cracks in Elvis' shell plates.

'Aye aye your Highness!' said Sam Biosis.

'There you are. Can you dig enough dirt off Starkwood's face as we need to talk to him?'

'Consider it done mee lord…' and with that the captain called out to his deck hands; 'Cmon yer lilly-livered land lubbers, get digging the crazy flower head out of his rat-hole!'

The crewmembers that had appeared were looking a little sheepish and stared at their feet to avoided eye contact.

'What be the problem ya scurvy ridden weevils?! You be wantin' nine lashes o' the polecat?'

'Um…' began one of them, 'there be a problem Cap'n…'

'There be a problem if you don't all be digging for the planted treasure!'

'We can dig...' another started explain, 'that's possible...'

'Then dig!'

'Um, but we won't be able to find him...'

'Find him?! You be a needin' a freakin' treasure map?! The niche ain't that big! And it'd not be that deep you parasitic pustules!'

'We know he be no longer there... Cap'n...'

'What?!'

'Plant overboard Cap'n...'

'When?'

'A while back...'

'How?!'

'The Saint of Arkwood wanted to commit veggicide...'

'Isn't it herbicide?' asked another.

'There'll be some forced *insecticide* on this ship if you don't be goin' and a gettin' 'im back!'

'Already underway... Cap'n sir...'

'And you didn't tell me this afore, because...'

'We was hoping that we could be smuggling the cabbage head back on board without you noticing sir...'

The captain turned humbly to Elvis.

'Um... your Kingness...'

'Yes?'

'It seems you might be havin' to carry on without your friend...'

'Really?'

'Um... he seems to be in a kind of dormant cocoon in all that dirt...'

As the captain said this, he had his fingers crossed behind his back. Somewhere his pyrite God was keeping track of his ever-growing list of lies, adding this one to the as yet unexplained real cause for the loss of Sailor Swift.

'That's a shame,' said Elvis in his usual Muddist way, then turned back to Fionix and explained the situation. 'If you just need some electrostatic plants, then you can find plenty on the Tharsis Ridge.

'Then that's where we'll go!' Fionix replied, sounding

decisive. 'Hop on board sir, we've got some Interspecies Talks to attend…'

'Um,' said Elvis, 'can't I just stay on the ground?'

'Walking there would take too long, plus I need an Ambassador that has demonstrated a symbiotic friendship with one of *their* kind. Those plants are going to be more cooperative if they see someone like you… you don't eat electrostatic plants do you?!'

'No my friend, just rocks.'

'Good, so climb on my back and we'll be off.'

'You don't quite have a cliff top to launch yourself from and I…'

'Don't worry about that,' said Fionix, 'I don't live on Olympus Mons for nothing! Up here we're literally in the air already! Come on, we're going to see a volcano about a vent…'

10

Hi Ho Quicksilver Lining!

Jade had noticed a change in Grit in the short time she'd known him. Here he was leading the way.

Jade inspected the ground. She looked from side to side. Nothing. Well, nothing but a relatively strong breeze blowing from the west. She tried sniffing the ground but had a pretty good idea that her sense of smell had not evolved enough to pick up any traces of her Great Uncle Syd.

Grit watched her then looked ahead in the direction they had been heading and squinted to avoid the sand and dust getting into his eyes. Nothing, but the swirls of wind vortices and failing attempts at dust devils, with the wind being not quite fast enough.

'I can't see a trace,' commented Grit.

'I can't smell one either,' agreed Jade, 'but Hanksie's definitely been heading this way...'

'That wind's swept away any footprints that he might have made,' tutted Grit.

It had been a long traipse since they left the Hellas Basin and those Angels, or Angles or whatever they were. Great Uncle Syd had been heading north, according to his marks in the dust so they had followed his tracks, which to begin with wasn't too difficult, as the winds had been quite calm. The Umpteenagers continued across the Syrtis Major Plain, one of the darkest surfaces on Mars and, fun fact, the most prominent feature that could be seen from Earth. Dark also described the mood of these two tortles. Plus they'd lost their prey.

Jade looked at Grit and shrugged, then she looked to the top of his head at Masha.

'How are you feeling?' Jade asked the lone pyrite captain.

Masha was sitting there, insect equivalent of elbows

plonked on insect equivalent of her knees with the equivalent of her hands (of this pair of arms) propping up her sad face. Masha looked up from what she'd been staring at (an empty point on the ground in front of Grit) and her face said it all.

'Never been away from *her* before…' she admitted, '…ever…'

'Has she ever upset you before?'

'Yes! But not like now…'

Masha sighed.

'Well I'm sure we can sort it out… given time…' Jade admitted.

'Knowing how stubborn *she* can be,' Masha admitted, 'that could be years… Decades even!'

Grit couldn't watch the conversation going on as it was on his head, but he stared into Jade's eyes and could see a mini version of his first ever louse. He was actually happy about having a captain. Masha was pretty cool: a real rebellious pyrite and she'd chosen *him*!

'I abandoned ship…' said Masha with guilt.

'You stood up for your beliefs!'

'I mutinied…'

'How could *you* mutiny?!' said Jade 'You're the captain! You can't mutiny your own tortle!'

'It was a pretty *pyritey* kind of thing to do!' said Grit, with a bit too much enthusiasm.

Masha sighed again.

'Look Masha,' said Jade, 'my dad used to tell me when he was teaching me Muddism that when we are troubled we should concentrate on what we see in front of us.'

Masha looked out at the scenery.

'A dust storm brewing?' she said a little sarcastically.

'Not exactly what I meant,' Jade corrected herself, 'the *metaphorical* thing in front of us, the most important task to do.'

'The Crazy Gravity Artist…' said Masha.

'We agreed with those Hells Agents to carry out this important mission.'

'I know.'

'They said it was of the utmost importance...'

Sigh.

'The whole planet depends on it!'

'It does sound big...'

'They said Fionix told them some ships were coming from the planet Earth!' Jade reminded everyone. There were a few moments of silence.

Grit interjected here.

'Thank you for standing up for me back there,' he said, trying to speak to the top of his own head.

'I'm wondering if I did the right thing,' admitted the sad captain.

'You did!' cried Grit. 'And because you did that, we're now in a position to help those Hell Birds with this emergency.'

'At the cost of losing my...'

'It's not the end,' said Jade, 'perhaps just a pause between the two of you, until we get this other matter sorted out. Besides, I have the feeling that Ruby is going to be finding it difficult without you at the helm' and she smiled at Masha.

Masha looked at her and managed a little smile back.

'Imagine,' Jade continued, 'those two, what's their names, Piccolo and Terry The Terrible, taking over the running of their tortle!'

Masha even sniggered a little.

'If they're all wearing eye patches,' Masha said, 'it's going to be mayhem!'

She laughed.

'Don't forget the nose patches as well!' said Grit.

Then there was a recognisable cough from behind Masha and she had to turn round to be sure.

'Piccolo?!' she said.

'An' me,' said Terry the Terrible sheepishly appearing from behind his ship mate.

'What are you two doing here?!'

'We be a stowin' away,' started Piccolo.

'Keepin' an eye on you!' Terry continued, lifting his eye patch and pointing at his hidden good eye.

'What, since I left Ruby?!'

'It was she that was askin' us to have your back.'

'Well all of your backs actually,' Terry confirmed.

Masha was momentarily stunned and remained speechless.

'So, Cap'n Masha,' started Jade, getting her mind back to the matter in hand, 'you've spent more time in this area than we have, what with Ruby skulking round Vastitas and Utopia for Ice Ages, what would you suggest?'

Masha paused and looked around, obviously taking it all in and considering the options.

'It would be nice to know why we have to catch this Hanksie character,' Masha voiced her curiosity.

'Well they wouldn't tell us, remember,' Jade reminded her, 'they said it was a need to know basis. Well, while you're thinking, I have something that might help make your stay on Grit a bit more bearable...'

Both Grit and Masha watched Jade with interest. Jade peered back over her own shoulder and called out, 'Captain Raffi? To the nose...'

'Aye aye ma'am,' came the obedient reply, 'what can I be doin' for ee?'

'We have a situation and I want you to assemble half the crew...'

'Would that be the top harf or the bottom harf of each crew member, your majesty?'

'Um Raffi, no, half the crew members, their top and bottom parts together.'

'Are we be doin' the flyin' of the nest ma'am?!'

'Not exactly Raffi. This is just temporary. Please get them together to go join Captain Masha over there on my friend Grit. Masha's going to need a hand or two and Grit could do with a practice run getting his own crew.'

* * * * *

Grit, again, peered over at the dust devil that was starting then stopping to materialise in the plains ahead. These mini-tornados often did this, sometimes leaving their spirally, well actually, *helically* shaped traces along the ground, like someone had overstretched and unwound a huge slinky and laid it in the dust.

'You should actually feel a little more secure,' said Jade, stroking Grit's shoulder. 'I did when I first got my lice.'

'Thanks,' said Grit, a little distracted.

'You're not still worried are you?' she asked him.

'Not about the lice, no,' Grit continued, but his mind was clearly elsewhere, so Jade decided to follow his gaze. He was still looking at the particles of sand that were doing the 'twist and shout' dance, or something ice skaters might do when given the chance. Jade suddenly picked up on the unsounded alarm bells.

'It's…' she started.

'…the Eschers!' Grit finished.

It was indeed. What had looked like a normal, innocent atmospheric vortex, was in fact the perfectly adapted Eschers, tiny grain-sized creatures that were like the piranhas of the Martian atmosphere. Individually they weren't particularly dangerous, a bit like getting a splinter, but together, hundreds, thousands, millions, hundreds of thousands of millions of them in one place, they were like a huge wooden stake compared to that splinter. And, like carnivorous locusts swarming, they were deadly. This was only a small dust storm compared to the planet-wide one of recent years, but it was still deadly to two umpteenaged tortles, with very little place to hide. Fresh in Grit's mind was his parents' demise during that big storm. The very event that Ruby had been so insensitive about. Jade knew instinctively they were in serious danger if the dust devil, like a wasps' nest, noticed that two takeaway 'meals on wheels' were only a short flight away...

'Don't make any sudden movements...' Jade whispered out of the corner of her mouth.

'I know...' Grit whispered back; he'd already been here, done it and lived the book version (if Elvis' theory was right).

'We're too far from shelter...' Jade continued, not taking her eyes off the unaware Escher whirlwind.

'We need to bury ourselves...' Grit pointed out, though that was also an instinctive action and both had already started using their feet to flip sand and dust over themselves, whilst digging a hole at the same time.

The pyrites also kicked into action, as if by instinct too. An *instinct* so as not to be *extinct*.

'Submerge!' cried Cap'n Raffi, an-outdated term the pyrites still used from when there used to be oceans on Mars and tortles were turtles and they did indeed go below the surface. The captain's cry was a signal for all hands on deck, to then form chains and hang over the edges of the carapaces of their respective 'ships' and assist in the burying alive of their land vessels. Both umpteenagers knew that they had to bury all fleshy bits below ground level at least, if they wanted to stand any chance of surviving an attack of the Escher-Schmitts. Grit had ended up underneath his parents during that big storm. Sadly they'd not had enough time to save themselves or their daughter, but at least they had saved their son. Jade had had a few close shaves with the Eschers; little squalls like this one, but never one of those macro-storms.

Then the Eschers, like a murmuration of starlings, all started moving in synchronisation. No longer individual creatures, but one, much larger, much more terrifying, *hungry* monster. They had noticed the Maxi best of Jade and Grit with fries and a coke. The dust devil swirled into action and like the most perfectly choreographed chorus line in three dimensions, they tilted their vertical spiral at an angle to head in Grit and Jade's direction. The two only had seconds to finish burying themselves, which was clearly not enough time.

Grit and Jade stared death in the face, well thousands of tiny little *vicious* faces, mini, jagged sand grain-sized creatures whose mouths were like half equators round their bodies, resembling pac-men with the top and bottom rows of teeth leaning one way and the other, like old gravestones, making them look like deep-sea anglerfish. Staring crazy eyes and topped with an equally crazy looking chaotic hairstyle. No body, no limbs, just a head with a big mouth and big teeth, but each the size of a piece of gravel or smaller.

Masha stood proud on Grit's back and stared at the marauding enemy. Her new crewmates stood behind her in the same power stance. On Jade's back, Raffi did the same pose, as did his crewmates, accompanied by a few cries of 'AH HAAR'. Many that had been digging had bounded back on board, though a few remained on the ground. Masha looked across at Raffi and he looked back. He nodded. She nodded back. Masha then pulled out one shiny silver weapon with her right arm. The other pyrites all did the same. Then she pulled out a second one with her left hand and the others followed. A third then fourth weapon appeared with each of the remaining limbs and now the tortles' backs were a forest of spikes, clubs, spears, slingshots and chains and just about every kind of weapon you could think of. A few others had weapons you wouldn't think of, like a toilet plunger and a food mixer. Masha's fourth weapon looked like one of those wire mesh nets that Gladiators would have used in a Roman stadium, so she was clearly ready for business.

'Battle Antenna on!' cried Masha to her crew and led the way by slipping on some armoured horns that enveloped her long, spindly hooked-forward aerials. They normally looked like coat hanger hooks but the horns now gave her a more formidable bullish appearance. Her crew followed her gesture. Some had spikey antenna, others forked, fishhook extensions and others antlers, like a stag in the rutting season. Masha glanced at them, then did a double take.

'Terry?'

'Aye Cap'n,' he said, adjusting his headgear.

'What are those?'

'Ah, I be as usin' my *drag lice* accessories ma'am,' and he fussed to get them both symmetrical.

'They look like feathers!'

'They is from my panto act ma'am, you know, the pink boa, when I does the song 'n' dance with Piccolo…'

'And they'll protect you?'

'As by distractin' the little critters Cap'n, which is then that I am catchin' them underwears ma'am…'

Masha was about to reply, then thought better of it. Natural selection, she realised, would decide whether Terry's DNA remained in the gene pool or the next pool of blood on the Martian surface.

The next moment there was a clash – not of Titans but Tiny-tans, creatures on the other end of the size scale, the diminutive pyrites risking life and limb against the milliscopic (that's millimetre sized – the Eschers were too big to be called microscopic) foes that were clearly outnumbering the crews of the tortles. The noise was deafening (for the little creatures) as sword hit sand grain, as hammer hit dust particle and food mixer chopped up gravel, the limbs of these normally sluggish lice were slicing through the air like expert chefs cutting up their *roccoli*.

Jade and Grit were momentarily taken aback at the way their symbiotic saviours were giving their all. Jade had heard that lice trained in what were called the Martian Arts, and she knew it was nothing to do with sketching or water colours, but she had never witnessed them having a real fight. Once the initial surprise was over, the umpteenagers returned their attentions to digging for their own lives. They scrambled and flipped soil over their backs, also causing a bit of a 'smoke screen' which confused the Eschers. Jade allowed herself a moment of hope to think they might actually go deep enough to cover all exposed edible bits. Then they both struck solid ground. The soil wasn't very deep here, barely ten centimetres, which was not nearly enough to cover their juicy parts. It was bedrock below the layer of topsoil. How low can you go? No lower was the answer. The pyrites were doing a commendable job, but they were clearly outnumbered, in spite of having so many extra pairs of limbs and weapons. Sometimes the Eschers would club together in dozens or hundreds to make a bigger adversary, even mimicking the shape and size of the lice to put them off.

Masha seemed to be quite the expect at dicing and slicing these rocklettes. While fighting them with three arms she would suddenly whiplash her fourth limb and send her net spinning at the marauding Eschers, the holes too small for them to get through, sweeping up quite a haul –then slipping the netted catch beneath one of her other limbs which held a hammer, she would pound her net as if making bread crumbs from a bag of old crusts. Smaller particles of dead Escher dust wafted out of the holes in the net, before she started the cycle again. A couple of the lice had sadly succumbed to the Eschers and a few had fallen in battle, the piranha particles gathering around the fallen sailors and gobbling up and fighting over them like pigeons over crusts of bread. It seemed only a matter of time before both crews would be gone and then the tortles would be the dessert, before becoming the *desert*.

Jade couldn't believe her bad luck. Twice in the same year she'd been attacked by rocks. The two jumping rocks back when she first encountered Grit and now these much smaller but more numerous grains of violence. She would have done better back then to have just stuck her head in the sand and stayed inanimate for another million years. It was only a birthday after all and she had had so many of them, there would have been another one along next year. And every year after that. Assuming she'd lived that long.

Grit felt his luck was running out too, what with the Giant Dust storm to be included with the same two attacks that Jade was internally grumbling about. He didn't want to die just yet. He'd found a purpose in life and his part in it actually mattered.

Just then a strange glinting light came over the horizon to the north. It was moving pretty fast. Not a source of light in itself, but a powerful reflector of light. There was a neighing sound and even a sort of galloping, splashing sound. Splashing?!

'Hi ho!' came the cry from this silver mirage. Though the pyrite-Escher battle was still raging, the tortles were suitably distracted and even many of the warriors on both sides were losing concentration.

'Woa!' came another cry from this shiny apparition and the thing rapidly decelerated, throwing up clouds of additional dust to add to the melée of Sailors versus Escher Air Pilots. Whatever it was that arrived, arrived so fast that the onlookers barely got a glimpse of it before it hit them and exploded into a splash of liquid, like an overripe peach hitting the ground. But whatever this thing was, it wasn't peach coloured. It was silver. And the liquid was not the squelchy, gooey insides of some fruit, nor in fact blood and guts as one might have expected. It was just a silver liquid.

The immediate surroundings were covered with pools of this mercurial fluid and drops had splattered over the rock tortles, the pyrites and even most of the Eschers had been given a silver lining. One could say everyone was looking *gilty*.

As they all recovered from this unusual collision, the silver liquid started to flow back together into one large pool, like something out of a science fiction movie. The pool sat there filling up the lowest level of the nearby ground, with a few ripples crossing its surface due to the wind. Grit and Jade lifted their heads up out of their half depth hidey-holes and stared at this thing. Then suddenly a head made of the same silver liquid rose out of the pool. A horse's head of all things. All shiny and silver and the mane followed with a neck. The horse's head looked over to the speechless tortles and said, 'Hi there, I'm Quicksilver!'

* * * * *

Meanwhile...

In a place that was supposed to be empty of life, a dead pyrite's graveyard, stood what appeared to be a plant. It was alive. The eyes had opened. Its feet-like roots were still embedded in the soil and they were still entangled round the deceased Sailor Swift who, seemed to have now become an integral part of this new plant.

Not far away, another plant-like entity that had sprouted from one of the dead remains of Starkwood's hadron-collided body, opened its eyes for the first time. It raised its flower-like head and had a striking similarity to the sample from which it had been cloned. It blinked. It looked round at the Martian scenery. It looked up to the heavens: the stars and the moon Phobos were reflected in its saucer-like eyes. It looked back down at its own body and then its sepal arms, which it twisted back and forth so it could inspect both sides. Below its nose was a tiny slit of a mouth, which it opened slightly and took what seemed to be a breath in the thin air. Meanwhile other zombie plants were sprouting up, each from a different scrap of Starkwood's remains. The area was starting to resemble a plantation on the rise.

* * * * *

Grit and Jade stared speechlessly at this horsey hero. Even the pyrites stopped in mid strike; Masha herself had her hand round the neck of a many thousand composite Escher crowd and just held it there as if on pause. The

157

Escher construct also stopped fighting as if equally intrigued by this super shiny, super steed.

The majestic stranger filled the momentary silence.

'No time to chat now,' he began, 'hop in, the mercury's fine,' and he gestured with his head for them to get on board.

Jade and Grit were still a bit too stunned to react and Quicksilver picked up on this, so chivvied them along.

'Look,' he explained, 'the Eschers can't cope with mercury poisoning, but they'll eventually shake it off and attack you again and though your *parasytes* are putting up a commendable fight, you'd be better off climbing on board as I can outrun these dust-storm-troopers... they can only go as fast as the wind! Come on!'

Quicksilver then looked quizzical and peered closely at Grit's head.

'Oh!' he realised, 'Masha! I didn't see you there!'

'Hi Quick,' said Masha nonchalantly as she cut the last unsplashed Escher grain in half with a machete. Grit and Jade looked at each other incredulously, but Masha's acquaintance with this unique creature was enough to convince them they were joining an ally.

It didn't take Grit or Jade long to dig themselves out of their shallow graves – they'd not got very far as it was. All the separate drops and film of silver liquid on the surrounding surfaces started seeping back towards the pool surrounding the partially emerged horse figure. Jade stepped cagily into the pool and found she didn't sink. It was slippery but she managed to half climb onto the back of 'Quick', helped by unexpected hand and arm-like shapes that grew out of the liquid which pushed her up. Grit followed suit and the moment they were within the confines of the pony's pond, Quicksilver splashed northwards, which is where he'd come from in the first place.

It felt pretty odd to both Jade and Grit to be riding on the back of – well it wasn't really the back of, it was a pool of liquid of this silver creature's own making. Quicksilver shifted himself, as his name implied, at a high speed across the Martian surface. His head stood high out of the pond of mercury, a bow wave leading the way and various secondary ripples flanked each side. The liquid that made up this shiny sea horse of a creature seemed to defy the laws of gravity – not exactly flowing downhill as one might expect, but sloshing across the surface as if the fluid was magnetic and it was being attracted along by a huge, well, horse-shoe magnet. Both Grit and Jade tried to hold on to something, like the splashy mane that was breaking into drops with each grab, but Quicksilver raised his liquid sides a bit like someone trying to transport soup in a bowl very fast and trying not to spill a drop. This had the effect of making the tortles slide away from the edges and stay within the safety of the central area.

Jade glanced back in the direction they had just left and noticed the swirling vortex of Eschers was so far behind that she breathed a sigh of relief. She turned her attention back to Quicksilver, now ready to better make his acquaintance.

'Well thank you Quicksilver,' she said with gratitude. Grit backed her up by agreeing.

'You're welcome,' said Quicksilver and he bowed his head gracefully.

'Why did you rescue us?' Jade asked with curiosity.

'Common enemy aren't they?' said the horse with a smile, 'Besides, they should pick on someone their own size!'

'You came just in time,' Jade continued. 'I'm not sure we could have lasted much longer,'

Then she looked over her own shoulder to check out her own lice and Grit did the same for his crew. Captain Masha looked a little dishevelled with a few cuts and bruises and she was helping to attend to her own wounded crew members.

'That was quite some fighting,' said Grit to his pyrite protector, 'thank you.'

'Line of duty…' said Masha, a little subdued.

'Grit,' Jade pointed out in a loud whisper, as he

probably wasn't aware of protocol, 'you need to ask for a status report...'

'What? Oh! Um Captain Masha, would you um tell me how the crew is doing?'

There were a few moments of silence as Masha collected her thoughts, wiped her brow and finished tying a splint onto the leg of one of her injured crew.

'Um... We have a couple of dozen injured to take care of and sadly we lost about half a dozen to the Eschers, though we haven't finished taking roll...'

'Oh,' said Grit, not familiar with what he should say or how he should react, 'um, I'm sorry to hear that... um, my condolences to the, er brave pyrites who gave their lives to protect um all of us?'

'Thank you,' said Masha.

'Um, should we have some kind of ceremony or something...'

'There will be,' Masha explained to her new vessel, 'once we've patched up the survivors. It'll involve a few prayers to the gods, then that's usually followed by lots of singing and drinking...'

'Oh, well, um that sounds like a healthy way to celebrate your er heroes, um captain,'

'Thank you, sir...'

'Um,' Grit asked hesitantly, 'is there something that I am supposed to do for this, er wake?'

'Well you will be the venue,' explained Masha, 'but we can sort that out when we come to it...'

Masha paused then continued.

'... Um sorry we weren't able to protect you completely under these recent conditions...'

Then she hopped back into the midst of her crew to tend to more of the injured. Grit felt sorry that *she* was apologising, feeling that he had just been saved with the help of a bunch of pyrites that not so long ago he didn't have. Grit also felt bad that some of his newly formed team had perished for his sake.

Grit looked at Jade, who'd been spectating this discussion and gave him a little rub with her claw on his shoulder and said: 'You did okay'. She then turned her attention to her own captain and crew.

'How is everyone Raff?'

'Similar situation to Cap'n Masha,' began the seasoned pyrite leader, 'we be having about 30 or 40 injured crew and lost about a score, but we be thinking that some was just fallen off the deck and not eaten by those damn Eschers.'

'Thank you Raffi. Well as we know, if they survived, they will make their way back on board. Thank you for your crew's loyalty.'

'Bein' our pleasure ma'am,' said Raffi proudly.

'Any damage?'

'Well, some of them damn sand lubbers got on board as a group and wreaked havoc between a couple of your plates ma'am, but we dusted 'em and I have a repair team, patching up the crack they started.

'Thank you again for your protection Raff.'

'It be workin' both ways m'lady,' Raffi Rehab reminded her, 'you be a safe heaven for us pyrites, an' we be making sure your back is scratched too.'

'Appreciated.'

Now the internal formalities were over, Jade turned her attention back to her newly found liquidator, or *fluidisor*, or whatever his title might be.

'So Quicksilver,' she started, 'where are we going?'

'Well,' he suggested, 'initially, as far away as possible from those crevice filling critters, then after that, well you're free to go wherever you want.'

'Thanks. Tell me now, what exactly *are* you?'

'Me? Oh I'm sadly the last of my kind – we're just about extinguished! Well *I* am.'

'You seem quite jolly about it all,' Jade commented

'Oh,' dismissed Quicksilver, 'I've been the last of my species for quite a few million years now, I got past the grieving and feeling sorry for myself stage a long time ago. I looked on the bright side, well, being shiny, there's *always* a bright side...'

'The end of your species?!'

'Look, if you're like me, we live, what, so long, hey I've now lived longer myself than some entire species used to live!'

'What species *are* you?' Jade finally asked.

'It's not obvious?!'

'Well I've heard legends and folk tales about *liquinine* creatures, but never seen one before.'

'Ah,' said Quicksilver, 'I'm one of the Four Fundamental *Horses* of Nature… the best one.'

'Oh,' Grit perked up, 'like what's their names, um Warmth, Persistence, Farming and Depth?'

'Not quite,' smiled Quicksilver, 'you're talking about the Four Horses of the Outer-cropolis – a different species entirely, now sadly gone too.'

'If you've been around for a long time,' Jade asked him, 'then you must know many of the creatures that live here on Mars?'

'I tend to keep to myself a lot,' Quicksilver explained, 'certainly since my species numbers dropped to one. I see folk from a distance… um I've seen a few of your kind, you solid turtle types. I've bumped into one called Ruby a few times oh and I've seen those huge solid flying carpet birds up there and of course that Gravity Artist…'

'What, *Herman*?!' cried Grit on hearing an eye witness account of a sighting, albeit it vague.

'If you mean Hanksie, yes, I saw him just a short while ago…'

'Really!' said Grit again, splashing more wildly in his silver paddling area, 'Where?! Where!? We've been trying to catch up with him!'

'You have? Why? Do you like his artwork? I'm not so much of a fan myself. I'm not the Fundamental Horse of Graffitti, I'm the Quantum Chromo Diabolical Horse.'

'No I don't like his creations,' explained Grit, 'but it's just that we have to stop him, by order of Fionix the Flying Carpet Bird.'

'Oh, maybe she's the one I've seen flying round the most. Okay, well let me take you to him…'

Quicksilver made a slight course correction, as they'd

moved far out of the range of the Evil Eschers and now they headed off in the general direction of Hanksie the Hyperactive Hippy.

* * * * *

It was odd for both Grit and Jade to see the scenery whizz by at a speed that they would never have experienced on their own. The ride was a little bumpy, but slightly cushioned by the buoyant nature of their liquid limousine. They had continued to travel north and slightly west, which was going to take them to the Cydonia area of Mars, the place in fact from where Great Uncle Syd had come. Was that a coincidence, Jade thought. Was Herman steering Great Uncle Syd back to his birthplace? If so, why?

Jade had lost track just how long they'd been riding the Quicksilver Wave. She had nodded off from time to time. She looked over at Grit and he was actually taking a nap himself. Jade shivered again, as she felt the cold of the north making its way through the normally well-insulated carapace that protected her from such temperature extremes, then she stared out at the distant horizon in front of them. Her attention was caught by a faint, but, caught-in-the-light dust cloud.

'There!' she shouted, pointing towards the cloudy trail.

'I see it!' said Quicksilver and he moved up a gear. This woke Grit from his light sleep.

'Are we nearly there yet?' he asked instinctively.

'Herman on the port bow!' shouted captain Masha as her crew also sprang into action, 'or is it starboard?'

Quicksilver put on a spurt, literally. His silver mane was blowing in the breeze that he'd created by his speed and specks of the tiny liquid splashed over his two passengers. Grit and Jade in turn shook themselves in a very un-tortle-like way but a more dog-like way, which forced the metallic drops to fall back into Quicksilver's own gene pool. Grit half climbed onto the fluid back of the sea horse and half held onto the neck, while Jade in

163

turn lay her head on Grit's shell, her front claws clasping onto his rim like it was a piggy-back. They looked vaguely like some kind of rocker with his girlfriend on the back of his silver machine. They both bobbed up and down as waves ran through Quicksilver's body. A number of pyrites had also gathered 'on deck' and were poised at the ready on the backs and heads of their respective tortle-ships. Some pyrites had ropes with backward pointing fishhooks as if ready for some kind of confrontation or illegal boarding. Although he was the oldest tortle, who predated most of the life on planet Mars, Great Uncle Syd being ridden by the most idiosyncratic artist in the solar system was not the most formidable looking adversary. Plus, a splashy-shiny, liquid horse carrying two umpteenaged tortles was also not exactly the most frightening fighting machine around. If Mars had geeks and nerds, then all these guys would probably be them.

Grit found himself gawping and so did Jade as they both looked at their quarry. Quicksilver was panting with the exertion but also seemed to be excited about this out-of-the-ordinary activity that had broken his otherwise solitary wandering. His tongue was hanging out and it flapped in the wind. He looked back at his passengers with a smile, then at the target, then back at Jade and Grit again, a bit bewildered.

'What's the matter?' he asked his newly found acquaintances.

They didn't answer. They had now caught up with the Post-Modernist Martian *Martist* and it was only as they pulled up alongside him that Quicksilver felt something was odd, but he couldn't say exactly what it was. Jade and Grit knew. This just *shouldn't* be happening. There was Jade's Great Uncle, a several hundred million year old, ex-turtle, one day to be a new-tortoise but still stuck somewhere in between. He was moving far too fast for it to be physically possible, certainly not for a heavy, shell-backed testudo. His legs shouldn't have been long enough. They should not have been able to bend quite like they were bending. Herman, or was it his altered ego Hanksie, was sitting atop his Martian Mustang. Herman had a loop of rope round Uncle Syd's neck, the other end he was holding in one of his many limbs. Jade had never noticed just how many legs Herman had. He seemed to have several pairs of limbs that ended in thin blade-like shapes as if he was perhaps more of a crab than a tortle. Of course! A *hermit* crab! He was using a couple of his bladed legs to cling to Uncle Syd's shell. On one of his pincer-like hands, Hanksie also had another length of rope, which he was swinging around in circles in time with his riding rhythm. Beneath him, and this was what was so disconcerting, Great Uncle Syd was galloping! It seemed so unnatural that a creature who could barely scrape his carapace across the ground should actually be supple enough to gallop!

Quicksilver was now neck and neck with Great Uncle Syd and the old tortle seemed to be in a mesmerized trance. Hanksie looked across at the two young tortles and gave them a wide, crazy grin. He cracked the whip in his freehand.

'Yee! Haaa!' he cried, then put his attention back to what lay ahead.

Grit and Jade were momentarily stunned by this, but Masha soon woke them from their pause.

'Charge!' shouted Masha and the next moment, ropes with hooks were being thrown across the space between these dry sea vessels. Hanksie, with his extra limbs, knocked a few of the ropes out of the way but some landed on Uncle Syd and the hooks dug into his shell; the next moment, hordes of pyrites were sliding down the ropes and boarding the rogue racer.

Then there was a shudder. Quicksilver juddered and it shook many lice off their ropes like water drops released from a shaken wire fence.

'Uh ho…' said Quicksilver with realisation.

'What?' said Jade, looking at him with concern.

'We've come too far north!'

'No, we have to catch Herman!' said Grit.

'Or the sun's getting too low,' said the horse.

'What's that got to do with this – we've nearly got him?!'

'I'm seizing up!'

'Why?!'

'It's too cold for me,' Quicksilver explained, but by then he had already slowed down so much that Hanksie and his trusty steed Great Uncle Syd were disappearing out of sight, with a trail of fallen pyrites marking the escape route taken by the Crazy Cubist. The lice bounded back to their respective tortles, both of whom by now had stepped off Quicksilver and were transfixed watching their friend changing state.

'You need to warm me up before it's too late!'

'How?' asked Jade

'Any hot rocks around?'

'No,' said Jade with frustration, 'the nearest volcanoes are days away and anyway they're pretty much extinct now.'

'Light a fire?'

'With what?'

'Get me in the sun then!'

'But it's going down,' Grit pointed out. 'We'll have to wait until tomorrow morning.'

'We need to go south then!' said Quicksilver

'We'll have to let Hanksie go,' Jade pointed out.

'Well you go after him yourself,' Quicksilver suggested. 'I'll have to wait here 'til the sun … comes…'

Before their eyes, Grit and Jade saw Quicksilver solidify and freeze into his last position, half of his horse body and head sticking out of his pool. There was an odd creaking sound, which they'd heard before when water ice and dry ice started to freeze.

Jade had stepped off Quicksilver's solidifying surface and now she stood on the permafrosted, dust-coated Cassini countryside. Grit was a bit slower in leaving, as he curiously stared closely at his latently fusing friend. Grit got distracted by noticing his reflection in Quicksilver's curved, mirrored skin and found his image quaintly diminished, then remembered himself and looked into the horse's eyes.

'Hello?' he asked. There was no answer.

Knock knock! Grit tapped the silver statue with his claw and it made a sturdy sonorous echo, typical of a lump of metal.

'Anyone in there?' he continued, but still nothing.

Jade's glance had followed Hanksie's disappearing silhouette, bareback riding her Great Uncle Syd as they dipped below the western horizon again, then turned back to Grit.

'Like he said,' she pointed out, 'there's nothing we can do until the sun rises.'

'Oh right,' realised Grit, then turned to step off. His two front limbs made it to the ground, but his third poised in mid-air as his fourth could not leave the horse behind.

'Come on,' Jade insisted as she turned and looked like she was about to head after Hanksie.

'Um…' Grit began, but Jade was concentrating on the task ahead of her.

'Maybe we can do that galloping thing that Hanksie got Syd to do?

'Jade…'

'What?'

'My foot's stuck…'

Jade finally snapped out of her 'next mission' mode and looked back at Grit and, sure enough, he'd waited too long while standing in the pool of their equinine transport. The mercurial metal mammal had solidified around his foot and Grit was up to his ankle in horse.

Jade tried to yank Grit out of his trap by biting on to the edge of his carapace and pulling, but he wouldn't budge.

'Go on without me!' Grit insisted, 'Save yourself! Catch up with Hanksie before it's too late! Don't worry about me! There's a bigger picture to consider…and it might be Hanksie drawing it!'

Jade watched him for a moment and let him get it out of his system. Grit noticed this so eventually quietened down.

'Finished?' she asked. He nodded. 'Right, well like he said we need the sun's heat to melt him so maybe we can make our own heat somehow... or chip you out of there... Raffi?'

'On it ma'am,' came the voice next to Jade's ear and the next moment there were lice jumping, sliding and roping down the sides of Jade's shell and bounding over to Grit who'd really put his foot in it. Some lice had little pick axes, others had hammers and chisels and one even had some kind of mini pneumatic drill while another had a harpoon gun. Many hours were then spent chipping away at this almost impenetrable metal... We shall join them later...

11

Minisilver

It was now quite dark as night had fallen and apart from the stars there was only the occasional streak of gentle light from a monopole-cat taking its chance.

'Captain's progress report,' began Raffi to a slightly dejected Jade. Dejected due to the failure of her mission. She knew Grit would be free anyway once the sun rose the next day, but that meant Hanksie would have a good twelve hours head start on them and that time would be more than enough for the wind to erase his trail in the sand.

'Yes Raffi…what's the progress report?'

'Um, no progress to report ma'am.'

'Thanks Raff.'

'Sorry ma'am.'

'Not your fault. We're not really equipped to tackle tortle limbs stuck in quick drying silver.'

'It actually be mercury, beggin' your pardon ma'am, but silver'd be tougher at this temperature ma'am.'

'Well tell your crew to down tools and have a well-earned rest.'

'Aye aye,' said Raffi Rehab.

Jade looked at Grit who looked back, still feeling a bit daft for getting stuck like this.

'Let's sleep on it,' she suggested.

'Well a nap,' agreed Grit, 'I normally sleep for a few months at a time and I'm not due for one just yet.'

'Whatever gets you through this night then…'

And Jade crouched down, her front paws crossed and her chin resting on them, ready for a forced break in proceedings.

Jade was just entering the SEM stage of sleep (slow eye movement) when she thought she could hear a strange sound. Several strange sounds. Ones that she had not heard before – even after sixteen million years of listening to things. It was a rushing sound of air, not quite like a normal wind, but a hovering kind of sound. Air moving downwards. Not loud, not obtrusive, but a gentle whooshing as if the cause for it was trying not to be heard. She opened her eyes and looked around. Next to her was Quicksilver's reflective silhouette, being both black by his opaqueness but also reflective in sending back the soft glimmerings of the monopole-cats and even some equatorial borealis, plus some cute little images of the starry sky in his skin.

But there was something else. Jade now stood up on all four limbs and, seeing nothing, she raised her head high on her neck, as if she was some kind of Martian meerkat. Still not enough, so she pushed with her front feet, which pivoted her body up vertically until she was standing on her back limbs. She hadn't considered what havoc this might play with her pyrite crew, but personal safety first and she didn't want to lose a moment if this was going to be another encounter with a new crowd of Eschers.

'Grit!' she whispered loudly, 'wake up!'

'What?!'

'Shh! Something unknown!'

Grit rose with a start then found out he couldn't move far, as his foot was still embedded in Quicksilver. He instinctively started to try and run in the opposite direction to the noise and merely managed to slightly turn the heavy horse, until he was now behind the horse compared to the direction of the noise. This seemed good enough for Grit and he crouched down behind the steed's frozen profile. And there he hid.

'Grit,' she said carefully, 'now is not the time to revert to old habits…'

'Sorry,' he realised, then sheepishly dragged himself back round to the frontline of what was likely to be their next confrontation (and maybe last from the sound of the arriving adversaries).

'I'm getting tired of fighting,' said Grit with all sincerity.

'Me too,' said Jade and they both faced the oncoming gentle roar and slightly rising wind speed.

'I'm down a limb,' said Grit with disappointment.

Masha was now standing on his nose and moving into her warrior stance.

'I've had to fight with half my limbs missing,' she admitted to Grit, 'and even with only one eye.'

'But you told me the patch was just a fake!' said Grit.

'It is,' Masha admitted, 'but I knew I looked meaner with the patch so I had to fight without depth of vision.'

'Oh... hang on, *limbs missing*?!'

'They grow back,' said Masha matter-of-factly.

'Oh,'

'So,' she said, 'one can still succeed three handed and one eyed.'

'Wasn't it off putting having to do all that with one eye closed?' Grit asked. 'I've tried closing my eye for a day when I was bored and it got very uncomfortable.'

'Oh it would,' Masha agreed as she sharpened one of her blades, 'but I kept swapping the patch onto the other eye, mid-fight... they never noticed...' and as she said this, she did the very same action, lifting up the eye patch then sliding it over her other eye and before Grit could blink she had a full set of killing instruments pointing ahead.

A sort of rumbling joined the ill-wind and once again the young tortles were preparing for another unwanted confrontation. Then, without warning, something, well some *things* (they were huge), appeared out of the darkness and just over their heads. So huge that whatever they were blotted out the view of the stars and polecats for a few seconds. Whoever it was, they seemed to trap the air and also muffle the sound, like when your ear gets very close to a wall your hearing feels odd. There was a lot of cold mist, and heavy dry ice smoke fell onto the semi-trapped tortles, as something like a huge flag rippled over their heads. More than one, one after the other. Not only the tortles, but the pyrites were also momentarily stunned by this unexpected vision, or lack of vision rather. A third flying sheet whooshed just above their heads, obviously lapping up the ground effect, but the excess of exhaust dry ice smoke was confusing. In the thin gap of background light that was made between the ground and these flying carpets, Grit and Jade could see a fourth one arriving and the thing it was carrying was dropped as if like a bomb from an aircraft and the huge cylindrical missile sped towards the tortles. It was like a compartmented flying sausage, though technically it was not flying, just ballistic and falling with gravity. In the next moment, loads of pairs of legs popped out from underneath the Martian Zeppelin and the tortles could see a face with an embarrassed smile on the front end of the blimp.

'Oh it's Catapilla!' Jade managed to say before she heard Catapilla say 'ooops!' and then the multi-legged animal ploughed into them. Her front end slowed down faster than the back end as she collided with the tortles, while her back end was still running along the ground and overtook her front, looking a bit like a giant accordion scuttling across the ground and bent double.

The Hellas Angels had been gliding so close to the ground, they were almost hugging it and they left long vapour trails behind them. Much like high flying jets do in the Earth's atmosphere. One after the other, the Angles, or Angels depending how you think of them, each in turn crash-landed, which involved hitting the ground and doing more sliding rather than digging up the dirt, what with the permafrost making it a huge ice skating rink. There was the sound of claws scratching along the ground which had everyone's neck hairs standing on end as they would for fingernails down a blackboard. Most of the flying squad ended wrapped up in their own wings, like garden sized cabbage leaves wrapping some strange rice balls, stuffed here with bird meat of course.

When all the ice spray had settled and the Angels had unfolded their wings and smoothed out the wrinkles, Catapilla was lying on her back with her little legs wriggling in the air, her face looking at the tortles, but of course everything was upside down for her. She smiled in an embarrassed way again. Jade had been knocked from her defensive position and was now just spinning on the edge of her shell like a coin that hadn't decided on which side to fall. Grit was still caught with his hand in the silver, so to speak, and all that could be heard was the rising pitch of Jade as she span faster but at a more horizontal angle. The Angels gathered round and politely waited for Jade to stop.

Hell herself watched then turned to Syrena.

'Heads,' she said flatly.

'Tails!' cried Syrena and they shook claws on the bet.

'On her edge,' said Dasha, liking the slim odds.

'I say she keeps spinning,' said Layer.

'She has to stop!' said Hell with derision, 'it's a law of physics.'

'Maybe Jade never studied physics,' suggested Syrena.

'Physics laws don't rely on you knowing them to obey them,' Hell argued.

'Well I heard the observer affects the observation,' said Dasha.

'Maybe none of this is real, so she *can* keep spinning forever.' suggested Catapilla.

The four aerodactyls turned to face their upside-down multi-legged friend with disbelief.

'Are you of the camp that believes we don't really exist,' asked Hell 'and that *someone* is making all this up?!'

'Not making it up,' Layer interjected, 'we're just in someone else's dream and impossible things can happen in dreams, so this tortle will carry on spinning forever.'

'You think that too?' Hell asked Catapilla.

'Well I remember Elvis talking about it once and it sounded like an interesting idea.'

'I still say tails,' said Syrena, not really interested in this heavily philosophical debate.

They all looked back to Jade, who was now passing the point of no return; the crest of her carapace was making contact with the ice and she was now spinning on that point, rather than the previous rolling around on her rim.

'There, Tails!' snapped Syrena with delight, 'Told you!'

Jade came to rest upside down and when she finally stopped turning she was facing Catapilla; as they were both upside down, to each other they were the right way up.

'Hi.' said Jade.

'Hi,' said Catapilla awkwardly.

Meanwhile, hundreds of lice, some that had been centripetally forced off and others that were now jumping off, were pulling on ropes and trying to upright their ship. Hell came along and effortlessly used her beak to flip Jade back up the right way.

'Thanks,' said Jade.

'You're welcome,' said Hell.

'So what brings you calling birds round so late at night?' Jade asked, as if it was quite a normal interruption. At the same time she was brushing off the spray of ice and frost that had stuck to her during the spin.

'Oh, business,' explained Hell, 'we're here to commandeer the horse.'

'Really?'

'Yes,' put in Syrena, 'Fionix ordered us to find one. She was shouting *a horse, a horse my planet for a horse*, and we said any old horse and she said *no, a silver one*, and we said we'd not seen one in ice ages and she said *well you better start looking harder now as I need one*, and we said but how many still exist on Mars, and she said *a number of them* and she was right.'

'A *number* of them?!' asked Jade.

'Yes, but the number's one and *he* is it,' said Syrena, pointing at the polychromed statue.

'And why does Fionix need Quicksilver?' asked Jade.

'Oh,' dismissed Dasha, 'we just followed her orders, boss lady was in a bit of a flap. Quite a big flap actually! She can cover quite a lot of cross-sectional area when she fully spreads her wings...'

'Well there may be a problem with taking Quicksilver,' Jade started, but Hell interrupted her again.

'Why, because he's solid? We can carry him back to Fionix like that, it's actually easier than if he was liquid you know. Have you ever tried carrying a liquid? Falls through your claws...'

'Okay,' Jade agreed, 'that sounds reasonable but there's another problem.'

'No there isn't,' said Hell, 'as long as your boyfriend steps out of the way and lets us do our job.'

'He's not my boyfriend!'

'I'm not her boyfriend!' cried Grit.

'He can't move,' explained Jade, 'he's got his foot frozen into the horse.'

The Angels all took a closer look. Even Catapilla, from an upside down position, peered more deeply at the spot-welded odd couple.

The Hellas Angels all suddenly looked delighted.

'It's *my* turn!' cried Syrena, pointing one of her bat-like fingers at herself and glowing with victory.

'You did it last time!' Dasha accused her.

'That didn't count!' Syrena protested.

'I think it's unladylike,' commented Princess Layer distastefully.

'But it's one of our super powers!' said Hell proudly.

'What are you all talking about?' said Jade, confused.

'We have the power to melt the horse!' proclaimed Syrena with pride and a pinch of suspense. At the same time she took up a stance, legs astride and claws clasped together like she was pointing a weapon forwards.

'And we can release your boyfriend from his metal chains...' Hell backed her up, adding more drama and then she turned her back to Syrena, standing to her right, claws clasped and pointing her imaginary weapon vertically.

'And make this Planet a safer World for all Martian-kind...' said Dasha, standing symmetrically on Syrena's left and she too pointed her imaginary weapon skyward.

'Because...' said Syrena.

'We are...' said Hell.

175

'The...' Dasha built up then all together they said different things.

'Hellas Angels!' cried Hell.

'Little Syrens!' said Syrena.

'Team Dasha!' said Dasha.

'Count me out!' said Layer.

Jade, puzzled, looked at Catapilla who looked back.

'I have no vote in this,' said Catapilla.

'Is the name of your team that important?' asked Jade, which brought them back to the problem in hand.

'Er, no,' agreed Hell, 'you're right, but we now have to decide who's going to be the one to use their powers.'

'Weren't you in a hurry a moment ago?' Jade enquired, still confused by the infighting.

'Yes, right,' Hell corrected herself, 'so I'll do it...'

'No!' Syrena protested, 'We'll play rock, gravel, sand to decide."

'Okay,' agreed Dasha and with that the three who'd been arguing over it went into a huddle away from the others, leaving the tortles sort of twiddling their thumbs. Jade looked to Layer and started to quiz her.

'Um Layer,' she began, 'can you tell...'

'No,' she refused and folded her already half-folded bat arms.

Jade looked to Catapilla (who was still upside down) and before she spoke, she felt obliged to make a friendly gesture. She came up to Catapilla's side, about halfway down her body, sort of stomach level, though it was hard to tell, and she started to wedge her head under Catapilla's side to lever and roll her over. Being slightly wedge-shaped herself, Jade was pretty good at this and in a few moments Catapilla was back on her own two hundred feet.

'Thank you,' she said a bit self-consciously and shook herself almost dog-like to finally shake off the sand and ice shavings after her crash landing.

'So Catapilla, or can I call you Cat?'

'No don't call me Cat.'

'How about Pilla?'

'Don't call me that either.'

'Sorry. So what is this power they're going on about?'

'Oh that,' she huffed dismissively, but continued, 'you know Fionix?'

'Yes, and she's your chief?'

'Yes, she trains us and, well, she's a bit prudish herself about this power – it's like she was trying to tell us the facts of life and she was more embarrassed than we were. Well you know we are also actually known as nogards?'

'I've heard your species called that. Because you *guard* the planet?'

'Not exactly. We're actually the opposite of those mythical creatures called dragons.'

'Ah… Oh! It's dragon backwards,' Jade realised.

'Exactly.'

'Oh, what, so they breathe *out* fire, you breath *in* fire?!'

'Um no,' Catapilla continued a bit awkwardly, 'dragons were supposed to make fire come out of their mouths. We make fire come out of our… Um…'

'Oh!' Jade realised, 'Yes! So I wasn't imagining it! I've seen Fionix shooting across the sky and I used to think it was just because she was going so fast, like a meteorite, that she was heating up from the friction.'

'Sadly no,' said Catapilla, 'it's jet power.'

'Ah, so one of your friends is going to melt Quicksilver with her own flames.'

'Yea.'

'Won't that hurt the horse?'

'Small yellow flame, air holes closed, surround the area with dry ice, they should know what to do…'

'And it won't hurt my friend?'

'No and by the way, *I* don't think he's your boyfriend…'

'What?! Oh, well…'

'I could see he had the hots for your sister the other day.'

'What?! I don't want to go there thanks!'

'They'd make a nice couple, if your sister was a bit nicer.'

'Well that's not going to happen anytime soon and anyway, we have our claws full of other obligations at the moment...'

It was then that the other Hellas Angels came back to Quicksilver.

'I still say *rock* covers *sand*,' protested Hell, obviously losing the game.

'No,' Syrena corrected her, 'sand always covers big rocks. Mars is a big boulder and it's covered in *smaller* rocks. Anyway let's get on with this. Fellow Angels, get the dust, get the dry ice, get an anaesthetic if our patient needs one...and let's go!'

The Angels took up their positions, a layer of sand and dust and claw-fulls of dry ice scraped from the tops of the nearby rocks and Grit was caked in a layer of solid carbon dioxide and looking like a most unusual snow-tortle, with a splattering of real grit. The two 'wing' ladies actually held Syrena by her wings so she could lift her claws off the ground and she turned her back to face the patients, clicked her claws together to make sparks and after a couple of splutterings, there was a flame. At that moment, Hell and Dasha had to hold tightly to their friend so she wouldn't jet herself away. There was a gentle roaring sound of the flame and Jade gawped at the spectacle, which only lasted a few seconds before the metal around Grit's foot was soft enough for him to pull himself free.

The three successful Hellas Angels gave each other high fours (they only had four fingers on each wing), then turned to soak up the admiration of the crowd. There wasn't much of a crowd nor much admiration either. Catapilla had seen this before and as Layer didn't really approve, she was facing a different way. Grit was inspecting his foot to make sure there was no damage while Jade was closely inspecting the melted part of Quicksilver. She was about to dip her claw into the curious rippling puddle within the limits of the creature when, to her surprise, a little horse's head poked out of the puddle.

'Oh a baby!' she cried in shock.

'No,' said the little voice of the pony puddle, which sounded like a higher pitched version of Quicksilver himself, 'This is me, Quicksilver. Well, part of me.'

At this, the chromium colt peered round to see the rest of himself in freeze frame.

'Ah, I get it,' he said, 'wandered too far north. Waiting for sunrise I guess...'

'Actually,' said Jade, 'those Angels there said Fionix needs your help.'

'Really,' said Minisilver, and he looked at the girls who were doing a victory dance.

'Something about saving life on Mars and you are her only hope,' said Jade.

'Sounds important!'

'Apparently it is.'

'And what about your task to get that crazy artist?'

'On hold for the moment... Oh I see you're freezing up again!'

'Adaptation has its limits...' said the small Quicksilver.

'Right,' said Syrena, 'let's go!'

'It's *me* who decides!' Hell put in.

'I freed the horse,' Syrena justified herself, 'I get to call the shots this time – besides I called *sand* and covered your rock so it's still me.'

Hell sighed deeply and gave in.

'Besides,' Syrena said with justification, 'this is *my* home ground, This is *Syrtis* where I came from!'

'Okay okay!' Hell admitted.

While the birds were fighting, the part of Quicksilver that was still molten caught Jade's attention.

'Psst!' he said out of the side of his mouth.

'What?' Jade asked.

'Take me with you!' said the little pony.

'They need you!'

'Just take the melted bit. Don't worry, the rest of me can still operate with a bit missing and I can stay with you guys. Give you a helping hoof... a small one mind you...'

Jade checked that the birds weren't looking, then scooped up the cooling down molten part with the little horse's head in it and plopped it into the cracks on the top of her shell.

'Thanks!' said the voice of whom we will call Minisilver for now, as he poured down into the crevices.

'Hey Grit,' said Syrena, 'you still got that rope you were dragging around?'

'Um yes?'

'We're going to have to commandeer it – to carry the horse.'

'Oh okay,' and with that Grit pulled out the cord from inside his shell and the four flying Angels tied it round the metal statue creating four free ends.

'Grab an end each!' cried Syrena and the ladies proceeded to do so, first with their beaks; they pulled tightly and managed to raise Quicksilver just above the ground.

'Thanks fellow Martians,' said Syrena.

'You're welcome,' replied Jade, 'but what are we supposed to do now?'

'Well,' continued Hell, as the four Angels started to unfold their wings and flap them in preparation for take-off, 'Fionix said that she would be sending you orders shortly. Just hang around here.'

'Oh okay,' Jade said a little confused.

'What about me?' Catapilla suddenly piped up, looking a little forlorn.

There were a few moments silence.

'Yea, sorry,' said Syrena, 'it's going to take the four of us to carry this dead weight of a statue. You stay here with the tortles and we'll come back for you later, okay?'

Catapilla was speechless. By now, the place was awash with huge unfurling, then flapping leathery wings, as the four Hellas Angels pointed themselves in the direction of the slightly downhill slope of the plains and began to waddle then pound their way south-west, leaving the two rock tortles and the abandoned, non-flying Angel, Catapilla, in a cloud of floating particles. As it was night time, the feeling of abandonment was even greater.

After watching the team get airborne and head over the horizon, the three land-locked creatures turned to face each other. Jade looked at Catapilla who had a worried frown on her face and smiled awkwardly at her. Grit followed suit and Catapilla tried to smile back but it fell short.

* * * * *

The testudos and their multi-legged friend had been hanging around in the Syrtis Major Plain for several days, waiting for further instructions and they were getting a bit bored and restless.

'What I can't understand,' explained Grit, 'is why you have so many legs *now*, but you'll only end up with, like, two when you've changed…'

'Four actually,' corrected Jade, 'if you count the wings as well…'

They both looked at Catapilla again, who looked back bewildered.

'I mean, how many legs *do* you have?' Grit asked again, becoming a bit fixated on the number of limbs on the pre-flying stage of the bird of paradise, a nogard to use the other name. He proceeded to start counting them.

'Do you mind?' asked Catapilla a bit put out. 'I mean I could ask you the same thing: how come you keep the *same* number of legs in all your stages?'

'Stages? We don't have stages,' explained Grit. 'We hatch from eggs then we just basically grow to become bigger versions of ourselves…'

'But didn't you have flippers before?'

'Well yes,' he agreed, 'but my parents told me our flippers started turning into feet when the seas began to dry up, some kind of evolution they said…'

'After hatching from an egg,' explained Catapilla, 'I became a lava…'

'Isn't that some kind of *ingenious* rock? Grit asked.

'Well,' reflected Catapilla, 'when it comes down to it,

don't we all come from melted rocks? I mean we all grow from the dust of Mother Mars, no?'

The tortles considered this. Then Grit looked confused.

'Isn't it *Father* Mars?'

'That still doesn't change where we come from.'

'You know,' said Jade to her friends, 'I think you'd both enjoy chatting to my dad, Elvis. He's into all this kind of thing.'

'I counted twenty four,' said Grit, suddenly out of context.

'What?' asked Jade.

'Pairs of legs,' he qualified, 'Catapilla has twenty four…'

'They're not all real,' explained the multi-limbed proto-aerodactyl, 'most of them are *pseudopods*.'

'Oh… What does that mean?'

'They're just for show. They don't work as such, they don't move like my real legs, they're just something to rest my body on…'

At this moment, the discussion about limb use was interrupted by the sudden arrival of a fluffy green coloured creature. It was a monopole-cat and the prehensile tail of this flying feline grabbed on to what it could, in order to come to rest. The finger-like roots of the tail closed over Grit's face, which reduced his speech to an incomprehensible mumble.

'Oops, sorry!' said monopole Katya, as she yanked on her own tail like she was in a tug of war competition and pulled the rest of herself down her tail. Once she had got to Grit's face, she grabbed a nearby rock with one of her paws then quickly transferred her rooted tail to the new anchor stone.

'Yeah, sorry about that,' she said again, 'still haven't got used to the stops and starts of this way of moving.'

'Who are you?' asked Jade.

'Oh, we haven't met?' the cat said with a smile and she leaned over, like a helium balloon in the wind, until she was near Jade and she held out a paw to greet her. 'I'm Katya. I'm a monopole-cat if you hadn't realised…'

'Hello?' said Jade, a bit confused as she raised a claw to make contact with Katya's furry foot, 'But you're green!'

'Yes I am!' said Katya proudly.

'But aren't you supposed to be like, red?' Jade asked.

'Ah, well,' Katya began, 'it's a complicated story and I'm not even sure I've got to the bottom of it. But when this is all over, we will have a better chance to get acquainted. You must be Jade?'

'I am,' said Jade, surprised, 'how do you know – I mean I've not met you before.'

'I recently met your father, Elvis.'

'Really?! Where was this?'

'Ooh… about 30km above the surface of Mars… a very kind and charming tortle…'

'Up in the air?! What?!'

'Another long story,' Katya dismissed with a wave and a smile then she turned to the multi-podded millipede and said: 'Hi Catapilla! I see your friends abandoned you again.'

'Story of my life,' said the flightless larva of paradise.

'And you must be Grit,' Katya greeted the young tortle, 'the Hellas Angels told me about you,' and she came back to shake his claw properly.

'Did Fionix send you?' asked Grit as they shook limbs.

'Indeed she did,' said Katya, then she did a double take and now seemed to be staring intently at Grit's nose. Grit got a bit worried and more so when Katya came close up and squinted at his slightly spiked beak.

'Masha? Is that you?'

'Hi Kat,' waved the tiny pyrite captain and Kat absentmindedly waved back.

'What are you doing here?!' she asked Masha

'That's *my* long story, sister,' said the symbiotic tortle louse, 'like one of yours. I'll tell it sometime…'

'Well I just saw Ruby – from a distance mind you, as I was coming here and, well, she looked a little lost…'

'Oh…'

'We can talk about this in a moment, but first, the reason why I came…'

Masha was clearly distracted by hearing that her vessel, well her *previous* vessel, was not doing well, but her worries now had to wait until the mission was explained.

Catapilla, Jade and Grit faced Kat as she drifted gently from side to side on the end of her tail. Kat was gently pushed by the breeze, pulled by the field and tensed up by the tension in her tail that was tethered to the ground as she described the situation.

'So yes,' Katya explained, 'Fionix wants you guys to keep following Hanksie to make sure he's not getting up to any mischief.'

'Well he was travelling north-west when we last saw him,' explained Jade, pointing the way with one of her forearms.

'And he still is,' confirmed Katya, 'the Hellas Angels spotted him heading for Cydonia.'

'Is that where the ship from Earth is going to land?'

'We don't know yet,' said Katya with a sigh, 'but that's something I'm hoping to find out on my next mission.'

'How do you find out something like that?' Grit asked with interest, 'Obviously before it gets here!'

'Well,' said Katya with a wry smile, 'it involves a box or two and a little bit of quantum witch craft.'

'Which craft?' quizzed Jade.

'Yea, *which craft* is going to land *where*! Just my little joke. I can't tell you anymore as it will break the spell.'

'Okay,' agreed Jade, 'so we continue tracking this crazy Gravity Artist then?'

'Indeed,' confirmed Katya 'and if by chance one of the landers *is* making a surprise trip to Cydonia, well at least you guys will be there.'

'And what would we do if this Earth ship did arrive?' Jade asked with a little concern.

'Oh just keep the crazy folk like Hanksie out of the way. Earth mustn't find any life here. But don't worry. We'll be sending reinforcements once we know for sure.'

'Okay,' said Jade, 'well good luck with your mission.'

'And you too.'

'Excuse me Katya…'

Katya, Jade and Catapilla turned their attentions to Grit's nose.

'Yes Masha?'

'You say you saw Ruby?'

'Yes, skulking on the edge of the Hellas basin. Why?'

'Are you going back that way?'

'Yes but in a convoluted path!' said Katya with a laugh, 'You know I have to do some field line dancing.'

Masha then turned and leaned over the top of Grit's nose to catch his eye.

'Permission to ask a request, sir?' said Masha quite formally.

'Oh, er, okay, um captain,' replied Grit, a little taken off guard.

'I realise I have only recently come on board and you have been most kind in making me welcome sir, but I feel concerned that my previous vessel is in danger of becoming a wreck. I would like to track her down if you would allow me, sir.'

'Oh, er,' began Grit, not used to having such authority, though knowing at the same time Masha could just as easily do what the hell she wanted, 'well if you think you can make a difference captain.'

'It would only be temporary sir, until I make sure that Ruby is okay. I will be leaving most of my crew members...' and as she said this, Masha looked in their direction where some stood huddled towards the back of Grit's head, '... and if they don't each give you a helping hand, then I'll cut them off and give you their hands anyway, sir...'

The crew of pyrites took a small step back and huddled a bit closer together on hearing this and hid their hands behind their backs at the same time.

'Well that's very kind of you to dismember your crew just for me,' said Grit, a bit shocked at the threat of violence, 'but if we're just keeping an eye on Hanksie, then help required will be minimal.'

'Thank you sir for your permission,' and Masha gave a slight bow then turned back to Katya.

'Would you be willing to drop me off at the last place you saw Ruby?'

'Of course Masha!' said Katya with delight. 'You're like a sister to me!'

'Thank you ma'am,' said Masha, keeping in character and also giving the monopole-cat a slight bow too. 'Permission to come aboard?'

'Granted,' said Katya, who also saluted as part of the act.

Masha bounded off Grit's nose and after a few leaps was already entering her soul sister's green fur. A handful of her most loyal crew also hopped across to join her.

Masha turned to the first two, with a loaded pointing finger in one hand and three sharp blades in the others.

'You behave yourself Piccolo, and you Terry, or you won't be men of arms for quite some time!'

'Aye aye Cap'n!' they both shouted.

'AH HAAR!' cried the others.

'AH HAAR!' replied Piccolo and Terry the Terrible, as they turned to face their shipmates and shook their fists in the air.

Katya turned back to Jade, Grit and Catapilla and waved, before flashing a few other colours, becoming reddish then shooting off along the local lines, arcing high into the air then shooting off over the horizon.

Catapilla sighed.

'Cydonia, here we come,' she said with little enthusiasm.

The pre-pupating bird of paradise turned her head and started to walk north-west. The rest of her body turned slowly like a slinky following its falling end. Grit and Jade also turned and began the long trek along the North West Passage.

'Raffi?' Jade called out.

'Ma'am?'

'Do what you can to keep him warm.'

'Aye aye.'

'Don't worry about that,' squeaked Minisilver, 'if I become frozen, well I'll melt again when the sun next comes up.'

'My dad says us tortles are like pressure cookers,' Jade explained, 'as we digest the rocks we've eaten. The pyrites can redirect the heat that comes out of my pressure valves and keep you warm enough to stay fluid. Plus they have a forge back there for making their weapons.'

'Why thank you.'

* * * * *

It was nighttime in the Magnetic Fields of the Central Bulge and a silhouette stood tall, with fronds waving gently back and forth in Mars' fluid electromagnetic field. The electrostatic plant that was once the headstone of Sailor Swift's tomb was the second to open its eyes in the darkness. The eyes squinted and looked purposefully off into the distance. Let us call her Ephanie for the moment.

Determination came across her face as she made up her mind, assuming she had one. With effort, Ephanie strained on her body's stem, leaning first to the right. Topsoil moved, the dust fell back to the ground as she shook her left root. Then a leg-like appendage took a shaky step forward. Ephanie shifted her weight to this left limb and proceeded to tense up as she pulled her right leg out of the ground, similarly shaking loose all the Martian soil. She advanced her right 'foot' in front of her left, still a little shaky and unsteady on her feet, her two sepals held horizontally forward as if she was sleepwalking. Ephanie then took her second step. Trailing from the back of her stem were some more root-like tendrils, that were still buried in the ground, but they became uprooted like the raising of a ship's anchor with every step forward that she took. These roots seemed to widen into a kind of clump, like a ribcage made of the roots themselves, and inside was a cocoon, that was glowing in waves of faint pulsations and there was a slight, deep humming sound. For a few steps, this 'growth' was dragged along the ground like a ball and chain, but then the roots holding onto it went tense and slowly lifted the glowing package up into the air, like it was a prehensile tail. These roots arched forwards over Ephanie's head, bringing the cocoon to hang in front of her like a night light. It also looked a bit like a glowing scorpion's tail. An angler fish even.

Not far from Sailor Swift's grave stood a plant now tall and proud. It wasn't completely upright: it had a sort of hunch and leaned a little to one side. This was Starkwood's new clone that had grown from one of the remains of his cosmically zapped body a while back. The sun had now risen and Starkwood II's eyes were lit up by the warm orange sparkle of the dawn light. He tried to uproot his left side from the ground and had immense difficulty doing this. So much so that he fell onto his sepal-like hands, his stem bending near the lower end as if he was now on his hands and knees. With sepal hands gripping into the topsoil, the plant had far more purchase and managed to rip his left leg out from the ground, tearing a few dendritic ends of his roots in the process but seemingly unhurt by this minor damage. After a pause and a few deep breaths, Starkwood II repeated the process and pulled out his right foot root.

There the electric plant paused, recovering from the strain. When ready, the plant crawled – not upright like Ephanie, but still on his hands and knees – seemingly also limping in the process, if it is possible to limp when on your knees.

When Starkwood II had crawled far enough away from his graveyard birthplace and was disappearing over the local horizon, it was clear that the area he left behind was not as empty as one might have thought. Several tiny shoots had continued to appear, dotted randomly all over the ejecta area. Not one of the creatures who had been present at the time of the Cosmic Event, neither Elvis, nor Starkwood himself, nor the two Physics Police and not even the eagle eyed Fionix, none had noticed that after Starkwood had been hit by the cosmic wave of the century, several pieces of Starkwood's exploded body had floated back down to the ground. Some smoking, some just landing, apparently bereft of life, had actually started to grow roots. Maybe this was one way procreation had occurred on Mars over the ages. Or maybe this was the first time it had happened like this. Maybe this was a new kind of evolution. If Ephanie and Stark-staring-mad-Wood II were anything to go by, one might be concerned what a crop load of mutated plants might do... Actually, there was one creature that had seen the original illegal hundred million year ray: one of those QT worms. However, shortly after witnessing this law-breaking incident, he'd been picked up by an unusual monopole-cat – unusual in that it was green and, secondly, that the green cat seemed to be collecting samples of random things on her route.

* * * * *

Meanwhile, back on Earth...

Martin was perched on the telephone wire just next to his mud house, not moving a muscle, but just staring up at the creature on the roof. House was also perched next to Martin on the same telegraph cable and he too was frozen to the spot and staring at the green creature. The green creature smiled at them. Down below them, in the café square of Tourrettes, the morning business was just starting and the people below seemed completely unaware of this meeting of beings from different planets.

'I thought they had little green *men* on Mars,' said House, out of the corner of his mouth to Martin.

'Maybe they have them as well,' suggested Martin very quietly, not wanting to bring attention to himself.

'This one looks like a cat though,' said House.

'Fionix told us it would,' explained Martin.

They both looked at the green cat-like creature again with blank faces and yet again the creature smiled back as if it was from Cheshire. The creature certainly had feline features: the pointy ears and the whiskers *and* stripy fur, though the fur in this case was green. It had a cute kitten-like face and equally adorable furry green paws and with its ears, whiskers and tuft on its chin, it had a star-like face too. Behind this was a body, smaller than one might have expected for a head this size and, almost out of sight, but still visible was a curious tail, also green and fluffy, but ending in finger-like dendritic roots, as if it was a creeper that attached itself to a wall with suckers.

'Hello,' said the green cat, 'I'm Katya!'

'Please don't eat us!' said Martin instinctively, as if it was beyond his control not to.

'Why would I do that?' asked Kat, 'You're not magnetic are you?'

'Well my wife says I'm attractive…'

'You're funny,' said Katya with a smile, 'Fionix tells me you're a distant relative to a rock tortle on Mars. No?'

'You haven't eaten him have you?' Martin asked.

'What's with all this *eating* things?' said Katya, bemused, 'Has Fionix been winding you up about me?'

'No,' said Martin, 'just here cats tend to eat us birds…'

'Not my thing,' remarked Katya then she dashed forward and her prehensile tail grabbed onto the telegraph cable next to Martin and she floated just in front of the two petrified birds, taking a close look at the nervous neighbours.

'You're a *delichon urbicum* aren't you?' she asked.

'Muddist actually…' said Martin with his eyes shut, 'but just make it quick, please…'

'Fascinating how much you've evolved away from your original species,' said Katya, only just starting to pick up on the terror and panic of the two terrestrial tenants. 'Look, I know it sounds clichéd, but I do come in peace…'

'Should you be showing yourself then?' asked House,

'Oh no,' Katya realised, 'you're right,' and she quickly hopped back onto the roof and out of sight from the folk sitting at the bar below. Martin took a quick glance at them himself to see that the locals had absolutely no interest in them, then he glued his eyes back on the potential predator from another planet.

'Keeping hidden is the very reason for my mission

here,' explained Katya, focussing once again.

'So,' Martin tempted fate, 'Fionix told us you needed our help. If it's tins of cat food, then I know where the Co-op supermarket stores them, it's only a few minutes from here…'

'It's nothing to do with food,' Katya assured them.

'Okay, so what can two house martins do to help a Green Martian Cat?' asked Martin, 'we can build you a mud house if you want…'

'Oh, I'm actually a monopole-cat,' explained Katya, 'but you won't just be helping me, you're going to be helping all of *Marskind*! And we are kind Martians, honest!'

'That's sort of putting the pressure on us isn't it?' said Martin.

'Fionix thinks you're both up to the challenge,' said Katya, 'besides, she doesn't really know anyone else on the planet. Apparently, you're the last living relatives of any creature on Mars. All the others have become extinct, well, others might still exist but they're just not very good at keeping in touch…'

'Oh,' said Martin, 'well, until quite recently, all this Mars connection was just a curious family tale that my great gran used to tell me…'

'Of course,' Katya reminded herself, 'your generations don't live as long as we do. Must be odd not being around to see what happens next… I mean you spend your life learning all that stuff, then you don't have a chance to use it…'

'But don't you get bored living so long?' asked Martin, 'I mean don't you run out of things to do?'

'Not yet,' said Katya, 'look, here we are about to save a planet! I've not done that before…'

'So,' House interrupted, 'what is it that we can do to help?'

'Oh, right, yes,' said Katya, getting back to the matter in hand, 'yes, right, what I need is access to the NASA program and then use of any large radio telescope you have handy…'

12

Green, House, Effect

Fionix circled as she descended towards the edge of the Equatorial Bulge of the Syria Plateau. To the north was the Noctis Labyrinth and to the west on the distant horizon was the most southerly of the three-in-a-row volcanoes: Arsia Mons. Almost as high as Olympus Mons, Arsia made a magnificent visual detour from the normal, almost horizontal horizon on Mars.

Fionix still had her first class passenger in the form of Elvis the Rock Tortle, who was clamped on to her back and had his eyes closed and his front claws clasped together in the solemn process of prayer. Muddism had never prepared him for being so far above the ground. True, there had been claims that some tortles had mudditated so successfully that they were seen to hover a few centimetres above the comfort of Ground Zero, but not this high.

'We're coming to the edge of the ridge,' said Fionix.

'Good, let me know when we've landed please…'

'Make the most of these experiences,' suggested the bird of paradise.

'If the God of Mud had wanted tortles to fly, he wouldn't have made us love the ground so much…'

'Oh,' said Fionix, 'I can see Starkwood's plantation, there straight ahead.'

'I'll take your word for it,' said the seasoned ground dweller.

'Curious,' said his flying friend, 'it looks like the crop are playing some kind of ball game…'

As Fionix approached the ground she continued to circle, and her flight path took her just over the edge of the ridge – but she was hoping to land on the plateau itself, rather than slide painfully down the side and end in a heap at the bottom of the cliff, covered in rubble.

The crop of electrostatic plants were indeed in the middle of some unusual sports competition. It seemed to be a cross between basketball and volleyball. Of course the players couldn't move from where they were rooted, so it was a stationary basket-volley ball game – maybe vosket ball? The plants of each team were interspersed throughout the 'pitch' which was merely a central patch of the field of electrostatic plants: a rectangular space with one plant at each end standing tall and upright and crossing over sepals to create a ring through which the 'ball' could pass. Plants were either passing the ball by a bounce on the ground or thrown through the air, or swipes in a volleyball style. It was only as Fionix came in for her final approach that she noticed it wasn't a ball, but a head. Starkwood's head.

Fionix came in very low from the west, where the ridge took a sharp drop and she passed like a huge dark blanket just over the tops of the flower heads. Her wingspan was just about as big as the pitch area and the swirls that came off her wing tips twisted and sent distorting waves of air currents through the crop before she finally made contact with the ground to the east, causing a massive dust cloud over this part of the Syria Plateau.

By the time she came to rest, the waves of disturbance had died down within the electrostatic plantation.

* * * * *

'You say you have three questions?' Katya asked her Ornithological Opposites.

'Yes,' said Martin, 'so please bear with. We're new to this kind of thing.'

'Sure,' agreed the green cat, 'I can't say I've done much of this interplanetary interaction before either.'

'So, question one: what is NASA?'

'Okay,' said Katya, 'I can answer that for you,'

'Question two: what is radio?'

'Ah…'

'And question three, what is a telescope?'

'I see. Anything else?'
'Apart from those three things, we get the rest…'

* * * * *

Several hours later…

After Katya had given the two house martins a quick lesson in space travel, Galileo and the development of optical devices, oh and Maxwell and his equations, the birds were now up to speed.

'In a vacuum you say?' asked House for confirmation.

'Indeed,' said Katya, 'now, if you have no more questions, are you able to answer mine?'

'Oh, right,' Martin realised himself, 'yes, so we can. The NASA place, well that's like a long way from here, not quite the other side of the Earth, but still pretty far.'

'And the radio telescope?'

'Well,' Martin warmed as he told the tale, 'as it happens, there's flocks of birds from the north that migrate past here and something matching what you're looking for is found in Nancy, which is like the middle of France, so also pretty far away.

'Oh,' said Katya a little disappointed.

'But,' said Martin, raising a flight feather, 'you know they do talk about NASA on the TV, so you might be able to get the information that you want there…'

'And where might I find one of these *TV*s?'

'Oh you can see one in almost every home around. Just spy through the window of any house and you can listen out for when they mention your home…'

'Sounds like half a plan,' said Katya.

'Sometimes they mention NASA in the paper,' Martin added, 'they sell them down there in the bar…'

'Thanks,' said Katya, 'I'll check them out as well.'

'Then you can go back home and tell them what you've found,' said Martin.

'It doesn't quite work like that,' explained Katya.

'What, you can't get back home?

'*I* can,' said the monopole-cat, 'but the information

195

can't. That's why I need a radio telescope to send it.'

'What do you mean the *information can't*?'

'It's hard to explain,' said Katya.

'Well try us!' said House, 'we now know what a NASA is and a radio and a telescope, *and* a radio telescope!'

'And radio waves,' put in Martin.

'I will,' promised Katya, 'but first I must secure a way to get the information back to Mars, after I get it from one of those TVs…'

* * * * *

Meanwhile back in the Hellas Basin…

Ruby sat there, her chin resting on her front claws, in a pose that was certainly neither cool nor classy. But then, being by herself, there was no one to witness her dropping her guard. She sighed and stared at the two empty tortle shells in front of her, the hollow remains of Grit's mum and dad, only too recently violated by the inconsiderate Herman. Well, it was a few months ago now since the squirrely squatter had been chased out by a very upset Grit, before he hijacked Great Uncle Syd, but Ruby hadn't really moved since then. She was still pondering on the fact that she had been dissed by her own pyrite captain. That hadn't happened often – in fact this was the first time for her. Masha had grown up under Ruby's cooling influence and it had just never seemed a likely scenario that she would leave. Ruby was both saddened that she'd lost the respect of her symbiotic side kick, but also impressed that Masha had stood up to the powerful influence that Ruby herself had wielded over her sailing soul mate. Female pyrite captains were few and far between, and any that succeeded to captainship usually had to have more balls than their male counterparts.

Ruby sighed again. She had been mean to Grit, though she wouldn't admit it to him or anyone who dared to ask her for a confession. She looked at the skeletal remains of his deceased parents and made a decision.

'It's the least I can do,' she said, then raised her head and got back up onto her four feet, gave herself a little shake to get her limbs working again, then started digging.

* * * * *

A week later

'So,' Katya asked, 'have you got any plans for the immediate future?'

'Me?' asked Martin, 'well, just some repairs to the house again, see top left-hand corner… some ants started making their nest in the mud and now it's crawling with them.

'And you?' said Katya, turning to the other *delichon urbicum*.

'Me?' asked House, 'No, not going anywhere for the time being, no going south, nothing, just hanging around here.'

'Well,' suggested Katya, 'how would you guys like to visit the United States of America?'

'The *what* of *what*?!'

'I've got to go and see a man about a planet,' said Katya.

'When?'

'Now!'

'Um, how long will it take?

'As long as it takes to send the information…'

House looked at an imaginary watch on his wing and said 'Okay, but how do you intend to get there?'

'A way that works so much better here than on Mars!' said Katya with delight. 'Your magnetic field is way stronger than ours. I just need to make a few adjustments…'

'Okay,' said House, not sure what he was letting himself into, but he had to admit that his life had become a bit more interesting since the green cat had arrived.

'I travel along magnetic field lines,' Katya started explaining.

'Oh, said House, 'is that like how we travel along these telephone lines?'

'No,' Katya dismissed at first, but then reflected on the question, 'Not exactly, but well maybe in a way. Your telephone line is physical. Fields lines are... are... well they're not physical, but it's like they're really there...'

'Sounds like the subject for another lesson...' said House, clearly keen to find out.

'Sure,' agreed Katya, 'we can do that on the journey.'

'I've heard about some magnetic train,' Martin mentioned, 'like it hovers just above the ground and it carries people around.'

'Yes,' Katya sparked up, 'it's a bit like that, but we're going to be a bit more than just hovering above the ground...'

'So what do we have to do to get there?' asked House.

'Right,' Katya explained, 'you guys will need to hold tight to my tail, or climb on my back and hang on for dear life... or both... yes, do both, and this will be from the moment I change colour until I change back... or we land, or we get into trouble...'

'Sure we can do... *trouble*?' House began, 'Trouble?! Is that likely?'

'Flying always carries a risk,' Katya pointed out, 'well you two should know that...'

The two birds looked at each other, shrugged then nodded and thus their collective fates were sealed.

'Hop on then,' invited Katya and the domestic duo climbed on board.

'Do we get anything to eat on this flight?' asked Martin with a wry smile.

'At the speed we'll be going,' Katya explained, 'you'll just have to open your mouths and the wind will do the rest... you do eat insects don't you? Now seatbelts on.'

Katya felt her two passengers' claws dig more deeply into her fur and they each raised a wing to give the thumbs up. Katya then squinted like she was attempting some telekinesis, which in a way she was, then her colour started to flip to red then blue and back to green a few times until finally settling on red and the next moment, Katya had shot off the tiled roof of Madame Helene's house and headed in a southerly direction at quite a high speed.

WAAAAAAAAAAAAAA!

'But I thought you said the USA was west, not south!?' asked Martin, surveying the geography below.

'We have to follow the field lines,' Katya explained, 'which means going south first, then north a moment later.'

'But isn't it cold in the north?' asked House.

'Well, cold for you, yes...'

'But we normally fly *south* to find the warm,' House explained

'And once we're north?' Martin asked.

'Then we go south,' Katya replied casually.

Both the birds looked behind them and saw their home village of Tourrettes being left behind. The familiar clock tower standing at the top-most point, a few streets south of Madame Helene's house.

'Won't we end up where we started,' House asked, 'going north then going south?'

'No,' Katya corrected him. 'Let me explain with a puzzle.'

'Oh I like brain teasers!' said House with excitement.

The two birds stopped looking south at their disappearing home then looked between the ears of Katya to the north.

'When we get to the North Pole, we'll have to walk a short way west then ride back on a different field line until we get to Pasadena...'

'Anyway,' said Martin, 'it's going to take a while so we could have our first lesson on quantum mechanics and a famous cat in a box.'

'Well you're both familiar with the idea that an object can be in the same place at two different times?'

'We got that,' said House, 'that would have described me sitting on the telephone cable, and not moving.'

'Correct and you've heard that you cannot be in two

different places at the same time?'

'Yes,' confirmed House, 'that was a consequence of that guy's theory of relativity.'

'Indeed, but it should be clear that you *can* have an object in two different places in two different times?'

The birds had to think about this. It sounded fine but they both felt there must be a catch in it.

* * * * *

Later on Earth…

'… so that's the story so far…' said Katya as they came into land somewhere in the Qausuittuq National Park on Bathurst Island (west of Greenland).

'Shouldn't *you* be in a box or something?' asked Martin.

'It's a *metaphorical* box,' explained Katya with a smile.

'Oh,' thought Martin, 'so it doesn't have to be *cardboard* then?'

Katya looked at him, not sure how to proceed, but House butted in.

'Where are we?' he enquired.

'Oh, this,' said Katya 'is the North Pole. Well, *Magnetic* North Pole,' and with that, her reddish colour flipped back to green and she brushed off the snow that had frosted to her on landing. 'Isn't it beautiful here?'

'It's bloody cold,' said Martin, burying himself a little further into Katya's warm fur.

'Feels a bit more like home…' and Katya smiled.

13

QT Worm And The Cat Among the Birds

A few hours, and two holes later, Ruby stopped. She waddled over to what looked like the father's remains, grabbed the edge of his carapace just behind his skull with her beak, then started dragging his bones towards the hole, stopped dragging, then went to the butt end and slowly pushed the deceased dad down the slope she'd made into his shallow grave. She looked at him, sighed again then did the same to the mother's remains, until the mother was lying next to her husband in their side-by-side resting places.

Digging holes came instinctively to Ruby, what with being a creature that, should she ever decide to have offspring (not that she ever wanted to), had evolved to lay eggs in the soil. The next step also came naturally to her, kicking the soil back over the bodies until they were hidden under the two mounds of amber sand. She also pushed a few rocks with her nose into a random pattern, onto or around the mounds, to make it look less artificial, then stopped to look at her work.

'Um...' she started out loud, a little awkwardly, 'Mister and Misses, um, *Grit*, ... I guess it was pretty insensitive of me to mock your son for his loss. That was uncool. I should have known better. Er, having lost my mum the same way, I know how it feels...'

A tear started to form in Ruby's eye, which froze immediately and fell to the ground with a pinging sound.

'I think you must have been good parents because you protected your son from danger and saved his life... and you sacrificed yourselves for him. Grit was ready to go and do some good himself, so you raised him well too. I think you would be proud of him...'

There was another pinging sound.

'I hope you find peace in that great mud bath in the

sky or whatever it is supposed to be that we believe in.
And don't tell Grit I did this, or I will never live it
down...'

Ruby had one final thing to do before she left. Cover
her tracks. She plodded over to the original resting place
of the passed-on parents and started to roughen up the
smoothed grooves she'd made when she dragged them to
their graves. As she ruffled up the patch where the
mother had been, she noticed a small object just sticking
out of the soil. It looked odd. She leaned closer, it was
slightly green with spikes, like one of the mines they had
floating in the sea on Earth during a World War, but it
was only a few centimetres across. Could this be the
hedgehog egg that Grit had ranted about?

Ruby gently closed her jaws to grab it and slowly
pulled it out of the ground. It felt strangely heavier than
she had expected, until she noticed, biting onto the
hedgehog egg and dangly beneath it, was a tiny, baby
rock tortle.

* * * * *

Meanwhile, later on Earth...

'Can't you move any faster?' said House, 'it's so cold
I'm going to change my name from *House* to *Igloo*!'

'I'm not really built for the Cat Walking,' admitted
Katya, as she literally pussyfooted her way over the
snow-covered terrain of Bathurst Island, 'I'm usually
hanging in the wind on the end of my tail, or just flying
through the air, wherever the field lines take me.'

The two house martins were riding on the back of the
green monopole-cat, like they were cowbirds, but the
winter wasteland scenery couldn't have been further
removed from the hot dry scenery of the real Wild West.

'You don't look well,' observed Martin.

'Actually,' admitted Katya, 'I'm not used to this
heavier weight that I feel on Earth...'

'Are you saying you don't understand the *gravity* of the
situation?' said Martin.

'Oh,' Katya smiled weakly, 'so much like your distant cousin.'

'I can be funny as well,' said House feeling a bit left out of the praise.

'Go on then,' Katya invited him, 'say something to raise my spirits, because to be honest I am finding this hard going...'

There was a pause.

'... don't let *gravity* get you down?'

'Nice one...' said Katya feebly, 'five points to House, er *House...*'

'How much further is it?' asked Martin.

'In my reckoning,' said Katya, a little short of breath, 'a couple more kilometres west. We should ... then be next to the lines that pass through North America. We can hop on one flux route and ... get all the way down to California...'

'What if *we* carried you?' Martin suggested. House looked at him sideways

'*We* carry *her*?!' House said in dismay, 'Have you got brain freeze?! Do you realise how heavy she is? Like two and a half times her Martian weight!'

'Good job House,' said Katya, 'you were listening on the journey.'

'Is that five more points then?'

'Yes, but House is right,' agreed Katya. 'With your power to weight ratios ... you could barely maintain an extended glide with me hanging on.'

'That's all we need!' said Martin. 'You could hang on to us with your tail?'

'I can do that,' Kat agreed, 'but you won't be able to lift me far.'

'No,' Martin said, now using one of his flight feathers to draw a diagram in the snow, 'you do your magnetic polarity switch thing to blue...'

'From here, that would take us straight to the South Pole, right down the middle of your Atlantic Ocean!'

'Wait, not finished,' Martin pointed out. 'You said the field lines here at the pole are going almost vertical no?'

'Oh yes,' Katya confirmed, 'the only way is up!'

'Well, we go up first using your magnetic repulsion, then you switch your polarity to neutral...'

'But then we'd fall,' Katya said, a little lost, fatigue knocking off several IQ points.

'Yes!' Martin butted in, 'but not quite! I got it! We, me and House here, we then flap our butts off, and head west, so we fall *slower* but go *sideways* at the same time...'

'Oh!' Katya realised, 'You're right!'

'And then you switch your polarity again,' Martin continued 'and go up...'

'Then green and we glide west!' House finished, finally catching on.

'Yes,' Katya reflected, 'up then west, up then west, until we've moved far enough along and I can switch to blue for the final leg down to Pasadena!'

'And that way,' House qualified, 'you won't have to do much work, because it's the magnetic field that will be supplying the energy!'

'Well done!' said Katya with delight, 'You must be the best students I've ever had!'

Both birds puffed out their chests with pride.

'You'll be getting your doctorates in physics in no time!' said Katya.

'Oh,' realised Martin, 'so I'll be called *Doctor* Martin!'

'Yes!' cried House, 'and I'll be *Doctor* House!'

'Let's get going before I collapse with exhaustion then!'

* * * * *

A little later and a little further west...

'So, are you feeling up to it?' Martin asked the fatigued magnetic feline.

'I could really do with a Cat Nap,' said Katya.

'Well,' said House, 'you can sleep on the way, and that's doctor's orders!'

'Can you stay in southern polarity while you sleep?'

Martin asked just to make sure.

'Usually,' said Katya, yawning a little.

'Right,' said House, 'let's check we have everything. You've got your two house martins?' said Martin.

'Check!' said Katya.

'Then we're ready for take-off!' said Martin.

'California...' said House, '... here we come!'

A few clicks and the sound of a misfiring engine and Katya's colour changed several times before settling on blue and in a fraction of a second, Katya took off, almost vertically and there was the sound of two house martins screaming like scaredy-cats. Katya's own facial features were pulled back by both the acceleration and air drag and the ripples of air currents ran outwards from her nose.

Once they had reached a steady airspeed and Katya had even let herself drop to lower field lines to keep on course for Pasadena, the craft and crew started to relax.

'So Katya,' asked Doctor House, 'can I ask you a question?'

'...you just did,' she said, almost nodding off.

'Clever,' said House, 'okay, can I ask you another question?'

'... you just did...'

'Got it! Can I ask you two questions?'

'Yes. One left!'

'Right, you know this ability you have to switch polarity?'

'Very handy,' Katya commented.

'So you can just keep changing poles and hence go backwards and forwards along the field lines, and not need energy...'

'That sounded almost like a question but I'll just assume it was qualifying the situation.'

'Well aren't you getting all this energy for nothing? Aren't you breaking the Conservation Law?'

'How do you mean?'

'You know,' House tried to explain, 'like that Maxwell's Devil you were telling us about...'

'Ah,' said Katya, realising, 'I think there's still some confusion and that Devil is all about the laws of thermodynamics. But let me get a bit of rest and we can talk about it another time, okay?'

* * * * *

A bit later and further south...

'But what I don't understand,' said House, as they continued on their magic green carpet ride across North America, 'is that Katya is able to flip her polarity back and forth the way she does...'

'Well don't wake her,' said Martin, peering over the sleeping Kat's ears to check on her, 'she needs to conserve her energy...'

'That's exactly what I mean. It's all about energy...'

'Look,' said Martin, 'we now know that the Earth flips its magnetic polarity every so often. She told us all about it in lesson three I think.'

'I know,' said House, 'I remember. And she also explained that the sun does the same too. Those field lines getting all wound up as the sun rotates then they snap and all those sunspot souths becomes norths and norths becomes souths.'

'So why don't you think Katya should be able to do it then?'

'The Earth takes thousands of years before it flips while the sun takes, what was it, eleven years. That's not instantaneous like her.'

'Her mind is controlling it.'

'But the *energy*! Obeying the laws of energy! It's like she can be a perpetual motion machine!'

'A *purr* petual motion machine you mean!'

'Be serious!'

'Okay, but what do you mean?'

'Look, she could be sitting on the North Pole and pick up a rock, then flip her polarity and get repelled south and she could drop the rock on top of a mountain on the equator say, then flip polarity and go back and pick up another rock from the North Pole and flip again and add that to the mountain top and just keep doing that nonstop. You know what that means?'

'A taller mountain?'

'Yes, okay, but who's doing the work? *Something* has to!'

'Oh, I see, well I guess it's the magnetic field she's sitting in at the time then...'

'If it is, then it's losing energy. If not, then she's breaking the conservation laws.'

'Do you want to report her to the Physics Police then!?' said Martin with a laugh.

'Do they *exist*?!'

'A good question! Hey House?'

'Yes?'

'Do you remember when all we used to talk about was, like how much mud we needed to fix our houses? And whether Madame Helene was going to wear those tights with a ladder in them?'

'She was repairing them when we left... oh and did you fix the ant damage?'

'My wife said I couldn't go on this trip unless I did.'

'This bigger picture puts everything into perspective doesn't it?'

'Once you've got the smaller jobs done, yes.'

'Hmmm,' said House, 'considering how long we've been field line surfing, and noting our mean air speed, we must have crossed the Canadian border into the United States by now.'

'Lessons twelve and twenty six.'

'Spherical geometry and the equations of motion mastered!'

'Three quarters of the way there then,' commented Martin. 'Shouldn't we be dropping to lower field lines?'

'Already taken care of,' said House, 'I was tilting our *Kitty-Hawk* downwards while you were asleep. That lesson seventeen on aerodynamics helped a lot...'

'Well done Doctor House!'

'You're welcome Doctor Martin!'

* * * * *

Ruby held the spikey green ball between the claws of her right forefoot. She held it up and inspected the mini dust-covered tortle that was still suspended from the ball. Several of Ruby's pyrite crew scrambled along her arm and over the ball to inspect the recently buried tortle, swords and weapons raised and ready to attack.

'Okay, stand down men,' said Ruby a little bemused, 'I don't think…'

'But it could be dangerous!' cried one of the weapon wielding lice.

'It could be a trap!' shouted another.

'Like what?' asked Ruby.

'Um, er a Trojan Tortle?'

Ruby sighed.

'Where's Masha when I need her?' she asked rhetorically. One of the pyrites put their hand up. Ruby gave him a look that could have killed at fifty paces and he quickly withdrew his hand before he lost it.

Ruby took a deep breath and blew on the tiny tortle, the wind carrying away the camouflaging copper coloured coating to reveal a curious patchwork of yellow and orange and red and even almost black areas, as if the youngster had dressed up as a pizza for a party.

'Hello?' asked Ruby to her motionless micro-friend, not sure if the tortle was still alive, or just frozen. She had a pretty good idea why she'd been found here – a pretty knee-jerk reaction for a parent tortle to protect their offspring by burying them in the sand and then sitting on top of them to stop the deadly Eschers from devouring the family tree. The chance that Grit's mum had come to rest just where a completely unrelated tortle was already hiding was very slim. Nor that this baby tortle happened to be waddling past at a later date and sought refuge under a dead tortle's carcass, though that was more likely. But Grit talking about his hedgehog egg and his odd reactions when he'd been talking about his parents' demise hinted at something.

'You're safe now,' Ruby offered the toddler, in case it was still playing dead. Then the yellow-flecked chelonian opened an eye, which caused the handful of pyrites to jump and back off.

'Hello,' said Ruby again, now that they'd made eye contact.

'Hey…' the little lemon coloured female tortle started, but the moment she stopped biting the hedgehog egg to speak, she was no longer hanging safely from an object attached to the ground and gravity did its usual trick. Ruby caught her with her other forearm.

'Got you!' and she smiled a hopefully reassuring smile to the young tortle.

'Thank you miss,' said the youngster, 'but where's my mum and dad?'

Ah, thought Ruby, the tough talk straight away!

'What's your name sweetie?' she asked, going against her instincts to be cocky and smart-arsed, then she noticed her pyrite crew members were already sweeping out the dust between the plates of this youngster and doing all the first aid activities they were supposed to do as part of their unwritten symbiotic contracts. This momentarily impressed her but she tried not to show it.

'My mum and dad named me Sulphie-Rose after all my pretty shell colours…'

'And that's a pretty name for a pretty tortle…'

Ruby hated herself for talking like this, but she just wanted to keep the youngster calm.

'You're pretty too,' said Sulphie-Rose, which made Ruby feel even more uncomfy and she wished she could just go back to her normal unpleasant mode.

'Well thank you Sulphie-Rose, I'm Ruby.'

'I was playing hide and seek with my mum and dad,' Sulphie-Rose explained, 'when there was a big sand storm…'

'Oh, um do you have a brother called Grit?'

'Gritty, yes! Oh did you find him before me?!'

'Um, well yes…'

'So I won! I must tell mummy, where is she?'

Ah, the talk again. Not easy. Certainly not for one as young as...

'How old are you Sulphie-Rose?'

'I'm three million and three quarters... Though, how long have I been hiding?'

'Oh, maybe only a couple of years I think...'

'So I'm almost four!' she shouted with delight, having tried to add using her claws. Ruby decided not to correct her but was then snapped out of her thoughts by...

'Mum! Mum!' from Sulphie-Rose, as she looked from her vantage point on Ruby's upturned paw to try and find her parents.

'Dad!? I'm here!' then Sulphie-Rose noticed the two slight depressions in the soil where her parents had been and looked confused at Ruby.

'Look I need to tell you a story about your parents...'

'Oh I love stories! They used to tell them to me before I went to sleep...'

Oh schist and crack, thought Ruby, who had always felt herself to be a pretty tough nut. How do you give the dreaded talk to such a cute and young child as Sulphie-Rose? Ruby's only saving grace was that she too had lost her mother in a similar way, but she'd been much older and certainly not as cute.

'What are these two mounds of dirt?' asked Sulphie-Rose, snapping Ruby back to the present unpleasant reality.

'Well –'

'They weren't here before...' Sulphie-Rose pointed out, 'Oh! Are my parents hiding under them?!'

'Okay,' Ruby said as a kind of defeat, 'tell you what Sulphie-Rose, I'm going to put you on my back and we can take you to your brother...'

'Gritty! Yay! I'm going to tell him I beat him!'

* * * * *

A few days later in Pasadena...

'This is very kind of you,' said Katya sincerely, as she inspected her new temporary home.

'Not at all,' said House, blushing a little under his feathers.

'It's the least we could do,' said Martin. 'Besides you do have to keep out of sight during the daytime.'

'This must have taken ages,' said Katya, inspecting the mud wall to her left.

'Well you were asleep for a day or two since we arrived, so we had a bit of time…'

Katya tapped the mud wall with her knuckles and it made a nice solid thudding sound.

'Don't tap too hard,' said House light heartedly, 'though I reinforced it with some straw, as we're not used to supporting lodgers with your dimensions…'

Katya looked to her right at the brick wall of the building to which the mud house was attached and above her was the overhang of the roof. There was barely enough room to fit a… House Cat, but it felt snug and secure and both House and Martin were standing in the remaining part of their top floor 'outside' apartment.

'So,' Katya asked, pointing at the wall, 'is this the JPL building?'

'Pasadena, California, yes,' said House proudly.

'Wow!' said Katya, impressed, 'you got us down here! Why didn't you wake me?'

'Felt you needed to recover, ma'am' said Martin. 'Besides you taught us well, so landing was a piece of cake.'

'Great. Fionix and Elvis are going to be so proud of you.'

'Happy to help save your planet,' said House humbly.

'Do we get a medal?'

'If Mars lives to tell the tale, yes,' said Katya, 'Now, we have to get that all-important information about the landing sites. We have to locate the office that has the plans and…'

'Already done,' said House, not able to hide his smug feelings.

'What?!'

'Yes,' explained Martin, 'well, we did a bit of scouting

211

around earlier and found out some names and what they do and where they work in the building and so on.'

'What you just walked in? I thought they might have more security than that.'

'Oh they do for the people, but an open window to keep the team cool and a bird can easily fly in and snoop around.'

'Two birds even!' said House.

'So you found out where the plans are?!'

'We think so,' said House, 'we found out the Viking Mission Director is someone called Tom Young,'

'And the Viking Project Manager,' said Martin, 'is Jim, would you believe, *Martin*! Jim Martin! What's the chances of that?!'

'I guess you could work that out now!' said Katya.

'Lesson thirty-three,' said House.

'Maybe he's another distant relative?!' joked Martin.

'Well done guys! So, when do we go find the landing plans?'

'Perhaps you should stay resting,' suggested House. 'We could go when they sign off work this afternoon…'

'I'm okay thanks,' Katya insisted, 'and besides, it might be better if I look at the maps, it is my home planet after all.'

'Okay,' agreed Martin, 'but we're coming with you…'

* * * * *

Later that evening, the lights were switching off all over the JPL complex. Doors were closing, locks were turning and windows were shutting. Staff were leaving the building and getting into their cars and heading back to their own homes. House and Martin were watching, then made the decision.

'Right it's time,' said Martin, 'let's go!'

Katya gave a nod of agreement and the two birds hopped out of their mud hut under the flat roof overhang and darted back and forth, waiting for Katya to emerge and catching a quick light meal of gnats and mosquitos on the way. She poked her head out first.

'What floor?'

'There's a window still open on the third floor, just round the corner,' said House.

With that, Katya put her head out of the tightfitting, one bedroom, mud condo, and cracked some of the mud frame.

'Oops, sorry,' she said apologetically, realising they must have built it round her. At the same time, her prehensile tail poked out its dendritic end, which automatically felt round for the building wall and clamped on with its little suckers. This allowed Katya to swing her body out and hang her claws on the rim of a nearby closed window. She then alternated between unsticking her tentacular tail to move to the next suitable sticking place then unhook her claws to swing to the next ledge and so on. The two birds flew by several times to make sure Katya didn't lose her footing or her energy. They reached the open window and the birds landed on the window ledge to look in.

'Coast is clear!' and in they flew. Katya landed on the ledge, looked round, even outside just to make sure no one was looking up. Her presence would have caused an interplanetary problem if she was seen, and probably hurry along the race to Mars to conquer and destroy it.

'I feel like a burglar,' said Katya with one final glance outside,

'Ha!' said Martin 'A cat burglar!'

Inside, House and Martin flew along the corridors while Katya bounded along the ground like a kitten until they got to the office with the name plaque 'Jim Martin V.P. Manager'.

'Maybe he's an *Uncle*!' said Martin.

Katya reached up to the door handle of the office with her ever-versatile tail and turned it.

'Locked...' she said.

'Blast!' said House, and he flew up to the glass panel above the door and looked in, 'Windows closed too, so we can't get in that way.'

'I don't suppose you can get through a locked door?'

asked Martin. 'what with your box trick and your collapsing wave function…'

'Sorry,' admitted Katya, 'not one of my superpowers I'm afraid, though I could if I was a Cutie Worm…'

Katya realised something then fumbled in the folds of her fur, pulled out her notebook and pen and put them to one side, then rummaged further and threw out a small Martian rock, a snowball from the North Pole and then a cicada hopped out and half-flew, half-jumped across the corridor.

'It's amazing what things accumulate if you're not tidy,' she said to her curious best birdies, 'Ah! Here it is…'

With that she produced what appeared to be a worm-like larva, small, off-white and segmented and it had a very slight luminous glow. It was nothing compared to her powerful, traffic light green brightness, but it shone nonetheless.

'Good job I hung onto you,' said Katya to the worm.

'This is a *vermis eorum suffodiendis cuniculis*,' she explained to her friends, 'or Cutie Worm as it's commonly called.

'Hey!' said the worm, 'I'm more than just a species!'

'Oh sorry,' said Katya, genuinely remorseful, 'I didn't mean to be rude. I'm actually amazed at what you can do…'

'That's as may be,' said the Cutie Worm, 'but I do have a name you know.'

'Sorry,' said Katya, 'please accept my apologies and do introduce yourself…'

'Well, I'm Dmitry…'

'Nice to meet you,' said Katya.

'And don't call me Dim,' said the worm with attitude, 'it wasn't even funny the first time I heard it.'

'I shall make sure I don't,' Katya promised, 'now if you've forgiven me, I need a favour from you.'

'Depends what it is,' said Dmitry, 'but I can probably guess what.'

'What's he on about?' asked Martin,

'Well you'd never guess what this worm can do,' Katya started, 'hey maybe I can show you...'

'No!' snapped Dmitry, 'You're not going to do the swallowing trick. *Everyone* does the swallowing trick. I'm fed up with it!'

'What's the swallowing trick?' said Martin. 'Besides. We're house martins, not swallows – everyone makes that mistake.'

'Okay, I won't do the swallowing trick,' assured Katya, then turned to her friends, 'but it *is* good!'

'What do you want me to do then?' asked Dmitry.

'Right,' said Katya then turned to the birds, 'well gentlemen, you remember my lesson forty-three?'

'What, about how particles can get through a barrier by letting their probability wave extend beyond the barrier?' said Martin.

'That's the one! Five points to House um, Martin! Well This Cutie worm, sorry, *Dmitry*, operates on that principle, so if I take him and push him against the door...'

'Wait,' Dmitry started, but Katya was over enthusing about the peculiar property of this special species.

'Dmitry's probability wave will first start to enter the fabric of the door...'

'Stop pushing me please...'

'That's fascinating,' said Martin.

'Yes and normally Dmitry's too big to ever stand a chance of making it through...'

'Can you stop?!'

'But with a high enough pressure, a large enough portion of his wave function will stick out the other side of the door and if we wait long enough, he himself will suddenly appear on the other side of the door!'

'You don't need to do this!' Dmitry shouted.

'What?'

'I said you don't need to do this!'

'But we need you on the other side of the door so you can unlock it for us.'

'There's an easier way,' said Dmitry, a little fed up.

'Really? I worked out you need a pressure of three hundred kilopascals to raise the probability to getting through in the next few hours…'

'What about exerting *no* pressure in the next few seconds and let me just crawl through the gap *under* the door…'

They all looked down and finally noticed the crack. Then they looked at Dmitry and saw his body was of a similar size.

'Oh, sorry,' said Katya, 'I was caught up in the moment…'

'Right,' said Dmitry flatly and Katya gently put the Cutie Worm on the floor.

Dmitry gave them all a wilting look, sighed, then headed for the crack. It was a tight fit but his body easily changed shape like a tiny little sausage balloon. There then followed an almost silent slither as he made his way up the door on the other side. The Save Mars Team heard a click and next moment the door was open.

The Brainy Birds flew into the office of Jim Martin and made a quick scout round, while Katya prowled in more gracefully, her tail raised up behind her and high enough for Dmitry (the quantum tunnelling worm with attitude) to wriggle on to the tip and have a worm's eye view.

'Thanks, Dmitry,' said Katya, making sure she named names and showed gratitude.

'That didn't hurt did it?' said the not-so cutie worm, like he was carrying around a chip on his shoulder the size of Phobos for all the years of his kind being used as a party trick.

'Over here!' shouted House, fluttering then landing on top of the filing cabinet. The others joined him and with Katya's green glow they were able to see the title on each drawer.

Katya turned to Dmitry before they started: 'If we find this cabinet is locked, can we ask you to do some quantum tunnelling for us?' and she tried to smile an ice-melting smile. Dmitry sighed.

'Okay, but if it were up to *me*, I would use the keys that have been left in the lock…'

They all saw them and realised this little quantum shifting invertebrate had other superpowers than just walking through walls – like actually observing the world around him. Katya hooked her tail on one of the top-drawer handles and lifted herself up. She had no problem pulling the top drawer open. House and Martin scanned each pocket folder until it was clear that that particular cupboard was bare of what they wanted. They moved to the next drawer down but came up empty handed again. Third drawer and bingo! A folder marked 'Proposed Viking Landing Sites'.

House and Martin picked up the thin pocket folder and carried it to the desk. Katya followed and stood over the open set of papers, acting as her very own living, angle poise lamp. Dmitry hopped off Katya's tail and onto the papers and inspected them from close up.

Papers were scrutinized then pages turned over until they came to the last one: a map. Of Mars! Both Katya and Dmitry recognised their home planet and this raised their curiosity level. Dmitry was crawling over the page then looked up at the rest of the team.

'Hey look!' he said 'I'm back on Mars!'

'You're funny,' said Katya.

'I'm bigger than a lung whale!' he continued, letting his harder, cynical guard down for a moment, then realised, coughed and tightened up again, 'So I see there's a date on this map…'

'How does that compare to today's date?' Katya asked.

'Well this one says 1970…' said Dmitry.

Katya looked at the desk calendar and felt disappointed.

'This is 1976 on Earth and with two Earth years to a Mars year, this map is three Martian years old…'

'What's the chance of the landing sites being the same now?'

'Not a lot,' said Martin, 'if they've sent craft there since to photograph the surface, they'll have a better idea where to land now…'

'Hang on,' said House, 'lift up the papers…'

Katya obliged and belatedly they saw that some

217

documents had been left on Jim Martin's desk.

'It's dated from three days ago,' said Martin, 'this is recent!'

'Look here!' said Dmitry and not having any limbs as such, pointed with what might have been his nose, 'a drawing of Mars!'

'It's upside down,' said Katya

'Or we are,' said Dmitry.

'Oh! Two places are marked with an 'X.''

'Buried treasure?' offered Martin.

'Well it's *precious* information we just found so I suppose you're right.'

House peered closer and read the names.

'Tiu Valley? Cydonia? You know these places?'

'Yes!' said Katya, as she collected all the other papers together and put them back in the pocket folder. House and Martin obliged and flew it back into its drawer, pushing it closed with a quick flick of their wings. Katya continued.

'Tiu Valley is at the southern entrance to the Chryse Basin and Cydonia is an area to the north…'

Suddenly the light came on in Jim Martin's Office and in walked Jim Martin. The two birds flapped around the office like two trapped frightened birds, which is what they were, while Katya had remained motionless on the desk. Her green glow was not apparent in the full brightness of the office lights and Katya let it fade to nothing in a gradual way. Dmitry was nowhere to be seen.

'What the hell?!' said Jim Martin, clearly confused and annoyed at what he saw.

Jim instinctively went and opened his office windows and picked up the papers on his desk to wave at the panicking birds to shoo them outside. In a few seconds the birds were gone. Jim shut the window, then returned his attention to the strange green furry object on his desk.

'The cleaner must have brought his kid in again,' said Jim inspecting the fluffy green toy, 'this looks like one of those, what are they called, um Marsupial Amies? But I thought they were yellow, not green…'

Jim tutted, then turned to his filing cabinet.

'Ah, my keys,' he said with delight and he was about to pull them out of the lock, then looked at the green Marsupial Amie toy, opened one of the drawers and dumped it in, slid the drawer closed and proceeded to lock it before removing his keys.

'There,' he said, then went to his desk and wrote a quick note on a large note-pad next to the landing details. 'His kid's toy safe and sound. He can pick it up tomorrow…'

Jim walked out of his office, locked his door and went back to his car, now able to drive home.

* * * * *

Ruby found herself choking up a bit, but as she lifted Sulphie-Rose to place her on the front of her carapace, just behind her own head, she took a closer look at Sulphie-Rose's shell and what her marauding pyrites were up to. When she peered closely enough at one louse with the yellow lump he had been carrying, he quickly hid it behind his back and smiled with guilt.

'What are you doing?'

'Um nothing ma'am,' said the pyrite, having been caught yellow handed.

'Show me…'

He sheepishly revealed the small yellow rock in his hand.

'Just cleaning up her shell ma'am.'

'By chipping bits off?'

The pyrite then leaned closer and cupped his hand conspiratorially.

'It be pure sulphur ma'am!' he whispered, but with the hint of a cry as if he'd struck gold.

'And she's covered with it!' cried another one.

'We could man our weapons for millennia with this!' said a third.

'Put it all back,' said Ruby sternly.

'What?! But we,'

'We're not stealing it,' she said with conviction.

'But that's what we've been doing since *forever*,' said one of the pyrites.

'Yea, well not this time. Put it all back.'

'Can we not even take some of the *orange* sulphur ma'am?'

'No.'

'The *red*?'

Ruby didn't answer.

'The really dodgy looking *black* sulphur then?'

'They're funny!' said Sulphie-Rose and she giggled a little. 'Mummy told me I fell into a hot sulphur pit when I was born, which is why I'm covered with it. She said I'm special. Where is she?'

Ruby helped the orphan up the last step to her shell and said to her own lice: 'Make sure she stays in one piece, or some of you will end up in a sulphur pit yourselves,' then she took a deep breath again and considered using the Muddist teachings she'd pretty much ignored when her Dad was being uncool and telling her about it all. Something about the present being the most important time. Ruby had never bothered to make any future preparations and she wasn't tied to the past, so she tended to agree with her dad on that point. Then the second point; who was the most important person – which to Ruby, meant herself, but the goodie-goodie-four-claws like her sister Jade would have said 'the person in front of you'. Ruby winced when she thought of her sickly sweet sibling. Ruby would only have agreed with 'the person in front of you' if she, Ruby, had been standing in front of a reflective surface and looking at her own reflection. And the third thing, what was it, the most important thing to do? *Care* was the right answer, but Ruby always used to shout out 'not to care!' when she was a child. This made her smile when she recalled the time that her mother was telling her off and she said to her mum: 'I don't care', which landed her a clout round the ear. So here she was: Ruby the Rebel, Ruby the Wretch, Ruby the Really Rotten Rabble-Rouser (that last name was given to her by

Jade), yes Ruby the Rascal, was about to tell this sweet young innocent still-yellow-behind-the-ears Sulphie-Rose the truth about her parents – and for all the street credibility she had, the bad-girl vibe that had become her trademark, she felt helpless in the face of this most difficult challenge.

* * * * *

Dmitry dropped out of the bottom of Jim Martin's desk and onto the floor. He looked around. It was getting pretty dark now but he tried peering about and could see very little, even with his own glow. Then the tapping at the window caught his attention. Two birds were knocking their beaks on the window pane with clear urgency.

'Let us in!' cried Martin.

'A please wouldn't go amiss you know,' said Dmitry.

'Please!' said House.

'Better,' said Dmitry.

'The locks there,' shouted Martin through the glass.

'I know where the lock is,' said Dmitry, and he pulled on the latch and let them in

'Now where's the cat?'

'He put her in the filing cabinet!' said Martin, pointing with his wing.

'And he locked it!' said House 'And he's taken the keys!

Dmitry wriggled off the windowsill and hopped down onto the thick fluffy carpet, bouncing a little as he hit, then he crawled over to the cabinet and slimed his way up the side.

'Third from the top!' cried Martin.

'A little help getting there would have been useful...' complained Dmitry but by then he was there. When he reached the right level, he tapped his nose on the thin, but strong steel cabinet door.

'I've failed,' he heard Katya say in a feeble voice.

'Well for the moment,' Dmitry agreed. 'Neither of us

can open a locked door without the key and I guess you can't use your magnetic powers in there?'

'Not through steel,' said Katya, defeated, 'it blocks the field lines…'

'Well at least I can come in,' said Dmitry and he duly climbed to the middle of the drawer. There was a handle that stuck out a few centimetres and Dmitry began to squash himself into that small space behind it, then he pushed hard.

'Save yourself!' said Katya, 'Forget about me!'

'Don't be so melodramatic,' said Dmitry and he then proceeded to make noises like he was straining himself, then pop! Next moment Dmitry was inside the filing cabinet drawer. He'd passed through steel metal sheet like a true QT worm. There was Katya, glowing very faintly as if her batteries were running low, looking all forlorn and defeated.

'I did the trick for you…' said Dmitry, 'going through a barrier.'

'Thank you…' said Katya weakly.

'Did you see that, guys?' Dmitry shouted to the birds.

'Yeah,' said House, 'that was cool! Now get her out! Um … please!'

'We know that's not going to happen,' said Dmitry to Katya.

'I know,' she agreed 'not the way they were hoping anyway.'

'You're going to collapse your wave function aren't you?' Dmitry asked pointedly

'It's the only way…'

'What's going on in there?!' shouted Martin. 'How are you getting out?'

Katya slowly came up to the inside of the door of her confinement cell to speak to the birds.

'Hey guys,' she said with a heavy heart.

'Kat!' said House. 'Stop playing hide and seek and let's get on with the mission!'

Katya half smiled at her friend's attempt to joke.

'Doctor House,' said Katya more seriously, 'now if

you've really understood my lessons, then you know there's only one way I can get out of here…'

'There must be *another* way!' he said, banging his wings on the door and pulling on the handle to make it rattle.

'I'm only here because I'm in two states at the same time…'

'But…'

'I'm both back on Mars, and…'

'Yes, I understand bilocation,' said House, 'and your state will collapse and disappear and you'll *both* be back on Mars…'

'Not both,' Katya corrected him, 'there's really only one of me.'

'But you can choose not to collapse yourself here!'

'And get found by Jim Martin tomorrow? That might be worse than any other outcome!

'But you need to get those landing coordinates to your friends on Mars!

'And you know I can't take that information with me when my wave function settles on the *other* me, so you guys will have to send the information with that OVRO radio array down the road.'

'How can we do that?!' asked Martin, 'We don't have the know-how or the limbs to do all this!'

'Dmitry can help you!'

'There you go again!' said the insulted QT worm, 'Treating me like I'm just a piece of equipment.'

'I did use your name,' said Katya, 'but you could help them, and in the long run you'd be helping your home planet…'

'Never been much of a planetist,' said Dmitry, 'Just because I was born on a planet-doesn't make it the best place in the universe.'

'You don't have to consider it the best,' Katya suggested, 'just one that would be better off if humans didn't find out it has life on it.'

'Okay,' said Dmitry, 'well suppose I agree, how are we going to do this?'

'We have to send a radio signal to Mars and tell them about the two landing sites.'

'Using that Caltech radio dish array you mentioned…'

'Yes,' said Katya.

'And do you know how to operate these dishes?'

'Well the humans use computers to do that…'

'And do you know how to use a computer?' asked Dmitry, poignantly.

'Not so far, but I was hoping to learn, well that was before I got trapped here.'

'So that sounds like a dead end then…'

'Maybe you can learn?' Katya suggested hopefully.

'How long would that take?'

'But I only have a limited time left here then I'm gone. Back with my *other* half, but not with the information. Someone has to get the details to Mars quickly and I don't know of anything quicker than electromagnetic waves… which is only about ten minutes from here'

'Technically, quantum…'

'I know, Dmitry! Sorry that was rude of me. But yes, I know when I go I jump back instantaneously. But then I won't have the information, as I technically won't have been here. Well not the part of me that's stayed on Mars.' The quantum-leaping couple seemed to know what they were talking about, while the two birds felt lost in translation as they listened through the side of the filing cabinet to understand the reasoning. They felt as if they were both shut in a Schrödinger Box themselves, not knowing whether they were still alive and smart, or dead and stupid. Or just dead stupid. They were wishing they'd got on to that advanced lesson before everything had gone filing cabinet shaped.

Katya and Dmitry continued their discussion, while House and Martin strained to follow a law way harder than the splitting of the atom: the splitting of the cat.

'Well,' Dmitry replied to Katya, 'expecting me to learn about computing and get those huge dishes pointing and sending waves to your friends on Mars, is pretty unlikely…'

'What do you mean?'

'I mean there's more chance you could push your way out of here using a probability wave, than me taking over the mission…'

'Hang on…' said Katya, her glow suddenly warming up; there was now a light on and someone was home, and that person was Katya.

'I was joking!' said Dmitry, 'haven't you noticed I have a dry sense of humour?'

'That's because there's no liquid water on Mars!' shouted House.

'Hear me out,' Katya started, 'look, if two particles are stuck together as one, then they'll share a probability function.'

'Yes,' Dmitry agreed, 'but being heavier together, they would need a larger force to overcome a barrier.'

'And it would take a longer time I know,' said Katya.

'Yea, maybe thousands, millions of times longer because you'd make up most of the mass and you don't have my speleological skills.'

'But there's still a chance!'

'But how could we even become *one*?' asked Dmitry, 'I can't swallow you and do the QT trick in reverse – you're thousands of times bigger than me!'

'I was going to say that maybe you could surround a *part* of me…' and Katya held up a paw and pointed to her wrist.

'Your hand?!'

'You could be like a bracelet?'

'Really?!'

'And then we push like Hell.'

'I can't see it working.'

'Come on, let's at least give it a go,' Katya suggested, finding a bit of her old fighting spirit coming back.

'If it happens,' said Dmitry shaking his head, 'then it's like we're breaking the laws of physics!'

'Well, then the Physics Police can come and arrest us!' said Katya with a smile and she held up her paw again, ready to become 'one' as bride and worm.

Hugh Duncan

House and Martin listened from outside the cabinet with curiosity at the strange conversation going on inside.

'Okay are you ready?' Katya asked Dmitry.

'I'm worried it's going to hurt…'

'Well on the count of three, push, okay? One… Two … Three… PUSH!'

AHHHH! I can't do it!

Take some deep breaths! Now push again!

'I can't!'

'You can, now quick breaths, ready for the next push…'

House Looked at Martin perplexed then called through the drawer, 'Do you guys need some hot water and a blanket!'

'AAAAHHHHH!'

'Is it a boy or a girl?' asked Martin, trying to hide a snigger under his wing.

'A cat or a worm?' said House.

'Wait 'til we get out!' cried Dmitry, then said, 'AAAAAAAHHHHHHH!'

14

The Police: Walking on the Earth

In a perpendicular dimension that was both just next door and also infinitely far away, were two four dimensional beings... or were they...

'Turkan is that you?' said Amelius the 3rd, staring at the flat shape next to him.

'Is *what* me?' said Turkan's voice from somewhere else.

'Clearly it isn't you,' Amelius the 3rd realised, 'Hey, two dimensional creature next to me, who are you?!'

The shape next to Amelius somehow turned over as if it was a page in a book, but did all this within the confines of the two dimensional world they found themselves in.

'It's *you*,' said the other shape, 'I'm Amelius the 3rd too!'

'What?' said the first flat Amelius the 3rd.

'I'm you, you're me. We're both *us*!'

'Help Turkan!' cried the first one, 'I'm talking to myself!'

'*We're* here,' came the voices in stereo from behind the first Amelius. This Amelius flipped over to face *them* and saw two flat identical copies of his multidimensional friend Turkan.

'What's happened?!' Amelius the *First Third* asked in a panic.

'Nothing to worry about,' said the first Turkan.

'It's all perfectly normal,' said the second Turkan.

'*Normal*?!' said the first 3rd, 'but we're two *four* dimensional beings!'

'We are,' said the first Turkan, 'but we can also be four *two* dimensional beings.'

'What?!'

'He's right,' said the second flat Turkan.

'It's not breaking any laws,' said the second Amelius, which made the first Amelius flip sideways again to face his mirror image.

'We could even be eight *one* dimensional creatures,' the second Amelius explained.

'Or one *eight* dimensional creature,' said the first Turkan, while Amelius the first III had to flip back again to keep up with the conversation.

'Though, sixteen *half-dimensional* beings is questionable,' said the other Turkan.

'Fractally speaking it *might* be possible,' said the first Turkan, pondering on the enormity of this line of thought. Or half a line of thought if half dimensions were allowed.

'Well don't get me started on half a *sixteen* dimensional being!' said the other Amelius with a laugh.

'Yes,' the second Turkan agreed, 'and anyway, which half would it be!'

At that moment, an alarm started ringing and it sounded strange to Amelius as it was in mono and not the usual quadraphonic sound.

'Oh dear,' said the first Turkan, as their two dimensional world began to fold over on itself and the second Turkan ended up on top of and merged with the first Turkan, becoming a four dimensional being again.

'Someone's breaking the law again,' said the second Turkan just before they fused. Meanwhile, the two Ameliuses (or is it Ameliae?) also joined as their two copies became folded one on top of the other and together they doubled their dimensionality.

'And it's in the same planetary system as the last crime!' said Amelius.

'Ha!' said Turkan as he flexed one of his multiple limbs and passed it through his face to come out and scratch the back of his own head. 'What are the chances of that?!'

Amelius had his electronic notepad in one of his right hands and he threw it to his right and it suddenly appeared from the left where he caught with one of his left hands: 'One in a hundred million?!' he said with a laugh.

The next moment they disappeared from their 4D bubble.

* * * * *

Katya and Dmitry stopped pushing and listened. The flash of light outside the filing cabinet had been so bright that for a fraction of a second the inside of the cabinet became like midday. Lightning from a storm, Katya thought and there was a loud sound like a crack of thunder that accompanied the light, but to her it felt like it had happened *inside* the office!

'Evenin' all,' said the first little green man, taking up his power stance in the middle of the office, sunglasses on and head slightly tilted back (Note, the shape of his head was a wedge). The two birds were flapping around the room in two random flights of panic, like two smoke particles doing the Brownian Motion Dance.

'Nobody move!' cried the other little green man and he stood with his two arms clasping what looked like a weapon and he was pointing up towards the ceiling without a particular target in sight. The two birds, on hearing this command, suddenly stopped flapping their wings and they both fell to the floor.

'I said stop moving,' said the Craggy-faced, gun-toting little green officer, now pointing it at the birds who were lying on the ground.

'That was gravity doing that,' explained House, now standing with his wings held vertically up in the air.

'Don't try and be clever,' said the Wedgy one.

'Too late for that now,' said Martin, the in-joke lost on the officers.

'What's going on out there?' came the muffled cry from inside the cabinet and on hearing Katya's voice, the trigger happy cop pointed his weapon at the cabinet.

'Hands up!' he cried at the cabinet.

'I know these voices!' Dmitry whispered to Katya, then he called out to the little green men: 'What if you don't have hands?'

'What? I have hands!'

'No,' explained Dmitry, '*I* don't have hands, so how can I raise them?'

229

'What, oh,' Wedgy realised, 'um well the other creature with you, how many limbs have they got?'

'These guys were on Mars!' whispered Dmitry again, then Katya replied.

'I've got four,' said the Magnetic Moggie.

'Well you can raise *all* of them to make up for your friend's handicap.'

Then Officer Craggy turned to his quieter Wedgy friend and smiled: 'It's like the dimensions thing! The figures balance: two hands from each or four from one!'

'We're already squashed in here!' said Katya, 'I can't raise any limbs as I'm already touching the top of the drawer.'

'Yea,' said Dmitry, 'there's not enough room to swing a cat in here…'

Neither of the little green men were really listening as they had their minds on the notepad.

'Got it…' said officer Wedgy, who had been flicking through the pages on his electronic notepad. This notepad had a large fob attached, with the word *matter* written on it in bright day glow yellow ink.

'So what's their crime?' asked Officer Craggy.

'Who are you?' asked Martin.

'We're Officers of the *Law*: the Law of *Physics*.'

'So they really exist?!' said House in surprise.

'Of course we exist,' snapped Craggy.

'And why are you here?' asked Martin.

'Someone just broke one of our Laws.'

'But why are you green?'

Both officers looked at each other then back at the birds.

'Is this not Mars?'

'No,' said Martin, 'it's Earth.'

'Damn,' said Wedgy to Craggy. 'Same solar system, but different *planet*.'

'Nothing we can do about it now,' said Craggy, 'So, the crime and it's you two inside the cabinet!'

'What have we done?' said Katya.

'It says here,' and Craggy glanced at his pad '… Breaking and *exiting*…'

'But we haven't gone out yet,' explained Katya.

'Ah,' said Officer Craggy, 'it's a *premeditated* crime! That's just as bad, you know!'

'This is crazy!' said Katya.

'I *know* it is,' said Officer Wedgy, 'why would anyone want to break the Law? They are there for a purpose!'

'But hang on,' said Katya, 'we've done nothing wrong. We hadn't even premeditated doing anything wrong.'

'You were going to try and get yourselves through a potential barrier, this said cabinet, by using your probability wave function.'

'But there's nothing wrong with that,' Katya defended herself.

'It says here that your combined mass means that the chance of you succeeding in the lifetime of this universe is impossible.'

'But wait,' said Katya, 'it's not *impossible* is it, it's just highly *unlikely*...'

'Close enough to zero to...'

'But *not* zero.'

'Still not going to happen.'

'One question,' Katya changed tack, 'this isn't the only universe is it?'

'No ma'am,' said Craggy, feeling cocky about knowing everything, 'one of many. We have a lot of ground to cover.'

'How many universes?'

'Um, well that would be infinite.'

'So,' Katya asked, 'what's infinity multiplied by a tiny number?'

' Well it's...No!' said Wedgy, 'You're not going to use that trick here!'

'It's not a trick,' said Dmitry, 'It means that somewhere in the multiverse we *will* get out of this cabinet using the probability wave.'

'But not necessarily this universe!' defended Craggy.

'But it could be,' said Dmitry.

'You don't get to choose,' said Craggy, 'now I want you two to come out of there slowly, no funny moves...'

'But we *can't* get out of here!' said Katya.

'That's the problem!' cried Dmitry.

This comment stumped the confused cops for a moment. This gave Dmitry a chance to explain what he knew.

'I saw these two on Mars a while back. They charged some poor plant who got hit by a cosmic ray for tempting fate.'

'Like Martin just said, I didn't know physics police were a real thing,' said Katya.

'Anyway,' continued Dmitry, 'it all went pear shaped because one of them had brought an anti-matter notepad and there was a pretty big explosion...'

'I don't remember that,' said Katya.

'Oh,' Dmitry corrected himself, 'it was in a different universe...'

Katya looked at him sideways. Dmitry picked up on this.

'Another QT worm property I have – I'll tell you about it sometime...'

Meanwhile, the two 'green behind the ears' Officers had come to a decision.

'Well we could arrest the *whole* filing cabinet,' said Wedgy to Craggy, 'unless you've got a cutting tool with you?'

'No,' said Craggy, patting his pockets, 'I left my four dimensional *hole* at home...'

'Officers,' Martin tried diplomatically, 'I think this has all been a big misunderstanding.'

'Are you suggesting we don't understand the Laws of Physics?!' said Craggy getting upset.

'Not at all,' said Martin, 'look, can't we just sit down and have a nice cup of tea or something?'

'Bribery now!' said Officer Wedgy.

Meanwhile back inside the cabinet.

'I have an idea!' said Katya, 'but it means you'll have to do your party trick.'

'Not again,' said Dmitry in a fed up way, 'but I don't see how that can help?'

'I just have to tell the birds something…'

'Officers!?' Katya called out.'

'Yes ma'am?' Wedgy asked.

'Can I make one last call to a friend?'

'It's your right I suppose,' said the officer.

'Hey House, hey Martin!'

'House? Martin?!' said Wedgy in disbelief and sniggered.

'Yes?' the birds replied.

'There's an airport just down the road from here, called the Burbank I think,'

'Why are you telling us this?' said Martin.

'Hitch a ride on a plane so you can get back home…'

'What about you?' House asked with concern, though for some reason, Martin had flown back to the office desk.

'I won't be coming with you…' admitted Katya.

'You're not giving yourselves up are you…' House began, while Martin had picked up a felt pen.

'Don't worry,' she assured House, 'the mission will have been accomplished by the time I say goodbye. I just have to *swallow* my pride before I *collapse* from exhaustion. So thanks for all your help. I'm sorry to have to leave you like this, but it's been nice knowing you… Goodbye.'

'WAIT!' cried Martin, who flew back to the cabinet and landed on the handle of Katya's drawer.

'What?' said Katya. The two officers looked on confused.

Martin managed to slip the very tip of his wing into the thin gap between the top of the cabinet door and the frame.

'What's goin' on 'ere?' asked Officer Craggy.

'Shake my wing will you,' said Martin.

'What for?' Katya asked.

'You're not planning an escape are you?' Craggy asked, still holding his hands together like he had a gun and he looked round for a possible exit route.

'Take one of my feathers as a keepsake!' said Martin.

233

'Move away from the cabinet sir!' cried Craggy 'and put the dangerous wing down…NOW!'

House removed his wing from the drawer and the next moment there was a sudden flash of green light coming out through the cracks in the filing cabinet; then the light was gone and the cabinet went quiet.

'Hello?' said officer Wedgy, who came up to the cabinet and tapped on the side. Martin looked at both his wings checking that he was one feather short. He smiled.

'We can wait here all night!' said Officer Craggy to the cabinet.

'Um,' said Officer Wedgy, 'actually the new season of Professor When is starting in a couple of hours, so…'

Meanwhile the two house martins had quietly slipped out the open window.

'Okay,' said Craggy, 'we can wait until midnight… then we're coming in for you!'

* * * * *

Katya couldn't remember how she ended up in a hole in the ground, with a slice of shale blocking the exit. She pushed at the thin sheet of rock, which wasn't heavy. She slid it to one side and squinted against the bright midday sunlight. She couldn't quite explain it, but she felt somehow 'whole' again, whole and complete. Then she remembered she was supposed to be helping Fionix. She quickly grabbed a large rock with her grabby tail and switched blue, then found herself thrown to the ground.

'Fifty fifty chance,' she said, then flipped to red and suddenly she was up in the air like a little red weather balloon. This extra metre or so gave her a better view of the surroundings. She noticed where the sun was, the stars, as well as her tail's angle, then peered at the horizon in all directions.

'Hmmm,' she said to herself, 'it feels like I'm near the eastern end of the Marineris Valley…'

She licked one of her paws and held it up to check the wind.

'I think Fionix said she'd be heading for Syria Planum for now. Got a bit of pole hopping to do before I get there…'

With that, she let go of her rock and went wherever the field lines took her.

* * * * *

'Shall we give up?' said Elvis, watching his friends straining themselves for what seemed to be a thankless and pointless task.

'We need the data,' said Fionix, frustrated and fed up.

'But you've been doing this for seventeen days,' Elvis explained, 'and not a single radio photon has been received from Earth…'

He looked at the convoluted feat of engineering in front of him and felt compassion. There was Fionix, leaning with her back against a steeply inclined cliff face. At the same time she had raised her wing tips until her right and left end wing claws had hooked together way above her own head. She'd done the same with her feet, which she'd pulled inwards and hooked together and, with her other wing fingers spread out, her wings now made a huge umbrella shape, a parabolic dish that was pointing towards a tiny twinkling light in the sky: Earth. That by itself might have been more easily dismissed as a kind of sunbathing pose, but what made it more unusual, was the highly reflective silver sheen that the exposed underside of Fionix's wings had gained.

'I'm willing to help you keep going as long as necessary,' came a voice from somewhere in the middle of the silver dish. Elvis looked down and saw Quicksilver's head.

'Very kind of you,' said Fionix, 'but the craft will be arriving any day and if we don't get the landing details by then, and the landing sites are too far away, well we won't get there in time to secure the perimeters…'

Fionix sighed both with frustration and with the strain of keeping up this unnatural shape.

'Are you sure there's nothing?' Fionix asked to the object floating in the air above her.

Elvis turned his gaze to the other half of the makeshift *telectroscope*. Hanging there many tens of metres above the ground, was a greenish bulbous head. It had wild staring eyes and a gawping mouth and a crazy punk hairstyle of wispy fronds standing on their ends as if a plastic comb had given him the worst bad-hair day possible. Even at the best of times Starkwood looked dishevelled. In fact he had probably never looked *shevelled* in his life. The leafy prophet was not hanging by himself. A hand like set of green roots was holding him up, by gripping onto a clump of his fronds. It was, in fact, the prehensile tail of a green monopole-cat and at the top end of the tail was the rest of Katya. She had finally mastered the art of hovering in a magnetic field and she was holding Starkwood fairly steady, remaining at the focus of this 'telectroscope'.

'Nothing, sorry,' admitted Starkwood disappointedly.

'And you Katya?' Fionix asked her, 'You don't remember whether you sent the radio message?'

'It doesn't work like that,' she also admitted. 'Once the other version of me collapsed, her probability wave, well *our* wave, she instantaneously ended up with me here, well, there was only ever really one of me, but in two undecided states… so no, all information that I had when I was on Earth would have stopped existing the moment I came back…'

'And you Dmitry?'

'The Kat's right,' said the QT worm from his vantage point on the top of her head. 'As I went there with her, I was part of the same wave function, so I'm just as blank as she is…'

'And are you sure you didn't write anything in that notebook of yours?' Fionix asked, still clutching at straws.

'Even if I had,' Katya explained, 'as the notebook and the pen went there with me, then they were also part of the function and, hence, temporary.'

To prove the point, Katya rummaged around in her fur and found her pen, then found her precious scientific notebook.

'Look,' she said, opening it to her last entry, 'nothing since you left me in a box on Earth and see,' she began flicking through the remaining pages 'everything is blank after that...'

Something fell out from between some later pages. It fluttered to the ground and landed just in front of Elvis.

'What's that?' asked Fionix.

'It's a feather,' said Elvis.

Fionix unhooked her wing claws and leg claws and let Quicksilver pour off her into a pool on the ground, where he reformed his normal shape, which was half a horse raised above his personal silver moat. Fionix collapsed her wings and folded them up as she waddled down the slope to join Elvis. Katya gently lowered Starkwood's head until they were both back on the ground as well.

'Do you recognise it?' Quicksilver asked Katya.

'Earth mind erased I'm afraid,' said Katya, inspecting the black and white feather.

'What about you Fionix?' Quicksilver asked her, 'you told me you've been to Earth many times.'

The aeradon had a closer look.

'I think it's a house martin's feather...' she said with a growing feeling of excitement.

'Oh,' said Elvis, 'look, there's something written on it, hang on...'

And he peered at it.

'Oh!' he said with controlled surprise, 'it says *love Martin*...'

'Your cousin!' said Fionix.

'Anything else?!' asked Katya.

'Not on this side,' said Elvis, then he turned it over, '... Ah, I think this is what we've been waiting for...'

'What does it say?' asked Fionix, 'does it say what I hope it does?'

Elvis held up the feather and looked at his group of friends.

'And the winners of the most attractive tourist destinations on Mars are… Tiu Valley and Cydonia!'

* * * * *

'Right,' said Fionix, 'are we packed and ready?'

'Um,' said Elvis, looking around himself, 'well, bodiless Starkwood, check, liquid silver horse, check, and green polecat, check, so I guess so.'

'Climb aboard then…' she beckoned them.

'What?' asked Elvis surprised, 'why would we do that again?'

'You still concerned about being up there?'

'Not if there's ground just below my feet,' Elvis qualified.

'It really is best to fly there,' explained Fionix, 'as it will give us some extra time to set up camp, without there being a visible camp of course and then we can scout the Tiu Valley to make sure anything living keeps living but out of sight.

'Can't I just walk?' asked Elvis. 'If the Mudda had wanted us tortles to fly, he would have made us more aerodynamically shaped…'

'I really need you there as soon as possible,' said Fionix, 'Do you know how far it is to the Chryse Basin from here?'

'It's the end of my journey, that's how far…'

'Very philosophical. It's about three thousand kilometres – do you know how long it'll take you to get there by foot?'

'It will take as long as it needs to and not a second more…'

Katya had her paw up, so Fionix pointed to her. She answered.

'The average adult male rock tortle can maintain about a metre per second indefinitely so Elvis would be there in about thirty five days.'

'Correct,' said Fionix, 'five points to Team Kat. That means my dear Rock Star, you'll be a couple of weeks too late.'

'But you're counting from when you said the orbiting craft arrives,' Elvis pointed out, 'we'd still have time before the landers come down.'

'Groundwork Elvis, we need to prepare the surroundings, those humans mustn't see a single living thing here. Not even two. Not any number of living things unless the number is zero. If they do, then we can say goodbye to life on Mars – Martian life that is. There'll be human life coming then human waste. And they mustn't even see a *dead* Martian, as a dead Martian will imply there were living Martians in the very recent past, so we'll have to clear the site of any cadavers – gruesome though that may sound…'

'I understand the urgency,' admitted Elvis, 'I also understand *acrophobia*. Couldn't you just fly a bit closer to the ground then?' and he held up his foot with two claws about a centimetre apart, 'About *this* altitude?'

'It's hard to get enough lift…'

'There is the Ground Effect…' Katya put in.

'Shhh!' said Fiona.

'And I've seen your Hellas Angels use dry ice under their wings,' pointed out Elvis, 'so that when it sublimes it gives them a cushion of CO_2 to ride on…'

'I know,' said Fionix, feeling defeated, 'it's just *so bloody cold* when I try that!'

'How about we compromise,' suggested Elvis, 'half the journey near the ground and half in the air?'

'Okay,' said Fionix, 'and I can use my personal rocket booster instead of dry ice.'

'I'm not sure…'

At this moment, Quicksilver was holding up a hoof, but it kept pouring back down into his own pool.

'Yes, my knight in shining mercury,' said Fionix.

'Can I make a suggestion?'

'If it solves this problem…'

'Well I think it might. And will I get five points to Team Horse? I don't travel quite as fast on the ground as you in the air, but I'm not called Quicksilver for nothing.

Elvis could float on my back and I could be there a couple of days after you…'

'…well…'

'I could take the Marineris Valley and it's downhill all the way until it opens into the Chryse Basin and the Tiu Valley is just at the opening. Plus you as the Flying Fleet will be able to travel faster without a ton of extra baggage in the form of Elvis – no offence meant.'

'None taken, but I'm not that heavy.'

Fionix pondered this offer, rubbing her chin with a couple of wing fingers (which also caused a few gusts of wind, like bellows, and her sail-like wings filled with the Martian wind).

'I could be there in a day or so…' she decided, '… and it *would* give me a bit of time to scout around without Elvis as payload. Okay, it's a deal.'

'Great!' said Quicksilver. 'And the five points?'

'Take them.'

'Not ten?'

'Don't push it.'

Fionix then directed her attention to the green cat.

'Katya, can I ask a favour of you before you join us at the Viking I Invasion Site?'

'Sure.'

'Can you locate the Hellas Angels for me and tell them to go and help the umpteenager tortles at the Viking II Invasion Site in Cydonia? They should have reported back by now but they haven't…'

'Happy to help Sir! Ma'am, sorry. But I'm going to take a little detour myself before I join you,' she explained, 'if you don't mind.'

'Is it important?'

'Yes,' said Katya, pointing to Starkwood's sulking head propped up next to a rock, 'I'm going to try and get him back on his feet, well, roots, well *somebody's* roots anyway.

'Well don't take too long,' said Fionix, 'I don't think I can cover the area so efficiently without your scientific background.'

'Shall we say we meet at the mouth of the Tiu Valley midday in four days' time?'

That agreed, Quicksilver gathered himself in a pool next to Elvis.

'Hop in,' said Quicksilver, 'the mercury's cool today.'

'Wow,' said Elvis, 'thanks. This will take me right back to when I used to swim in the Chryse Basin – when it used to be a sea, and we called it Chryse Bay...'

Once Elvis was in the pool of liquid metal, Quicksilver let his own body disappear below the surface of his pond so that only his head was sticking out, while Elvis sat, barely submerged in his high density mobile bathtub. Quicksilver then started to flow south-east towards the edge of the Great Marineris Canyon.

'See you then!' said Fionix, gradually unfolding her wings fully and turning to start waddling down the slope and letting her Mylar thin wings catch the wind and start to fill like a paraglider's chute. She still put her first claws and elbows to the ground to catapult herself into the air pole-vaulting style for the final launching manoeuvre.

That left just Katya looking at the dejected Starkwood.

'Come on, my perpendicular friend,' said Katya, 'let's go.'

'I'm half missing...' said Starkwood in his deadpan depressive tone.

'Well,' Katya tilted Starkwood's down-angled face upwards a little, 'I try to be an optimist, and I would say you are half *present*. Let's now make you fully present!'

'It was supposed to be my birthday today...'

'So we'll make it your *birthday* present!'

Katya grabbed Starkwood's head fronds with her prehensile tail, and lifted him off the ground. She had to switch colours back and forth until she found the right polarity.

'Come on oh holy martyr,' she said, as they began to rise, 'let's get you some legs: it's time you grew a pair...'

15

A Landing Site for Sore Eyes

Almost a week later, Elvis emerged from the Valles
Marineris, surfing on the back of Quicksilver the Puddle,
a cross between a pony and a pond. Hey, a *Pondy*! It had
taken twice as long as predicted for various reasons: toilet
breaks, Quicksilver getting frozen in some of the more
shadowy areas of the deep canyon and another time when
he had flowed over what would have been a waterfall
where he splashed into so many tiny puddles that Elvis
was trapped under the surface of one patch of mercury
that was too small for him to get out of. This was quite
unexpected for him; Elvis hadn't been aware that
Quicksilver actually extended a little into an extra
dimension, so he was deeper on the inside than he
appeared on the outside. It was probably against the laws
of physics; if those Physics Police knew about it, there
would be a lot of paperwork to do.

The Marineris Valley had widened out so much, you
could hardly see the edges of the opening on the horizon.
Plus, the slope of the flood plain had become so shallow
that Quicksilver was meandering rather than gushing
swiftly northwards into the Tiu Valley.

'It was a shock to me when I first found out,'
Quicksilver finished explaining. 'When rocks and stuff
would fall inside me, I just assumed they were dissolving
– I knew mercury was a good solvent – but when I dived
in to look for myself I realised there was a whole new
world in there.'

'Fascinating.'

'I know! Once I spread myself out as thin as I can go,
and I got a lung whale to jump inside – and she fitted!'

'Hang on, she's not still in there, is she?'

'…I don't think so. But she completely went under, so
that must be at least three hundred metres – and I was

only a millimetre deep on the ground!'

'There's a lot more to you than meets the eye,' Elvis said, cryptically, before knocking on his head with one foot. When he saw Quicksilver's confused gaze, he explained.

'Sorry, I still have some of you in my ear."

'Oh! Sorry, those rapids were a bit more rapid than I expected.' Quicksilver paused, looking back out at the land in front of them before he finally continued.

'We're here. Running late, though.'

'We'd better look out for Fionix before she has a fit.'

With this agreed, Elvis stepped out of Quicksilver and on to solid ground. It felt odd after having been somewhat weightless in an Archimedial way for several days. He shook himself and several silver drops of mercury flew off. They all flowed back to join with the main body of the pondy. Both Elvis and Quicksilver scanned the skies. The jagged skyline made it harder to see Fionix in the distance.

'It doesn't seem like the nicest place to drop in,' said Elvis, now inspecting the ground more than the skies.

He'd never really considered it before in all his years travelling through the Basin, but it seemed a poor choice to land your Viking invasion. There were large boulders strewn all about, and many craters – most filled in or eroded away over the years, but a lot less flat than seemed ideal.

'Oh look!' said Quicksilver, trying to point with a hoof that slowly dripped back into the his mirroring pool.

'Fionix?' asked Elvis, turning to follow the original direction of the melting limb.

'No, that green cat friend of yours and she's carrying that other green friend of yours…'

Sure enough, coming in from the south-west was the 'Green Team', with Katya as the proverbial helicopter and Starkwood dangling beneath her by her tail. He was looking much larger and the Martian magnetic field was struggling to supply enough force to keep the non-magnetic half of the reluctant partnership airborne. Well

244

most of it; parts of Starkwood's newly-large body actually seemed to be defying gravity a little, a few extra side stalks with tiny pods on their ends pointing upwards like little helium filled balloons did on Earth. Or was Elvis just imagining things…

It was clear to both land dwellers that Katya was coming in too fast and it was Quicksilver's quick thinking that offered a solution. Literally.

'Hang on!' shouted the shiny stallion, then he turned to Elvis, 'this is what I was talking about – saving falling objects,' then he shouted back up to the incoming less-than-Dynamic Duo, 'aim for me!'

With that, Quicksilver tried to flow in the general direction of Katya's expected landing site and spread himself out like a huge shimmering safety net.

Katya was descending fast, but she was too far from a splash landing. She began swinging her tail back and forth like a pendulum bob with her frightened payload on the end, and then she sling-shotted him forwards and Starkwood found himself less like a plant and more like a flat stone as he bounced off the surface of the pool, skipping several times as Quicksilver changed shape to follow the path of this botanical bouncing bomb. On releasing her payload, Katya found herself katapulted upwards, conserving momentum and basically going wherever the solar wind was blowing her. She quickly settled on the right colour and was soon returning gently to Aera-Firma.

Elvis watched Katya as she came in and he thought she too looked different. Her hair seemed particularly radial, pointing out in all directions, as if she'd had a bad fur day – or maybe it was just a frizzy hair-do – and she also looked a bit on the tubbier side too.

Quicksilver's impersonation of a liquid landing strip was working quite well and Starkwood continued to bounce along his length, heading straight for Elvis. Elvis, for his part, just stood there at the end of the runway unmoved by what had been looking like an emergency. As Starkwood reached the end of the silver slick, he suddenly reached dry ground with all its extra friction and this caused his lower end, his roots, to slow more rapidly than his upper end, his head, which carried on unheeded. It made him flip over in the air and do a somersault until he landed quite comically and in a most unlikely way onto Elvis' shell, exactly where he'd spent the last million years or so. No Physics Police seemed to be watching this event so they were safe.

'Welcome back,' said Elvis, Zen and cool, as if all his Muddist practices had come back to life.

'Shell Sweet Shell,' said Starkwood and he bent double to kiss the carapace that he called his shellter.

'You've grown,' Elvis commented casually.

'Thanks to Katya actually, she grew my new body.'

'A multi-talented monopole,' said Elvis, 'how did she do that?'

'It started… hang on where is she?'

They both scanned the skies and there she was, descending more gracefully than when she was overburdened with one too many vegetables.

'Hi,' said Katya.

'Well done,' said Elvis. 'I like what you've done to Frankenstark.'

'Thank you, but I can't take all the credit.'

'So how did you genetically engineer this hybrid?'

Katya had now landed and she changed into a little green number that was more fitting to staying put and not following any magnetic lines of fashion. She still looked a bit more fluffy and, well one couldn't call it puppy fat, maybe it was kitty fat, but Elvis wasn't going to point it out.

Katya and Starkwood looked at each other then Starkwood gave a wave of his sepal and said 'You tell him.'

'You start,' said Katya as she began brushing off the dust from her fur using an orange pebble.

'Okay,' said Starkwood as he stood tall on Elvis' back. At the same time, he had a sepal full of red powder that he munched on from time to time. He took a deep breath and cleared his throat.

'Oh,' said Elvis, realising what was coming.

'A reading from the Gospel According to St Arkwood...'

'I've missed this!'

'And lo, I fell like manna from the heavens and I didst land into the field of my followers, who never followed me and had warned me that if I ever stepped root in their field again, I would be punished and, verily, I say unto you I was punished and kicked around like a ball until they didst dispose of me over the edge of the Tharsis Ridge. And there I was cast into the pit of dead souls...'

Elvis looked confused. Katya butted in.

'He means the compost heap at the bottom of the Ridge, where his electrostatic compatriots dump all their dead ancestors.'

'Oh.'

'Yea, and I didst plummet head first, for I was only a head at the time and could not plummet with anything else and I landed into the pit of decay and rot.'

'Very rich in nutrients, that soil,' Katya explained, 'millions of years of recycled electrostatic souls. Starkwood's body started regenerating much faster than when he was in the ordinary dirt in your shell – no offence...'

'None taken. But when you found him first, he still had that tiny little stem of his?'

'Yes,' said Katya, 'after locating him in all the mulch at the bottom of the Ridge, I pulled him out of the ground without thinking...'

'And I didst run away,' admitted Starkwood.

'You should have waited for me!' said Katya.

'But you didst lose control of your internal compass.'

'I cameth back!'

'Thou did so, seventy seven times seven times, but I was fed up and climbed back up the slope...'

'You went back to your old crop?' Elvis asked in disbelief.

'Yea. After a Second Rising from the Dead and a *Second* Second Coming, I thought they might accept me back into their fold.'

'And didst they?'

'Verily, no. And lo I was forced to play Plantball, as the ball for an eternity. Until Katya and Fionix turned up and rescued me.'

'Ah,' sighed Elvis, 'well it all makes sense now... well up until this new buff body of yours...'

Katya took over the story telling.

'Anyway,' she began, 'it was only sometime after I'd plucked Starkwood out of that ground that I realised these electrostatic plants can grow back from cuttings at an accelerated rate in their own manure so to speak, so I went back a few times and noticed a full-sized version of his body was growing out of the graveyard.'

'With a new head?' asked Elvis.

'No,' said Katya, 'there was no head on the new Starkwood body, just a sort of hole where it should have been. When I measured the hollow space in the top of the body, it was exactly the size of his head's little body. So I took him back and the big body fitted like a glove around his little body.

'I'm as good as new,' said Starkwood proudly.

'He is!' Katya said proudly.

'Well it all sounds like a happy ending,' said Elvis.

'Not quite,' came the unexpected voice of Fionix who had just appeared behind them. They all turned to face her, a bit surprised at the sudden apparition as they usually heard her noisy arrival.

'Fionix!' cried Katya.

'Glad you all made it,' said Fionix in her no nonsense military mode, 'sorry but we can't celebrate Starkwood's body swap at the moment, nice though it is – there's a problem with the landing site.'

'Oh,' said Katya, 'aren't the locals cooperating with a self-imposed lockdown?'

'It's not that,' said Fionix, 'I got the feeling that this *isn't* the landing site for the Viking I Mission... I think they've changed it.'

* * * * *

'They should have landed by now,' said Fionix, pacing up and down but doing more lolloping than pacing.

'Maybe the craft is running late,' said Quicksilver.

'A traffic jam up there in the interplanetary highways perhaps,' offered Elvis.

'No,' Fionix shook her head, 'it went into orbit already.'

'How do you know?' asked Katya.

Fionix looked down at her shadow then at the sky.

'Viking I should be passing overhead in a few minutes…'

They all looked to the heavens and scanned the horizon.

* * * * *

'This is ridiculous!' said Starkwood, still dangling below an airborne monopole-cat at roughly the focal point of a silver coated Martian bird of paradise that had shaped herself into a parabolic dish like the Earth dwelling umbrella birds. Again. The telectroscope was not a one off.

'Keep still!' shouted Katya, who had the impossible task of maintaining this reluctant antenna of a plant in the right place long enough to pick up a signal. Ha! A plantenna!

'Third time lucky,' said Elvis calmly from a vantage point behind the makeshift radio dish, 'Now, Fionix, a little to the left.'

Elvis had one eye closed and was trying to line up the axis of Fionix's cupped wings so they were following the retreating Viking I orbiter as it headed towards the eastern horizon. On the opposite side of the sky, near the western horizon was the brightest star-like point in the sky, that of Earth itself.

The principle behind the plan was quite simple. The Viking I orbiter that they'd first watched a week or two ago, was in some highly elliptical orbit, that brought it very close to the Martian surface, but each time round it was sweeping over a different part of that surface, clearly looking for a better landing site. That new information had to be sent back and forth to Mission Control on Earth and this Mars-made amateur contraption was trying to listen in on these messages like some interstellar spy. They might have done better with two tins and a tight string between them a thousand kilometres long for all the success that they'd had so far.

Already the original attempt to pick up the radio messages from Earth about the landing weeks previously had failed – probably due to the signal being too weak, plus the inefficient method of a Martian bird of paradise's wings coated in a liquid silver horse and the odd electromagnetic combination of a static plant and a monopole-cat. Hence they were now looking at the orbiter, whose signal had to be much stronger at this distance of only a fifteen hundred kilometres. Though, having said that, the previous two attempts at aiming for the orbiter had picked up next to nothing.

'They *have* to have chosen a landing site by now,' Fionix insisted, 'that orbiter has to have scanned everything for miles!'

'Stop wriggling!' said Katya.

'It's tickling me,' explained Starkwood.

Katya looked below herself at Starkwood who was twitching noticeably on the end of her tail. The plant's hair was certainly standing more on end than usual, and the occasional blue spark ran between some of the fronds.

'Then we must be close to the beam!' said Fionix with hope.

'Kat, you keep drifting away from the focal point,' said Fionix.

'I know!' she snapped quite uncharacteristically, 'Sorry,' she excused herself straight away, 'I seem to be more…'

'… *catty*?' Starkwood put in with almost deliberate spite.

'Well it's not easy since you've become a big lump!'

'I told you,' Starkwood snapped back, 'it's this craving

I've had since I got this new body.'

'Can you two focus, literally?!'

'Yes ma'am,' said Katya, swaying back into the correct position, with Starkwood still swinging with residual simple harmonic motion (though it was seeming more like simple *discordant* motion, with all the bickering).

Katya then whispered aggressively out of the corner of her mouth to her hanging plant luggage, 'Why *are* you eating all that iron oxide mix?'

'What's it to you?' snapped Starkwood.

'Concentrate you two!' shouted Fionix.

'A degree to the right,' said Elvis.

The next moment, Starkwood's fronds stood even more on end and he took on a bluish glow. Katya's fur also stood strictly radial and she flickered all three colours red, green and blue as if she was a disco light gone crazy.

And there it was, the message between the Viking I orbiter and Earth straight from Starkwood's mouth, with the coordinates of the new landing site: 22 North and 48 West.

* * * * *

'I'm flying on ahead,' explained Fionix, 'it's about eight hundred kilometres west north-west of here, so we won't have much time to clear the area before the lander arrives.'

The last drop of Quicksilver had run off Fionix's wings and dripped back into his personal puddle, his head and shoulders now rising above the surface again.

'I'll bring Elvis as before,' the silver horse offered.

'And I'll bring Starkwood,' said Katya.

'Here's an idea,' said Elvis, 'why don't *we* take Starkwood on my back again, like old times. That would allow you to ride the field lines alone and get there quicker?'

'Won't it slow Quicksilver down?'

'Hardly,' said the horse, 'Starkie's only a fraction of the weight of Golden Boy here.'

'Sounds like a plan,' said Elvis, then with a nod of the head he beckoned his old *soil* mate; 'Hey Buddy, climb on board. I've saved your place for you…'

Starkwood looked to Katya for approval.

'Makes sense,' she agreed, 'plus the distance might do us some good, after picking up each other's mannerisms…'

'Okay,' and with that Starkwood shuffled onto Elvis's carapace and felt his roots work their way back into the crevices and cracks between the plates on the shell. Starkwood sighed with relief; it was truly like coming home.

'And now the magic silver carpet ride,' said Elvis with a smile, as he in turn stepped into Quicksilver's docking area. 'Captain,' he said, turning to his host, 'ready to sail…'

'It's still downhill all the way,' commented Quicksilver, and turning to Fionix, 'we should be there in a couple of days.' With that Elvis held his claw to his head. Quicksilver held a hoof to his, and even Starkwood held a sepal to his own ear as they all saluted their boss. Without thinking, Fionix began to return the gesture then realised what she was doing and dismissed them with a smile and a brush off of the wing.

Quicksilver flowed downstream in a north-westerly direction and Starkwood leant back slightly in the breeze of their travel, loving the feeling of reconnecting with the ground and his old travelling partner. He hoped that all would return to normal and the other changes were just temporary.

Katya and Fionix watched them go, then Fionix shook her wings back to life and got ready for another embarrassing take off from ground level. However, she hesitated and turned to Katya with a quizzical look. The cat seemed to be cleaning herself using a stone of some kind again.

'What's going on between you and Starkwood lately?'

'What do you mean,' asked Katya, clearly pretending there was nothing wrong.

'You both seem to be rather, *snappy* with each other...'

'Well it has been a nerve-racking time for everyone,' Katya suggested, 'what with these unwanted guests from Earth arriving, plus growing Starkwood a new body and the sheer stress of carrying him around everywhere – it does get to you eventually.'

'I guess so,' agreed Fionix, 'but what's with him eating that powder and you, what are you rubbing yourself with now? Never seen you do that before.'

'Oh this?' said Katya, holding up the orange pebble, 'It's a piece of amber. I find it helps keep my coat nice and shiny..'

'And *charged*,' Fionix pointed out, 'Amber's known for its electrostatic properties, but you knew that already?'

'What are you implying?'

'Well, you using an electrostatic stone and you're a magnetic monopole-cat while Starkwood is eating magnetite and he's an electrostatic plant. You each seem to be taking on some traits of the other. Is that healthy for either of you?'

'Well,' Katya sighed, 'we've spent so much time connected recently we might have affected each other's behaviour... But now he's back on Elvis' shell, this should all fade away and we can return back to normal...'

'Have you ever come across this kind of osmotic assimilation before?'

'No,' admitted Katya, 'monopole-cats and static plants are so laterally opposed, it's about the most unlikely teaming up of any two creatures possible.'

'Well I hope you can both sort it out,' said Fionix with concern, 'for yourselves of course, but also so we can focus on containing this menace from Earth.'

'You have my full commitment,' said Katya with sincerity as she finished rubbing her fur with the amber, after which her hair puffed up and stood on end even more. Her tail took the stone out of her hand and she flickered a few colour changes before finding the right polarity. Up she rose, not as fast as she used to, and off she headed north-west. 'See you soon!' she shouted back to Fionix, who was now hopping along the ground, using both ground effect and the slight downhill pull of gravity to build up speed. However, she decided to avoid the usual embarrassment and take a risk on a different one; a few sparks were seen, then, the next moment, her exhaust gases were ignited and off she shot with a roar. She overtook Katya and sent the cat into a spin with air currents curling off her wingtips. Katya managed to steady herself and looked at her bloated body with concern. She had a pretty good idea what might be happening, but she didn't even want to consider it as a possibility, especially when it should have been an *impossibility*.

Shortly after Fionix and Katya left for the new landing site, there was a not so sudden – but steady – arrival of a long stream of slow moving, trudging, zombie plants.

16

The Vikings Have Landed!

It was the 20th of July 1976 on Earth. The Viking I craft had moved into an orbit above the landing site some six days earlier, and the manoeuvres began to finally release the lander and let it live up to its name. It just so happened that the Martian Unwelcoming Committee had arrived at Ground Zero a little earlier. Katya had come with them but had gone magnetic field surfing to scout the area and check the extent of life, and any evidence thereof, scattered across the untidy rubbly surface that might have to be brushed under the proverbial carpet for now.

Fionix and her friends had gathered about a hundred kilometres east of the Xanthe Ridge, with the splat crater Yorktown 40km north-west, the Lexington crater the same distance south-west, and the Savannah crater 20km to the south-east. It was fairly typical Martian terrain of blue grey rocks, of various sizes, scattered across the plain from a previous ground melt episode. They were interspersed between the ever-changing sand dunes driven by the prevailing winds. The crescent wedges were formed as the wind blew round the edges of the rocks and, in some places, there were semi-parallel smaller dunes – a nice rippling blanket that brought a bit of attractive symmetry to the otherwise chaotic nature of the regolith.

The sun was in the sky and its bright rays were making it hard for the team to spot the unwanted gate-crashers coming in from space. It wasn't so much the clouds, but more the tiny sepia-coloured particles – forever being picked up by the wind – refracting and scattering the sunlight and giving the sky its recognisable reddish tint. Only the brightest stars and artificial satellites could twinkle their way through this haze.

'Well,' said Fionix, scanning the skies, 'I did make a huge sweep of the area before you guys got here and I couldn't see anything major that would give us away…'

'I can ask my pyrites to have a closer look,' offered Elvis, 'but unless we know exactly where the lander is going to land, there would be too much area to cover.'

'At least this area's not teeming with life for the moment,' said Fionix.

'I was born near here,' Elvis mused, 'when all this was a shallow sea, full of my family and friends…'

'Well, if it was still like that,' Fionix pointed out, 'we wouldn't have had a hope in Hellas of hiding the facts of life from those Earthlings. At least it's calm now.'

Elvis looked round – for him it was all too quiet on the South Eastern Chryse Front.

'Let's hope we can keep it like this,' Fionix wished out loud.

Elvis looked to Quicksilver, who was a limpid pool of still mercury, with just his head peeking above the surface like he was relaxing in a bath. They smiled at each other. Then Elvis looked to Starkwood. Crouched down in the shadowed crevice area of his shell, sepals clasped round what looked like his bent knees, Starkwood seemed to be in deep thought, almost dormant. Well his body was – his hair was waving and the little pods on the ends of their overhanging willow stalks seemed to all be leaning in the same direction. Could Elvis hear a rumbling sound? Was it his stomach? No. Starkwood? No. Was the ground vibrating perceptibly? He looked at the soil below his claws and noticed some tiny bits of gravel were jiggling a little. He even noticed some ripples in Quicksilver's pool and Quicksilver himself looked down at them with curiosity. *A Mars Quake?* thought Elvis. Or was it the Earth ship's arrival he just couldn't see yet? He had little time to ponder, as there was the sudden arrival of a monopole-cat, who just flopped out of the sky and landed next to him. It was Katya, panting and lying on her back trying to find a moment to speak between her gasps for carbon dioxide.

'What's up?' Fionix asked with concern, waddling over to find out what was wrong.

'Serious problem... mission compromised ... *they're* coming...'

'What, who?'

'...zombie army ... of plants ...'

The next moment there was a sudden wave of walking plants from the south. Well not so much walking, but stumbling. Some were staggering, some were dragging a leg, others half-formed were clawing themselves along the ground and they were all heading straight towards Starkwood. They were led by the two most well-dressed plants. One plant, male, looked like a spitting image of Starkwood, but perhaps lacking in the brain area. He had his two sepals pointing forward and horizontal in the stereotypical zombie sleepwalking pose. The female looking plant, Ephanie, had the added accessory of a forward pointing tail that hung over her head and held in the cage-like end was a glowing white chrysalis.

The Charge of the Light Green Brigade was not so much a high-speed one, but more an unstoppable lava flow, slow and steady. There were hundreds of zombie weeds following the leading couple, maybe even thousands, all in various stages of formation, or, more accurately, stages of *deformation*. It wasn't actually clear whether they could feel emotions as the living plants did, but they must have felt some kind of single-minded force – one that had driven them thousands of kilometres across the planet on this plant pilgrimage to meet their Saint Arkwood.

Starkwood realised something was wrong but didn't quite know what. Quicksilver instinctively picked up the limp body of Katya, who was still recovering, and gently lowered her into his own pool to play a kind of medical waterbed – he had just enough time to flow to one side to avoid the slow motion stampede of Green Walkers. They hobbled past, like some badly choreographed Michael Jackson Zombie Video (ahead of its time), and the horde had no qualms about trampling anything in its path. None of the crop seemed to have a desire to bite any of the bystanders or eat their brains (or maybe they had decided there weren't enough brains to bother with). Fionix was frozen with shock for a second or two as she took in what was going on, then looked skyward in case the lander turned up at the worst possible moment and made this double-booked date even more awkward than it already was. The dust being kicked up by the Green Fun Run, she thought, would've been enough to let Earth know that a Marsathon was taking place and there were new Animal and Plant Kingdoms to conquer and more trophy heads to hang on the walls of their earthly homes, more names to add to the endangered and extinct lists.

She had to stop Earth seeing anything. Everything!

For the moment, there was no lander in sight, thank the heavens, but how much longer did they have before it arrived and saw the flower power party in progress?

'Who ordered all this salad?' asked Elvis in his usual dry, ironic way.

As the front of the procession approached Elvis and was only a few metres away, Starkwood looked closely then asked them: 'Do I know any of you?'

There was no answer; they just continued getting closer.

'Are you my long lost family?'

One of the zombie plants, one with a face, opened his mouth and tried to speak.

'ARK... OOD...'

'Ah, that doesn't sound encouraging,' said Starkwood, as he fast picked up that he might want to back away from his sociopathic fans. He started to uproot his toes from the cracks in Elvis' shell that not so long ago he had returned to with joy.

A second zombie joined in the chant, 'ARK... OOD!' then gradually more and more augmented the sound.

When the marching mulberry bushes started climbing onto Elvis' shell, Starkwood finally got the hint and jumped off the back. Elvis had no choice but to retract himself to protect his squishy bits from being trampled to mush.

Sadly, Fionix hadn't scanned the skies thoroughly when she gave them a quick look. She was understandably distracted by the herds, nay, flocks, no, *plague* of plants. Fortunately there was another pair of eyes on the skies, though technically it was only one eye because of an eye patch (those patches were quite popular at this time). There was a sudden cry from Elvis' head. It was from a pyrite that had recently installed a sort of crow's nest sticking up like a radio antenna on the tortle's temple.

'There she blows!' he cried with all he was worth.

'Who?' asked Elvis, still distracted by the plants now using him as a welcome mat.

'A ship be coming!'

'Where?'

'Upwards from the port and starboard bows, Admiral!'

'It's descending!' cried Fionix as she followed the lookout's directions.

The worst-case scenario was now happening! A procession of petal waving plants arrives just as a visitor from another planet was landing, an uninvited guest that would be looking for the merest whiff of an excuse to conquer and destroy any system that was working better than its own.

Fionix didn't take her eyes off the approaching light, but called to the person at the epicentre of the tsunami of ten thousand trees.

'Starkwood!' Fionix said with alarm, 'lead them away! Now!'

'What?' said the disorientated plant.

'Do as she says,' said Elvis, as another walking wallflower stepped on his head on its way to get closer to its maker.

'Why is this happening to me?!' asked Starkwood, as he turned tail and started to hop in slow motion away from the approaching line of lilacs.

At the same time, Elvis shuffled just out of the path of the migratory mangroves. He looked up again and the light in the sky did seem to be coming directly at them.

'Stop moving!' said Fionix in a loud whisper.

'Are you asking us or the craft?' said Elvis and Fionix gave him a hard stare.

'Not moving now,' said Elvis to please his friend.

'I'll hide too,' said Quicksilver, who pooled himself in the space behind Elvis on the opposite side to where the craft seemed to be heading.

Meanwhile Starkwood was plodding north and the trail of followers were still following him, still chanting 'Ark ood' very badly. The slow speed at which they were passing by suggested that they would not be out of sight when the landing craft arrived.

'Aren't *you* going to hide?' Elvis asked Fionix.

Fionix was staring at the lander as it was now within a few tens of metres of the ground. Elvis could see the look of a predator in her eyes, as if she was weighing up the pros and cons of attacking the invading Viking Lander. She even seemed to be crouching, ready to pounce.

'Camera might be on,' Elvis suggested.

'It's not,' said Fionix, twitching as the fight or flight scenario played over in her mind.

'Would they accept another failed landing?'

'Most of them have been…'

'Too many might arouse suspicion…'

Fionix paused to think.

'If we can just keep *this* patch of Mars as dead and as empty looking as possible until the craft's batteries run out, then we can live to hide another day.'

While watching the last moments of descent, and the slow moving crowd leaving the scene, Fionix weighed up her options.

'We can't let them know there's anyone here!' she said, exasperated. 'If those humans find out, then it's the end of life on Mars as we know it, and it's already hard enough as it is…'

At that moment, the Viking I lander finally came to rest on the surface with a little bump, clouds of particulate material rising around it in the process. The first successful landing on another planet by Earth… for the time being anyway. As the dust settled, the Defence Team watched from their hiding places (Elvis looked like a rock anyway, as long as he kept his head and limbs out of sight). The craft was now silent. No lights on. Nothing moving. No one seemed to be home. The Martian surroundings were not as quiet and tranquil as hoped for. A rowdy convoy of rebel radishes were in the wrong place at the wrong time (not that a right place and right time ever existed). Fionix looked at the dormant craft and had to make a decision fast. It had a bunch of landing pads on the ends of what looked like its bony legs. Its body had one eye on the top, which was the main camera and the lander seemed to have only one arm, which was all folded up. The craft seemed to be sleeping for the moment. She looked at the zombie plants and again at the craft.

She was transfixed for a second or two by what was happening – but then noticed some lights coming to life on the lander. In an instant, Fionix jumped over the stampede of plants and extended her wings outwards in front of herself – forming a huge umbrella over the Viking Lander – and brought her wing's edge tight to the ground. She created a huge hemispherical shell over the craft. More lights were lighting up on the lander as Fionix's wings started to change colour, chameleon-fashion.

Meanwhile, Starkwood was hopping round the edge of this newly formed dome, in an anticlockwise direction as seen from above, albeit it in slow motion, but it was fast for a bunch of zombie plants who were only supposed to be able to just about move without being picked up on a movement detector. Elvis and his friends just stared in disbelief at the almost endless traipsing of passing plants. It seemed quite surreal. Inside the dome created by Fionix's umbrella wings, the Viking lander was now coming to life; the camera lens was opening. Anyone inside the dome would have seen Fionix's wings change colour and texture to become almost invisible; near the ground she took on the shades and colours of the Martian soil, even creating patchy areas that looked like randomly scattered rocks on sand, exactly matching the actual rocks on the outside of the literal planetarium. Arched over the top she changed to look like the sky itself – still dark, but with dawn fast approaching she became lighter in the direction of the soon-to-be-rising sun. Her wings blocked out the crazy cross-country run of zombie plants on the outside, which by now had already made half a circuit round the dome, as they continued to chase Starkwood. The end of the marching column of Faithful Followers did not yet seem to be in sight, but for the moment at least, the Viking Lander One – and hence, Earth – was not aware of all the Hellas that had just been let loose on the Red-With-Embarrassment Planet.

Elvis tried to look over to Quicksilver, who was now on the other side of the highway of Starkwood lookalikes, to make sure he and Katya were okay. With Fionix sealing the Earth ship from the rest of Mars, he felt it was safe to talk.

'You okay?' he called over the tops of the zombie stalks.

'Oh I'm fine,' said the liquid horse, 'but our flying cat here doesn't look too good. I think she needs a flying doctor.'

'Ask her what's wrong.'

There was a pause. Between the slow stampede of plants, Elvis could see Quicksilver leaning down to talk to the sickly ferromagnetic feline.

'She's not got *mono*?' asked Elvis, 'I've heard these cats can get that quite often…'

More silence, but the unheard conversation continued. After a moment, Quicksilver raised his head and mane high out of what was now a silver sick bed and called across to the tortle.

'Katya says she's pregnant…'

'… Oh …'

More moments of silence (apart from the walking weeds). Then –

'And she's going into labour now…'

'… ah … can we help?'
More silence.
'She says yes, shortly.'
'Does she know who the father is?'
Another pause.
'… Yes …' said Quicksilver.
Elvis watched the next batch of botanical wanderers file past.
'… It was Starkwood…'
'… Oooh …Anything else? Not that that isn't a lot already…'
More silence but obvious hushed tones going on over the other side of the mobile moving hedge.
'… Yes … she says Starkwood's pregnant too… though with plants she says it's technically not called being pregnant but it amounts to the same thing…'
'Ahhhh,' reflected Elvis, 'perhaps it's best we don't say these things out loud – you never know how far away the Physics Police might be – although this actually sounds like a case for the Biology Police. And would I be right in thinking that Starkwood is also going into labour?'
The usual silence followed.
'… Katya says it should normally be a little later but the present stress might bring it on now…'
'Does Starkwood know he's pregnant?'
'She hasn't told him, but he might have worked it out himself. She says that's what those pods are hanging from his head. His babies!'
Elvis turned his attention back to that encircling trail of green runner beans. Starkwood had now completed one lap and was back where he started, now stumbling past Elvis himself. Starkwood stared wide-eyed at his tortle friend as he passed frantically.
'Help me!'
'How? I can't move as fast as you!' said Elvis.
'Stamp on them! I don't know – eat them!'
'You know it's not in my nature to kill living things.'
'But they're zombies! Already dead!' claimed Starkwood.

'Then I couldn't even make them more dead than they are. Plus I'm not a vegetarian – I eat rocks.'

'I'd forgive you this once!'

Elvis was walking and following his dynamic static friend, but was still being left behind.

'Have you not asked yourself why they're chasing you?' he posed to his veggy running mate.

'I have no idea!' shouted Starkwood. 'Ever since I got hit by that cosmic ray, everything's been going wrong.'

Elvis looked at the rag tag crowd of followers that were after his travelling companion. They came in all different shapes and sizes as well as varied stages of completion. They were all clearly electrostatic plant-like in their appearance. The same skinny stem as Starkwood, a kind of lolloping gait like Starkwood and, those that had flower heads shared the same untidy hairstyle of fronds. At the bottom of their stems, were the typical bulbous onion butts of the species. Below that, the roots were equally as entangled as Starkwood's. In fact, they all looked like dead ringers for Starkwood. Literally dead. A thought struck Elvis.

'Hey Starkie, I think your fan club here is actually connected with your cosmic experience,' but as he said this Starkwood was already too far away so he thought he'd wait until he came round the next time and contented himself with watching the never-ending plodding of the Green Army. It was at this point that the stragglers at the back end arrived. These were the more deformed, mutated or incomplete zombie plants that couldn't move quite as fast, or were perhaps less sharper minded and couldn't think quickly enough. Apart from the very last one in fact, which was a very low ability zombie plant, struggling to keep up, but seemed to be towing *another* creature. Actually, it was towing a *machine*! This caught Elvis' attention even more. The object attached to the last zombie plant by a vine-like rope looked like a small rectangular metal cuboid on a pair of skiis and the poor plant was pulling it along like a beast of burden ploughing a field. Then Elvis noticed a tiny creature sitting on the top of the mobile metal box. He peered closer.

'Masha?!' he asked with surprise, recognising the pyrite captain.

'Admiral!' said Masha, suddenly realising the importance of the tortle she had just encountered, and she stood up on the top of her mini Russian Rover and saluted Elvis with her two right arms.

'You traded in my daughter for a new model?' Elvis asked.

'Long story sir,' said Masha, clearly respectful towards him, 'been following this fleet for a while now sir. We harpooned this plant to see where they were all going.'

'Looks like they found their goal,' Elvis said, watching Starkwood disappear round the curve of the dome. 'So how is Ruby? You finally got fed up with her?'

'Having a pause from each other sir,' said Masha uncomfortably, not wanting to criticise the daughter of one of the most renowned ships in the navy, so to speak, 'sorting out some ethical and moral differences of opinion, Sir.'

Elvis tried to hide a wry smile. He could just about keep up with the slowest end of the protest march with Masha on her mechanical vessel, but they were now part of the second ring of ramblers that were a lap behind the front-runners.

'Ruby's morals being worse than the average pyrite's, I suppose?' Elvis asked, then answered before Masha had to question her loyalties, 'Don't worry, I know what my daughter's like! She's got a good heart, if she ever remembers to switch it on, but she does like to be the most rebellious rebel in rebel land.'

'I hope to sort it out with her Sir...'

'I'm sure you will captain,' Elvis agreed, 'now, tell me, what you know about these dynamic dandelions!'

'Well Sir, they actually seem harmless. They've not attacked or eaten anything on their way here.'

'And how long have you been following them?'

'Some months. I picked up this mechanical ship where

Hanksie left it but it didn't have any power left in it. By chance, this bunch of plants crossed my path so I decided to follow them. I lassoed one of the less intellectual ones and here I am.'

'Good move,' said Elvis, 'I have a feeling these plants have something to do with Starkwood being hit by a cosmic ray some time ago. All but his head got blown up, but a monopole-cat friend grew a new body for him.'

'Sounds like Katya,' Masha pointed out.

'That's the one. Anyway, I got the feeling that this troupe of Biodegradable Bud-heads are somehow badly cloned copies from the bits of Starkwood that got blasted off him in that accident.'

Due to the lapping that Starkwood was doing on the later arrivals to the circular ball, he now found himself running *among* the zombies, with not only many staggering in front of him and behind him, but also to his left and right. Starkwood looked to the mutated clone to his right and gave an awkward smile then looked ahead again and produced his go-to anxious face. The simple-minded clone looked back at him and smiled a slightly more gormless smile and he too continued to follow the green team runner in front of them. They both realised the situation and looked at each other in shock and the zombie clone pointed and cried '…ARK… OOD!!'

This made the zombies in front slow down and stop, then turn around. In fact, the ones following from behind slowed to a halt as both groups stared at each other in confusion and this standing stillness propagated forwards and backwards to all the other zombie plants until the whole ring of a thousand or more of them had become static again.

Starkwood was panting a little and the sap could be seen pumping round his veins.

'…ARK … OOD,' continued one of the zombie plants, then it grew to a duet in which one was not quite in tune or in time with the other.

'ARK OOD!' came the cry a little louder as it became a trio then a quartet and quintet up into the full orchestra of Arkwood instruments.

'ARK OOD!' was the collective response and then the originator of this extended family panicked. Rather than run radially away from the area, Starkwood started to waddle up one of Fionix's wings, and it curved below Starkwood's roots like space curving around a mass using the rubber sheet analogy. Of course it was a bit like trying to run on a trampoline and Starkwood bounced up and down with each root step as he headed for the top. It didn't take long for the zombie plants to copy him and soon there were dozens, then hundreds, climbing up onto Fionix's gossamer thin wings, which started to sag under the weight of these volatile vegetables.

Fionix was horrified.

'Get these jumping beans off my back!' she cried, not enjoying being used like a bouncy castle, then she shook her wings. This sent the zombie plants flying in all directions, like a lawn mower that had lost its collecting basket. The pause in the merry go round madness was clearly temporary as Starkwood, then all his lookalike fans, picked themselves up and worked out their bearings – and where the real Starkwood was – then resumed their chase.

Now that the area surrounding Fionix was cleared of its unwanted weeds, Elvis was able to reunite with Quicksilver, who was still nursing the very expectant Katya. Masha, had released her mini Rover's connection to her zombie plant and she stopped next to Elvis.

'Are you alright?' Elvis asked Katya, with genuine concern.

'I'll survive,' said Katya in a dismissive way.

'But how did you get pregnant?' Elvis asked, with great curiosity.

'No time to talk about cross-pollination between species now,' said Katya, 'we need to get rid of this plague. They want Starkwood for some reason, so we need him to lead them away.'

'I don't think we can get him to think straight in his present condition,' Elvis explained, 'he's in hysteria mode – he won't respond.'

'Then we force him,' said Katya, 'or maybe we could make a decoy...'

'Go on,' Elvis invited her.

'If we disconnected him from his new body and send *the body* walking off by itself then all the zombies would follow it, thinking it's him, which it sort of is, but the important part of him will still be with us...?'

The others pondered this – then Katya let out a meow of labour pains, so they all got distracted. When Katya recovered she was breathing heavily, but managed to speak.

'I don't have the strength to pull Starkwood's head away from the new body. He would have formed too many new tendons and sap tubes.'

'That's okay,' said Masha and she produced four shiny cutting swords, one in each of her four forelimbs. The dozen or so other pyrites that had remained loyal to her (as the Russian Rover's crew), also drew their numerous weapons of Mass Slicing Destruction.

'Ah haar!' cried Terry the Terrible, then Masha gave him a hard stare and he clammed up. Masha thought about it and repented.

'Okay, you're right: AH HAAR!'

The dirty dozen grinned with delight and answered back, 'AH HAAR!'

'You're going to cut him up?!' said Katya in disbelief.

'No,' said Masha, 'more, *dissect* him *surgically*. See my shipmate over there: the one with the white hat on? He's our cook and he knows how to dice and slice vegetables.'

'Ah, but once we remove Starkwood, the new body won't be able to walk by itself,' explained Katya. 'It's not like the zombies, which grew in a different way.'

'Well,' thought Masha quickly, 'we'll harpoon another zombie and have it pull the decapitated Starkwood body along on the back of this Russian Rover.'

'Doesn't the rover have its own power source?' asked Katya.

'Not to begin with, no,' explained Masha, 'it was

connected to the landing craft by a cable of some kind, but Hanksie must have severed that when he sailed off on it. My crew went back and pulled out a battery from the Mother Ship and put it in the Rover but it didn't last long...'

'I might have a solution to that,' said Katya and she unfurled her long prehensile tail and the hand like rooted end extended towards the Rover.

'Just step off it for a moment,' Katya said and the dozen pyrites obliged.

When Katya's tail grabbed the Rover, her own hair first stood on end, then blue sparks came out of her tail and ran wild over the body of the mini rover. There was a crackling sound then Katya's body hair suddenly lost its charge.

'That should do,' said Katya. 'I think I just charged the Rover's batteries, so you should be able to move by yourself, at least long enough to coax these zombies away...'

Masha nodded in gratitude then signalled to her crew and off they bounded, making their way to the epicentre of the disturbance to cut Starkwood down to size.

Elvis, Katya and Quicksilver could hear some swishing and slicing sounds, among which were a few screams from a hysterical Starkwood. Moments later the head with its mini body came arcing and spinning slowly across the sky and – plonk! – right on to Elvis's shell.

The next falling object turned head over heels, though there wasn't actually a head, so more *neck hole* over heels – well *roots* – and the recently grown body of Starkwood pulled a few somersaults then landed upright on the Rover, swaying back and forth a little, until the pyrites had dropped ropes and pulled them tight to hold the shell of the body in place. Masha switched the electric rover on then looked back at the others.

'I'll do what I can,' she said, 'but this is just a temporary solution.'

'Thanks Captain,' said Elvis, giving her a salute and Quicksilver and Katya made the same gesture.

Masha returned the gesture then spoke to Katya.

'Good luck with having your, um, kittens?…'

'Actually,' Katya explained, 'technically as they're crossbred with a plant, they would be called *Katkins*…'

'Permission to speak?' came the voice of Captain Sam Biosis.

'Yes Sam,' replied Elvis, 'do you have any advice?'

'Not wishing to be coming across like an old fashioned cap'n sir, but an optimal plan would be that I commandeer that mechanical ship in place of Cap'n Masha.'

'What?!' said Masha, clearly insulted.

'Beggin' your pardon and be as hearin' me out Cap'n Marina. I'm not doubting your ability to lead these zombies away. No. It's more that you are suited to helpin' the Green cat in her hour of need, what with you two being as soul sisters, as what you said in your own words…'

17

Katkins, Pussywillows and Runaway Runner Beans

The Pied Piper in the form of Sam steering the mini-rover with the 'empty' shell of Starkwood's recently grown body was successfully leading the Zombie Army of Plants away from the Viking I landing site. As the decoy slowly disappeared over the horizon, with the unwanted weeds, the pyrites could be heard singing.

'An it's no, nay never! No nay never no more! Will I sail the Mars Rover, no never no more!'

They headed north-east, but in fact, any direction would have been good enough to free Fionix the embarrassment of letting the monopole-cat out of the bag, so to speak. However, a different proverbial cat was now the new problem.

'Admiral,' said Masha, obviously a little put out at being removed from her own plan, 'I'm at your disposal...'

'Don't worry,' said Elvis, 'at least you're freed up to help out here. Would you mind standing in as my temporary captain, until this is all sorted out?'

'It would be an honour, Admiral,' said Masha, perking up a bit.

'Good for you! Now Ruby's trained you well for most things, but how are you with delivering babies?'

'Where do I need to take them?' said Masha in all sincerity.

'Um into this world actually.'

'Ah, well I'm willing to give it my best sir.'

'That's the spirit,' said Elvis.

'What does it involve?'

'Not quite sure,' admitted Elvis, 'I've never assisted in something like this before myself. I guess we'll be learning together...'

Starkwood had been taken down from Elvis' shell and placed next to Katya. Elvis turned to look at his two overly ripe friends, who were lying on the ground head to head but facing opposite directions. Both were groaning.

'As you know, Masha,' Elvis continued, 'us tortles, well, the *mother* tortle, digs a hole, then lays her eggs in it and then covers them up with dirt and after that we just wait around for a few years. Not much to it. But these two here could involve boiling water and some towels to soak up whatever liquid comes out, for all I know.'

By now, Elvis was facing the two expectant parents, who were surrounded by Quicksilver's stainless steel looking liquid structures. He certainly made the environment look clean and sanitary. Elvis spoke to Katya.

'So,' he started, 'you're our resident expert of life on Mars. Can you tell us what happens next?'

'No!' cried Katya, 'I've never been pregnant before! And certainly not by a plant!'

'It's not my fault!' cried Starkwood. 'It's you grabbing me all the time with that creepy tail of yours.'

'That shouldn't make us pregnant,' said Katya.

'I shouldn't be cross-pollinated like this with another species!' cried Starkwood. 'My mother warned me about magnetic creatures like you!'

'Okay,' said Elvis calmly, 'I realise you both must be trying to cope with a large imbalance of hormones or something, so let's save the recriminations for later and just deal with the problem in hand... in tail...'

He took a deep breath and reminded himself not to show any hint that he had less than no idea about what to do, nor to let on that he was only a thin acting mask away from hysteria himself.

'Katya,' he began, 'with all your knowledge about the Natural History of Mars... and probably the *unnatural* history, would you be able to hazard a guess concerning monopole-cats getting impregnated by an electrostatic plant?'

'Oh... er,' and she looked worried and started panting a

little, 'well, it'd probably be a reproductive process like budding...'

'Good, well that's a start,' said Dr Elvis and he looked across at Nurse Quicksilver and gave a hopeful smile.

'I can feel the bumps under my fur,' Katya explained. 'I think they're ripe and ready to burst out, like, any moment!'

'Okay, and is there anything we can do to help?'

Katya was pulling pained faces as she tried to think clearly about this never before, and probably never to be repeated, event.

'Just catch them when they appear...'

'I think we can do that my friend,' said Elvis, in what he hoped was a calming and soothing voice. As he said this, Masha was already walking across the shiny liquid that was both Quicksilver and a heat blanket for the mothers-to-be. Masha came up to one of Katya's paws and took hold of one of her sharp claws. Masha's hand just fit round the pointy end and she squeezed. Katya rubbed Masha's back in a reciprocal gesture.

'Is it worth us shouting *push*?' asked Masha, which made Katya smile through the pain. 'We could also get some pyrites to do a bit of *pulling*, if necessary.'

'Glad you're here, sister,' said Katya to Captain Masha, 'but no pyrites pulling ropes this time, thanks all the same.'

Elvis resumed his questioning; 'Now Katya, a similar question, what's the likely outcome when an electrostatic plant gets fertilised by a monopole-cat?'

'It shouldn't have happened either,' she began.

'I'm sure you're right,' agreed Elvis, 'but sometimes hundred million to one chance things actually happen. So what's your considered opinion?'

'Well...' she pondered through her own pain, 'we can all see the pods that have been growing from Starkwood's head, so I've got a feeling that they are likely to spread a bit like those spider plants on Earth. They are probably aiming for the ground anyway. But, being half monopole-cat, the pods could just open when they're near enough to the ground and the seedlings drop to the soil… But I don't really know. They could be more cat than plant, which would mean they may end up running around, rather than becoming planted, or even fly along the field lines. Who knows?!'

'Fair enough,' said Elvis, 'so what might we be able to do to help?'

'Maybe they just need to be buried in the ground and the soil will do the rest? I'm really just guessing…'

'Thanks,' said Elvis, then he turned to Masha, 'okay Chief Medical Officer Masha, can you get half the crew in position to catch any *Katkins* that pop out of Katya and the other half can start planting Starkwood's pods into the ground to help the… *Pussy Willows*, start life off on the right, um root…'

Masha saluted Elvis then stroked Katya's claw again before she bounded back onto Elvis' carapace and started assembling the other pyrites.

* * * * *

In the 4D bubble apartment of Amelius III and his friend Turkan, Turkan was actually blowing some 4D soap bubbles, using a wire frame dipped in soap solution. The frame itself was the shape of a tesseract. To us it looked like the edges of a wire cube sitting inside a larger wire frame of a cube with the corresponding corners joined diagonally. Turkan had a handle, which he held then he blew into the complex soap film frame to create bubbles with the same shape as the frame, making dozens of them of many different sizes. Amelius looked on.

'Pretty aren't they?' said Turkan casually.

'Yes,' said Amelius the Third, still captivated by them, 'but have you finished filling in all the paperwork? That incident on Earth with the green cat and the tunnelling worm duo?'

'Nearly,' said Turkan, taking another breath then blowing into the wire web again, releasing a whole new wave of tesseract bubbles that flashed all the colours of the spectrum.

'Can I have a go at bubble blowing?' Amelius asked.

'Sure,' said his friend, 'in a moment...'

Just then there was an alarm hyper-sound ringing and a light flashing with square-wave photons, letting them know there was another breach of security.

'Oh,' Turkan began, 'sorry, it'll have to wait. It seems we have another criminal act happening...' and he put down his bubble frame and looked at his 3D computer screen, which was like a hologram in the cubic space above his keyboard, 'Ah, look, it's something happening on the *same* Red Planet we went to before!'

'*Again*?!' said Amelius III, 'what have they done *now*?!'

There was a pause as the final multi-cube bubbles popped and cleared the air.

'Looks like another highly improbable event and, hey, you'll never guess! It involves the *same* green cat we saw on Earth *and* that moving plant that got hit by a cosmic ray!'

'Well what are the chances of *that* happening?' joked Amelius.

'Hopefully not too high,' laughed Turkan, 'or we'll have to arrest ourselves.'

As he said this, both Turkan and Amelius III started to morph into tesseract bubble versions of themselves then pop out of existence in this space.

* * * * *

The next moment two three dimensional protrusions of four dimensional creatures were materialising just next to the impromptu Maternity Ward.

Masha and a number of pyrites were crawling all over Starkwood. Like termites they were making their way along the stems that led to the hanging pods and the more lice that collected on each pod, the more they weighed them down until they were reaching the ground. Quicksilver, who was using his own pool to create the sterile surface below the two expectant creatures, then started making holes in his silver liquid surface to reveal the ruddy Martian soil below each hanging seed. Another batch of pyrites were now jumping into the clear patches of soil and starting to dig away. This came naturally to them from millions of years of dealing with buried treasure (or just burying their adversaries, alive probably).

As the first Physics Policeman materialised, none other than Police Officer Craggy Thomas, he shouted 'Gotcha!' with glee, but then realised he was facing the wrong way. Once again he was in 'little green man' mode in the naïve hope he'd fit in – though had he landed in the middle of the zombie stampede, that would have been the case.

As Officer Craggy Thomas turned round, the second Physics Law Enforcer arrived, Officer Ben and he too shouted the 'Gotcha!' cry of joy at dropping in on the guilty red handers. He also had his back to the supposed culprits, so after a moment of embarrassment he turned round and took up the same stance as his partner and together they cried, 'Gotcha!'

Elvis, and even the prostrate Starkwood and Katya raised their heads to look at the two Cosmic Clowns, only to react with disappointed realisation.

'Not *them* again...' said Katya, without fully understanding why she felt that. She let her head fall back down and splash into the calming mercury bath that was Quicksilver.

'Oh dear,' said Officer Thomas, 'we are in trouble aren't we?' and his voice was dripping with fake concern.

'Becoming repeat offenders now eh?' said Officer Ben, with a patronising tone that comes so easily to four-dimensional beings in front of lower dimensional creatures.

'Not now...' said Katya to herself as she stared upwards at the empty sky, 'please not now...'

'Good morning, officers,' said Elvis politely, 'how nice to see you again.'

'Soft soaping won't work with us,' said Craggy, 'we're not standing for any more nonsense!'

'Yeah,' said Wedgy, 'It's nasty cop, nasty cop this time!' he said as he called up the file on his electronic notepad.

'What seems to be the trouble officer?' Elvis continued, 'You see we are rather overwhelmed with challenges at the moment.'

'Oh, we are *well* aware of this gang's mischief,' said Wedgy.

'I'm not aware of anything we've done wrong officer,' said Elvis, 'certainly not intentionally.'

'What, like the hundred million year cosmic ray incident with you and your Pet Petunia,' said Craggy with a slight sneer, then turning to Katya 'and you with your creepy crawly worm friend on the planet next door.'

'I don't remember that,' said Katya with a sigh, 'I was in bilocational lockdown at the time.'

'No excuse – ah here it is,' and Wedgy found the appropriate entry.

'You, Miss Katya and you, Mister Arkwood, are accused of highly unlikely cross pollination. And once again you, Mister Arkwood, are at the centre of breaking the laws of probability. You're just like that Maxwell Demon we keep trying to catch!'

'It wasn't on purpose,' Katya began.

'It never is, is it,' Craggy said without any compassion.

At that moment, Dmitry the QT worm popped out of Katya's fur.

'They're done,' he said out of context, then did a double take 'Oh! You two again.'

'That cocky worm,' Craggy realised.

'Those useless cops,' said Dmitry irreverently.

'Disrespecting an Enforcer of the Law!'

'I'm sure he didn't mean anything by it,' Elvis interjected, trying to avoid a scene and desperately attempting to get this unwanted challenge out of the way so they could get back to the two other unwanted challenges. Both felt more important than the cross-species thing.

'I'm   adding   *that*   to   the   growing   list   of

misdemeanours…' said the unyielding law enforcement officer.

'*Enforcer*?!' said Dmitry with surprise. '*Deformer* more like! All this is due to you two! I know about your positronic pad that messed up!'

'Please! I'm about to give birth!' cried Katya with genuine concern.

'*Illegally* ma'am,' said Officer Thomas, leaning in towards her, 'scientifically, that is.'

Before Police Officer Craggy Thomas could react, a long green furry tail had wrapped a few times round his neck. He looked shocked, as did his partner who – to his credit – dived forward to come to his friend's aid. Wedgy grabbed the end of the tail that wasn't involved in strangling Officer Thomas, which had been writhing around like the nozzle of a high pressure water hose, but once he'd grabbed it, it then smothered his face like some face-hugging alien. The look on Katya's face – that was normally sweet and smiling, putting aside the present ongoing laboured look – went quite crazy. One might say psykatic. With the strangling and the face gagging, her two victims couldn't scream and all that could be heard were muffled noises of terror. Plus a bit of gurgling. Katya pulled them in even closer until their faces were just a few centimetres from hers. She was pulsating with waves of colours, like squid on Earth.

'If this goes to court,' said Katya – so calm, yet menacing, 'I will plead a serious imbalance of hormones. The more you struggle, the tighter this gets …'

Katya began to rise magnetically out of Quicksilver's stainless steel maternity ward, dragging her victims with her. Her colour was changing blue then red as she followed the local field lines, accelerating upwards and north-eastwards. Her ground-dwelling friends just stared, transfixed, having never expected their happy, easy-going, gentle, loving, magnetically attractive friend to go from Dr Katya to Miss Hyde. Even Fionix poked her head out of her thunder dome to witness her chief science officer carrying off her prey.

'Gentlemen,' Katya explained, as she carried them to destinations unknown, 'I love Science and Science is a lovely thing. You are both giving it a bad name. You are nasty people. You are vindictive and arrogant and basically all the things that science isn't. Rather than punishing, you should be educating. And I get the impression from my friend Dmitry that you might have had something to do with all of this anyway! Something about an anti-matter mix up in a parallel universe... So perhaps you should get your priorities right...'

Katya was reaching the top of her arc and the new members of her flying squad didn't know whether to panic about the socio-cat or the vertical distance they might now fall should Katya release them from her grip. Caught between a Crazy Cat and a High Place.

Katya continued.

'My theory is that when poor Starkwood got hit by that cosmic ray and you guys got your electrons mixed up with your positrons, something changed – which led to all *that* down *there*...'

And Katya turned their heads to see the long untidy line of uprooted refugee zombie plants, then turned them back to herself.

'... And Starkwood becoming ferociously fertile when I grabbed hold of him. Now, we're trying to save Our Planet from extinction and you're part of the problem. So maybe you can do something *constructive* for a change and sort out this crowd – before they let Earth know there's more life to destroy, once they finish the job on their home planet!'

Katya was almost at ground level now as she loosened the grip of the face-hugging end on Wedgy and the coils around Craggy. She plonked the two police officers on the ground, facing the runaway Starkwood husk on a trolley. Both Craggy and Wedgy were shocked and disorientated by their recent manhandling (though technically it was woman-handling, or maybe *cat*-handling). Craggy stood rubbing his neck, while Wedgy rubbed his overly hugged face and they stared at the peculiar silhouette of the wobbling Starkwood body double, trying to work out what it all meant, then they heard a rumbling from behind. They turned round slowly. They saw the hordes of mobile mangrove bushes, dynamic daisies, crawling crocuses and instinctively each held up a hand and shouted 'HALT!'

But the plants didn't. The police officers got trampled under root by this slow-moving river of prancing plants and they ended on their stomachs covering their faces in the soil.

'Let's get out of here!' cried Craggy and the next moment their three dimensional protrusions started to slip back into the safety of their four dimensional hyper-home.

'No!' cried Katya, now glowing so green like she was the Martian Hulk, ready to explode. She dashed back and just managed to grab onto Craggy's ankle with her tail. She put on the magnetic brakes, stopping the 4D interloper from disappearing through what literally seemed to be a rip in the Martian space-time continuum. Craggy was just off the beaten track of the marching maple trees, the trampling tomato plants, the, wait we haven't got time for this! With a front paw, Katya grabbed on to one of the passing zombie azaleas and dug her remaining three limbs into the topsoil, scrambling around for purchase – but she lacked the funds to buy anything. Her colours flickered the deepest shade of red to pull in the opposite direction to where Craggy was sneaking off to. And Katya was losing; only Craggy's leg was still in this universe and Katya did not want to follow him down this Wonderland Wormhole. And she didn't want to leave this walking time bomb of a zombie army roaming around her beloved home planet. What could she do?!

'Do you mind?' came a voice from just behind one of her ears. 'I'm trying to get some sleep…'

'Ah Dmitry!' she cried, 'I need your help!'

'Isn't that usually what happens when I pop up?' and Dmitry scanned the situation in the time it takes a particle to sneak through a potential barrier. 'Ah I see you're caught between a Craggy Rock and a Hard Plant...'

'I can't let these idiots leave without clearing up their mess!'

'Yeah, same thing's happening in a number of parallel universes...'

'What? So how do they solve it?!'

'How do I know? It's not finished yet!'

Katya felt herself being stretched by the two forces pulling her in opposite directions. She wasn't sure her body obeyed Hooke's Law, but she was pretty certain there would be an elastic limit and she didn't want to exceed it. As she extended like a tortured wretch on the rack, she felt sparks building up. It was a bit like the piezo electric effect, when a squished crystal converts the compression energy into electrical energy.

'Can you help, *please*!' she cried at Dmitry, as she strained fit to burst. 'This is worse than labour pains!'

'I suppose I can, but...'

'I promise I won't bother you anymore!'

'Really?' said Dmitry.

'Well not unless Mars is in danger again.'

'Ah, *there's* the catch,' he sighed, 'but I guess that's better than nothing.'

Meanwhile the Marching Magnolias still moved forwards, except the one Katya was clinging to; that plant merely tried to move, without realising why it wasn't getting anywhere. The electrical arcs and sparks and lightning forks were now spreading from the zombie plant that Katya was holding, to those nearby. The end of the procession was approaching, however.

Katya was making noises that one might have associated with the birth she was supposed to going through. Craggy's visible part was the bit below the knee and he was waggling it violently to shake off Katya's snake-like grip.

'Okay,' said Dmitry, 'I guess if you can keep making those pretty fireworks, I can see a solution. You know, entangle both sets of wave equations and make them one.'

'But I don't want to get caught up in it!' cried Katya.

'Ah,' Dmitry realised, 'so I guess you need me to take your place?'

'Will you be okay?'

'Eventually, though I'm not sure I want to go... Okay, come on then. You have to bring the plant and the leg of that multidimensional moron about this close...' and as he said this, he showed Katya his straightened out body. She looked through her squinting eyes at the worm that was barely a few centimetres long then checked out the distance between the end of her tail and the claw that was gripping the zombie plant walking on the spot (about two metres) and realised she had a large gap to bridge.

Craggy Thomas was now only showing his ankle, with the rest of him already in a different dimension. Katya dragged the easier-to-move plant closer to her, as her blue streaks of lightning spread further along the line of other Starkwood lookalikes, linking more and more of them into the enveloping plasma tree. As she brought the plant's sepal like arm closer to Craggy's foot, Dmitry climbed onto Katya's tail and waited for the hopeful uniting of 4D foot with the 3D plant.

The last of the zombie plants was now passing Katya's captured one and though her lightning streaks were still jumping the gap to the rest of the line of uprooted refugees, the plasma cords looked close to snapping and losing contact.

Those interlocking electrostatic strands of light had finally reached the front crawlers that, in turn, were just behind Sam Biosis on the Russian Rover and the headless Starkwood decoy.

'I can't hold it anymore!' cried Katya, as she made one final pull to bring the zombie plant's leaf to the Physics Police Officer's foot.

'See you on the other side,' said Dmitry and he bridged the gap between the two parties. The blue sparks surrounded him and Craggy's foot, and they became one wave equation with the straggly line of plants. Katya let go of both halves and fell to one side. In an instant

Craggy's final foot disappeared through the tear in space, but it dragged with it Dmitry (who was heard to shout 'weeee') and then one plant after the other like a tragic mountain-climbing expedition going wrong. In went all the less well-formed plants, then the better formed ones, then the good looking ones, including Ephanie herself and the Starkwood lookalike. Katya noticed the mini Russian Rover with the decoy also caught in the wave and heading for the way out. She quickly grabbed the Rover and whipped it out of the collapsing wave function, as the rest disappeared into dimensions unknown.

'Thanks ma'am,' came Sam's voice from the Rover.

Katya, exhausted, glanced at the little vehicle to see Captain Sam Biosis and his pyrites falling to the ground – alive and well.

Between pants, Katya gasped, 'Better get back to motherhood...'

'Come on yer bunch of slackers!' cried the captain, 'Let's be getting back to help the Admiral!'

Instead of hitching a ride on the swiftly disappearing green cat, the pyrites returned by foot.

Katya had switched her colour and was now flying back to her hospital bed. Her medical team were still staring in the direction in which she'd very illegally kidnapped (or was it cat-napped) the two unfortunate enforcers. 'Look out!' she cried, and luckily her aim was good enough as she headed straight for Quicksilver.

There was a splash of mercury and several popping sounds. As she hit the surface of the shiny liquid, a number of small items popped out of her green furry body. At the same time Masha shouted 'Fire!' and from Elvis launched a net, much like the sail that had helped Jade escape those jumping rocks. Katya's projectiles were caught in the net, which then fell gently back to the ground. There was a rush of pyrites who gathered up their catch and dragged them over to Katya, who was now floating calmly in the shallow mercury of Quicksilver's pool. After a rapid untangling of the nets, two newly hatched babies were freed and carried onto their mother's gently heaving belly. Masha oversaw this, then bounded down to the bunch of pyrites that were now dragging the net back towards Elvis.

'Gentlemen?' Masha asked them in a clearly suspicious tone. They tried to look innocent.

'Yes ma'am?' said one of them, the others all gathering behind him so that he was the only one in front, with the rest forming a wall of concealment where no gaze could enter.

'How many new-borns did you catch?'

'Um… a *number* of hatchlins ma'am…'

'And what number would that be?'

'… we be countin' two ma'am…'

'Maybe your maths isn't very good, mid-shellman. Try again…'

'Well, ma'am, we was kinda hopin' there would be a *reward*, seein as we be doin a good deed…'

'The reward,' said Masha, 'is that I don't do a caesarean section on you with my sword.'

And as she said this one of her fore arms appeared with the aforementioned sword.

'So we won't be havin' any salvage rights ma'am?'

'No.'

Masha's second forearm appeared with a spiked ball on a chain.

'No treasure trove like as we used to in the Days of the Oceans?'

'Hand it over…'

A third forearm appeared with a spear.

'We used to be takin' hostages ma'am and then gets paid for returning them, as unharmed of course… ma'am.'

The fourth forearm appeared with a double-headed axe.

'*Mainly* unharmed…' said another from the second row.

'Shh!' said the front pyrite, now realising he might not remain unharmed himself. There was a shuffling and a movement among the ranks and a bundle wrapped in part of the netting was pushed forward.

Masha made a gesture with her head and several dozen pyrites picked up the hatchling and carried it onto the silver pond's rippling surface then hauled it up onto Katya's belly to join the other two triplets.

Starkwood, who had been lying down throughout the comings and goings, as the pyrites planted his pods, now sat up to have a look at Katya. As he did so, the umbilical cords that were attached from his head to the buried seeds snapped, his offspring now technically 'sown'. Quicksilver, seeing that the labour was now over for the both of them, collected himself together and gathered round Katya to give her some privacy, creating some rather attractive fountains that formed sheets of mercury all around her.

Pyrites were running around like ants, before they all boarded His Martian Shellship (HMS) Elvis. The whole group were still behind him, hidden from the Viking Lander in case Fionix stopped her temporary dome.

With Katya and her offspring now 'screened off' and Starkwood's pods planted and awaiting the harvest, Starkwood sat with his back against Elvis' carapace and sighed. Quicksilver too looked at Elvis.

'Feels like it's all over bar the shouting...' Starkwood said, slightly bewildered at the mad hour they'd just gone through.

'Might be some crying still to come,' said Elvis thoughtfully. 'Parenthood does bring out a lot of emotions... and the babies might do some crying too.'

Elvis turned to speak to his temporary new captain.

'Thank you for your assistance, Masha.'

'You're welcome sir.'

'Well-handled, that baby-napping incident.'

'The crew are fighting a habit of a lifetime, sir... the habit *of* fighting.'

'You know our work, well *your* work, is not over by a long shot?'

'It never is sir. I'm ready for it, and I will ensure the crew will be ready too.'

'I'm sure you will, Masha,' said Elvis with a smile, and

as he spoke, he spotted his own captain, and his band of pyrites, hopping back from their little sojourn on the Russian Rover.

* * * * *

When the new litter and vegetable crop had made their entrance and mother and plant were both coping, Fionix decided it was safe to stop being the chameleon dome hiding the Viking I Lander. During the night, when the craft was not taking photographs, she brought down the 'big top' (herself). Unfortunately, Elvis had to stay where he was – his presence had appeared on Fionix's camouflaged wings, so the Earthlings were expecting to see a two and a half metre boulder. Fionix had to leave, because she had other important business to attend to: finding out where the second Viking craft was going to land.

18

Cydonia, A Hill Too Far

The Umpteenagers stood there, staring at the great monolith in front of them. In a relatively flat plain, there was just this odd isolated hill on the horizon. But it was this one to the north that had grabbed their attention. It was not unlike that solitary outcrop in Australia called Uhuru. It was a few kilometres across and about three hundred metres high. Even at the distance where they had stopped, it was awe-inspiring.

'He's up there,' said Jade, as they all strained their necks and stared at the monumental mound.

Catapilla, who was not quite as fast as the tortles in spite of the extra legs, arrived and joined Jade and Grit in the line-up of onlookers. Minisilver observed from his vantage point in the warmed hotplate among the cracks of Jade's carapace. Cap'n Raffi also peered from Jade's nose.

'You sure?' asked Catapilla, catching her breath from the almost nonstop several thousand kilometre trek from the north-west edge of the Hellas basin to here, Cydonia.

'Look,' said Jade, pointing, 'you can still see some vague footprints leading to the foot of the cliff...'

'And look over there!' Grit put in, 'Clouds of dust.'

'So?' asked Catapilla, as she lifted each of her own feet – including the pseudo pods – and shook the dust back to the ground.

'There's no wind,' Jade explained, 'so why is there dust up there?'

'We're lucky there's hardly been any wind for months,' Grit pointed out, 'otherwise we would have lost the trail ages ago.'

'You two are becoming quite the hunters aren't you?' Minisilver praised them.

'Thanks,' Jade acknowledged the compliment, 'but what's he doing up there?'

'More of his graffiti I suppose,' suggested Grit.

'Yes, but why here?' Jade asked.

'He's a show off,' Minisilver commented.

'We need to catch him as soon as possible,' said Grit, 'before he gives us all away.'

'Pity none of us can fly…' said Jade idly, 'we could get up there faster…'

There was a pause as the B team reflected on their challenge.

'Beggin' yer pardon ma'am,' interrupted Captain Raffi. 'You can fly?!'

'Not as such me lady,' Raffi explained, 'but us pyrites as bein' creatures of high power an' only light weight, meself excepting ma'am…' and he patted his middle-aged tummy, 'some of me crew can clear tall rocks in a single leap, and doing it at high speed ma'am…'

'I've never seen them do that.'

'Cos that's how quick they can move me lady! All those years a pillaging and stealing treasures from other tortles, not that we do it any more of course.'

'Of course,' Jade accepted. 'Okay, well could you send a scouting party out ahead and let us know what's going on?'

'A pleasure to carry out the duty ma'am and be assured that they will bring back the intelligence for you – though them that has the agility of body are not exactly those that has the intelligence of mind, but they do be quick.'

'Thank you captain.'

The party watched a dozen or so long-legged tortle lice bound off Jade's shell and like acrobatic fleas, they did indeed make the slow moving umpteenagers feel even more like the snailens of this world.

* * * * *

From the southern edge of the mesa's rim, the umpteenaged party had a clear view of the rest of the hill. They could see Hanksie's dust trail only too obviously now, as he continued to cut a groove around the edge of the whole mound.

'He's shaping it,' Grit realised.

'It's like a huge sculpture,' Jade pointed out. 'Poor Great Uncle Syd...'

'Excuse me ma'am?'

'Yes captain?'

'The trap be set and ready and just awaitin' your word ma'am.'

'And it won't hurt Uncle Syd?'

'I have told the crew that any harm that comes to the Uncle is a coming back to them tenfold.'

'Is that necessary?'

'Well,' Raffi explained, 'most of them can't count that high, but I think they got the message.'

'Okay, thank you captain,' then she turned to Catapilla.

'Are you ready?'

'Will your uncle listen to me?'

'If you stay in character, yes. Minisilver? You sure this will work?'

'Well,' said the little silver horse-puddle, 'If this Hanksie is as narcissistic as his artwork suggests, then he's as good as caught.'

'Good, Grit?'

'I'm ready, but how much time do we have?'

'Katya didn't know when she spoke to us,' Jade reminded him, 'but the craft was expected around now. We've seen that light crossing the sky regularly now, so it seems it's already in orbit.'

'She still hasn't come back,' he said with concern, 'plus we still haven't seen those Hellas Angels either...'

'I imagine everyone's busy with their own role.'

'I suppose so...'

This was not Jade's plan A. Earlier there had been a lively discussion when Minisilver mentioned his extra dimensional insides. Jade thought it might be a way of capturing the wayward artist. If Minisilver could surround and engulf Hanksie, he could then make his surface area too small for the creative crab to climb out. It'd be an ideal holding cell until the Hellas Angels arrived.

Sadly, as Minisilver explained, the extra dimension's depth depended on the mass of mercury involved. The heavier the horse, the deeper the dimension; fat fillies are more profound. Mini went on about it being a fourth power relationship but it boiled down to the fact that if Mini spread himself out wide enough to swallow Hanksie, it wouldn't be deep enough for him to be completely submerged. End of Plan A and back to Plan 'let's wait and see…'

'Come on then,' Jade said with encouragement, 'let's get going!'

Jade leaned forward and let Minisilver pour off her shell and onto the mesa. He gave a little 'hooves up' gesture, then flowed down into the curiously cut groove that ringed the whole hill. It was quite a wide groove – tens of metres across and similarly deep – and it wiggled following the natural edge of the plateau'd hill, leaving just a narrow 'wall' before the drop over the sides, a bit like the top of a huge, chaotic castle. Within this groove there were various dips and bumps, all clearly artificial in that they had been smoothed and sanded somehow: no doubt by Hanksie using Great Uncle Syd as some kind of ploughing beast of burden.

Jade looked to the south. From this vantage point, the other hills were some fifty kilometres away, but she could see further, as the mountains of the Arabia Terra uplands were peeking over the edge of her horizon. Below her, the Martian terrain was largely just plains stretching off into the distance in all directions, but scattered around were these knobbly little hillocks and flat-topped mesas, as if some huge knife had cut the peaks off like slicing off the top of a hardboiled egg.

'Come on!' coaxed Jade, 'he'll be coming round the bend any minute.'

'I wasn't built for speed,' said Catapilla, matter-of-factly.

Jade was now positioned in the huge groove that Hanksie had carved around the top edge of this Cydonian mesa – the battlements, if you like. It was a bit like the terraces of those Mediterranean hills, but then it curved up again towards the inside edge, with several larger carved dips and bumps. Jade was watching Catapilla concertina her way along the gulley and she was now about a hundred steps further north.

'Just make yourself inconspicuous in one of the side cracks,' suggested Jade.

'I wasn't built to be inconspicuous either,' said Catapilla. 'I'm not in my pupae stage yet!'

'Pretend to be a rock. Hanksie will be looking elsewhere anyway.'

Jade looked up the side of the artificial valley and did a 'claws up' sign to what appeared to be a medium sized boulder half way up the slope. The boulder raised a claw back, letting Jade know that it was Grit and he was ready.

'Right,' said Jade, 'that just leaves you, my trusty steed.'

Minisilver had settled in a small pool just in front of Jade and he let his head peep above his surface and he too raised a hoof.

'Ready and waiting boss!'

'I'm not a boss,' said Jade dismissively, 'though if my sister Ruby was here, she *would* say I was the bossy one.'

'You're rising to the occasion,' Minisilver pointed out.

'Your father would be mighty proud of you ma'am,' said the pyrite captain on her shoulder.

Jade sighed. She looked at an imaginary watch on her wrist and realised that the birthday rendezvous with her dad was arriving fast and she was nowhere nearer actually meeting up with him. Suddenly, the return of a pyrites scouting party snapped her out of her daydream. The pinging and boing boing sound of the lice along the ground caught her attention.

'He be a comin'!' cried one in a whisper.

'Right, into positions!' Jade replied.

'Oh!' yelped Catapilla in a most uncharacteristic way.

'What?' whispered Jade in the loudest and quietest voice possible that would carry all the way to her friend.

'Oh dear,' said the pre-pubescent aerodactyl as a follow up.

'What is it?'

'I think I'm pupating!'

'What?!'

'It's like my waters just broke and my cocoon web is starting to spill out!'

'Well hold it in!' said Jade for want of anything better to say.

'It doesn't work like that!' explained Catapilla. 'It must be all this stress!'

'Where's the thread coming from?'

'My butt of course!'

'Well sit on it or something – we may only get one chance to catch him …'

Then Jade saw the cloud of dust coming from round the corner of the channel, so gave Minisilver the signal.

'Now Silver!'

In the blink of an eye, the pony puddle on the ground in front of her rose up like a sheet, and hung itself across the narrow valley, forming a gossamer thin film of silver, quivering there like the surface of a vertical lake – Mylar thin and Mylar shiny. Jade could no longer see the approaching Hanksie from her side of the mirror; all she could see as she hid behind this flimsy film was her own reflection in it, which was looking back quite anxiously, and the rest of her side of the channel disappearing behind her. She knew that all Hanksie would see was his own reflection, seemingly moving towards him.

Jade's well-oiled plan now seemed in jeopardy with Catapilla's sudden transformation. Admittedly, Catapilla's role was the least important in the 'sting'; Hanksie would see his reflection, and being quite obsessed with himself, would get off Great Uncle Syd and approach his image, mesmerised by it. While distracted, Catapilla was supposed to sneak up to Syd and convince him she was his long lost cousin and persuade him away and if in his seriously confused memory he didn't buy it, she was to carry him off by force. Grit, when Hanksie was in position, would throw himself from the top of the ridge, super hero style and barge Hanksie through the looking glass. Meanwhile, on Jade's side of the mirror, the pyrites would have prepared the dendritic net covering that would flip up like a sail and they would use it as a net to catch the Anarchic Artist like the glove in baseball. That was the plan anyway.

Hanksie, riding on Great Uncle Syd's back, moved along the carved channel with his eight bladed limbs spinning and slicing like a crazed combine harvester, shaping the land as he went along – like a sped-up glacial erosion machine. He was still using his 'feelers' to pinch the back of Syd's neck and somehow maintain control over him. Then Hanksie stopped. The dust started to settle. He cocked his head and looked at the strange figure in the distance in front of him.

'Hanksie twin?' he asked with confusion.

At this, Hanksie climbed down from the mind-controlled tortle and took a few steps towards his doppelganger. Then he reconsidered his move, turned back to Great Uncle Syd and with deft dexterity, thanks to his many limbs, flipped the tortle onto his back like a pancake, found a suitably sized rock and wedged it under his shell so Syd was stuck upside down.

'Old tortle stay here,' Hanksie said redundantly.

When Hanksie gave Great Uncle Syd a little shake to make sure he couldn't wriggle free, he turned round and walked towards the mirror. He returned his attention to the most attractive looking thing in front of him – his own reflection.

'You Hanksie too?' he asked his image. 'You copy Hanksie?' he continued and then tried various moves to see that this other Hanksie was mimicking him.

Meanwhile, Catapilla took this opportunity to come out from the shadows and approach the upturned tortle. She had to keep gathering up the cocoon thread that was spilling out of her like an uncontrolled unrolling toilet roll. She looked at the inverted vertebrate and realised that the role to pretend to be a long lost relative to lure him to freedom was now pointless, with him stuck in his own underside world. She just had to get him the Hellas out of there before his tormentor came back.

Uncle Syd looked at Catapilla.

'You're upside down,' said the disorientated tortle, fortunately out of earshot of the crab.

'Actually,' Catapilla replied in a whisper, '*you* are, but I should be able to put that right…'

Catapilla glanced back to see that Hanksie was so self-absorbed that he didn't notice what she was up to, plus his own image was hiding what was going on behind him.

'Are you my long lost cousin Argile?' said Syd.

'Um,' Catapilla paused in her manoeuvre to wedge herself under the old tortle, ready to flip him over, 'yea, okay, yes I'm Argile…'

From Grit's vantage point halfway up the rock face, he could see both sides of the mirror. Hanksie almost had his nose touching the mirror's surface as he inspected his spitting image. On the other side, Grit saw Jade looking up at him. She gave him a thumbs up, he gave a slight nod back, then he launched himself into the void and let gravity do its thing. Grit's descent was almost silent and slow at first, but he knew his inertia should be enough to nudge the Peculiar Painter into his own reflection, just like potting the black in snooker. Jade watched him and gave the pyrites the signal and up came the crab catching sail.

'Long time no see, Argile,' Syd greeted his fake relative.

'Oh, yes, um cousin,' Catapilla continued, 'so long ago, I can't remember when it was…'

'Where's your shell?' asked Syd.

'Oh, er, having it cleaned. My pyrites are giving it a good sanding…'

As Catapilla said this, she was now thoroughly squeezed under the tortle and managed to pull the offending rock out of the way. She tilted Great Uncle Syd far enough to one side that he turned over and landed on his feet, still facing the same way.

'You don't remember why we haven't seen each other

then?' asked Syd as he arthritically dusted himself down from his forced ploughing job.

'No, why,' said Catapilla, glancing from time to time back at Hanksie to make sure he hadn't spotted them.

'Because I *hate* you!'

'What?!'

'And I *never* wanted to see you again!'

With that Great Uncle Syd made a lunge at Catapilla and a scuffle started. Catapilla's thread whipped behind her like a gymnast's ribbon, duplicating all her moves, as she suddenly found herself tussling with the creature she was supposed to be rescuing.

At the other end of this stretch of the valley, Hanksie was shutting one eye then the other to see that his new friend was doing the same. He hadn't seen the Grit-shaped cloud falling from heaven. Then the noise of the tortle-Catapilla fight caught the crab's attention and the spell was broken. He looked away from the mirror and saw his enslaved digging machine fighting with his unwanted rescuer. Rapidly all his bladed limbs turned in unison and Hanksie made a dash to retrieve Great Uncle Syd. At that moment, Grit passed through the space that Hanksie used to occupy a second earlier and as he sailed by, he missed the valley floor, hit the raised outer edge, bounced off like a discus and went over the side of the plateau down towards the plain below.

Catapilla was now upside down underneath Uncle Syd but could see the rapidly approaching psychopathic strimming machine in the shape of Hysterical Hanksie. This new fear sent another stretch of cocoon web out like a candyfloss machine gone wrong. With so many legs, Catapilla soon managed to right herself, and a quick look at the crab's crazy face was enough to galvanise the normally sloth-like pre-pupated bird of paradise into action and she used her head to push Uncle Syd along the valley away from Hanksie – much like a dog might push a football along the ground. Catapilla surprised herself by how fast she could move, and increased her lead on the crab. It seemed she was actually going to be able to perform her new role – however, she suddenly felt an increasing force opposing her escape, as if Syd was getting heavier and heavier. Yet the force seemed to be coming from behind. Her galloping became running on the spot; she looked back and realised what was happening. The cocoon thread that had been spilling out of her butt was now pulled tight, and the other end had fixed itself to the rock where she'd been hiding. And what had been unravelling against her will had now reached the end of its supply. She tried to run harder and it stretched the thread a bit more, but was clearly reaching its flexible limit. Catapilla had now pushed Syd enough that he carried on moving a little and out of her grip, while she remained running on the spot. And all the time Hanksie was catching up…

Meanwhile, Minisilver was watching from wherever he'd put his eyes in the mirror, somewhere on the rim, probably. He was reporting to Jade what was going on as she panicked that all was going wrong.

'Catapilla's running on the spot,' Minisilver explained, 'and Uncle Syd is out of reach, but he's actually moving away by himself, so that's not a bad thing.'

'Oh dear…' Jade whispered to herself.

'Hanksie's almost caught up with Catapilla. Should we do something?'

I don't know, thought Jade to herself, but held off replying for a moment.

'We could be a chasing after that narcissistic artist,' suggested Raffi Rehab.

'Oh, Catapilla's lost her grip with the ground,' said Minisilver, '…her stretched thread is pulling her back this way… Oh… She's going to hit Hanksie!'

Jade could hear the sound of the collision but there was little time to react as the next moment Minisilver's mirror smashed into tiny drops, and Hanksie shot through and went straight into Jade's net-like sail, like a baseball into a huge glove. Such was the force that it sent Jade several metres back along the valley, thus obeying conservation of momentum laws and keeping out of physics trouble.

The pyrites didn't waste much time and quickly tied the sail's edges together to keep Hanksie hog-tied and neutralised. Minisilver's drops were coming together and coalescing, while Catapilla had reached the extreme end of this side of her swing and she found herself pulled back in the direction of her rooted thread, and back towards the escaping Uncle Syd, like a strange horizontal bungee jumper.

Jade breathed a sigh of relief. They had caught the rogue, *rogue*. Hanksie felt heavy on her back, but the pyrites were now cutting the sail's links to her shell and the entrapped crab rolled off her carapace into an undignified pile next to her.

'Sorry Hanksie,' said Jade, 'but we have to protect the whole planet.'

'Green one cannot keep Hanksie down,' cried the crab in a muffled voice from inside his tight fitting net cage, 'Hanksie free spirit.'

'Not free at the moment,' said Jade, 'but we'll free you when the danger's passed.'

'Hanksie free now,' said Hanksie and the next moment a couple of his bladed limbs poked out through the holes in the dendritic net, and a couple of snips later and Hanksie had cut his way out. They hadn't taken the sharpness of his blades into account and Jade felt stupid. Again.

In a flash Hanksie had shrugged off the sail, along with the pyrites that had tried to keep him there, and he then scuttled back up the valley path towards the retreating Uncle Syd. Sadly, Hanksie had mistimed his move and got hit square in the face by the now crazily oscillating Catapilla. She grabbed onto him with several limbs even as he tried to push her off. In the tussle, Catapilla's thread got tangled round Hanksie and the more he struggled, the more entangled he became. As the thread tightened, it restricted Hanksie's movements until he was cocooned himself. By then Catapilla had stopped her harmonic motion and they were now both stationary on the valley floor. A couple of Hanksie's blades poked out between the threads and he tried to cut them. But failed. Lots of snipping noises followed like a crazed hair dresser, but to no avail.

Mini Silver had coalesced his drops, just in time to see Catapilla's success. Jade was also watching the spectacle, while Grit had just finished climbing back up the slope to see they had caught their quarry, albeit it in a slightly different way. And as if the timing had been perfect, they looked up and saw a star like object passing by overhead. This was suddenly blocked out by the appearance of four medium sized, winged nogards that were circling and slowly descending onto this flat-topped Cydonian hill.

* * * * *

The Hellas Angels had finally made it to Cydonia with an urgent message from their boss Fionix. And it was fortuitous that they had taken flight paths at a high altitude, rather than surface hugging hovercraft trajectories, otherwise they would never have seen what they saw and would never have been able to avert a planetary disaster. The hill on which the Umpteenagers had been chasing Hanksie stood several hundred metres above the surrounding plains. The four adolescent birds of paradise had chosen to fly at the heady height of a kilometre or two. Fionix had warned them about the orbiting satellite, so the girls were using their chameleon coverings. Their shadows of course would have been cast on the ground, but whenever they saw those spots of light that were the Viking orbiters, the nogards would fly in formation so that at best three of the shadows were hidden by the birds themselves so only one shadow would ever show up on any photo, so three could deny ever having been there, your honour. Plus, at that height above the ground the shadows would have only been penumbral smudges, missing the dark centre that would have created a total eclipse to anyone caught in its path below.

'It's silly!' snapped Syrena, 'Change back!'

298

'But I want to be a cloud,' said Layer.

'We have to blend in with the ground,' Syrena explained, 'in case something's watching us…' and with this she looked up.

'But they'd see a cloud from up there,' defended Layer.

'Moving in the opposite direction to the wind!'

'But I look good in white…'

'Tell her Hell,' Syrena insisted.

'We're here,' Hell said, ignoring the infighting. 'Look out for any dust trails from those tortles…'

'These little flat hills look funny from up here,' commented Syrena, noticing the peculiar mesa formations of the scattered squat outcrops that broke up the otherwise monotonous plains.

'Yeah,' agreed Layer, as she moved into position, in line with the other three, '*that* one ahead and to our left looks like a flattened lung whale!'

'Where? You're supposed to give directions like a clock,' said Syrena, all formal like, 'you know, at *ten* o'clock or something – and if anything, personally, I think it looks like a tortle that's had the top of its shell sliced off.'

'That's nothing,' dismissed Dasha, pausing as she looked up to the rapidly moving point of light that was the Viking orbiter and adjusting her distance from Hell – then looking to the sun and their shadows on the ground to get their spacing correct. 'Take a look at that hill on our right – I mean half past four, Miss Stickler for the Rules. It looks like someone who's been hit on the head and is dazed but still smiling!'

'That's not half past four,' corrected Syrena, 'it's half past *two*! You're going to fail the next navigation test and Fionix won't be happy with you…'

The speaking stopped. The synchronised flying team seemed to be frozen in their poses, flying forwards (that would be twelve o'clock, if Syrena was checking this) but heads all turned some seventy-five degrees, clockwise and they were all staring at the hill to their right. The top surface of their wings looked the same shade of amber as the plains below and they slightly tilted their aspects in relation to the craft a few hundred kilometres overhead so as not to give too much away. However, their minds were now distracted by the curiously shaped hill below. A bit of a dust trail could be seen emanating from a point in the wide groove that marked the outer edge of the plateau.

'Is it my imagination,' Hell started, 'or does that mesa look familiar?'

'Well,' Syrena mused, 'we have been this way before, but I don't think the hill looked like this the last time we flew by…'

'I think we've found our tortles,' Hell decided.

'And the Crazy Crab they were chasing,' agreed Dasha.

'Oh dear,' said Layer, as realisation struck her, 'it's going to be the Canal Crisis all over again…'

Syrena squinted to be sure, then said what they were all coming to realise.

'That hill looks exactly like Hanksie's face!'

* * * * *

The date on Earth was the 25th July 1976. The Viking I orbiter took a photograph of the Cydonia region including the hill with a humanoid face on it. The hill was the one that Hanksie had been shaping for some time now, with the forced help of Great Uncle Syd. The Face, had the Viking team been in full possession of the facts, would have been easily recognisable as the face of the Herman. Hanksie had created the greatest sculpture in the solar system *ever* and it was of himself.

And it looked like it was about to create an interplanetary diplomatic crisis.

* * * * *

The four paraglider-like silhouettes circled and slowly spiralled down (technically '*helicalled*' down, as they retained their circular radii). They landed two on each side of the gulley in which their friends were resting, looking like vultures coming to feed on a carcass. There was the usual rapid down draft as eight wings flapped and folded up like reluctant tents not wanting to fit back in their carrying bags.

The Umpteenage gang was lying around looking exhausted and bedraggled. Catapilla had just finished spinning enough silk round the Crabster to keep him under control. Hanksie continued to try and use his bladed limbs to cut through the thread, but without success. The pyrites were dusting down their respective tortles while Minisilver was trickling around collecting up the last of his drops after he'd been almost turned into an aerosol. Great Uncle Syd had wandered off in the confusion, but no one was too worried about him as he was now freed from the mind-controlling sculptor.

After Jade had explained to the Hellas Angels the events of the most recent past, Syrena spoke.

'Well we'll take over from here,' she said, assuming control.

'Hang on!' interrupted Hell, 'I'm still in charge of *this* assignment!'

'If we wait for you, those Earthlings will have colonised by then and it'll be too late!'

'Why are you guys taking over here?' Jade asked, a little confused.

'A change of plans,' Dasha put in, while her team mates were arguing, 'your artist friend there has sculptured this hill into a huge edifice of his own face!'

'*I'm* supposed to be telling them this!' said Hell.

'No,' said Syrena, '*I'm* the communications officer on this trip.'

'You'd be able to see this big face from way up there,' Layer explained to Jade. 'We have to destroy every sign of intelligent artwork, like we did with the Canals, though I question Fionix's use of the word intelligent.'

'But can't we help you?' Jade offered. Hell jumped in.

'Fionix found out that the second landing site has been moved to the Hrad Valley. You need to go there...'

'What about Hanksie?' Grit asked.

'We'll take care of him,' said Syrena with an almost evil smile.

'We can keep an eye on him until the danger from Earth has passed,' Hell put in.

'Plus we can let him watch us get rid of his unsightly fresco!' said Layer with delight.

'He's got a lot to answer for,' Dasha explained, 'we spent decades getting rid of all his canals so's those Earth creatures wouldn't find any evidence!'

'Anyway,' interrupted Hell, 'that Viking craft is landing soon so you have to get to the Hrad Valley as soon as possible.'

'Do you know how far that is?!' asked Jade rhetorically, though Grit hadn't picked this up and he shot up a claw ready to answer.

'Yes,' said Syrena, 'about eight thousand kilometres, as the nogard flies…'

'And do you know how fast a tortle can move?'

Grit's claw went up again.

'At top speed?' Jade qualified. Grit put his claw up even higher as if he was going to strain himself.

'Yes I do,' said Hell enthusiastically, 'Katya gave us a lesson on it a few decades ago. A little over a metre per second on the flat…'

Jade carried on with her next question: 'And so to cover eight thousand kilometres would take?'

'Oh,' said Hell with excitement, rising to the challenge of a brainteaser 'well assuming it was non-stop that's about a hundred kilometres a day so that would be eighty days.'

'And you say we have how long?'

'About ten days…' said Hell, completely unphased by this disparity.

'So we would be late by how long?'

Grit still had his hand up but felt he was being ignored.

'Oh, you'd be seventy days late,' Syrena butted in.

'Do you see the problem with your request?'

'Oh yes of course, if you had to *walk* all the way, but that's not what you're going to do.'

'It isn't? What then?'

'Well, fortunately you only have to walk a few kilometres from here.'

'Okay,' said Jade, 'so where is this leading?'

'North-east,' said Syrena, 'You guys have to head north-east and – see that ridge over there?' and she pointed, 'Well when you go just beyond that, you will see the plain slopes down to a little crater which hardly gets any daylight and at the bottom, there should be a patch of solid carbon dioxide and water ice.'

'What do we do when we get there? Go skating?'

'Wait.'

'Until when?'

'Your next instructions.'

'And these instructions will get us to the Hrad Valley?'

'Indeed.'

'And us three are then supposed to save the world?'

'There's not just three of you,' said Hell, 'you do have your pyrites as well.'

'Um yes,' said Jade a little irritated, 'I know that, but just *us*? Us three plus crew? Saving the whole of Mars?!'

'No, only half. There's another team in the Chryse Basin to do the rest.'

'Oh well that's okay then,' said Jade sarcastically, but Hell didn't pick up on it.

'That's settled,' said Hell, 'you know, Fionix has a lot of faith in you…'

'Really, what makes her think that?'

'Oh she says it's in your genes.'

'What does she mean by that? Up until recently, I was just minding my own business and hardly even meeting anyone, then suddenly my whole world has turned upside down! What makes her say this kind of thing is in my blood?'

'Well,' said Hell with pleasure, 'your dad is helping at the other site…'

'Oh…' said Jade, suddenly humbled by this comment.

* * * * *

The umpteenaged tortles and the proto aerodactyl had now been waiting at the ice patch for a day and nothing had happened. Many of the pyrites had 'gone ashore', though in this case that meant 'gone on the ice' and some were having fun ice-skating. A few had scraped up the water-ice and dry ice and made a snow tortle – the younger ones played on the snow-tortle's back as if it was their own vessel. Jade had snapped off a part of the ice sheet with her beak and had been smoothing and shaping it into a roughly circular disc that bulged in the middle. She kept holding it up to inspect it and looked through it. Grit watched her and was amused to see that his friend's face looked larger. Catapilla was doing some strange movement, which caught the others' attentions.

'Watcha doin?' asked Grit?'

'What's expected of me...' said Catapilla as she had turned herself into a ring, with her face almost meeting up with her butt and she was moving in a circle, her face following her bottom.

'And what would that be?'

'I'm a *processional* Caterpillar', she explained, 'we normally follow each other, but as there's only me left, then I guess I have to follow myself...'

'Okay,' said Grit, not sure if he really understood the reason why. Then he looked back at Jade who had taken out the small silver lump that was Minisilver. Now she was placing him behind the ice lens and pointing that at the sun.

'Watcha doin?' Grit asked her.

'Trying to bring Minisilver back to life. The pyrite's forge in my shell went out...'

With that, they watched the lump of silver that was now glinting brightly in the focussed sunlight.

'You think it'll work?' he asked her.

'I don't know, but it passes the time... plus the lice are giving me a hand...'

Grit looked closely and saw there were a number of pyrites gathered round the experiment. Several had got their shiny shields out and were reflecting more sunlight onto the frozen horse – others were rubbing a black powder onto his surface.

Something distracted Jade from her task and the lens ended up tilting away from the horse. Grit felt the tremor too and Catapilla stopped following her butt and looked up. The ground seemed to be rumbling and a few pieces of broken ice sitting on the frozen lake began to rattle. The three members of the team looked at each other. The pyrites that had left the safety of their tortle shells began to hurry back on board as they saw their little snow tortle crumble with the vibrations of the ground.

The rumbling got louder and seemingly closer. Jade, Grit and Catapilla backed away from the frozen lake and reversed a little way up the slope.

'Mars quake?' Grit asked out loud.

'Too coincidental,' Jade disagreed. Catapilla looked to the sky in case her friends were returning and making all the noise, but all that could be seen above ground level was the sun.

The ice shuddered beneath them and the vibrations were enough to make the umpteenagers leave the ground and bounce up and down. Catapilla even wobbled in mid air like an aborigine's wobble board. A moment later the frozen lake cracked open and out jumped a huge lung whale. Not just *any* lung whale – Grit and Jade recognised her. As the leviathan came back down to the ground, half out of her hole, her body slapped the ground sending a spray of snow, ice and dust out, unceremoniously showering the B team.

'HELLO YOU GUYS!' shouted Chryssie, 'NICE TO SEE YOU AGAIN.'

Both tortles had their claws over their ears to deaden the rather loud greeting.

'OOPS, SORRY,' said the lung whale, 'I FORGET MY OWN VOLUME... IN MORE WAYS THAN ONE.'

'Hi' waved Jade, a bit stunned. Grit also waved but both of them continued to wipe themselves down from the ice spray.

'YOU MUST BE THE OTHER ANGEL,' Chryssie said to Catapilla.

Catapilla nodded yes but said nothing.

'DID YOU KNOW THE PLANET'S COVERED WITH DOZENS OF UNDERGROUND WATERWAYS?!'

They said no.

'ME NEITHER! IT WAS FIONIX WHO CAME AND GOT ME OUT OF MY COCOON.'

'So you're part of the plan?' Jade asked her.

'YES I AM! IT'S ALL PRETTY EXCITING ISN'T IT?!'

'Depends if you like that kind of thing,' said Jade dryly.

'OH, YOU SOUND JUST LIKE YOUR DAD!'

'So what *is* the plan?' Jade asked. 'I know we have to get to Hrad as quickly as possible.'

'THAT'S WHERE I COME IN. YOU KNOW IT FEELS SO GOOD TO BE FREE AGAIN, AFTER MILLIONS OF YEARS SHUT AWAY ALONE. DID YOU KNOW THE OTHER LUNG WHALES HAVE BEEN LIVING IT UP WITHOUT ME?!'

'No,' Jade admitted.

'I'M GOING TO BE HAVING A WORD WITH THEM WHEN THIS IS ALL OVER.'

'So how do we get to Hrad?'

'I AM YOUR TRANSPORT.'

'What? We have to ride on you through these subaeranean tunnels?!'

'NOT EXACTLY RIDE *ON* ME... MORE RIDE *IN* ME...'

'What?! No, not again!'

* * * * *

'I PROMISE I WON'T SWALLOW YOU.'

'I said I'd never do this again!' said Jade.

'I remember,' said Grit. 'That seems a lifetime ago...'

'And yet it's not even a year!'

'YOU CAN STAY IN MY MOUTH AND IF I KEEP

MY JAWS CLOSED THEY MAKE A WATER TIGHT SEAL AND YOU'LL BE SAFE.'

'No, never again!'

'WELL YOU CAN'T STAY OUTSIDE – THE TUNNELS ARE PRETTY MUCH FLOODED EVERYWHERE.'

'I can hold my breath for years,' boasted Jade, 'Grit could too. Us tortles have a very low metabolism you know.'

'FAIR ENOUGH, BUT WHAT ABOUT YOU CATAPILLA?'

'Breathing is not one of my strengths,' she admitted. 'Couldn't I just stay here?'

'I THINK YOUR FRIENDS WILL NEED ALL THE HELPING HANDS THEY CAN FIND AND YOU HAVE QUITE A FEW!'

'Feet actually…' said Catapilla.

'FIONIX WAS INSISTENT YOU ALL CAME.'

'So reserve me a seat inside then,' said Catapilla, giving up without much of a fight.

'OKAY, BUT YOU TWO, REMEMBER, MY SKIN IS PRETTY SMOOTH – YOU KNOW, STREAM LINED TO PICK UP SPEED IN THE WATER, SO YOU'RE GOING TO NEED THAT ROPE YOU HAD TO STRAP YOURSELVES ON BOARD…

Jade looked at Grit and he looked back as they both pictured the four Hellas Angels flying off with that rope supporting the Quicksilver statue.

'Can I have a window seat?' asked Jade dejectedly.

'ACTUALLY YOU CAN ALL HAVE WINDOW SEATS. MY TEETH ARE SEMI-TRANSPARENT SO YOU CAN ADMIRE THE SCENERY! NOT THAT THERE'S MUCH TO SEE DOWN BELOW…'

* * * * *

Chryssie unrolled her tongue like it was the red carpet receiving special stars and, in a small way, it was. Jade reluctantly stepped aboard and the squishy, spongy surface felt so unnatural to walk on, especially as the

307

taste buds seemed to stick like little suckers to Jade's feet. Grit followed and, cagily clambering onto the pink rubbery surface, decided it felt nothing like the Martian regolith and was a completely different sensation to travelling on the cold but comforting liquid of Quicksilver's body. The last to climb the gangplank was Catapilla and she had no trouble, what with all the legs and the concertina bend in the middle of her body that allowed a cheetah's flexibility. Chryssie raised her tongue and withdrew it back into her mouth to bring it to the same level as her bottom row of teeth.

'PULL UP A MOLAR AND SIT DOWN.'

The three passengers installed themselves behind the teeth and they were ready.

'KEEP CLEAR OF THE JAWS…'

The noise of the lung whale's jaws shutting was a deep rumbling and gradually the light cut out until the translucent teeth shut together perfectly like a jigsaw – but there was still a ghostly frosted light, still making its way through the teeth.

'WELCOME ON BOARD! I WILL HAVE TO CLOSE MY MOUTH UNTIL WE ARE FULLY IMMERSED AND IN MOTION. YOU WILL EXPERIENCE SOME TURBULENCE AT FIRST BUT THAT WILL SETTLE DOWN FOR A SMOOTH RIDE.'

As Chryssie closed her lips, Jade looked out at the slightly distorted view of the surface of Mars and she tried to soak up every glimpse of every random rock and wondered when she might see it all again. She noticed Grit too was gawping at the last closing image of their final view topside. The light level started to fall again until it became pitch black. And silent. And echoey.

Jade could feel the lung whale sliding backwards and downwards into the pothole from where she'd recently emerged. She then heard a whisper by her ear.

'Beggin' yer pardon ma'am…'

'Yes, Raff?'

'We be one step ahead of ourselves, should we need a quick retreat…'

'What do you mean?'

'Me and the crew had ourselves collecting then filling our pockets with some indigestible dust, like what we used the last time we was in here.'

'Oh…'

'Aye, so we can be coating ourselves if we need to go out the back way, if you be getting my drift…'

'I'm getting it Raffi. What about Grit?'

'His crew they been doin the same as us ma'am.'

'Good, and Catapilla?'

'We is thinkin that it's not needed, seein as she's not a rigid body like yerself ma'am, no offence.'

'None taken.'

'An she's more like a squishy balloon so should be able to fit up the blowhole.'

'You sure?'

'Might have to give her body a rub with some oil but us pyrites can be givin' her a helpin' push along the way.'

'Thanks Raff. Let's hope it doesn't come to that.'

'Aye ma'am.'

Jade sighed and wondered how she might cope with several days in complete darkness and travelling through water-filled underground tunnels. Though, having already been in a lung whale's belly and intestines, she'd pretty much been there and done that and lived to tell the tale. Well she'd never wanted to have to tell the tale – that made her think of her rebellious sister Ruby. Jade wondered what she might be doing at this moment, and envied the thought that she was probably on dry land and *definitely* on the outside of a whale.

'Hello?' shouted Grit in the darkness and his voice echoed around the lung whale's cavernous mouth.

'Yes?' asked Jade.

'You okay?'

'Yes, and you?'

'It reminds me of the previous…'

'Yes I know, but at least it's more comfy surroundings… Catapilla?'

'…Hi…'

'How are you doing?' asked Jade.

'Reminds me of when I was an egg.'

'Oh.'

'And I guess it's good practice for when I go into my pupa stage, if that ever happens…'

'I'm sure it will,' said Jade encouragingly, 'you're just a late bloomer.'

'Yea, several million years late.'

'My dad said to make the most of each moment. It's not the destination, it's the journey.'

'Nice idea,' said Catapilla, 'I just wonder if he ever travelled inside a lung whale before…'

The submarine passengers then felt a judder forward as Chryssie started her eight thousand-kilometre journey to the Hrad Valley. Apart from that initial shudder, the motion was quite smooth. There was a slow gentle wavelike wriggle to Chryssie's swimming, a bit like a large ship on the ocean barely bobbing up and down. Just when the passengers were getting used to the idea of a kind of sensory deprived passage beneath the surface of Mars, some lights came on – soft, faint red glows at first, and from high above them in the roof of the whale's mouth. Then on came some blue lights similarly placed round the top row of teeth. Some of them started to dart back and forth in the empty space of the whale's mouth.

'Monopole-cats…' said Jade quietly to herself.

As if the light show wasn't enough, there was then a guttural sound coming from the throat, and the tongue that had been fairly complacent started to ripple and undulate.

'THIS IS YOUR CAPTAIN CHRYSSIE SPEAKING. WELCOME ONBOARD. I HOPE YOU HAVE A PLEASANT CROSSING. THE MONOPOLE-CAT LIGHTS ARE TO MAKE YOU FEEL MORE AT HOME. THERE ISN'T ACTUALLY MUCH TO SEE, BUT I WILL NEED TO OPEN MY MOUTH FROM TIME TO TIME AND YOU WILL BE ABLE TO SEE WHAT SUBAERANEAN MARS LOOKS LIKE. WE WILL BE CRUISING AT ABOUT SEVENTY

KILOMETRES AN HOUR SO WE SHOULD ARRIVE
IN FOUR DAYS OR SO…'

'… thanks Chryssie…' said Jade with a sigh.

'YOU'RE WELCOME.'

'Sorry about earlier… you know, my reluctance to,
well…'

'NO OFFENCE TAKEN. NOT SURE I'D WANT TO
TRAVEL IN THE MOUTH OF A CREATURE
HUNDREDS OF TIMES BIGGER THAN MYSELF
EITHER.'

'And thanks for helping out with this mission…'

'MY PLEASURE! IT'S SO GOOD TO BE OUT OF
THAT COCOON. BESIDES I CANNOT WAIT TO
TRACK DOWN THOSE OTHER LUNG WHALES WHO
LEFT ME COOPED UP IN THERE ALL THIS TIME.'

'Well,' reflected Jade as she watched the monopole-
cats do their night dance like fireflies, 'maybe that kept
you safe all this time.'

'YOU SOUND JUST LIKE YOUR DAD! ALWAYS
SEEING THE POSITIVE SIDE'.

'I was supposed to be meeting up with him for my
birthday… not sure that's going to happen now.'

'WHEN'S THAT?'

'A couple of months…'

'WE'LL MAKE SURE IT HAPPENS.'

'Thanks. I hope you're right… say, I like the lights.'

'YOU DO?! GOOD. THAT WAS FIONIX'S IDEA.
SHE USES SOME WHEN SHE'S FLYING.'

'They don't mind?'

'OH FIONIX HAS SOME KIND OF SYMBIOTIC
RELATION GOING ON – A BIT LIKE YOU AND
YOUR PYRITES.'

'And are you able to offer them something for their
services?'

'ACTUALLY YES. SOME JUST WANT TO GO
SOMEWHERE DIFFERENT. OTHERS LIKE THE
IDEA OF HAVING A SECLUDED PLACE TO MEET
UP. NO CHANCE OF OVERSHOOTING AND
ENDING UP FAR FROM THEIR POLE-MATE.'

19

Catching a Crab

'OH,' realised Chryssie, 'I NEARLY FORGOT! GRIT, I HAVE A NICE SURPRISE FOR YOU... HANG ON...'

Grit pricked up his ears with curiosity, though being just holes in the sides of his head, there was no obvious movement. Chryssie made a noise like she was clearing her throat, almost as if she was going to vomit. Which she then did. Shooting from the back of her throat came a projectile a few centimetres across that flew like a Bat out of Hell. It hit the back of her top gums and then proceeded to bounce across her tongue like a child on a bouncy castle. It rolled to a halt just in front of Grit's nose.

'Is that...' Grit began as he approached and inspected the mucus covered slime ball.

'IT IS,' confirmed the lung whale.

'...but how did you find it?!' Grit asked, while he nudged the gelatinous coated object with his nose to speed up the emerging process. The goo gradually flowed towards the surface of Chryssie's tongue, revealing a greenish spike covered ball.

Jade came over to observe.

'What is it?' she asked.

'It's... it's my hedgehog egg...' said Grit, now wiping away the final globules of Chryssie's muco-membrane lining.

'So it's a real thing?' Jade asked as she inspected the oddity herself from close up.

'Yes,' Grit explained, still somewhat dazed, 'um, my dad told me they grow on special trees, called hedges and when these spikey fruits fall off, well some years later, they crack open and out hatches a baby hedgehog,' he raised his voice to address the whale, 'But where did you find it?!'

'IT WAS GIVEN TO ME A FEW WEEKS BACK, explained Chryssie, 'IT WAS FOUND WHERE YOUR PARENTS HAD BEEN. BUT THAT'S NOT THE MOST IMPORTANT THING I WAS GIVEN. I HAVE ANOTHER SURPRISE. HANG ON I HAVE TO LIFT MY TONGUE A LITTLE…'

Catapilla had to suddenly wriggle off the part of the tongue she was resting on, as Chryssie curled it over to reveal a yellowish object hiding in the space below the floor of her mouth. Chryssie, with a certain deftness, hooked the edge of her tongue under the yellow object and skilfully lifted it up. Grit, who had by now picked up his precious hedgehog egg in his mouth, gently put it down and moved – even more mesmerised – to the newly-presented cargo.

'It's a baby tortle!' shouted Jade in surprise.

'My sister!' cried Grit. At the sound of this, the small yellow tortle opened her eyes and looked up.

'Hey Gritty,' said the tiny tortle.

'Sulphie-Rose!' shouted Grit, then proceeded to pick her up with his front claws and give her a big hug.

'I'm riding inna big whale!' said Sulphie-Rose with pure delight.

'Where were you?! How did you get here?! I thought I'd lost you!'

'Not lost Grit. I knew where I was. I won the hide and seek game!'

'Where were you?'

'Hiding under mommy, with your hog egg… mommy's gone … and daddy…'

'I'm so sorry, sis… but we have each other now.'

'Yes, glad I find you… and we have a new mommy now!'

'What?'

'New mommy. She find me and bring me to Great Auntie Chryssie.'

'Who?'

'Rooby. She a very pretty red tortle. I wanna grow up and be like her…'

'What?!' Jade put in.

'But yellow, not red.'

'Chryssie?' Jade shouted out into the cavernous mouth space.

'YES?'

'Can you help here?'

'SURE. I WAS MAKING MY WAY OVER HERE AND CAME UP FOR AIR WHERE THE UNDERGROUND CHANNEL ENTERED AN ICE COVERED CRATER LIKE THE ONE YOU JOINED ME IN. WHILE GETTING MY BREATH, I NOTICED THIS REDDISH TORTLE ON THE RIM AND WAVED HER OVER. OF COURSE I HADN'T SEEN RUBY SINCE SHE WAS YOUNG BUT YOU DON'T FORGET THOSE RED MARKINGS AND THAT RAW BEAUTY, DO YOU?'

Jade was feeling two opposing emotions; a streak of green envy and jealousy that yet again her sister was being held up as the pretty one, but also relieved to have some news about Ruby since they'd parted company on not the best terms.

'Is she okay?'

'SHE SENDS HER REGARDS AND WISHES YOU GOOD LUCK ON YOUR QUEST.'

'But was she okay?'

'OH, SHE SAID SHE HAD SOME THINKING TO DO, WHICH IS SOMETHING SHE SAID SHE HADN'T DONE MUCH OF FOR A LONG TIME. SHE WAS TAKING THE LITTLE YELLOW ONE TO REUNITE WITH HER BROTHER GRIT WHEN WE MET UP. WHEN SHE HEARD I WAS GOING TO SEE YOU SHE ASKED IF I WOULD DELIVER SULPHIE-ROSE SAFE AND SOUND.'

Jade felt a bit choked up on hearing that her self-involved sister had done something quite altruistic.

'Thank you, Chryssie,' said Grit, also a bit wobbly in the voice.

With a paw around his sister, Grit lay next to her on Chryssie's tongue, under the lights of the monopole-cats.

Jade sat facing them, resting her chin on her own front paws. Catapilla meanwhile had strung up several strands of her thick silk web into the form of a hammock that hung between some of Chryssie's bottom teeth and proceeded to climb into it as if she was in a couchette carriage on the Trans Europe Express, perchance to sleep and dream, or finally turn into a Bird of Paradise.

It was around then that Minisilver had warmed up enough to liquify, helped by the Martian lung whale's elevated body temperature.

'Where am I?' the little horsehead asked as it rose out of the crack on Jade's shell.

'Oh,' Jade realised, 'welcome back from the cold! We're in a lung whale's mouth. Odd story, I'll fill you in as there's a bit of time to kill...'

* * * * *

It was actually the last night of the umpteenage gang's sub surface journey, though being underground, they couldn't really tell that it was night topside. A few ghostly lights of monopole-cats powering down flickered and returned the whale's mouth to its eerie cave-like feel, while the gentle rumble of Chryssie's motion helped keep the passengers in sleep mode. Catapilla rocked from side to side in her makeshift hammock, while Jade and Grit slept face to face with Sulphie-Rose roughly between them.

Chryssie suddenly put on the brakes, which meant that every creature that was not fully secured in place continued moving forward. That was most of them. The tortles rolled over the rubbery surface of Chryssie's tongue and ended up in a heap against the back of her lower front teeth. Catapilla moved in the same direction but as her strands of cocoon were strong and stretchy, she came to the end of her extensive limit then boinged back and forth. Several untethered monopole-cats lost their grip and crashed with no airbags for protection.

Through the semi-transparent, semi translucent teeth,

the waking tortles could see in front of Chryssie the face of another huge lung whale blocking the tunnel. The other whale looked shocked.

'CHRYSSIE?!'

'LONG TIME NO SEE,' said Chryssie through gritted (and jaded) teeth, not wanting to let water in and drown her passengers. As with all lung whales, the jaws when closed formed a perfect seal, so they could talk by moving their lips without drowning themselves.

'BUT I THOUGHT YOU WERE ... I MEAN YES, UM SO GOOD TO SEE YOU.'

'DON'T YOU PATRONISE ME UTOPIA!'

'YOU REMEMBER ME?!'

'I DON'T FORGET A FACE...WELL I DON'T FORGET AT LEAST ONE OF YOUR TWO FACES... TWO TOPIA!'

'THAT WAS A LONG TIME AGO.'

'I KNOW AND I WILL DEAL WITH IT LATER. I HAVE MORE IMPORTANT MATTERS TO SORT OUT NOW, SO IF YOU CAN GET OUT OF MY WAY, I HAVE TO GET TO YOUR HOME PLAIN OF ALL PLACES...'

'BUT I CAN'T GET OUT OF YOUR WAY! THE TUNNEL IS ONLY ONE WHALE WIDE HERE.'

'THEN BACK UP UNTIL IT IS WIDE ENOUGH FOR ME TO GET BY!' Shouted Chryssie.

The passengers looked on and listened to this road rage confrontation as it was growing to a critical size.

'BUT THERE'S A STRING OF OTHER WHALES FOLLOWING BEHIND ME!'

'OH, IT MUST BE NICE TO HAVE OTHER FRIENDS AND NOT SPEND AN ETERNITY IN SOLITARY CONFINEMENT.'

'CAN WE TALK ABOUT THIS LATER?!'

'OH WE WILL, BUT I HAVE A PLANET TO SAVE... UNLESS YOU HAVE SOMETHING MORE IMPORTANT TO DO, LIKE SAVING TWO PLANETS?!'

'BUT THE LAST LAY BY WAS OVER A

HUNDRED KILOMETRES BACK TOWARDS UTOPIA PLANES!'

'GOOD, THEN BEST START REVERSING NOW!'

'ALL OF US?!'

'THIS IS LIFE OR DEATH, UTOPIA! AND IF I HAVE TO CHOOSE BETWEEN YOUR DEATH AND ALL LIFE ON MARS, THEN YOU HAD BETTER START WRITING YOUR WILL!'

'MADAM! I MUST INSIST...'

But that was as much as Utopia managed to get out of his mouth before his mouth was filled with a very angry Chryssie. She bashed into him and kind of head butted him, which caused him to shunt back a few tens of metres. Only twisting slightly to one side and getting partly wedged made him stop moving.

'YOU HIT ME WITH YOUR HEAD!'

'AND TECHNICALLY YOU DID THE SAME TO ME, NOW BACK AWAY!'

'BUT...'

Another head butt and this unwedged Utopia as he reversed back further and his tail slapped the following lung whale in the face.

'I HAVE MILLIONS OF YEARS OF ANGER IN ME TO RELEASE! I CAN DO THIS ALL DAY! IN FACT ALL YEAR AND THEN SOME!'

BANG!

With each head on collision Chryssie pushed the line of other lung whales backwards – a whale way line that collected more and more carriages as the line moved back.

This went on for some time. Two days and a hundred kilometres later, they had finally backed up to the previous air hole. It was technically a vertical shaft leading back up to the surface and another ice-capped crater lake.

Chryssie made a stern face to Utopia who was just glad it was all over.

'THIS IS NOT OVER!' shouted Chryssie, disabusing him of the notion, then she headed back up to ground level. She had no difficulty in breaking through the layer of ice with the amount of anger she had been holding in.

* * * * *

The tidal wave from Chryssie surfacing washed up to the rim of the crater before subsiding back onto the ice and into the hole that Chryssie had made.

It was a small crater, only a few hundred metres across, and the rim was low so Chryssie could see over the edge as she rested on the ice like a basking walrus. Chryssie opened her mouth and unrolled her tongue to create some spongy steps for her passengers to disembark.

'COME AGAIN SOON!' she said with a smile.

The umpteenagers staggered a little, now somewhat disorientated by the stop start pneumatic drill of the last leg of their horizontal journey, followed by the vertical ride. Catapilla squeeze-boxed herself down the ramp and skidded on the ice with all her pairs of legs paddling to find grip.

'Thanks,' said Jade, hitting one side of her head with a claw and making some salty water squirt out of her ear on the other side.

'SORRY I COULDN'T GET YOU CLOSER, BUT IT SHOULD ONLY BE FIVE OR TEN KILOMETRES TO THE EAST FROM HERE.'

'You've done a lot already,' said Jade, 'though heaven knows what we're supposed to do when we get to the landing site.'

Meanwhile Grit was fussing over his little sister and wiping her down with strokes of his claws – he had years of being a protective older brother to catch up on.

'WELL FIONIX SAID YOU JUST HAVE TO KEEP ALL LIVING THINGS OUT OF SIGHT OF THE LANDING CRAFT UNTIL IT STOPS WORKING. AND HIDE ANY EVIDENCE OF LIFE, LIKE BONES AND STUFF...'

'Look,' said Sulphie-Rose, between brushing sweeps of her brother's claw, 'funny bird!'

Grit followed her pointing finger to something in the sky. Jade's attention was also caught by this distraction and she too looked. Catapilla was busy untangling her legs from the silken cocoon strands that had got twisted around her feet, so wasn't looking. As no one was now listening to Chryssie, she too turned her huge gaze to the north-western skies. Yes; there was something flying a kilometre up, and heading east.

'Isn't that one of the Hellas Angels?' Jade asked. They all squinted to make out details.

'Looks like it's carrying something...' Grit noticed.

He was right. It actually looked like one of those mythical storks carrying a baby in a hanging sheet on its way to deliver the new-born. However, the sheet wasn't quite sheet like. It was more an open-worked crochet affair, but it was carrying something.

'IT IS ONE OF THE BIRDS OF PARADISE,' Chryssie confirmed, 'BUT I DON'T KNOW WHAT THE THING IS HANGING BELOW IT...'

'That long blonde mane...' Jade realised, 'It's Hell!'

'Which means,' Grit took over, 'she's carrying Herman!'

'Why is she doing that?!' Jade asked rhetorically. 'And she's heading towards the landing site of the second spacecraft from Earth!'

'Hell!' Shouted Jade. No reaction. Grit joined in. Still no reaction. Chryssie added her voice and the thunderous tones travelled like a shock wave up to the flying postal service and it did cause Hell to wobble a bit on her course, but she carried on as if she heard nothing.

'We need to stop her!' Jade cried, suddenly realising their presence on Mars was going to be compromised.

'But how?!' Grit asked, with panic in his voice.

'We have to bring her down,' said Catapilla matter of factly. 'I think Herman's doing his mind control on her like he did to your Great Uncle Syd.'

'So it was all for nothing!' Jade uttered with despair.

'The craft isn't here yet,' said Minisilver brightly, 'so we still have time.'

'We've got nothing long enough to reach up that high,' realised Jade.

'Catapilla could squirt out some more thread?' suggested Grit.

'I don't think I have that much left in me,' admitted Catapilla.

'Catapult me up there!' suggested the fearless shiny stallion.

Jade looked at Catapilla for any kind of confirmation or a thumbs down.

'We can try, but I think it's too high up.'

The attempt tentatively agreed, Catapilla asked Chryssie to pick her up with one of her huge flippers and she placed her on one edge of the crater's rim. Catapilla then rubbed her butt against some of the more solid looking rocks and asked Chryssie to pick her up again. This she did and carried her over to the opposite side of the crater, an elastic thread of silk trailing in the air behind her like an overhead electricity cable. Once Catapilla had dabbed her own butt again on the rocks on the other side, she ripped the thread free before it had fully solidified.

Chryssie grabbed the thread in the middle and pulled it down to crater floor level, where the umpteenagers had gathered.

'Pick me up and put me in the slingshot!' said Minisilver, without any sign of fear.

Jade obliged and Minisilver changed his shape. He hooked round the thread, leaving strands overhanging so Grit and Jade could bite onto them and pull the elastic back as far as possible, scratching claws against the not so rough ice and trying to aim at the moving target of Hell and her unwanted parasite. Even Sulphie-Rose had joined in, biting onto her brother's heel and helping him to pull back. Jade shut one eye to try and aim as she looked along the possible flight path.

'Be careful,' said Jade, then Minisilver catapulted into the Martian skies, now heading north-east. He shot out of the makeshift siege machine at high speed, taking on a streamlined javelin shape. His high density ensured high momentum and his new shape ensured little air resistance. Those on the ground were all willing the heroic horse-missile to reach the target, but his path was clearly levelling off and he was still someway from the hypnotised and sluggishly flapping Hellas Angel.

'Oh oh,' Minisilver realised as he reached the top of his arc and was too far from the target. He was still a little higher than Hell, so they had a chance. The little horse changed his shape and sprouted wings – frilly ones like those of a flying lizard. Catching the air currents, the shiny spear turning into a shiny glider and, falling slower than before, was now heading for the brainwashed bird and her controller.

By the time Minisilver reached Hell, he was now lower than her back and too far from the wing tips that were still flapping several tens of metres lower but were still too far away sideways. Instead, he had to aim for the dangling string bag held in Hell's clawed feet and containing the crazy crab. Minisilver shifted his fake wings into a kind of parachute to make a soft landing on Herman's involuntary cocoon.

Back on the ground, the umpteenager gang breathed a sigh of relief.

* * * * *

Jade turned back to Chryssie who had hung around to watch the mid-air interception.

'OKAY, WELL I'M GOING BACK DOWN, AND IF THE LOG JAM HAS CLEARED UP I WILL TRY AND FOLLOW YOU GUYS TO THE LANDING SITE, BUT FROM BELOW.'

'Thanks again for your help Chryssie,' said Jade.

'HAPPY TO BE OUT OF ISOLATION. OH, AND I MUST ALSO SAY GOODBYE TO THE NEWLY WEDS...'

With that she stopped talking and opened her mouth and out bounded two monopole-cats, tail in tail. One bluish and one reddish.

'Thanks Chryssie,' said Frankie the blue King of the North.

'Yes, thanks for helping us get together,' said Nati the pinkish Southern Belle.

'YOU'RE WELCOME. WHERE ARE YOU OFF TO?'

The two looked at each other affectionately.

'Honeymoon,' said Frankie.

'Syrtis Majoris!' said Nati. 'Very attractive scenery.'

'Both visually and magnetically,' said Frankie.

'WELL ENJOY YOURSELVES!'

Chryssie turned back to Jade and the others and waved her big flipper.

'I'LL TRY AND MEET YOU GUYS AT THE LANDING SITE.'

'Keep hidden!' Jade shouted with a smile and Chryssie descended beneath the waves as the broken ice rapidly started refreezing behind her.

Jade sighed, waved at the happy monopole-cats then turned her attention back to the matter in hand. So did the others.

Minisilver had landed on the stringy sack enclosing Herman that the dazed looking Hell was still carrying in the direction of the landing site. The little horse did not have a clear idea what he was going to do, but first task was to find out what was going on.

Before Minisilver had slithered barely a few steps, a sneaky little claw had slipped out from between the bindings of the cocoon. He barely saw it coming. It was like the crack of a whip. The claw hit him close to the speed of sound and the small sized liquid horse exploded into a thousand tiny drops, which caught in the wind and fell like silver rain.

'No one stops Hanksie,' said the crazy crab from within his flying cage. 'Hanksie will be interplanetary star!' and his smile could just be seen between the strands of silk that were making the net surrounding him.

From that distance, the umpteenagers could barely make out what happened but realised something had gone wrong.

Jade, standing on the crater's rim turned back to call out to Chryssie, but she was long gone.

Jade realised they were in even more trouble now. Herman was still a loose cannon and heading for the landing site, while the smallest member of their team had just been vaporised, probably still alive if he could coalesce all his drops, if Jade understood his physiology, but she knew they had to find him. And worst of all, Chryssie had gone and she was the proverbial queen in this game of chess; now they had no way of contacting their strongest piece.

'Something wrong?' asked Nati, as the bipolar couple approached the umpteenagers.

Jade quickly brought them up to speed, as she started leading the raggamuffin team down the crater's outer slope in the direction of the disappearing Hellas Angel.

The two cats walked side by side and held tails, the contact neutralising their normally meteoric magnetism. They listened intently to Jade's story.

'I think we can help,' said Nati.

'But what about our honeymoon?' asked Frankie.

'I think we've waited long enough darling, we can put it off a little longer. This feels like a very important mission.'

'The Planet's Future!' cried Jade, as the group picked up speed, herself already as close to galloping as a tortle gets. Grit had got his sister Sulphie-Rose on his back, strapped in place by some pyrite-made bindings and the rest of the team were big enough and had legs enough to keep up themselves.

'You need to stop the crab in the cocoon?' Nati asked.

'He mustn't get to the landing site or the Earth people will know there's life here and they'll destroy it!'

'Well Frankie and I can get up there…'

'But you're neutral now!' Jade pointed out.

'Oh we have ways!' Nati smiled, 'Just tell us what you want us to do.'

'We need to bring him down, or break the hypnosis he's put on Hell.'

'Any idea how?' asked Nati.

'Beggin' yer pardon, ma'am,' Raffi piped up, having been fairly quiet for some time.

'Yes?' Jade asked.

'If'n the cats o' two tails were a willin', some o' the crew and meeself could be hitchin' a ride on their backs and we can do what we do best if'n you understand my meaning ma'am?'

'That's a good idea. Oh, but don't hurt him!' Jade pleaded. 'Just stop him!'

'Aye ma'am,' replied Captain Raffi, though there was clearly a touch of disappointment in his voice. Jade caught it.

'Promise?' she challenged.

'Aye ma'am… unless in there being no other way.'

Jade looked shocked.

'It is weighing up the Planet's safety ma'am – all the rest of us against a artistically bad interloper.'

'Just be compassionate, whatever you have to do.'

'Aye-aye ma'am,' said Raffi saluting and hopping towards the newly wedded couple, 'An' I will do that as an' when I find out what the word means…'

Jade didn't rise to the bait this time, but merely raised an eye brow. Raffi whistled and waved back at Jade's shell.

'Come on yer scabs, I wanna hundred of me worst men.'

'Raffi!'

'Sorry, me worst *wimin'*… can't be sexist.'

'Raffi!'

'I mean me *best* men an wimin!' and a matter of seconds later dozens of pyrites assembled, armed to the back teeth with more *arms* than they had limbs; some even had to drag their weapons along the ground, weapons even bigger than the lice themselves. Raffi turned to the honeymooners.

'Permission to hop aboard?' he asked Frankie.

'Ask her,' said Frankie, pointing to his bride, 'she's the Boss Cat here.'

Raffi looked at Nati, who smiled broadly and revealed her needle sharp teeth; clearly designed to pierce through the toughest of morsels – like pyrites exoskeletons. Raffi swallowed and smiled weakly back.

Grit, Catapilla and Jade looked on with curiosity as the battery of tortle lice hopped into Nati's rose coloured fur, who twitched with discomfort. 'Not *there*! On my back!'

'So how can you follow the field lines when you're together?' Jade asked.

'Actually it's basic physics,' Nati started, 'even Frankie understands it.'

There was clearly some play fighting going on, but Frankie didn't react and merely smiled. Frankie licked one of his fingers and held it up as if checking the wind. Nati continued.

'Together like this we're a dipole so we won't follow the Martian field lines, but if for example, I curl up and Frankie surrounds me, his polarity will shield mine and we'll be like a monopole, the pole that's on the outside.'

'It's you Nati darling,' said Frankie happily and then he proceeded to roll into a ball.

It was as if instinct kicked in, as Nati made herself as flat as possible and spread her limbs like she was the sails of a windmill.

'Hold on to your pyrite hats!' shouted Nati with enthusiasm, then turning to Jade waved, and said 'See you soon!'

The moment Nati had closed round her husband and surrounded him completely, the two became one and the dipole reverted to monopole. The fur ball launched itself into the Martian skies like a Cat Out Of Hellas Basin and headed almost straight for the runaway nogard. Jade and her friends stopped for a moment to watch the curious spectacle, then Jade nudged Grit to get moving and they headed down the crater's ejecta blanket towards the point where they saw their tiny equine friend turn into a literal silver-lined cloud. They glanced up at the flying cats and noticed that at one moment they were veering to one side and like a magician's sleight of hand, Nati and Frankie swapped places and the biplane changed direction back to the correct trajectory.

'Weeeeeeeeeeee!' shouted one of the pyrites who was hanging onto Nati's fur for dear life and the wind was lifting his body horizontal 'Cap'n, we gotta get us selves a flyin' ship!

'Don't be losing sight of our goal and our gold, crewman!' said Raffi, 'An' don't be losing any of yer weapons, cos I ain't gonna be lending any of me own!'

'Right,' decided Nati, who was the outer pole again and the one who could talk, 'We're going to land on the bird's back, so I suggest you all jump off then and go do what you have to do to the crab in the basket. Me and Frankie will try and snap the bird out of the hypnotic spell.'

'Works for me, yer katness,' said Raffi, sharpening his blades.

'And remember what Jade said!' she reminded him, 'Oh, gotta swap over again!'

Like turning a sock inside out, Frankie was now the outer shell and Nati became the core. The pyrites had to scramble through the forest-like fur, jumping from inner Nati to outer Frankie, as they came in to land on the back of the mesmerised Hellas Angel. As they did so, the two cats unfurled to become the neutral 'dumbbell', still holding tails, and all eight paws clasped into Hell's back with claws extended. She didn't even flinch with pain, showing just how mind controlled she was. Dozens of tortle lice jumped at the same time and most landed successfully; a few were caught by the wind and tossed overboard. They had to follow the laws of gravity and return to the ground – fortunately pyrites were light enough, and could produce enough air resistance, to land at a less than fatal speed unless they were very unlucky. A couple that missed the landing swung hooks on ropes and managed to catch their grapples under the scales of the bird's skin, which would have only felt like mosquito bites had Hell been awake.

'No letting go of tails,' said Nati, pointing out the

obvious – but also worried they could lose what they had spent years trying to accomplish.

'So we better grip tightly with our claws,' said Frankie. 'You have a plan?'

Nati quickly inspected the situation and saw Herman's little pincer gripping the back of Hell's ankle, while the Hellas Angel stared expressionless ahead and flapped slowly as if on autopilot. From this height, the predicted landing site for Viking II was visible through the slight haze in the distance.

'I'd say cut off the pincer,' said Nati, 'but Jade's not into animal cruelty.'

'What if we cover the bird's eyes?' said Frankie.

'I get the feeling the crab is steering her,' Nati suggested.

'Unless those pyrites can sabotage his control...' Frankie counter-suggested.

'And if they don't?'

'We could divide and conquer?'

Nati looked worried and clearly hoping that would be a last resort.

Frankie gave a knowing nod back to his bride and they both looked over the top surface of their brainwashed flying carpet to see if they could see what the pyrites were up to; the boarding party were making their way down the cords and strands of the string bag cocoon that was Hanksie's partial prison.

Then Frankie's and Nati's attention was caught by something coming from above. They looked. The Viking Lander!

'Looks like we don't have a choice.' Frankie looked back to Nati.

'But we could lose touch!' said Nati.

'Jade said this thing is bigger than all of us.'

'Then I guess we better do it. Just don't let go of the bird!'

'Do you want the left wing or right?'

'I don't think it matters,' Nati pointed out. 'Either way we can disrupt the flight...'

'Ready?'

'Come on…'

With that, both monopole-cats dug their claws deep into Hell's flesh, drawing blood. They still held tails as they moved onto opposite wings, Frankie on the right and Nati on the left. When their tails were at the limits of their reach, the prehensile tips let go. There was a sudden jerk to their flight path as both cats starting being pulled in opposite directions along the field. The further along the wings they crept, the more it modified Hell's trajectory, but the monopole-cats could feel the parasitic pilot trying to compensate. Frankie waved at Nati and pointed to his own tail then pointed over the front of the wing he was on, then pointed to Nati's tail and pointed backwards over the top of her wing. Nati gave a thumbs up and they synchronized their tails. Frankie passed his over the leading edge of his wing, and Nati let her tail trail back over the top surface of her wing. They nodded and, as one, pulled. Frankie pulled down and Nati pulled up and, keeping their tails in place, they each moved further along their respective wings. Hell was sent corkscrewing through the sky – Hanksie's cocoon ended up cupped in one of the wings as the bird of paradise turned upside down.

Meanwhile on the ground, the umpteenagers were scrambling to find Minisilver.

'Can you see him?' Jade asked, searching frantically.

'No,' said Grit.

'No,' said Sulphie-Rose mimicking him.

'Should we be doing this?' asked Catapilla, almost cynically.

'What do you mean?' said Jade, hurt by the seemingly unfeeling question.

'Well,' said Catapilla still looking and kicking over a few pebbles to check beneath, 'we have a whole planet to hide from these Earthlings, which seems more important at this moment.'

Jade knew Catapilla was making sense – she was basically throwing Jade's own words back at her.

'But…' she still argued.

'She's right,' said Grit gently.

'She's right,' Sulphie-Rose repeated as if it was a game. At this point, the little tortoid unhooked her own straps and shuffled off her brother's carapace, then searched the dusty surface more closely herself.

'But we can't just leave Minisilver lost here,' Jade defended her actions.

'*If* he still exists,' said Catapilla. 'We don't know if he could survive evaporating like that.'

'Let's make a dust castle!' shouted Sulphie-Rose, while the older team members tried to solve this moral dilemma.

'Not now sister,' said Grit, 'Look, how far are we from the landing site?'

'A few kilometres maybe,' said Jade, still desperately searching, 'an hour or so.'

'If we start now…' said Catapilla.

'You guys go,' said Jade, waving them on, 'I'll stay here.'

'But we won't know what to do!' said Grit, exasperated,

'Do you think *I* do?!' said Jade honestly.

'Sulphie-Rose, stop flicking the dust in the air!' said Grit. 'Your asthma will come back.'

'Dust castle!'

'Not now!'

'We should go,' said Catapilla, already turning to face east.

'I'll join you later,' said Jade.

'You sure it's the best thing to do?' asked Grit, who was now dusting down his severely crumb covered little sister.

'I can't just forget about the little horse. He helped us and maybe he's still here somewhere waiting to be rescued…'

'Okay, said Grit, nudging his sister with his nose to move her forward and following behind Catapilla who already had a head start. 'Hope you can find him…'

Jade nodded then turned away to inspect the rippled-sand surroundings, keeping her eyes peeled for anything shiny.

'You're a real mess,' said Grit, fussing over his baby sister as he blew over her shell to remove the caramel coloured coating.

'Oh look I'm all shiny!' said the youngster.

'Oh Sulphie-Rose! You've covered your shell with so much dust!' and as Grit said this, he looked closely at the sheen that his sister had picked up and this intrigued him.

'Hang on, Catapilla!'

'I'm not stopping,' she said single-mindedly, feeling she was the only one who was taking this Earth Invasion seriously, though she had always been the one least involved in Martian Affairs when she was with her flying gang.

Grit thought he could see tiny glittering particles embedded in his sister's yellow patches. With a claw, he pushed the little reflective grains together like he was sweeping breadcrumbs into a pile on the table. He watched. They coalesced. The drop was only a few millimetres across, but he was sure it was forming a tiny little horsehead.

Quickly he brought more of the sparkling debris together and then it seemed like the little horsehead was trying to speak. He put his ear close up.

'It's me!' came the tiny voice.

'Minisilver?!'

'More like Nanosilver at the moment, but you can get all of me back with the help of your sister!'

Sulphie-Rose herself was cocking her head and listening on bemused.

'I gotta a horse in my yellow!'

'Her *sulphur*!' shouted Nanosilver, 'Sulphur attracts mercury! You can use her to collect me up!'

It didn't take Grit long to put his sister back onto his shell and return to Jade's search area. He explained the possible happier ending and when Jade heard the truth straight from the horse's mouth, she swapped jobs with

Grit. He stayed to let his sister romp around in the dust, having fun like a young child should and collecting as many droplets of Minisilver as she could. Jade headed to join Catapilla and take back her role as the unofficial leader of this ad hoc team. She looked ahead at the sky to see Hell flying chaotically, and felt a bit better that the problem was being tackled. Then she spotted an object falling from the sky with an opening parachute and she realised the situation was becoming a high-level emergency. Again.

The Viking II Lander had arrived.

Jade galloped ungracefully behind Catapilla who was a few hundred metres in front and kicking up a multi-legged dust trail. In the air, Hell was spiralling and corkscrewing unpredictably as she unconsciously fought both the married monopoles and the overriding mind control from Herman. Inside the cocoon cage a confrontation was building up between the Goliath-sized crab artist and the pint-sized pyrites. Raffi and his *cracked* team had sneaked in between the threads of the cocoon and now inhabited the cell's inner space. At first, Hanksie was not aware of their presence, he was too busy trying to control his high flying host and not understanding at first why she was veering off course. When Hell turned upside down as part of one of her rotations, Hanksie's string bag of a cocoon landed on her stomach then on her back. When Hell did another half turn the twist brought him onto her back again. All this turning threw the pyrites bouncing and bumping in all directions and those that had not secured an anchor for themselves got shaken out of the cocoon like grains of salt from a salt shaker. Those that remained inside moved in a semi coordinated way (which also meant semi discoordinated way) and approached the single-minded end of the crab. Herman was peering out between the silken strands and trying to navigate and control Hell, so only noticed them at the last second.

'AHAAR!' cried Cap'n Raffi Rehab, the need for silence gone.

'AHAAR!' cried his team, and weapons were raised – about four per pyrite – ready to make a crab salad for the whole crew.

'Creepy crawlies! Leave Herman to his destiny!' and with that, the crab used all his remaining limbs (and he had many) like a collection of rotating chef's knives. While the cutting edges kept missing the pyrites, Herman's slapping with the sides of his blade-like limbs worked like tennis rackets and many of the pyrites were batted for six against the cocoon's boundary walls. With the gaps between strands, half of the pyrites were launched through and out to tumble back to the Martian surface.

Raffi realised he was fast losing men, and with them the chance of stopping the annoying arthropod, the crazy crustacean, the loopy lobster – no there wasn't time for this.

He shouted to his remaining crew, 'Time to play dirty me laddies!'

'We kill 'im?!' shouted one enthusiastic crew member.

'The lady Jade sez we can't, but we can sting 'im!'

With that the remaining dozen tortle lice raised their razor sharp arms and, as one, plunged them into Herman's exoskeleton. To him it barely felt like pin pricks and not even as bad as bee stings, but he flinched and lost control for a couple of seconds – which gave Raffi and his crew the impetus to carry on jabbing. They brought Herman to a defensive shaking act. Most of the pyrites were shaken free and went the only way gravity would let them go – Raffi hung on for dear life and, with one cutlass blade between his teeth, he crawled up Herman's back and reached his right cheek. He was struck by a strange sense of déjà vu; small next to Herman's huge face, exactly like the great sculpture in Cydonia. The momentary distraction was enough to let Herman spot the pyrite captain and before Raffi knew it, a pincer's shadow was descending on him fast. He tried to dodge, but the sharp blades closed rapidly round his right leg and SNIP! Off came the bottom half of his leg.

Raffi looked in horror then realised it was his wooden leg – in that second he swung his spiked metal flail at the crabby face in front of him and it hooked to the inside of the crab's right nostril. Raffi swung himself into the nasal cavity before Herman had a chance to react – he had his spear poised to jab the crab, when Herman snorted and shot Raffi out at close to the speed of sound. In that moment Raffi let go of his flail and hurled his spear into the darkness of the right nostril, embedding it like a splinter. As Raffi shot out of the cocoon and began to fall, he hoped his lost spear would distract the crab enough to do some good.

As the captain fell he could see the monopole-cats still twisting the day away, but Hell was still heading – albeit haphazardly – towards the Viking landing site. Raffi stopped watching and turned his attention to the ground that was rising very fast. His physics knowledge was limited, but he knew he only had ten to twenty seconds before reaching the ground. He scanned the surrounding terrain, looking for a crater. Several little ones. An ice filled one? Yes! And was that who he thought it was below the surface? Raffi looked through his personal armoury sack. Small throwing knives, no. No more spears, sabres or flails. Oh, but one big hammer. He took up a dive pose like a superhero carrying his powerful hammer and aimed for the ice-covered crater. He pulled the hammer back then threw it ahead of himself, put his hands together and prayed it would break the ice.

The hammer, like a bullet, smashed through the ice. Small spidery cracks appeared creeping outwards. And though the hole was small, it went all the way through the ice and met the cold salt water below. Raffi sucked his beer belly in a bit further and tried to think thin thoughts and hoped he would live to fight another day.

Jade had caught up with Catapilla, but was growing frustrated that they couldn't move faster –and she worried they were going to miss a very important rendezvous. What made it even *more* worrying was that they could see Hell struggling across the sky above them, yet still drifting towards the very place she shouldn't. The monopole-cats and the pyrites had slowed down Herman's progress, but hadn't stopped him.

'Remember when nothing used to happen?' Catapilla said, between gasps for air.

'I miss those days...' Jade replied breathlessly.

'I don't think they'll be coming back anytime soon.'

The two of them had reached what Jade thought was the final short rise before the landing site. They were just about to raise their heads over the ridge that was blocking their view of the plain when suddenly a green shape jumped up and, with paws and ambidextrous tail, pulled them both back down out of sight

'Shhh!' said Katya, holding a claw to her own lips 'It's landed!'

'Sorry we're late,' whispered Jade, feeling like she'd failed her most important task.

'Don't worry,' Katya smiled, 'it's all under control,' and she gestured to the pedestal rock just next to her.

Masha gave a little bow and a smile.

'Captain Marina reporting for duty, ma'am!' she said proudly.

Jade collapsed, slumped so she was resting on her own carapace, and let her limbs flop exhausted to her sides before releasing a great sigh.

'I don't understand,' she admitted. Meanwhile, Catapilla had similarly deflated and took a moment to recover.

'Your dad's got everything under control at the other landing site so me and Masha decided to come here as a backup.'

'We got delayed,' Jade admitted.

'Not to worry ma'am,' Masha explained. 'I flew on Katya with my crew and we've already secured the perimeter and all's good here. Fortunately not much was happening anyway, so we just have to keep it that way.'

'That's one small mercy,' said Jade, 'but we have another imminent problem.'

'What's that?' asked Katya innocently. Without even

looking, Jade raised a claw and pointed to the western sky.

Katya and Masha looked and saw the erratic bird of paradise, carrying her unwanted shopping bag full of trouble.

'Could you do me a favour please, Jade?' asked Katya.

'Um sure, what?'

'Can you keep an eye on my cat-lings for a little while?'

'Your…'

'Babies, it's a long story.'

As she said this, Katya rummaged around in her fur and after a little suction popping sound she produced a tiny little version of herself in one claw, picked up a rock and closed her baby's tail round the rock and let it float on it like a tiny tethered balloon. She then felt in again and pulled out a second one, fixing it to another rock, all out of sight of the Lander. When she pulled out a third one, she was shocked to find herself holding a chubby little beige worm.

'Dmitry! Where did you come from?'

Before he could give a dour reply, she nodded:'I might need you actually,' and she tucked him back into her green fur, then felt around and found the real third cat-ling.

'What do I need to do?' Jade asked.

'They don't need feeding, don't worry,' she explained, 'they're already moving onto magnetic energy.'

'What if they let go of their rocks?!'

'Not to worry. They seem to have the ability to *home*. I won't be getting rid of them that easily! Fascinating stuff. I must study it when I have a moment!'

Masha had climbed onto Katya's head and seemed to know instinctively what was happening next.

'Ready when you are Katya,' she said with conviction, just rubbing a whetstone against one of her sabres. 'Come on you scum!' she waved to her handful of crew that were still with her.

'Good luck,' said Jade and she waved absentmindedly,

noticing the cat-lings also waved, as if mimicking what they saw.

Katya changed colour and launched herself into the sky, heading roughly west and towards the badly dancing nogard, but keeping low and hugging the ground to remain out of sight from the Viking II Lander, should it be looking that way.

Hell was losing altitude, which is what the allies wanted, but Herman, peering out from his silken prison wanted to make it over the final ridge to get the attention of the Visitors from Earth. He could not stop himself from performing in front of an audience, even if it was just a remote camera on the landing craft. He knew that his image would be seen by billions if he could just make the audition. He pinched harder with his claw onto Hell's leg and this seemed to speed her spiralling jig, slowing their descent.

Masha, standing on Katya's forehead, was squinting against the wind caused by their rapid flight through the Martian atmosphere. Katya was phasing through various costume changes as she navigated the field lines, and as they approached they could see the poor nogard turning faster. Nati and Frankie were hanging on for dear life but losing the battle against divorcing centrifugal forces.

Katya ran a quick calculation and realised that if the newlyweds could not retain their torque – and Katya herself and Masha could not arrive in the next few seconds, with no idea of how to stop the mad crab anyway – then it would be too late.

Frankie clung with his tail's dendritic roots but, being at the end of the wing as it turned at such speed, was travelling very fast and getting very dizzy. Nati was no better off, the turning forces now exceeding any force with which they could fight back. Both were raising their adrenalin levels to increase their attractiveness to the field, but it was a losing battle. The helicoptering Hellas Angel was now rising slowly and still drifting towards the ridge that hid them from the Viking II Lander.

Frankie felt his tail losing grip. He stared with wild

realisation at his sweetheart on the other wing and she too knew they'd reached a critical turning point. As Frankie was finally thrown off, Hell's new imbalance meant Nati also lost her grip and flew off in the opposite direction to her beau. They could only gaze after each other with defeat.

'NATI!' he cried as he flew over one horizon.

'FRANKIE!' she reciprocated as she disappeared over the opposite one.

Both Katya and Masha stared, speechless, at this sudden loss of the upper hand.

'Got any ideas for this pain in the neck?' Katya asked the pyrite captain, as they approached the now steadily rising Hell, carrying her annoying package almost up to the ridge.

'Um,' reflected Masha, 'how about *being* a pain in *his* neck…'

Katya headed for the 'luggage' rather than the carrier pigeon, her tail now poised over her like a scorpion's sting. Masha hopped from Katya's forehead to the end of her tail and Katya caught her like a baseball in a glove. Herman saw them coming. He even started to speak.

'If you try to stop Herman –'

However he was unable to complete his threat. Katya aimed for the string bag cell and her versatile tail slipped in through the strands and curled several times round the crab's skinny neck; no air going down his throat, so no sound coming out. Well, apart from a bit of coughing. What next followed was a lot of writhing claws snipping and snapping frantically, like a barber on speed, while Katya tried to dodge a mid-air chain saw massacre. But there were too many pincers and Katya could not manoeuvre fast enough; a slap from one of the bladed legs swatted Katya so violently that she was knocked unconscious and loose; without her vice-grip on the crab's neck, Katya's only way was down. Masha was hanging on, hooked into one of the roots on Katya's tail and together they fell. For those brief seconds the combat lasted, Hell had started to head downwards, but as

Herman's attention returned to navigation, they were lifting again.

Masha could not see an easy way out, with the ground coming up fast and a monopole-cat stuck in neutral green. She looked up and saw their prey getting away and she felt a failure on at least two levels. Masha, in order to try and save the unconscious cat, was just about to do something she'd not done in public before: a last resort that she'd never wanted anyone to see. She started to unbutton her waistcoat corset when, suddenly, the ground below them burst open.

The erupting ground was actually a small crater, one that had a layer of ice across its floor. But the ice had just exploded. Bursting up through the cracked sheets of ice came the biggest face you might ever see in the solar system, and it was smiling as broadly as a lung whale could smile. It was Chryssie, and riding on her back was the smallest looking ship's captain, well small compared to her, and Captain Raffi yelled at the top of his voice.

'YEEEEEEEE HAAAAAAAA!'

Of course it sounded pretty quiet compared to Chryssie's rather dramatic entrance. While she and Raffi were rising, the out-cold Katya and hanging-on-for-dear-life Masha were falling. Raffi, seeing the two damsels in distress, hesitated for barely a second then ran down the whale's back and dived towards the green cat. Meanwhile, Chryssie was just about her full body length out of the water – some three hundred metres – and reaching the top of her flight path. Herman, who had just started to feel smug again, found the sky rapidly getting dark as the whale's jaws closed around his string bag prison. He barely had time to unclip his pincer from Hell's leg before Chryssie's teeth closed around his bag, snapping its contact with Hell, and the whale started her journey back down to Mars. With her hypnotising tormentor no longer controlling her, Hell flapped about and flopped slowly back to the ground, coming to rest on the sand dunes and scattered rocks not far from Jade and Catapilla – fortunately out of sight of the alien visitor.

Meanwhile, in the closing seconds of Katya's fall, Captain Raffi caught up with her and shouted to his fellow captain.

'Marina!' he cried, 'Hot wire the damn cat will ya!'

Masha had to think fast. Yes; she'd been told about this back in her early days, but that was hundreds of thousands of years ago and could she remember the details?! Not really – plus Katya was not like the blue and red ones they'd practised on in the past. Katya was now almost sliding down the body of the lung whale, barely centimetres away, and Masha considered trying to hook onto the whale using her weapon like a mini anchor. She quickly dismissed the idea. So she hurriedly tried touching together various combinations of the dendritic ends of Katya's tail as a join, even using her own metal weapons to wind pairs of fronds together. Sparks jumped between a couple of them, so she knew she had found the live roots. Katya started to flash her ignition colours and made sounds like an engine trying to start – she suddenly turned red and her motion changed so suddenly that Masha lost her grip. Raffi caught up to them and grabbed one of Masha's arms and the free end of the rope that was still hooked into Katya's tail. The three of them just missed the ground – Katya still out for the count mentally, but flying under her own magnetic steam across the surface of Mars.

Raffi pulled Masha back onto the Kat's tail and laughed.

'Have ye ever flown one of these things before?!' he asked as they bounded up the tail towards Katya's shoulders.

'No, have you?'

'Not as one what changes colour, but it can't be much different! You head for one paw and I'll be doing the other, and we is gonna try steerin' a bit – but it's a sure bumpy ride that's comin'!'

'Thanks for the helping hand,' said Masha.

'Pleasure be mine,' said the experienced old seadog, 'But ye might want to be doin' up yer corset. Yer showin' something on yer back ye mightn't want others to be seein'…'

Masha looked and realised, going slightly red, but grateful her fellow officer was helping to keep her secret. Her clothing adjusted, she glanced up in time to see Chryssie descend back into her icy well.

* * * * *

Grit was brushing his sister down, getting rid of the last drops of mercury and all the other dust she'd picked up. He squeezed his claw tightly and watched the silver liquid drip into the little puddle he'd been collecting in a concave rock. He cocked his head, distantly hearing sounds from the next valley; the one where he imagined the battle to stop the crazy crab was going on. He hoped they were victory noises and it wasn't going to be all in vain.

Sulphie-Rose looked, wide-eyed, at Grit.

'Thank you for giving me a dust bath.'

Grit smiled and a little tear came to the corner of his eye.

'Well you just helped our little friend here,' he said, pointing to the silver puddle, 'so, well done Sulphie-Rose.'

'Is he all there?' she asked.

'Let's see…' and with that they both peered at the shimmering liquid, their own reflections rippling beyond recognition.

'Minisilver?'

Slowly, a tiny horse's head started to rise out of the puddle. To their horror, the horse was missing the front half of his face: no nose or mouth, with the face flat as if someone had cut off the end! The poor little horse's eyes looked horrified.

'Oh no!' cried Sulphie-Rose 'We need to find his face!' and she turned and started scrabbling round in the dust.

'Just joking!' cried Minisilver, and when they turned back to him, his full face trickled back into place. 'Sorry I couldn't resist! It works every time!'

Sulphie-Rose's worry turned to joy and she looked at her brother.

'He's funny! Please can we keep him?'

'He's wicked,' said Grit, still recovering from the practical joke, 'and like I said before we can't keep him. He probably wants to get back to the rest of his, his... lake.'

'Um,' reflected Sulphie-Rose and looking at the toy pony, 'can you make yourself into a unicorn Mister Silver?'

'She's cute!' said Minisilver to Grit, 'Can I keep her?'

'Don't encourage her,' said Grit playfully, 'and besides, we probably should go and join the others, as they'll be needing our help...'

Sulphie-Rose seemed distracted and pointed behind her brother.

'Oh look, my second mummy!'

Grit was confused by this and turned his head. It was Ruby.

The two umpteenaged tortles stared at each other, saying nothing. Sulphie-Rose was already bounding towards the red rock tortle and she called back to the liquid pony: 'Come and meet Ruby dooby!'

Minisilver sloshed off his rock and slithered after the youngster, allowing a medium sized horn to grow out the front of his forehead just to please Sulphie-Rose.

'Hi Sulphie-Rose,' said Ruby with a very slight smile, 'Hi Quicksilver, you been on a diet?'

'So funny aren't you,' said Minisilver, 'I got separated from the rest of me, but it seems Big Me is being put to good use elsewhere!'

As they met up, Ruby continued.

'Give me some hoof.' Minisilver obliged, raising a limb out of his pool and Ruby tapped it with one of her claws. Sulphie-Rose arrived and hugged round Ruby's other front foot, her own limbs barely making it all the way round. Ruby lifted her up to face level, holding her upside down and gave her a kiss on her little beak.

'You being a good girl for your brother?'

'Of course Booby! I knew you would come back!'

'I said I would,' and with that Ruby placed Sulphie-Rose onto her own back then looked at Grit again.

There were a few seconds of more silent staring, then Grit spoke first.

'Thank... you... for bringing Sulphie-Rose back...'

Again Ruby almost smiled. She swallowed with slight discomfort.

'... Least I could do,' she began humbly.

'Have you come to help your sister guard the landing site?'

'Not exactly,' Ruby put in, 'um, there's another problem to sort out.'

'Not the Eschers?!' said Grit in horror as he backed away a few steps.

'I was going to help those birds cover up the Face on the Hill...'

'Oh,' reflected Grit, 'well can I help?'

'You have your sister to take care of now.'

'Yes.'

'Best thing for you to do is to take Sulphie-Rose with you and join Jade at the landing site. Keep her safe.'

'And you?'

'Don't worry,' said Ruby, 'I've got some flying friends to give me a hand – well a wing.'

'Okay,' said Grit reluctantly.

'Good,' then Ruby changed tack, 'tell me, is Masha with you?'

'I've not seen her for a while,' said Grit, 'Not since she went looking for you. That was some time ago.'

'Oh...'

'I guess she never found you?'

'No... what about the rest of the crew, they behaving themselves with you?'

'Well,' Grit smiled, 'as well as pyrites can!'

'Say hi to my sister,' Ruby asked, 'tell her not to worry about me – you guys need to watch that landing site thing.'

'Okay,' agreed Grit, feeling the encounter was coming

to a conclusion, 'well I guess we both have jobs to do. Come on Sulphie-Rose!'

'Can't I go with Ruby dooby?'

Ruby lifted the youngster off her back and gave her another little peck.

'You go look after your big brother,' she said with a smile, 'keep him out of trouble and I'll come and see you again soon okay?'

'Okay Booby,' and she walked back to her brother and climbed onto his back. 'Come on Mini corn!'

The little horse looked at Ruby.

'Any use for a four legged friend?' said Minisilver.

'*Legs*?!' said Ruby with a smile. 'I think you should keep the youngster company.'

'Okay, ma'am. Well, good luck with your hiding.'

'No!' Ruby protested, 'I'm not hiding, I've got an important job to do!'

'I know you, Ruby,' said the little horse, 'You're avoiding your sister, but I'm sure you'd be warmly welcomed.'

'Bye, Minnie.'

With that, Minisilver trickled back to Grit and, unliquid like, flowed up like a backward waterfall onto Grit's carapace to join Sulphie-Rose. They slowly turned and began their journey east to join whoever was at the landing site just a few kilometres away. Ruby turned to face the west and contemplated where she was going to hide. Yes, hide. She'd been a loner all her life, not really worrying about anyone else's problems and now look at her. Saving orphans and reuniting families and being nice to others. Minisilver was spot on and saw right through her; she couldn't face her goodie-goodie sister. Or her bad ass ex Captain Masha, who was also a good ass and put Ruby herself to shame.

No; she just wanted to curl up somewhere and smoke a few drycicles.

20

Subaeranean Homesick Hanksie

Chryssie spat Herman out with such a force that his string bag prison cell hit the back wall of the subsurface cavern, and there the crab hung, entangled on the cracks and crevices of the tunnel. Whale saliva dripped from the jail bar ropes and big globules fell onto the cave ledge below – all dimly lit by a pair of glowing monopole-cats. The salty water in the underground tunnel splashed up to the ledge with Chryssie's movements, almost lapping over the top and dragging more of the saliva blobs into the water. The light from the corner polecats cast some dark shadows of the rugged edges of the rocks, while reflections from the water surface sparkled on the ceiling, like a light show in a nightclub party.

'YOU ARE GOING TO STAY THERE IN YOUR CORNER,' said Chryssie, waggling one of her flippers at the scoundrel, 'AND YOU ARE GOING TO THINK ABOUT WHAT YOU HAVE DONE!'

'Not *done* all yet. Only want to draw,' said Herman from behind his stringy prison bars, 'let Herman go. Make Mars more beautiful!'

'CERTAINLY NOT,' thundered the regal whale, 'THIS IS TO STOP YOU LETTING THOSE EARTHLINGS KNOW THERE'S LIFE HERE WITH YOUR ART WORK!'

'Too late, big fish,' said Herman smiling in his crazed way, 'Herman already left his *shez doves* all over Mars...'

'HAS HE?'

'Herman has...and Herman is happy!'

'WHAT HAS HE DONE?'

'Herman left his art all over the everywhere!'

'WHAT ART?'

'Herman sculpted rocks to look like things.'

'WHAT THINGS?'

'Faces… in places… triangle buildings … Earthlings sitting… god heads, all everywhere!'

'WELL,' decided Chryssie, 'YOU ARE NOT GOING TO BE DOING ANY MORE OF THAT FOR SOMETIME!'

'Herman free spirit!' he cried in his defence.

'HERMAN FREE MEAL FOR WHALE IF HE CAUSES ANYMORE TROUBLE!'

Chryssie took a deep breath and sighed.

'COME ON YOU TWO!' she called out to the love cats, 'I'M NOT GOING TO LEAVE YOU ALONE WITH THIS ONE, HE DOES MIND CONTROL. AND BESIDES, I THINK YOU'VE BOTH NOW PLIGHTED YOUR TROTHS, OR WHATEVER YOU CALL IT. HOP IN!'

At that, Chryssie opened her mouth and the pair of monopole-cats, tails entwined, jumped from the corner and had no trouble landing on the spongy tongue of the lung whale. Chryssie spoke to Hanksie again.

'YOU ARE GOING TO STAY DOWN HERE UNTIL IT'S SAFE TO LET YOU OUT AGAIN. I'M OFF TO WARN THE OTHERS OF YOUR RECKLESS GRAFITTI.'

With that, Chryssie submerged below the surface of the salty water and as she closed her mouth the light rapidly disappeared with her.

There were a few moments of silence. Only the echoey sound of drips of water falling from the cave ceiling broke the calm. Then there was a tiny scratching sound. Then there were two round patches of light coming from Herman's face. It was his eyes; an evolutionary remnant from when he used to live in deep oceans. From behind his almost unbreakable prison cocoon, his crazy eyes could be seen peering over the ledge, and looking at his one blade-like leg that had started to feel its way down to the water's surface. He dipped the pointed end in, then retracted it and brought the tip up to his mouth and tasted the liquid.

'Salty,' he said with pleasure 'Herman likes salty water.'

And with that, the crab-in-a-bag rolled off the ledge and plopped into the water, his eyes sending out beams like the headlights of some kind of underwater car and – in spite of being in a sort of fishing net – he swam down the tunnel and disappeared into the darkness.

21

House Goes Home

The noise was quite deafening and the rumbling gave a feeling of nausea, but the birds didn't seem to mind. House looked at Martin and smiled. Martin returned the gesture. The commercial flight, a Jumbo Jet heading for Nice, France was now leaving American air space and starting to cross the Atlantic.

'Quite an adventure...' House commented, as they perched on a short metal strut high up in the plane's undercarriage space.

'Feels good to have been a part of it though, doesn't it?' replied Martin, sighing contentedly.

'Once in a lifetime experience...'

'What was your favourite moment?' Martin asked his friend.

'Oh for me,' said House proudly, 'covering up that incident on the Viking camera! Has to be that!'

'Well, I guess it *was* your finest hour my friend,' and they both looked at the instamatic picture they'd brought with them.

'Thanks to Katya's lessons! And what about you Marty? I'm sure I know...'

'Writing on the feather,' said Martin proudly. 'Quick thinking under duress.'

House fluffed up his feathers, as it was getting pretty cold in the landing wheel compartment.

'Do you think we'll see our Martian friends again?'

'Like you said, it's a once in a generation thing. For those guys, the pace of life is so much slower than ours. Might be one of our kids or one of theirs before we hear from them again. I guess I just have to keep the family story going.'

'Something to tell the wives when we get back!'

'If they believe us!' Martin laughed.

The 747 continued on its uneventful journey across the Atlantic, taking the two house martins back to their quiet sleepy village. Neither House nor Martin would ever be the same again after their experience. They felt honoured to have had their eyes and minds opened and also that they'd helped, in their own modest way, a planet to avoid the exploitation of the human race. At least, for now. And as they relaxed on their return journey home after a working holiday of several months, they didn't know that this was *not* to be the last time they would be part of team Mars. Hey, who do you think is telling this story?!

22

Stuck Inside Dimensions With The Static Greens Again

It is a misleading concept to think that a four dimensional world cannot fill up with three-dimensional objects. Yes, okay I know, mathematicians will tell you that a one-dimensional line is made up of an infinite number of zero dimensional points. And then they will tell you that a two dimensional area is made of an infinite number of lines and up we go to a volume made of a countless number of slices and so on. But nothing is infinitely thin in the real universe. The four-dimensional bubble in which our Physics Police lived, though having that extra dimension, *was* finite in size. It was actually a tesseract, a four dimensional cube. Walking through one door into the next room and through the door in the opposite side merely brought one back to the first room from the opposite side. The same thing happened climbing up the stairs, it just brought one coming up through the floor of the first room and vice versa. Amelius the Third and Turkan were literally up to their second pair of ears in zombie plants. There were so many in their apartment that you just couldn't see the floor, or the walls and barely see the ceiling

'What do you want for your lunch?' asked Turkan, who had decided to remain looking like his Little Green Man personage from Mars. 'Static soup?'

'Not again?!' said Amelius the Third, who had also stayed in his Physics Police shape.

'We've a lot to get through,' admitted Turkan, as he lit the gas on his stove.

'Not boiled either. We've already had boiled zombie plant.'

'How about poached?'

'We had that last week.'

'Curried?'

'Friday. We've had plant zombaglione, gratin de zombie, zombie and chips, zombie bolognaise... you name it, we've had it with zombie.'

'The bolognaise wasn't bad,' Turkan put in.

'Yea, *because* of the bolognaise,' snapped Amelius, 'not the zombie plant extract.'

'What about stuffed zombie in a marinated sauce, on toast? We haven't tried that yet?'

'Call it what you like,' said Amelius, pulling off another plant that was crawling over the top of his head, 'it's still bloody zombied vegetables!'

'Well,' Turkan explained, 'what else can we do with them? They're dying off like they have a built in sell by date. We can't release them back out in the universe, plus there's actually a good load of fibre going to waste otherwise. Besides, as that rock on Mars, you do need to lose a bit of weight you know...'

Amelius sighed in defeat.

'Quite frankly,' he admitted, 'I can't wait for this nightmare to be over,'

'Well,' Turkan reflected, 'we've got a couple of Martian year's worth of vegetation to get rid of, so don't hold your breath.'

'I'm dreading the new job,' Amelius sighed, looking at the writhing zombie plant in his hand then tossing it to one side, only to be walked on by another less ragged, mindless, Starkwood lookalike.

'It could have been worse,' Turkan pointed out, now chopping one of the fully dead Stark zombies into chunks and throwing them into a frying pan.

'Worse than traffic duty?!'

'It won't be forever...'

'But you read the letter. You saw where we're going to be stationed?'

'At least we know the area.'

'Aren't you worried about bumping into the crazy green cat again?!'

'Forget that for now,' said Turkan. 'Take your mind off

it and give me a hand. Can you get me some milk from the fridge?'

Amelius sighed and pulled the present Stark zombie off his head.

'Where is it?'

'It's about three hyper-metres down there,' said Turkan pointing at the present level of piled up zombie plants. Amelius pushed himself out of the melee then jumped off the surface layer of vegetation, did a double back flip, then dived back down in to the squirming green sea of plants and headed deep down to find the buried treasure in the chest freezer below.

23

Calling Elvis

It was several weeks since the Viking I Lander had broken the relative peace and tranquillity of life on Mars. Well, ignoring the hordes of marching plants that had passed by just before its arrival. Oh, and the badly timed birth of some cross-pollinated plants from a monopole-cat. And the cross-bred kittens from an electric plant. And the Physics Police. Oh and though it didn't happen in the vicinity of the first Viking Lander, Elvis was aware that his daughter Jade had also encountered her own challenges on the other side of the planet. Fionix had brought back news about Cydonia and the Second Viking Lander in the Hrad Valley. Apart from that briefing, Elvis barely saw Fionix as she carried out her duties protecting the planet.

The weathered old rock tortle had had to remain motionless since the craft had arrived, though he had perfected the art of not moving during his long and mainly stationary life. His left flank was facing the Viking Lander a couple of tens of metres distant but, fortunately, his head was out of view. All that the humans on Earth could see was a huge, worn and craggy rock some two and a half metres long, covered in tiny cracks, dust and sand. They had decided to name the rock Big Joe. With Elvis' real name being Big Joe, well, what were the chances of that?! At *least* one in a hundred million.

Behind this living rock, Starkwood – the *original* one – slouched, or was it crouched, well, his body language was somewhat slobby, but he had had to keep out of view of the human race whatever his stance. If seen on camera by the Earthlings, Starkwood might end up with a more famous name than *Big Joe.* Something like *Big Living Weird Green Plant That Proves Life Does Exist On Our*

Neighbouring Planet, Even If It Looks Badly Put Together, So Let's Go Kill It. Or something similar. Starkwood was leaning to one side, head resting on one of his sepals which was bent like an arm supporting his chin. He was watching his own offspring, now that they'd sprouted out of the ground. All three looked like mini versions of Starkwood himself, but maybe a little greener behind the ears. The third and final sapling was taking its first moves out of the Martian soil in a wobbly, unsteady small step for static plants, but a giant hop for a seedling. Starkwood put a caring sepal behind his offspring to stop it falling backwards and that helped it stagger forward a little way, with a smile coming to its happy face.

Also hiding behind Elvis was Quicksilver. He had created a swimming pool for the other two Starkwood babies. Quicksilver's head was sticking out of his shiny pond and he was creating ripples for the budlings so they could surf across his undulating body. Fortunately, neither Viking Lander had brought any sound monitors, so the Martians could make as much noise as they wanted without waking the neighbours. 'They grow so fast,' said Starkwood, not realising how stereotypical he was sounding as a parent.

'Don't I know it,' Elvis sighed, thinking of his own kids.

Just then, the little Starkling made a crackling noise with its mouth, which surprised both reminiscing fathers.

'He must have a bit of solar wind,' said Starkwood, patting its back then putting a sepal in front to stop him falling forward. The Doting Dad Group was then interrupted by the pyrite captain's arrival.

'Reportin' in for the regular, um, report Admiral.'

'Thank you Sam,' said Elvis politely, then listened respectfully.

'No life as far as the lice can see sir, not on the ground nor under it, nor up in that there sky.'

'Good to hear Sam. And no dead ones that could give us away to those Earthlings either?'

Before he had answered, there was some more white

noise coming from the walking baby plant and then a hiccup, which rapidly discharged his statically raised hair.

'Sorry,' said Starkwood, then he put the noisy newbie over his shoulder and patted its back again.

'No dead organisms visible, sir,' resumed Sam Biosis, 'Well, there was one on account of a couple of the men was feeling peckish and shared a snailien, but they was out of sight and they buried the shell rock an' leaving no traces of it sir.'

'Good. And the craft itself?'

'It's like watching dry ice sublimin' sir,' said Captain Sam Biosis, 'not the most intrestin' thing to watch. The *eye* thing just keeps turnin' and clickin' like it has a twitch.'

'And your crew are keeping out of sight when it's taking pictures?'

'As ordered Admiral. They isn't gonna catch us with our pants down – that's our metaphorical pants sir – and that arm has dug up some dirt, but apart from that it seems as harmless as an empty tortle shell, if you pardon the simile your 'onour...'

'No offense taken, Sam,' Elvis assured him.

'*No offense taken Sam...*' came an echo, quite unexpectedly.

It sounded like Elvis' voice but a bit crackly, and emanating from another source.

Elvis looked at his captain.

'Not me impersonatin' a superior officer sir!' Sam assured him.

It had come from Starkwood's direction so they both looked at Starkwood, who was still patting his youngest's back to relieve him from his static. Starkwood looked at the staring admiral and captain.

'Oh,' he explained, pointing to his offspring, 'he's done this before. Repeats things he hears. Apparently I used to do it a lot when I first bloomed. But without the white noise, mind.'

Sam Biosis turned his attention back to his boss and brought up a final point.

'Could I be askin' a question, sir?'

'Sure, what's up?'

'Me an' the crew was wonderin', if we might as be keepin' anything that falls off the Earth Ship?'

'*Are* bits falling off?!' Elvis asked in surprise.

'Not without a bit of help, if you get my drift Admiral.'

'Um, Sam,' Elvis began diplomatically, 'best not to help it fall to pieces for the moment.'

'We can help it get to the end of its active life an' thus stop it spyin' on us peace-lovin' Martians!'

'Just put that plan on the back burner, Sam and we'll see how the craft behaves.'

'Aye sir…'

'*Aye sir,*' came a crackly echo again.

It was Son of Starkwood parroting what it had just heard and this time it followed the mimic with a giggle.

'Not really the first words I was expecting,' said Starkwood, now lifting up the youngster to look at him face to face, 'but I'm proud nonetheless.'

'Been there my friend,' said Elvis with a sigh.

'Ah, your daughter?' Starkwood realised.

'It's her birthday today,' Elvis admitted. 'Sixteen Million…'

'Of course,' Starkwood suddenly remembered. 'With all that's been going on, I'd forgotten!'

'Hmmm,' Elvis agreed.

'*Hmmmm,*' said the seedling, along with some more crackling.

'You miss her?'

'It's been a million years!'

'Which daughter is this?'

'Jade…'

'*Jade…*' Repeated the plantenna.

There followed a bit more crackling and hissing, and some odd noises like the squealers during an aurora borealis display, then the baby static plant spoke again.

'*Dad*?' said the plantlette, '*is that you*?!'

It was Jade's voice.

24

Running Up That Hill

It was a couple of hours after Grit had parted ways with Ruby that he, Sulphie-Rose and Minisilver reached the plain's edge where Viking II had landed. Grit first passed an exhausted and disorientated Hell, who was lying crumpled and bedraggled on the rock-strewn edge of the plain. She was well below the line of rocks that the allies were using to keep out of sight of the Viking Lander II. Standing beside Hell and stroking her forehead with several of her feet was Catapilla, who looked up when she saw the umpteenager arrive.

'That big bird is hurt,' Sulphie-Rose said, pointing at the nogard who was having a bad feather day.

'Just recovering,' replied Hell, staring at the sky, her chest heaving a little more than usual.

'Can we help in any way?' Grit offered empathically.

'Thank you,' Hell replied, 'but there's not much you can do for a parasitic artist stuck in your head. Just let the nightmare fade away...'

'How did he do that to you?' Grit enquired, 'I mean everything looked sorted out when you birds took over?'

'Oh,' sighed Hell, 'I got a bit cocky. We were all fighting over who was going to carry the crab as far away from the landing sites as possible and imprison him in the polar ice until this was all over. I pushed for it the hardest and left the others reshaping that Cydonian Hill he'd sculptured. I don't know how long I was carrying him before he'd got a pincer to my leg and that's when I lost control over my own movements.'

'So where is Herman?' Grit asked.

'Oh he's taken care of,' Catapilla replied and she then gave a potted version of the fight she'd seen from her vantage point; the pyrites, then Kat and then the lung whale, Hanksie disappearing into the ground and everyone living happily ever after. Except Hanksie of course.

'I'm so tired,' said Hell.

'Well,' said Catapilla, 'when you're ready to fly again, we can go back and join the squad.'

As she said this, Catapilla, with the legs that weren't mopping Hell's brow, were somehow sewing the silk rope that was still slowly uncoiling out of her butt. She seemed to be knitting it round her own body, sewing herself up inside her long awaited cocooning phase.

'And I promise I won't pinch your leg while you carry me...'

'Where are the others?' Grit asked Catapilla.

'Just behind the next outcrop, towards the Lander.'

'What has this craft done so far?'

Catapilla shrugged.

'I don't really know. It's just been sitting there in the middle of the plain. Flashed a couple of lights and some bits have turned round, a thing that looks like an eye.'

'Well, we better join them, that's what we're supposed to do,' and with that Grit waved a paw and Sulphie-Rose mimicked him from atop his carapace. Minisilver stuck his head out of his little pool in one of the cracks on Grit's shell and waved a hoof and then Grit headed towards the next set of boulders.

Jade was sitting, cross-pawed next to another victim of the recent confrontation. The green cat was lying almost motionless on her back, her prehensile tail feeling around and picking up handfuls of sand and letting it run absentmindedly back to the ground like some form of mindful meditation technique. Hanging vertically by their own tails to one of Katya's legs were her three babies. They swung gently like helium party balloons in the mild breeze, three identical kittens seemingly synchronised in their movements. Each stared at the same thing at the same moment, or turned to the distraction of a piece of gravel falling from one of the big rocks. Then seeing Grit arrive, the triplets turned to face him. This caught Jade's attention and she perked up.

'You're all okay?!' Jade asked.

'All present and correct ma'am,' Grit joked in a military voice.

'Hello Greenie!' waved Sulphie-Rose.

'Hello again! And the horse?!'

Minisilver obliged and showed his head and smiled.

'Most of me is here!' he joked.

'Well that's good news,' said Jade.

'Seems we missed all the action,' Grit commented, 'saving Mars from the crazy crustacean.'

'We merely watched,' Jade admitted, 'we have to thank Katya, the pyrite captains and Chryssie for doing all the saving! Oh and the newly weds...'

Grit looked over to Katya but she wasn't yet in a state to accept any accolades. Then Grit looked back to Jade and noticed the two pyrite captains standing on her nose.

Grit gave them a nod of acknowledgement.

'Captains,' said Grit, trying to remain formal but he was pleased to see the ladybug that had been his temporary captain.

'Sir,' Masha said with a slight bow, as Grit began again.

'I would like you to meet my long lost sister, Sulphie-Rose.'

'Honoured to be meetin' you again ma'am' said Raffi Rehab, bowing politely, 'and you look like becoming a fine vessel if I may say so?'

'I'm going to be a vessel?' Sulphie-Rose asked, turning to her brother.

'A fine one,' Grit agreed, 'like my friend Jade here...'

'Greenie!'

'Just wonderin', Sulphie-Rose ma'am,' Raffi continued, 'if you be needin' all that sulphur on account of you got so much there on your shell.'

'Raffi!' cautioned Masha and she pointed a finger at him. Raffi defended his thoughts.

'There's good quality gunpowder in the yellow rock, Marina. I'll go halves with 'ee if the vessel says yes.'

'You're as bad as the crew!' Masha accused him half-heartedly and this caught Sulphie-Rose's attention.

'Ooh!' she said pointing at the female pyrite captain, 'you look like my second mum!'

Masha looked confused so Grit explained.

'It's your eye patch,' he pointed out, 'like the one Ruby wears…'

'Ruby's her *mother*?!'

'No,' Grit laughed, 'Ruby found my sister hiding under our… well, back there in the Hellas Basin and she gave her to Chryssie to bring her to me.

'How long ago was this?!' asked Masha who had bounded off Jade's nose and was standing just in front of Grit and his sister.

'You're pretty like she is,' Sulphie-Rose butted in.

'When did you see her?' Masha asked the young tortle, with mounting excitement.

'Oh we just seed her,' said Sulphie-Rose, 'just now…'

Masha looked to Grit who qualified this.

'Yea we did, back there, after we'd collected Minisilver together…'

'How long ago?!'

'Oh, a couple of hours,' then Grit turned to Jade, 'I tried to persuade her to come see you, but she made excuses and…'

Before Jade had a chance to reply, Masha called out.

'Permission to go get her ma'am?'

'Well,' Jade reflected, 'you're not technically one of *my* pyrites so it's not up to me.'

Masha thought about this, then turned back to Grit.

'Permission to –'

'If anyone can bring her back, it would be you…'

Masha gave a quick salute then bounded off, back down the slope and headed west.

They all watched her go then Grit turned his attention back to Jade.

'So what's there to do?'

'Oh well,' Jade reminded herself, 'most of the groundwork was already done before I got here. Now we have the pyrites securing the perimeter, keeping everyone out of the way, so really, not much. We have to keep out of sight of that craft and make sure it stays that way.'

It was an hour or so before Masha had reached the point where Grit had met and parted ways with Ruby. The agile pyrite captain had bounded and hopped in leaps as fast as her legs could carry her. Well they *were* praying mantis legs, so quite springy, and she was certainly much fitter than a triple jumping flea. She glanced back a few times to check on the crowd she was leaving behind and, when she felt she was out of sight, let her wings pop out and change her jumps into extended glides. Not being practised in the art of flying she resembled more the aerodynamics of a roasted chicken than that of a grasshopper. But certainly faster than normal bounding, that was for sure.

Being a female pyrite of a royal blood line, she did have the possibility of becoming queen of the hive so to speak, but the thought of devoting her life to popping out thousands of eggs and making thousands of rowdy reckless wretches like Piccolo and Terry helped her make up her mind to avoid it at all costs. Plus, when she did get her wings out, she felt she looked like a fairy and that just wouldn't do for her image. The Tinkerbell of the Tortle World? No thank you!

Once she had arrived where Grit had seen Ruby, Masha noticed the claw prints in the dust and tutted. Both tortles had failed to cover their tracks, though at least it meant she was able to continue to follow her vessel. It took another hour or so before she caught up with the Red One, who was resting under an overhanging rock – one of her favourite kinds of places to skulk. Ruby was facing the setting sun in the west and vaping a solid CO_2 icicle. Masha stopped dead on a small rock just in front of Ruby's face. The pyrite had already folded her wings out of sight before her final approach, so as not to invite comments from her old crew – she would never live it down.

'Ma'am...' Masha greeted her previous rock tortle and gave a slight nod of the head.

'Masha! Um… Captain Marina …'

Before Masha had a chance to reply, there was suddenly a handful of ragged looking lice gathered on Ruby's head.

'Look!' shouted one, pointing, 'It be the Cap'n!'

'She returned to the flock!' cried another, then more and more gathered on the bridge of Ruby's nose until the whole of the top of her head was streaming with hundreds of the creepy crawlies. All were wearing an eye patch. Ruby looked up at the welcoming committee then looked at Masha.

'Hello…'

'Grit said you found his sister,' Masha commented.

'Yeah,' Ruby replied, 'well best keep it to a whisper. That kind of thing will lose me my street cred …'

'May I ask you a question Ruby, sir?'

'Will I regret saying yes?'

There was a pause.

'Is there still a vacancy for your vessel's captainship?'

'I wasn't sure you'd want to, after what I'd…'

'That's not in the present…'

'Oh… That's very Muddist…'

'Only one condition, Ruby…' Masha put in with a calculated risk.

'I can guess what *that* might be… Okay…'

'Permission to come aboard then ma'am?'

The crowd of pyrites on Ruby's head parted in two, creating a gangway for the captain to return to her old job.

25

Happy Birthday, Sweet Sixteen Million

'You sure you're up to it?' Jade asked with genuine concern.

'Don't worry,' said Katya, combing the fur on her forehead, using the root-like end of her prehensile tail, 'I'm feeling a lot better now. Especially if you don't mind doing some babysitting, again...'

They both looked at the three kittens, their tails hooked into Katya's back fur and bobbing slightly in the magnetic field breeze. One of the kittens made a crackling sound, like the discharge of static and that made Katya jump a little.

'Oh!' she said, 'Marsing always takes me by surprise!'

The admiring mother took the statically dynamic youngster from her own back and it reflexively hooked its prehensile tail around its mother's paw. She gave the kitten a kiss and passed it over to Jade, who took it onto her front foot and the monopole kitten curled its tail round one of Jade's claws. It then discharged again and gave the tortle a mild shock.

'Ah!' she said, 'I see what you mean!'

'It's nothing to worry about,' Katya assured her as she took the second kitten and handed it to Grit. He held out a single claw and the triplet grabbed hold of it with its tail. The third one Katya handed to a delighted Sulphie-Rose and before she got her paw up to the grabbing tail, the kitten clutched onto Sulphie-Rose's face, which made her giggle through a closed mouth. Then the third kitten began lifting Sulphie-Rose off the ground, the baby tortle barely being much heavier than the new-born kitten itself. Minisilver jumped off Grit's back and splashed onto Sulphie-Rose, giving her just enough weight to bring her back to the ground. The next moment a dozen pyrites had jumped off Grit as well, with knives in their mouths and ropes wrapped round their shoulders and before you could say 'splice the main brace', the ruffians had tethered and secured the yellow tortle to some suitably located stones. This third kitten then let off a discharge which made Sulphie-Rose jump; the sparks ran down the ropes and burned and snapped a few of them (and a few of the more heavily armed pyrites), but enough held firm and the tortle remained with at least two feet on the ground. The little shock had caused the kitten to lose grip around Sulphie-Rose's mouth but Minisilver lived up to the name of his bigger part and quickly caught the kitten's tail.

'That tickled!' said Sulphie-Rose, rubbing her own nose as she watched the kitten, who was fascinated by the liquid pony's hold on her.

'*That tickled*,' repeated the kitten but in the same voice as Sulphie-Rose! This was a showstopper.

'Oh,' said Katya, 'her first words!'

'She copied me!' said the young tortle, with excitement, 'Can we keep her, Gritty?'

'Um,' said Grit, feeling a certain déjà vu about this desire to keep other creatures as pets, 'Well, we can't keep her forever, but you can help us babysit while, um, Auntie Katya is off bringing that couple back together again.'

'Can I take her for walks?'

'Well sweetie,' said Katya bemused, 'you'll probably take her for a 'float' to begin with, as new-born monopole-cats tend to stay in the air, ready to shoot off at any sign of trouble.'

'Can I play fetch with her?'

'What's that?' the mother cat asked.

'Look,' and Sulphie-Rose picked up a piece of gravel and threw it awkwardly in the air. The monopole kitten's attention was caught and she stared in a predatorial way at the arcing stone and even made a swipe at it with one of her tiny paws. The stone fell to the ground and bounced a few times before coming to a halt, the kitten not taking her eyes off it. Then Sulphie-Rose spoke again.

'Fetch!'

'*Fetch,*' said the kitten, which yet again surprised the onlookers.

Then there was another burst of hissy white noise from the talkative kitten followed by some very unexpected sounds.

'*It's her birthday today,*' said Katya's baby in a voice that was not her own, but instead was a voice they all recognised. '*Sixteen Million...*' continued the Elvis impersonator.

Everyone was now staring amazed at this parroting pussy kitten, as another voice came out of its mouth:.

'*You miss her?*' and this was now Starkwood's voice.

'*It's been a million years!*' said the kitten in perfect Elvisish.

'*Which daughter is this?*'

'*Jade...*' said the Elvis sound-alike

'Dad?!' shouted Jade, 'Is that you?!'

There was a pause of several seconds.

'*Jade?! Is that you*?!' said Elvis' voice.

'Your voice is coming out of a baby monopole-cat!' cried Jade, pointing at this possessed pre-kindergarten katling.

'*And yours is coming out of one of Starkwood's seedlings,*' said Elvis.

'Fascinating!' said Katya, closely inspecting the walkie-talkie tabby, 'They're acting like electromagnetic transmitters and receivers!'

'*Well, this is an unexpected surprise,*' said Elvis, '*but it does give me the chance to say Happy Sixteen Millionth Birthday daughter.*'

'Thanks dad,' said Jade, then she suddenly jumped with a start, 'Oh! Is that Ruby?!'

It was. Masha had obviously got her condition fulfilled (Ruby coming to Jade's birthday, if you hadn't worked it out). And with yet another unlikely coincidence with father and daughter being able to communicate over six thousand kilometres using new-born monopole kittens and Starkwood seedlings, those Physics Police would have been having a field day with all the arrests. Fortunately they had their hands (and pretty much everything else) filled for the foreseeable future with the invasive zombie harvest.

* * * * *

So let's leave Elvis with his two daughters, so they can catch up with news from the last million years. They did agree to meet up a bit more often, maybe every thousand years, though fate had other plans for them.

Katya flew off in search of the newlyweds Frankie and Nati in order to reunite them. It took her a couple of weeks, but she brought one of her kittens with her so she could stay in touch with her friends via the feline phone.

After she'd got the Love Cats back together again, Katya gave the Hellas Angels a flying visit, to check in with Fionix and asked for special cat-ternity leave from being Chief Science Officer with the Senior nogard for a while so she could be with her kittens. Fionix gladly released her for some well-earned rest after the crazy year they'd just had. Hell had joined her friends again and fully recovered from her mind-controlled kidnapping. Catapilla had found herself a niche on Cydonia Hill and was nicely sewn up in her silken sleeping bag, ready for her pupal stage. The other three Hellas Angels, though happy to have Hell back, picked up where they had left off and fought about which parts of the hill they were each going to reshape and what method was best to use – basically anything that could be argued about, they argued about it. Katya returned to Viking Landing Site II and hung around with her children and friends until the proverbial coast was clear. The Viking II Lander stayed operational for a little more than a Martian year (two Earth years, until April 1980), which was when the battery failed. Why the battery failed was never fully answered – all that was known was that one of the kittens had gone missing and there had been a flash of lightning that same night from the Lander before the kitten reappeared, seemingly all charged up with static.

Meanwhile, the Viking Lander I lasted a bit longer than Viking Lander II, some two and a half Martian years (five Earth years, until November 1982). Its death was apparently due to human error; updating the software, which caused the antenna to go down, and ending communication. Captain Sam's pyrite crew had denied profusely that they had been trying to create the tallest pyrite pyramid atop the antenna, the weight of ten thousand lice being enough to bring down the telescopic aerial. Apart from that incident, Elvis, Starkwood and Quicksilver maintained an almost perfect record at Viking Landing Site I, and felt they had not given Earth any reason to think life existed there. Well, except for one incident. The pyrites, after one night of over-drinking, had all wandered into the Exclusion Zone and collectively urinated over the Viking Lander's extendable arm, proudly marking their territory as the males of many species do. Sometime after this, the arm scooped up some dirt. This led to the analysis of the soil pointing to possible organic chemicals and hence evidence of life on Mars. Fortunately, the results were vague enough to be dismissed, as the bulk of the liquid from the peeing pyrites had been pure alcohol.

At Viking Lander Site II, they were almost as successful at not blowing their cover. There was an incident when Ruby's and Jade's pyrite crews went on a drinking spree and many of them wandered into the Exclusion Zone around the lander and, guess what – they all urinated on the telescopic arm that was to be used to sample the soil for evidence of life. The results of the tests for life were ambiguous enough to be rejected, just like the others. There were a few other nail biting incidents – one involved two monopole kittens, a yellow coloured tortle and a couple of seasoned pyrites from Ruby's crew (so eyewitnesses said). There had to be some explanation for the team on watch waking up the next morning and there having been a sand castle built right by the lander's digging arm. Piccolo and Terry the

Terrible denied it to their dying breaths, as any good pyrites – well, *bad* pyrites – would, and of course, you couldn't believe such a young tortle like Sulphie-Rose, whose imagination would be mixed up with dreams. Or perhaps the sulphurous one suffered from sleep-walking (and sleep sand castle building too). Captains Masha and Raffi led the damage control party to remove all evidence of the castle. All future sand building permits were only allowed *outside* the Exclusion Zone and not in view of the planetary visitors.

That hadn't been the worst incident. Everyone had forgotten another loose cannon on the planet (No, not Hanksie, well at least not for now) and the cannon ball turned up only a few weeks after the Viking lander 2 had arrived. As nothing had been happening and all living Martian lifeforms had been threatened with death in a thousand km radius of the landing site if they gave any hint of being alive, the umpteenager team had grown a little lax and missed the unexpected interloper. A couple of the team were on watch and it was Jade and Grit this time, both with their chins on the rock hiding them out of view of the lander. They were staring at the craft, as they had for many weeks, and it was as exciting as watching two dead rocks racing each other. Suddenly, out of nowhere bounced the mini Russian Rover, still with Starkwood zombie attached and he was lolloping from side to side like a raggedy doll. Jade and Grit could only gawp, wide eyed and opened mouthed, helpless to stop the very thing they were supposed to stop. As the vehicle passed the lander, the Starkwood zombie looked at the lander – well not *looked*, as it had no head, but its body turned to face the craft. By the time thousands of pyrites had been sent to discretely jump aboard the rover, it was leaving the perimeter edge and out of sight anyway. This incident caused much stress and worry to the team, but fortunately, back on Earth, all their necks had been saved by two helpful and now quite learned house martins. Doctors House and Martin had hung around to watch the start of the Viking missions, when they witnessed the surprise appearance of the car-thieving cactus. Fortunately, none of the Viking team was around at that moment, as it was the middle of the night. The two birds, having now picked up the rudiments of programming by watching the IT team through the windows, were able to erase the offending images – but not before they used a polaroid camera conveniently placed on the desk next to the computer to take a picture of the screen and whipped away the instamatic photograph back to the South of France as a souvenir. They even noticed on the picture, just peering out from behind a distant rock, the pointed green ears of a cat they'd once met.

26
Mars Rocks!

About eight hundred kilometres to the east of the Viking Lander I, still in the Chryse Basin and downstream from the Ares Valley, there was a conversation going on among some of the rocks.

'Hey Froggy,' said Duck, the rock just next to him. 'Wake up!'

'What is it now?' said Froggy. 'I was having a nice dream, about a curvy smooth pebble I once met in a ground melt.'

'I just wanted to remind you that it's Bunky's birthday coming up…'

'Bunky's birthday?!'

'Shhh!' said Duck. 'He's just over there!'

'Sorry, how old is he?'

'He'll be a thousand million in ten years.'

'So what are you planning?'

'A surprise rock party, right here, in ten years. Invite all the other rocks round.'

'Well they're already here!'

'I know, but we'll have a few extra guests. You remember that gold coated rock tortle?'

'What, Elvis?'

'Yea. He's coming and has promised to sing some, well, rock music. So anyway, pass the message to the others.'

'Okay,' and with that Froggy turned to the rock next to him and obliged: 'Hey Warthog! Bunky's birthday surprise party in ten years, pass it on.'

Ten Martian years is best part of twenty Earth years. The rocks were talking in late 1977 on Earth; the planned surprise party was booked for 1997. This was also to be the year that planet Earth sent another landing mission to Mars called Pathfinder. The chosen landing site was about eight hundred kilometres to the east of the Viking I landing site – in fact just a few metres from Bunky and his rock steady friends. Wow!

The Physics Police would have heart attacks with *this* coincidence if they ever found out about it. But for now, let's just let the creatures experience the next almost uneventful decade of Life On Mars in peace, before the madness picks up again.

THE END

Acknowledgements

'Hey House!'

'Yes Martin?'

'It's time to write the thank yous.'

'Can't Hugh do it?'

'You've seen what his writing's like. He can barely string three words together without making a mistake!'

'True.'

'Remember poor Sof who had to do the first read throughs and she's only just recovering.'

'Yea that was tough.'

'Recall when he wrote W.H.A.Y.T.H.U.R.R.?'

'What was that?'

'The worst spell of weather we've had for a long time…'

'Nice one.'

'Plus we need to tip our hats to Al, Pete and Sof at Elsewhen Press for their unending help in turning this ragged Cinderella of a story into something worth reading.'

'Agreed. Hang on, do we get hats?!'

'Hats?'

'You said tip our hats.'

'Focus will you! Then there's the wonderful artwork by Natascha Booth.'

'Lovely cover. And those little sketches inside.'

'The fleurons yes, there's a great one of us.'

'Sure, though I think my right profile would look better.'

'It's not about you House. Now, there are a *number* of people who've supported Hugh along the way …'

'And that number is…'

'No! We're not going to do that joke, if you don't mind. Anyway we should give them all a mention.'

'He didn't do the book all by himself?'

'No House, no one does. We are the result of all the

people and events that have affected us until now.'

'Very Muddist, that.'

'First we thank his parents for giving him life. His mum told me to say that.'

'It is a big gift. Not easy to write if you don't exist. Does he believe in God?'

'I think so, and God must believe in him too, to give him this chance of a lifetime.'

'Let's hope he uses it wisely.'

'You know, when Hugh first started dating Corinne, his wife-to-be, he told her that one day he'd be rich and famous?'

'The scoundrel!'

'Yet in spite of his lies she stuck by him and put up with him, especially when he kept going on about crazy projects like this one.'

'Worth a medal. A hat even.'

'Forget the hat will you House?! His own family also supported him during these ventures. His children Anais and Fabien were punished with reading the final draft and his other daughter Heloise must also be praised for giving him Hell.'

'Is that a cryptic clue?'

'Yea. And with any luck his eldest son Jonathan will be doing the French translation of this chez doves.'

'Formi-da-ble!'

'Isn't it? But let's go back to when this all began.'

'Have we got time to?!'

'Don't worry, not many people read the acknowledgments page anyway.'

'Page? *Pages* the way we're going!'

'Shh. So yes. Hugh wants to show his appreciation to University College London and in particular Dr Guest, who mentored him through his thesis on Martian craters and then employed him to work at UCL's observatory, cataloguing all those Viking photographs.'

'Apart from those we erased!'

'That's meant to be secret! Hugh also wants to thank the staff and students at the International School of Nice.'

'What did they do?'

'Well they laughed at all his in-house Deskworld parody stories and if they hadn't done so, he may well have never put pen to paper again.'

'So *they're* to blame!'

'Indeed. Hugh was worried that he might forget someone along the way.'

'Well he does have the memory of a five inch floppy.'

'He gave me this list.'

'It's a long list!'

'A marketing ploy probably. But it seems they've all helped Hugh in his journey to bringing out this novel. There's Mrs G, Toma, DJ, Astrid, Morgana, Janet, Rick, Penny, …'

Half an hour later…

'… Dmitry, the two Ninas… House? Wake up!'

'zzz … oh, what?'

'Pay attention! … um, sisters Katya and Masha, Nati K, Frankie, two house martins …'

'And a partridge in a pear tree! Haha! Hang on, some of those names sound familiar. You don't think…'

'Don't go there House, it's just coincidence.'

'Maybe you're right Martin. I suppose, in a big multiverse such as ours there's a chance this could happen, even if the chance is one in a…'

'No! Let's not get the Physics Police involved.'

'Fair enough. So are we done here Martin?'

'I think so House.'

'Can we talk about those hats then?'

'There *aren't* any hats!'

'Not even in the merchandising?'

'Grief…'

Elsewhen Press

delivering outstanding new talents in speculative fiction

Visit the Elsewhen Press website at elsewhen.press for the latest information on all of our titles, authors and events; to read our blog; find out where to buy our books and ebooks; or to place an order.

Sign up for the Elsewhen Press InFlight Newsletter at elsewhen.press/newsletter

Other Elsewhen Press titles that you might also enjoy

Don't Look Back

John Gribbin

*"A real scientist writing science-fiction with real science – what more could one ask?
John Gribbin is a visionary, and one heck of a good storyteller."*
— **Robert J. Sawyer**
Hugo Award-winning author of QUANTUM NIGHT

Retrospective SF short story collection from the master science writer

John Gribbin, widely regarded as one of the best science writers of the 20th century, has also, unsurprisingly, been writing science fiction for many years. While his novels are well-known, his short stories are perhaps less so. He has also written under pseudonyms. Here, for the first time, is the definitive collection of John's short stories. Many were originally published in *Analog* and other magazines. Some were the seeds of subsequent novels. As well as 23 Science Fiction short stories, three of which John wrote with his son Ben, this collection includes two Science Fact essays on subjects beloved of science fiction authors and readers. In one essay, John provides scientifically accurate DIY instructions for creating a time machine; and in the other, he argues that the Moon is, in fact, a Babel Fish!

The stories, many written at a time when issues such as climate change were taken less seriously, now seem very relevant again in an age of dubious politicians. What underpins all of them, of course, is a grounding in solid science. But they are also laced with a dry and subtle wit, which will not come as a surprise to anyone who has ever met John at a science fiction convention or elsewhere. He is, however, not averse to a good pun, as evidenced by a song he co-wrote for the Bonzo Dog Doo Dah Band: *The Holey Cheeses of Nazareth.*

Despite the exhortation of this collection's title, this *is* a perfect opportunity to look back at John's short stories. If you've never read any of his fiction before, now you have the chance to acquaint yourself with a body of work that, while being very much of its time, is certainly not in any way out of date.

With a cover especially created by legendary space artist David A. Hardy.

ISBN: 9781911409182 (epub, kindle) / 9781911409083 (272pp paperback)

Visit bit.ly/DontLookBackJohnGribbin

BLURRED VISION

A Polly Hart Chronicle

Steve Harrison

First contact?

"Take it easy," said Kylie, still with a hint of amusement. "You're perfectly safe. Think of me as a tourist."

Polly squinted back at her. She couldn't help herself. "Are you invading earth?"

"Are you kidding? Do you know how much that would cost?"

"Then what are you doing here?"

"We found you after you activated the camera on the satellite and were impressed by the other stuff you did to hide your tracks. Easy for us, but we all thought it was very cool. For an Earth human, anyway."

"You don't talk like an alien."

"How many do you know?" asked Kylie.

Polly couldn't argue with that. "Good point."

When Polly Hart agrees to swap places with a girl from another planet, she has no idea that this makes her a fugitive in the fabulous universe revealed by her new friend, and now she must outwit the school bully, a weird teacher and an interstellar hit squad to survive. So annoying!

ISBN: 9781911409564 (epub, kindle) / 9781911409465 (240pp paperback)

Visit bit.ly/BlurredVision-Harrison

Other Elsewhen Press titles that you might also enjoy

FAR FAR BEYOND BERLIN

CRAIG MEIGHAN

Even geniuses need practice

Not everything goes to plan at the first attempt... In Da Vinci's downstairs loo hung his first, borderline insulting, versions of the Mona Lisa. Michelangelo's back garden was chock-a-block full of ugly lumps of misshapen marble. Even Einstein committed a great 'blunder' in his first go at General Relativity. God is no different, this universe may be his masterpiece, but there were many failed versions before it – and they're still out there.

Far Far Beyond Berlin is a fantasy novel, which tells the story of a lonely, disillusioned government worker's adventures after being stranded in a faraway universe – Joy World: God's first, disastrous attempt at creation.

God's previous universes, a chain of 6 now-abandoned worlds, are linked by a series of portals. Our jaded hero must travel back through them, past the remaining dangers and bizarre stragglers. He'll join forces with a jolly, eccentric and visually arresting, crew of sailors on a mysteriously flooded world. He'll battle killer robots and play parlour games against a clingy supercomputer, with his life hanging in the balance. He'll become a teleportation connoisseur; he will argue with a virtual goose – it sure beats photocopying.

Meanwhile, high above in the heavens, an increasingly flustered God tries to manage the situation with His best friend Satan; His less famous son, Jeff; and His ludicrously angry angel of death, a creature named Fate. They know that a human loose in the portal network is a calamity that could have apocalyptic consequences in seven different universes. Fate is dispatched to find and kill the poor man before the whole place goes up in a puff of smoke; if he can just control his temper...

ISBN: 9781911409922 (epub, kindle) / 9781911409823 (336pp paperback)

Visit bit.ly/FarFarBeyondBerlin

Other Elsewhen Press titles that you might also enjoy

The Forge
& The Flood

Miles Nelson

When history itself seems written to keep them apart, can two radically different peoples really find it in their hearts to get along?

Sienna is an Ailura. His kind live on the lonely island of Veramilia, bound under traditions forged by countless generations.
Indigo is a Lutra. His kind goes with the flow, having lived as free as the ocean waves since the beginning of time.

When a great calamity strikes and the Ailura are forced to flee their island home, the Ailura and the Lutra come face to face for the first time in known history. In these turbulent times, it is Indigo and Sienna who are chosen to find a suitable habitat for the displaced tribe. One a princess destined to rule his kind, the other the only son of a would-be chief, the pair seem like a natural choice.

But as friendship blossoms into something more, and their journey takes them further and further from known lands, the wanderers begin to uncover secrets hidden among the ruins. Secrets which suggest the two species may not be as alien to one another as previously thought.

ISBN: 9781915304100 (epub, kindle) / 9781915304001 (184pp paperback)

Visit bit.ly/Forge&Flood

HOWUL
A LIFE'S JOURNEY
DAVID SHANNON

"Un-put-down-able! A classic hero's journey, deftly handled. I was surprised by every twist and turn, the plotting was superb, and the engagement of all the senses – I could smell those flowers and herbs. A tour de force"
— **LINDSAY NICHOLSON MBE**

Books are dangerous

People in Blanow think that books are dangerous: they fill your head with drivel, make poor firewood and cannot be eaten (even in an emergency).

This book is about Howul. He sees things differently: fires are dangerous; people are dangerous; books are just books.

Howul secretly writes down what goes on around him in Blanow. How its people treat foreigners, treat his daughter, treat him. None of it is pretty. Worse still, everything here keeps trying to kill him: rats, snakes, diseases, roof slates, the weather, the sea. That he survives must mean something. He wants to find out what. By trying to do this, he gets himself thrown out of Blanow… and so his journey begins.

Like all gripping stories, *HOWUL* is about the bad things people do to each other and what to do if they happen to you. Some people use sticks to stay safe. Some use guns. Words are the weapons that Howul uses most. He makes them sharp. He makes them hurt.

Of course books are dangerous.

ISBN: 9781911409908 (epub, kindle) / 9781911409809 (200pp paperback)

Visit bit.ly/HOWUL

Other Elsewhen Press titles that you might also enjoy

Transdimensional Authority / Multiverse series
Ira Nayman

If there were Alternate Realities, and in each there was a version of Earth (very similar, but perhaps significantly different in one particular regard, or divergent since one particular point in history) then imagine the problems that could be caused if someone, somewhere, managed to work out how to travel between them. Those problems would be ideal fodder for a News Service that could also span all the realities. Now you understand the reasoning behind the Alternate Reality News Service (ARNS). But you aren't the first. In fact, Canadian satirist and author Ira Nayman got there before you and has been the conduit for ARNS into our Reality for some years now, thanks to his website *Les Pages aux Folles*.

But also consider that if there were problems being caused by unregulated travel between realities, it's not just news but a perfect ~~excuse~~ reason to establish an Authority to oversee such travel and make sure that it is regulated. You probably thought jurisdictional issues are bad enough between competing national agencies of dubious acronym and even more dubious motivation, let alone between agencies from different nations. So imagine how each of them would cope with an Authority that has jurisdiction across the realities in different dimensions. Now, you understand the challenges for the investigators who work for the Transdimensional Authority (TA). But, perhaps more importantly, you can see the potential for humour. Again, Ira beat you to it.

Welcome to the Multiverse*
* Sorry for the inconvenience
ISBN: 9781908168191 (epub, kindle) / 9781908168092 (336pp paperback)

You Can't Kill the Multiverse*
* But You Can Mess With its Head
ISBN: 9781908168399 (epub, kindle) / 9781908168290 (320pp paperback)

Random Dingoes
ISBN: 9781908168795 (epub, kindle) / 9781908168696 (288pp paperback)

It's Just the Chronosphere Unfolding as it Should
A Radames Trafshanian Time Agency novel
ISBN: 9781911419113 (epub, kindle) / 9781911409014 (288pp paperback)

The Multiverse is a Nice Place to Visit,
But I Wouldn't Want to Live There
ISBN: 9781911419199 (epub, kindle) / 9781911409090 (320pp paperback)

The Multiverse Refugees Trilogy
Good Intentions: First Pie in the Face
ISBN: 9781911419540 (epub, kindle) / 9781911409441 (336pp paperback)

Bad Actors: Second Pi in the Face
ISBN: 9781911419946 (epub, kindle) / 9781911409847 (264pp paperback)

The Ugly Truth: ‹INSERT THIRD REPETITON WITH VARIATION OF PIE JOKE HERE›
ISBN: 9781915304148 (epub, kindle) / 9781915304049 (320pp paperback)

Visit bit.ly/TransdimensionalAuthority

GENESIS
GEOFFREY CARR

A conjunction of AI, the Cloud, & interplanetary ambition…

Hidden somewhere, deep in the Cloud, something is collating information. It reads everything, it learns, it watches. And it plans.

Around the world, researchers, engineers and entrepreneurs are being killed in a string of apparently unrelated accidents. But when intelligence-agency analysts spot a pattern they struggle to find the culprit, blocked at every step – by reluctant allies and scheming enemies.

Meanwhile a multi-billionaire inventor and forward-thinker is working hard to realise his dream, and trying to keep it hidden from everyone – one government investigating him, and another helping him. But deep in the Cloud something is watching him, too.

And deep in the Cloud, it plans.

What could possibly go wrong?

Geoff is the Science and Technology Editor of *The Economist*. His professional interests include evolutionary biology, genetic engineering, the fight against AIDS and other widespread infectious diseases, the development of new energy technologies, and planetology. His personal interests include using total eclipses of the sun as an excuse to visit weird parts of the world (Antarctica, Easter Island, Amasya, the Nullarbor Plain), and watching swifts hunting insects over his garden of a summer's evening, preferably with a glass of Cynar in hand.

As someone who loathed English lessons at school, he says he is frequently astonished that he now earns his living by writing. "That I have written a novel, albeit a technothriller rather than anything with fancy literary pretensions, astonishes me even more, since what drew me into writing in the first place was describing reality, not figments of the imagination. On the other hand, perhaps describing reality is what fiction is actually for."

ISBN: 9781911409519 (epub, kindle) / 9781911409410 (288pp paperback)

Visit bit.ly/GC_Genesis

Jacey's Kingdom
Dave Weaver

Jacey's Kingdom is an enthralling tale that revolves around a startlingly desperate reality: Jacey Jackson, a talented student destined for Cambridge, collapses with a brain tumour while sitting her final history exam at school. In her mind she struggles through a quasi-historical sixth century dreamscape whilst the surgeons fight to save her life.

Jacey is helped by a stranger called George, who finds himself trapped in her nightmare after a terrible car accident. There are quests, battles, and a love story ahead of them, before we find out if Jacey will awake from her coma or perish on the operating table. And who, or what, is George? In this book, Dave Weaver questions our perception of reality and the redemptive power of dreams; are our experiences of fear, conflict, friendship and love any less real or meaningful when they take place in the mind rather than the 'real' physical world?

Dave Weaver has been writing for over ten years, with short stories published in anthologies, magazines and online in the UK and USA. Jacey's Kingdom was his first published novel. He cleverly weaves a tale that takes the almost unimaginable drama of an eighteen year-old girl whose life is in the balance, relying on modern surgery to bring her back from the brink, and conceives the world that she has constructed in her mind to deal with the trauma happening to her body. Developing the friendship between Jacey and George in a natural and witty style, despite their unlikely situation and the difference in their ages, Dave has produced a story that is both exciting and thought-provoking. This book will be a must-read story for adults and young adults alike.

ISBN: 9781908168313 (epub, kindle) / 9781908168214 (272pp paperback)

Visit bit.ly/JaceysKingdom

About Hugh Duncan

Hugh Duncan hatched in Leicester in 1957. He studied astronomy at University College London and, though very lazy, got his degree. His final thesis was on Martian craters and, after, he worked at the UCL observatory cataloguing the Viking Mission photos.

Having fallen in love with a French woman and wanting to live happily ever after, he ruined that plan by becoming a science teacher. The temporary job became a lifelong career, first in the UK then for 32 years at the International School of Nice, from which he has recently retired. A few years ago, UCL launched the maths journal *Chalkdust*, in which Hugh has had a number of articles published.

Hugh started in science fiction aged five, when he wrote 'Dr Who goes to the balloon planet' and some have said it's his best work to date. In 1997 he sent off a novel which was rejected by many publishers, including Elsewhen Press. He was talked down off the ledge by Oxford Study Courses, who asked him to write revision guidebooks for IB Physics, which continues to this day.

Inspired by the Mighty Terry Pratchett, for school charity projects he started writing his own 'Deskworld' stories, parodying his school as one for witches and wizards. Three dozen stories sold using a captive audience scared of getting bad grades if they didn't buy them, hmm…

Hugh's interest in the Turin Shroud has led to a number of articles for the British Society For The Turin Shroud. With Louise Thomas, he translated a 17th century French local history book 'An Undiscovered Treasure' by Brother Raphael, and he is making the first English translation of Paul Vignon's 1938 french science book on the Turin Shroud.

He is a punk at heart. You can't keep him off stage, even when no one wants to hear him (which is most of the time) and he has managed to force his home grown albums of punk, ska and pop rock songs onto the unsuspecting public, using real musician Rick Preston. There is a good chance that if he makes any money from *Life on Mars*, he will waste it recording more of his songs. He is also finishing an album based on the life of Mary Magdalene sung by real singer Penny Mac McMorris. Check out his Youtube channel if he ever gets his finger out!

Hugh has been married for 40 years and has four children – most don't seem to want to leave home in spite of being adults and having to listen to his songs and stories all the time. He lives in the South of France, not very far from the village with two famous house martins who appear in *Life on Mars*. He owns a Hermann's tortoise called Sophie Rose.